Rannulf of Sleaford was known throughout the land as a bold and ruthless warrior. Face to face with an oncoming army, he could decide matters of life and death. But now, face to face with one gentle woman, he was hopelessly confused and uncertain. Startled by Catherine's pale beauty when he first saw her, he was dumbfounded by her passionate radiance now, and he felt a desire far different from his usual impersonal need for a woman.

Look out for more romance based on historical fact by Roberta Gellis in Mayflower.

Also by Roberta Gellis

THE DRAGON AND THE ROSE

# Roberta Gellis

# The Sword and the Swan

This edition published 1994 by
Diamond Books
77–85 Fulham Palace Road
Hammersmith, London W6 8JB

First published in Great Britain
by Granada Publishing Limited
in Mayflower Books 1979

ISBN 0 261 66422 5

Set in Intertype Plantin

Made and printed in Great Britain

# Introduction

In every social group – insect, animal, or human – a power struggle exists. For the so-called nonintelligent creatures, it is simply a struggle to determine who is the strongest, and, by virtue of that strength, who will lead the group. In humans, however, matters are not so simple, and the power struggle is complicated by the fact that the clever are often more capable of leadership than the strong, as well as by theories of ruler-ship and of good and evil.

By the twelfth century, every possible permutation and combination of forms of government had been sampled in Europe; at one time or another, for one reason or another, every form had been found wanting. The democracy practised by the Greeks fell because the citizens did not really want the responsi-bility of government and would not work at it, because men placed their own profit above the good of the state in contra-diction to the theory of democracy, and because the form of government moved too slowly in times of crisis. The republi-canism of the Romans was destroyed by the same causes, and government once again turned to absolutism under the steady hand and relative benevolence of Caesar. Absolutism was no answer, however, for there is a flaw at the very heart of the concept: The absolute ruler, to be successful, must be both more and less than human, and there are very few men, in-deed, who can fill the role. With the destruction of the un-wieldy and bloated corpse that the Roman Empire had become, the people had a fresh taste of what amounted to anarchy. This plague, however, was worse than either the responsibility that came with self-government or the oppression that came with tyranny.

Slowly Europe began to pick up the pieces of what had been destroyed and thrown away, and experimentation in government started anew. There were small, remote, isolated hamlets and religious houses that practised perfect democracy. There were the shattered remains of great Roman estates where the descendants of rich or noble families continued to rule as petty but absolute tyrants. Some of the hamlets were not remote enough and were preyed upon by robbers, and some of the petty tyrants either had a lust for greater power or had not enough dependents to work for them. Out of this developed another system, not new (nothing in government can be new), but new to these people, in which the hamlets were protected from marauders by the petty tyrants who were paid for their protection in services. In turn, the petty tyrant sought security by alliance with other petty tyrants, and, as his position became assured, it became necessary to find someone to judge between him and his allies, lest anarchy return.

Thus it was, according to some authorities, that the concept of the feudal king arose. In theory, the feudal king was no more powerful in his own right, no richer in lands or money, than his major barons. He had only one strength that these men did not have, and that was that each of them swore to support him against the other barons. By this arrangement, it was believed, the individual barons could be prevented from preying upon each other – any man who was attacked had a right to appeal for protection to the king, who, in theory, could call up the other barons to help him suppress the attacker – and yet the king himself would be unable to seize absolute power.

In theory, again, this should bring about an excellent form of government. If the barons were united in any cause, the king would be forced to accede to their demands; yet, if any few should become rebellious for their own profit, the king could control them. Unfortunately, like all other theories of government, this one contained the seeds of its own destruction. Men often did not keep their oaths, and the kings, seeking to protect themselves against this human failing, tried to seize more power so that they could enforce terms of the feudal pact that were not willingly met.

And so the power struggle began anew. A strong king beat his barons into relative submission, generally after a period of civil war. A weak king was at the mercy of his own baronial factions and usually had to watch his country being torn apart by internecine strife that he was powerless to prevent.

In England, after the Norman Conquest, this power struggle and its results were remarkably clear. William the Bastard conquered the country by force of arms and ground the barons' faces into the dirt under his mighty heel. Some obeyed and some died, but where they obeyed, the land was at peace. William Rufus could not maintain his father's iron grip on the throats of his men. There were already rumblings of rebellion when a hunting arrow – whether deliberately or accidentally is uncertain to this day – put an end to his life. Henry I, a younger son of William the Bastard, inherited from his brother. He went slowly and softly, but slowly and softly towards only one end. By the time the lords of the land realized what he had done, he had them in an even more inexorable grip than that of his father. Under William the Bastard the land had lain still and groaned; under Henry I it did not even dare to groan.

Had Henry's plans come to fruition, the history of England might well have been different. Man proposes, however, and God disposes. Henry's only legitimate son was drowned at sea, and in desperation, Henry tried to force his daughter Matilda upon the barons as their queen. During his lifetime, even when he was old and sick, they dared not oppose him and he made them swear that they would accept her.

With the death of Henry I, however, the chains were broken, and the barons united to set aside the oath given under duress and appoint a king more to their liking. This man was Stephen of Blois, a grandson of William the Bastard; Matilda was William's granddaughter. Perhaps the barons hoped that Stephen would be the perfect feudal king, uniting mildness of temper with a strong fighting arm; perhaps they knew that he was weak and lazy and they only desired freedom. Certainly they obtained their freedom; but with that too-great freedom came anarchy again. By this time there was another claimant to the throne of England in Henry of Anjou, Matilda's son, who gave every sign of combining his grandfather's talent for governing and lust for power with a great deal of good humour and military skill.

This novel concerns the last power struggle between Stephen of Blois, a weak feudal king, and Henry of Anjou, who finally became Henry II of England, a strong feudal king. Unfortunately, the discussion offered above is a great oversimplification of the situation, and the line of demarcation between the opposing forces is far from clear.

Ranged on Henry's side were not only the barons who desired a stronger king to keep peace between them, but also those who were attached to his cause by the memory of the oath given to Matilda. Roger of Hereford's father had given such an oath and the son, for that reason as well as for reasons of personal liking and loyalty to Henry, was a rebel against the king of his country. There were also men who cared for neither cause but used the instability of a nation in the throes of a civil war for their own profit, raiding their neighbour's property and seizing his goods under the guise of supporting one side or the other.

The supporters of Stephen's cause had similarly diverse reasons for their actions. Some, like Northampton and Warwick, were truly honourable men who believed that an oath given under duress was not valid and that, therefore, the homage they had done Stephen was the oath that was binding upon their honour. Some merely had a hearty distaste for absolute monarchy and feared, with a great deal of justice, that Henry would try to bring absolutism back. Still others clung to Stephen simply because he was the king, and out of a weak and generous king there was profit to be made.

The hero of this novel is a totally fictional character, as are his wife and family. Fictional also are all conversations, all records of political manoeuvring, and all influence the hero has on the events that take place. The events themselves, however, are strictly historical, and are taken largely from the *Gesta Stephani* (edited by K. R. Potter, London: Thomas Nelson & Sons, Ltd, 1955), the best chronicle of the events of Stephen's reign. Other medieval chronicles and modern texts have been used as necessary to fill in characters or events and the surrounding milieu. Even with best of intentions, though, it is often impossible to be perfectly accurate in all things because of lack of information about many common matters: For this reason descriptions of housing, styles of armour and clothing, types of food and eating utensils, and even the exact wording of challenges and oaths – particularly since French was the language used by all the upper classes at this time – are only valid within about one hundred years.

Finally the author must admit one great liberty taken with history. Nowhere is there any historical indication whatsoever that the death of Stephen's eldest son, Eustace, was anything but natural. Eustace did die very suddenly after a bitter quarrel with his father and the majority of the barons, but people died suddenly in the Middle Ages because of lack of sanitation and medical knowledge.

The author offers, in amelioration of the liberty taken, the licence allowed in a work of fiction to produce an effect (when it does not actually alter an event in history) and the fact that the cause of Eustace's death was not the usual 'fever' that carried off so many medieval people. In fact, two different causes are offered. Roger of Hoveden and William of Newburgh say that Stephen's son strangled on a dish of eels. Gervase of Canterbury states, 'But when he sat down at table to eat, as we read in writings, at the first taste of food he fell into a miserable madness, and because of the arrogance he had shown to the Martyrs he underwent the dire pains of death.' It is possible that Eustace suffered either a heart attack or apoplexy, although he was a young man who had undergone the exertions of many battles without deleterious effect. It is also barely possible that one of the causes suggested by the medieval chroniclers actually did .terminate Eustace's life. Considering, however, how much Eustace was hated by both sides in the power struggle, the author feels justified in suggesting that Eustace was poisoned.

# Chapter 1

'Is this your thanks to me? Is this your gratitude for your son's life and freedom, for the crown upon your head?'

An expression of dumbfounded amazement covered the heavy, rather handsome blond face of the man addressed by those furious words. With the physical agility and instinct of a man of war trained by many battles, he caught the roll of parchment tossed at him by the mailed figure who had rushed in from the far door, scattering men-at-arms and serving men from his path, and who now stood panting with rage before the high table. Stephen of Blois, king of England, gaped with surprise and looked towards the dark, middle-aged woman who sat at his left hand. There was no visible surprise on the woman's face, for Maud of England, Stephen's wife, had absolute control over herself.

It was not that the words of the harsh, grating voice were rude, nor that both words and tone were scarcely those which a subject should address to a king. Rannulf Tefli, master of Sleaford, was always rude, and, Stephen suspected, would address God with as little ceremony as he used towards his earthly ruler. What had dumbfounded the king was that he had honestly sought a reward suitable to the deed, and, until this moment, had been highly pleased with what he had proposed. Rannulf had a sour temper, but what fault he could find with an offer that would more than double his possessions and make him an earl was beyond Stephen's imagining.

Now the king's eye ranged across and beyond the laden high table at which he sat in helpless bewilderment, as if he sought counsel from the great hall since there was none to be had from his wife. Ninety feet long and forty wide, the great hall of the White Tower had been built by his grandfather, William the Bastard, but the spirit of that mighty man who

11

had ruled his barons with a hand of iron had never infused Stephen. The noblemen sitting at the long tables nearest to the high table grimaced and fell silent at this most recent exposure of the king's indecisiveness.

No one was shocked by Tefli's rudeness. Most of the barons knew Rannulf well, and it was every man's right to stand up to the king and protest treatment that he considered unfair. The king could force the subject to his will or yield to the subject's protest, both without losing face; but he had to decide something quickly, and act forcibly if he wished to retain his men's respect. In this, Stephen of Blois had failed again, as he had failed time after time since he had assumed the throne of England in 1135. By the year 1150, the men who had fought for and against him through the thirteen bitter years of the recent civil war expected no more. The grimaces on the faces of the lords and barons of England were ones of disgust, not of tenseness or fear.

'We thought it a most meet and fitting reward, Sir Rannulf. It would double your riches, bring you an earldom which you greatly deserve, and, moreover, give you a young and beautiful wife to comfort your lonely estate.'

The person who spoke was not the king but the woman who sat beside him. No expression of surprise moved the watching men, although in general, it was the place of a woman to hold her tongue unless bidden by her male master to speak; but they knew that, if there were a ruler in England, Maud was that ruler. Her tone held no anger at what might well be considered an insult. It was pleasantly reasonable and suited her appearance, which was soft and matronly. Rannulf of Sleaford shifted his gaze to her, and while there was little change of expression on his hard face, the anger in his eyes lessened and the set of his lips softened somewhat.

'Aye, I should have known. Every woman goes about to make every other woman in the world a wife, be it to the pleasure of the man so trapped or not.' He waited while the burst of laughter that greeted his words died away, and spoke again more seriously. 'Madam, you know – I made no secret of it – that I have no lust for the married state. I have heirs to my lands and need no more issue. As for the land – land is

12

always good, but I have of that also sufficient for my needs. The title, any cur in the street is welcome to. I am Rannulf Tefli, master of Sleaford, and no title can lend me honour.'

No change marred the pleasant expression of the woman at this further insult, but she rose from her seat and edged around behind her son and daughter-in-law so that she could enter the space before the table in which Rannulf stood. As she approached, she held out her hand to him and a warm smile parted her lips. The gesture was graceful, surprisingly so, for one did not expect grace from that dumpy body, and the smile lit up a face which, without being ugly, was decidedly plain. There was no answering smile, but Rannulf took Maud's hand and kissed it with more eagerness than could have been expected from his angry words.

'How foolish we all are to stand here. A good greeting to you, my good lord. You are welcome to us glad or angry, but it mends nothing and mars all to talk when you are thus cold and muddied from your long ride. Bid your men come to table and refresh themselves, and do you come with me. When my women have bathed you and you have filled your belly, it will be time enough to quarrel if we must.'

'I would have the matter settled without delay—'

'I too,' Maud said softly, laying her hand on his arm, 'but is this a fitting time or place? These are not matters of state for all men to speak their minds upon but private things.'

To a great extent Rannulf agreed with Maud and was already regretting the fury which had driven him to expose his affairs and the king's weakness in public. He glanced quickly at the table, hoping Stephen would redeem himself by some decision, but the king only smiled encouragingly at him. He might have stayed anyhow to prod Stephen, but Eustace, the king's eldest son, growled and started to rise and Rannulf quickly turned away.

Eustace had never forgiven Rannulf for tearing him by force from a lost battle, and took every opportunity to insult his father's liege man. In his present temper, Rannulf could not trust himself to hold his tongue and, being too loyal a vassal to provoke his overlord's heir, sought safety in absence. His progress down the hall, however, was slow, for many men at

13

the top of the room, earls and dukes though they were, rose to greet Rannulf of Sleaford. Many of the greetings he acknowledged with no more than a curt nod, a few hands he pressed quickly – he was in no mood for civilities – but at the middle of the centre table he stopped.

'May I ask, Leicester, what you are doing in this fine company?'

Before the heavy, deliberate man to whom the remark was addressed could answer another voice intervened. 'Is that meant for me?' The retort was quick and hot in reply to the bitter sarcasm of Rannulf's tone, the voice clear and youthful. Maud's hand tightened on Rannulf's arm and she drew a hasty breath, but there was no need to speak, for the harsh laugh of her escort forestalled her.

'Nay, Hereford, you are an honest enemy and, though our swords may cross on the field in the future as they have in the past, I will break bread with you and welcome when we have space to breathe.'

Leicester had glanced up at Rannulf but still said nothing.

'Sit down, my cockerel,' William of Gloucester interposed in his silken purr. 'The barb was meant for me. But he who is well-armoured by righteousness need fear no feeble shaft of wit. I hope your arm is still stronger than your tongue, Tefli. Besides, I am no enemy to any man—'

'Except him who has a wife or a daughter or a young son—'

'My lord,' Maud pleaded softly, cutting off Sleaford's choking voice. 'We are all at peace now. Let us not unearth buried sorrows to bring us new grief.'

Indeed, there was little sympathy, even among his companions, for William of Gloucester's wanton provocation of Rannulf. Perhaps Tefli had not been civil – he never was – but it was no secret, considering his manner of entrance into the hall, that he was out of temper and the insult, if insult there were, had been directed at Robert of Leicester, who was well able to take care of himself. The earl of Hereford cast a glance of passionate dislike at Gloucester and stepped across the bench he had been seated upon.

'I give you thanks for those just words. I am not sorry to see you, Sir Rannulf, for I have long desired to tell you that I

14

bear you no ill will for the trick you played us at the battle of Devizes.'

For the second time in a few minutes, Rannulf wished he had controlled his hasty tongue. He should have known better than to play at talk with William of Gloucester, and he should, by now, have been able to control the inexplicable loathing he had for the man, who, after all, had never done him any more harm than to prick him with words. He turned now, almost smiling with relief to Hereford.

'Nay, why should you? I did my duty as you did yours. That we see our duty in different lights is no cause for ill will between us as men when the battle is over.'

'True. Moreover, I hope for the future that our paths will lie side by side rather than at cross-purposes.'

Rannulf looked at the young man who was now walking beside him and the lightness died out of his face. 'I do not think of the future, nor of the past, my lord Hereford. As each day comes to me, so do I live it, looking neither forward nor back. I am too old—'

'That you are not, and it is needful in these times to look forward.' Hereford checked his own hasty tongue, suddenly conscious of the silent woman who kept pace with them. 'Do you stay long in London? As my lady the queen says, it is useless to talk of any matter when the mind is clouded with weariness and the body restless with discomfort. I will leave you that you may take your ease, but I hope we will speak together again at a more suitable time.

'Here I am at leisure,' the older man replied in a more normal tone of caustic indifference, 'if you wish to speak; no doubt I will be constrained to listen. I know not how long I will stay, except that it be until my – private matter is settled.'

As Hereford left, Maud sighed. 'Alas, I do not know whether it is easier when they are in open rebellion or when they come here in "peace" to breed more war in those who are yet faithful to us.'

'Save your speech for those who have need of it, madam. From me you will get neither more nor less than I have ever given since the day I gave sword-oath to your husband.'

'Nay, my lord, I know you cannot be turned from the

15

true course, nor did I think of you when I spoke,' Maud said hastily, standing aside while Rannulf opened the heavy door to her quarters on the floor above the hall.

Only she did doubt, because Maud doubted everyone, and Rannulf had been seriously provoked by Eustace's behaviour. He had shown his consciousness of Eustace's hatred only by withdrawing from court, but to Maud it seemed essential to bind the vassal with new chains of obligation. Maud did not believe in oaths; she had broken too many herself, and there were signs and portents throughout the court. Leicester was more friendly than ever with the rebel lords – and Leicester was Rannulf's foster brother. If Robert of Leicester loved any man other than himself and his twin, he loved Rannulf of Sleaford; if he attended to any man's opinion, it would be to his. Maud did not really fear that Rannulf would turn on them, but he might slip into neutrality since he had no personal quarrel with the rebels.

Maud had guessed Rannulf's attitude towards the rebels accurately. True, it was Robert, the first duke of Gloucester, who had started the civil war when the barons of England had invited Stephen of Blois to take the throne in preference to Gloucester's half-sister Matilda, but Rannulf did not basically object to that. It was fit that each man should fight for what he believed to be right, and it was senseless to carry political grudges over into private life; the way things were, a man would soon have no one with whom to exchange a word. As far as Rannulf of Sleaford was concerned, war was the natural state of living, and it was in no way dishonourable to sit down at table, when the battle was done, with the man with whom you had just been crossing swords. It mattered very little to him whether one fought over political ideals, to conquer new territory, or to suppress the people one had already conquered. War was war, and, one side or the other, Rannulf hated no man who fought it honestly.

Shifting purposes Rannulf of Sleaford also understood, although he despised them. He despised them more in men like Gloucester than in the queen, being guided by emotion more than he realized; for their behaviour was almost exactly the same and for similar reasons. But in most things, Rannulf did not permit his emotions to run away with his reason. Just now, though, he had done so, cherishing his rage until it had overflowed in a way that was almost as detrimental to Stephen's cause as was the behaviour of the rebels of whom Maud complained.

The feeling was beyond his ability to express, however, since he was far more given to suppressing all thought of emotion than to discussing it. He took refuge, therefore, in a sullen silence, allowing Maud to direct her women to prepare a bath for him. With eyes stubbornly lowered and lips grimly set, he allowed the women to undress him and wash him in the hot, scented water. At last, as the maids wrapped him in a soft cloth for drying, feeling a difference in the atmosphere he looked at Maud and found her considering eyes upon him.

'Do you see something upon me that interests you, madam?'

Maud transferred her eyes from her guest's body to his face. 'In a way. To Hereford, below, you said you were old, yet I find you to look both fresh and young.' She rose and, without more embarrassment than if he had been her son, pulled loose the cloth to stroke the smoothly rounded, heavily muscled shoulder. 'Look here. This is not the stringy strength of active age. What are your years, my lord?'

Knowledgeable as he was in the queen's ways, and knowing that she loved her husband with an all-consuming passion that left no room for extra-marital desire, he reasoned that there must be a purpose to this admiration; even so Sir Rannulf was still flattered. His voice was as harsh as ever when he spoke, but involuntarily his eyes dropped.

'I have passed my fortieth summer. However I look, I am not young.'

'To one who has passed some few years more, that sounds most melancholy. I would that I appeared as fresh as you do. You hold yourself too cheap, my lord,' she laughed, 'and I will think twice before I leave you in my maidens' hands when I am not by. Did you not see their eyes upon you?'

'With five score young bucks to feast their eyes upon, I should not think you need worry over my influence with them,' Rannulf replied drily.

'The young have not what you have, Sir Rannulf. There is

17

a softness, even in their strength, that breeds insecurity. To look upon you is to be sure.' There could be no harm in building up his confidence. Sometimes a man of his age, when faced with a much younger and very beautiful bride, developed fears of insufficiency.

Rannulf moved restlessly. All this had a purpose, but what it was he could not, for the life of him, guess. 'Very well. A man of my age is a master of his own or no man at all. I did not realize that women felt masterfulness in a man to be an advantage.'

It was useless to press him further, Maud realized, because he was growing suspicious. She asked after his children instead, thinking with half her mind as he answered her inquiries that his sons were the weakest chink in his armour. Perhaps she could use them in some way as a weapon to get him well married. In addition to her political designs, Maud owed Rannulf a deep debt of gratitude and she was determined to do him a good turn in spite of himself.

A little less than a year previously, Henry of Anjou had come from France to try to wrest the throne by force from Maud's husband. Rannulf, together with those barons who were faithful to Stephen, had rallied to the defence of the kingdom, and Rannulf had been attached to the army of Maud's eldest son, Eustace. He had performed his duty well, as he always did; in addition, he had kept a rein on his young leader's enthusiasm and courage in a way that had recommended itself strongly to the mother, although the son had written home three times a week to call his mentor a traitor. In the autumn of 1149, Eustace had launched a massive attack on the castle of Devizes, one of Henry's major strongholds in England, and had sworn that he would take the castle or die in the attempt. In fact, he had done neither. Henry and his chief ally, Roger of Hereford, had returned in time to defeat the prince's force, and, although Eustace had been prepared to fulfil his oath, Rannulf of Sleaford was far past any belief in such vainglorious swearing. He had knocked the young prince unconscious with a single blow from his mailed fist and carried him off to safety.

It was not this deed alone for which Stephen and Maud wished to reward their liege man, however. Only a few days after Rannulf's rescue of Eustace, Henry of Anjou had mysteriously given up the fight and returned to France. A few months later the earl of Leicester had arranged to mediate a truce between the king and the rebel lords and peace, of a sort, had descended upon England. No reason had ever been discovered for Henry's action, and the king and queen had finally put it down to discouragement, crediting Rannulf with the final blow to Henry's hopes of conquest. Their sincere good will for him had caused them to consider long and anxiously a suitable reward. The continuing civil war had sucked them dry and they had little to give beyond empty titles which they knew Rannulf did not desire. In the midst of their perplexity a solution to their problem offered itself in the death of the earl of Soke, who left Lady Catherine, an only daughter, as his heir.

For once, Stephen did not vacillate or delay. Within hours of the time he had the news, he had set out alone with his household guard, leaving Eustace to marshal the barons if necessary, and had taken the chief castle at Bourne and the heiress into his hands. At that, he was only just in time, because Hugh Bigod, duke of Norfolk, had arrived the very next day with the same purpose in mind. The major portion of the lands of the earl of Soke stretched eastward along Norfolk's borders, and Bigod had desired to ensure the continued quiet of that border by marrying Lady Catherine to a man of his choosing.

Without sufficient force to fight a pitched battle, Stephen had raised the drawbridge and prepared for siege. News of Eustace's imminent arrival with a larger force and visual evidence that the vassals of Soke were gathering to his rear induced Norfolk to withdraw, and Stephen triumphantly returned to London bearing his prize with him. That the prize did not wish to go mattered little, for Lady Catherine in her overlord's hands was nothing more nor less than a prize of war. She was a prize treated with great courtesy, but nonetheless a prize to be disposed of like any other piece of property.

In truth, Stephen did not even realize Lady Catherine's unwillingness, for she made no protest against going with him. Both her father and her late husband had remained totally aloof from the court and the civil war; even so, rumours and snatches of news came by way of travelling knights errant and merchants, and she had heard a good deal about King Stephen and about Hugh Bigod. If she had to fall prize to either of them, Catherine considered herself lucky to have fallen into Stephen's hands. He was, she had heard, an exceedingly kind man – indeed, he acted kindly and spoke kindly to her – and Queen Maud was said to be very thoughtful and considerate of others when her family's interests were not involved.

This did not mean that Catherine thought any desire of hers would be consulted; she understood her position completely. It merely meant that, within the bounds of their own advantage, the king and queen would do the best they could for her. Had it been absolutely necessary to marry her to an ugly, brutalized mercenary, even to a monster of degraded cruelty, they would have done so – with regret, but done so nonetheless. As it was, when Maud told Catherine that she was being proposed as a third wife to Sir Rannulf of Sleaford, she congratulated the young woman on her good fortune. She pointed out that Sir Rannulf might seem to be a hard and bitter man and not young, but he had not actively mistreated his previous wives, he was just, honest beyond any doubt, and in excellent health and physical condition.

Privately Maud thought that it was unlikely that Rannulf would offer his wife either love or tenderness, but, on the other hand, he was equally unlikely to starve her, imprison her, steal her property, or beat her for amusement – all of which, if not common practice, were frequently enough encountered forms of behaviour among unscrupulous husbands who married heiresses.

Lady Catherine, unlike Sir Rannulf, did not cry out against the marriage; for this there were many reasons, none of which included any satisfaction with the proposal. Her religion and training, as well as her knowledge that she was a virtual prisoner, predisposed her to be submissive to the will of authority; above and beyond that, Catherine was in a state of emotional paralysis brought on by a series of shocks of grief. So many sorrows had oppressed the young woman in quick succession that her strong steady spirit lay inert and her mind was dulled.

In the same moment that Eustace was being carried senseless off the field before Devizes, Catherine was burying her young

20

husband and her three-year-old son. She had not been passionately attached to her husband, it was true. He had not possessed the strength or spirit that was necessary to arouse her love, but he had been chosen for her by her sweet-tempered, over-indulgent father because of his gentleness, and he had fulfilled his father-in-law's expectations in the treatment of his wife. Because he was kind and in love with her, Catherine had been fond of her husband, and her grief for him was sincere if not deep. Her feeling for her son was of a different order entirely. So violent had been her maternal agony at the loss of her child, that she had brought further tragedy upon herself and had miscarried, in the seventh month of her pregnancy, a desperately desired daughter. Received back into her father's keep with the tenderest sympathy, Lady Catherine had barely begun to recover some semblance of emotional balance when the final blow fell upon her – the earl of Soke also died.

Looking across the width of the fireplace at Rannulf of Sleaford, Maud wished irritably that he was as much a docile fool as the woman. She was tired and she did not wish to sit and reason with an unreasonable man who was ungratefully rejecting every offer made to him for his own advantage. If only he, like Catherine, would express neither joy nor repugnance, but sit with folded hands and eyes discreetly lowered, accepting as final all that he was told.

Maud almost giggled at the thought of Rannulf in such a position. The fool! He would not realize what a prize he was being given, and not in disposition only, for Lady Catherine was as beautiful as she was docile. A strong strain of Saxon blood had made her truly as fair as a snow maiden, her hair so pale a gold that it seemed silvery, her skin white and delicate as skimmed milk, and her large eyes of that soft, fathomless blue that makes the eyes of a very young child both infinitely mysterious and infinitely innocent.

Maud, however, had not yet introduced the lady into the conversation. By the time her inquiries about Rannulf's children were concluded, he was dressed. Instead of returning to the great hall, Maud had instructed her women to bring food to the solar and Sir Rannulf was now slumped in a cushioned, high-backed chair before the roaring fire, gnawing on the foreleg of a suckling pig. His eyes were not lowered, but fixed on his hostess, and their expression was an interesting mixture of fondness and caution.

'Nay,' Maud smiled at him, 'you need not regard me in that suspicious manner, my lord. You know and I know that I have kept you here to speak of my concerns as well as yours.'

'You do well to speak honestly to me.'

'I pay you that compliment, indeed, Sir Rannulf. You have been too long faithful to us for me to begin weighing my words to you now.'

Rannulf vented his harsh, mirthless laughter. 'If you have spoken an unweighed word to man or beast since you became queen of this realm, I will sharpen my sword on my own teeth before I next wield it in battle.'

Maud was touched to the quick because he spoke the truth, and spoke with what seemed to be a spark of malicious enjoyment. Her tone sharpened. 'Stephen and I do not pretend to be above other mortals, but why you should set us so far below them as to believe we cannot be honest with those we trust, I do not know.'

Trust was an unfortunate word. Rannulf was very fond of Maud, but he did not trust her. 'You have lost the habit,' he replied with his usual tactless directness.

Maud sighed, realizing now that he probably had not meant to hurt her and that it was useless to bandy words with a man who always said exactly what he thought, feared nothing, and sought no favours. He seemed sorry now that the subject had come up and she had a slight advantage. Tired or not, now was the moment to get on with obtaining his agreement to accept Catherine.

'I am exeedingly sorry that we judged so far amiss in the matter of the heiress and the lands of Soke, Sir Rannulf. Truly, Stephen and I had no thought that you did not love the married state as such. We knew, of course, that Lady Adelecia was not an easy woman to live with and that you wasted no grief over her loss, but—'

'You did not think that ten years of marriage to her might not give a saint a distaste for being a husband?'

'It might, indeed,' Maud replied drily, 'but you are no saint,

22

and, moreover, you were little enough in her company.'

'That little was too much.'

Although she had heartily disliked Lady Adelecia herself, Maud was annoyed by the pig-headedness that blocked every opening she tried to make to reason about this new marriage. 'You fathered a son upon her, nonetheless,' she snapped.

The harsh laugh cracked and was stilled. 'I would not lose her dower – what of that?'

It was true, of course, but Maud was frustrated again. If he had gone so far as to admit that there was a pleasure in be-getting children, even upon a woman one did not care for, she would have had a chance to expatiate on Lady Catherine's perfections. For a moment she sat staring at her hands in her lap and fighting her sense of fatigue, and then raised her head, realizing that he had given her a far more important opening. The dower of a woman who died childless reverted, under ordinary circumstances, to her family and Rannulf was too just and too honest to retain a childless wife's dower illegally – but Catherine had no family, none at all.

'Aye, that is just what I wished to speak to you about. Adelecia brought nothing in comparison with the lands of Soke. Wait – you have said already that you have need of no more land, but I am sure you wish to keep what is yours in peace and quiet. Bethink yourself, my lord, who among those men who are free to marry would you desire as so close a neighbour?'

Rannulf continued to stare at the flames in the hearth for a few seconds longer, but finally he turned to look directly at the queen, his broad brows drawn together in a considering frown. Maud studied the face turned to her more carefully, for she wished to be able to describe it in minute detail to the woman who would be – she was determined upon that – his wife. There was little enough in it to tempt a beautiful woman except its strength – a thin face, fortunately little marred by scarring, with a resolute jaw and a grim mouth. The beaked nose gave a predatory brightness to the clear grey eyes, and, although a full head of tangled curls showed no sign of thinning with age, enough grey was mixed with the brown to deny youth. It would not be easy, perhaps, to make that face sound romantically attractive, especially when coupled with Rannulf's deliberately crude manners, but Maud had struggled with more hopeless tasks.

'I see,' Rannulf was saying slowly, 'that there are no trusty men of weight available, but surely among the penniless younger sons you might find dozens who would suit your purpose.'

'Perhaps, although of that I am not sure. Soke was Henry's man. The woman shows no leaning in that direction, but she could hide what she thought would sit ill here. A young man might be easily led – she is very, very fair. But more important even than that, would a penniless younger son suit *your* purpose? We owe you much, Stephen and I, and we spent some thought upon this matter. Would it be to your taste to have a land-hungry pauper wield the lands of Soke?'

The frown of concentration deepened. Maud had no need to make the next point and she let the silence grow, studying her man. To the east and south of Soke lay the property of the earl of Norfolk. Hugh Bigod was by no means a peaceful man, and he was an open enemy to the king and queen, even while he was no friend to Henry of Anjou. Thus far Norfolk and the master of Sleaford had not come to blows, largely because they had a hearty mutual respect for each other but also because there was little chance for provocation between them. In spite of his attachment to the cause of Henry of Anjou, the earl of Soke and his vassals had taken little part in the fighting because of their geographical position. In addition, Soke had been an elderly, gentle man, given to religious and scholarly pursuits. His part in the civil war had been to supply money. Therefore, his lands had stood for many years as a buffer between Sleaford and Norfolk.

If a younger man, a loyal follower of the king, took those lands, it could not be long before conflict would arise. Either the young man would provoke Norfolk by trying to seize a little more land, or Norfolk would see in a younger man's inexperience an opportunity to add part of Soke's property to his own. Whichever man started the hostilities, sooner or later it was inevitable that Rannulf should be drawn into the battle. Sooner or later he would be engaged in fighting Norfolk to keep him off that buffer territory, and he would be spending his blood and substance for property that was not even his own.

Worse was the possibility that the vassals would not accept a young man who favoured the king as their earl. Again, and to even less purpose, Rannulf would be involved in war. If it were necessary to fight those men, he could at least do it for his own profit if he married Catherine.

For his part, Rannulf, who never forgot a favour, even if unintentional, had one factor to consider that never crossed Maud's mind because it was so tenuous and so far in the past. When the civil war first broke out in 1137, Catherine's uncle had been earl of Soke. He had considered the generalized hostilities a fine moment to swallow Sleaford, which Rannulf, then twenty-six, had just inherited. Under the pretext that Rannulf had declared for the rebels, Soke had enlisted Stephen's aid. The combined forces overwhelmed Rannulf's army, but not until Soke himself had been dispatched to his final reward.

After that, Rannulf had been unhorsed and beaten to his knees by Stephen, but that gentle man, with characteristic generosity, had exacted no retribution. Reversing his sword so that the hilt made a cross, the king demanded only that Rannulf swear to renounce the rebels and be his faithful man. Rannulf had, until Soke attacked him, been neutral. He felt no animosity towards Stephen, and life is sweet at twenty-six. He gave sword-oath gladly.

Unfortunately, Soke's brother, Catherine's father, who had become earl at the moment of his childless brother's death, had become a rebel at the moment Stephen pardoned Rannulf. To Rannulf's mind, he owed the loyalty of the vassals of Soke to Stephen because he had been the cause of their disaffection. There had been no occasion in the past to repay that debt, but he realized now that he must marry Soke's heiress. It would not be pleasant for him, but it was the best solution.

'There are other matters that you should consider, my lord,' Maud prodded gently when her experienced eyes told her that Rannulf had followed the proper line of reasoning to its logical conclusion. 'Remember there are no heirs to Soke except this girl. If you marry her, the lands and title are yours whether she bears you a child or not. If she does not please you, you may set her aside and, without wrong, still keep the property.'

Rannulf made no reply, but his face suddenly seemed to have turned to stone. Somehow, Maud knew, she had lost her advantage and she hurried on. 'No doubt you are wondering why I press you so to take what would benefit us to keep in our own hand. Perhaps if you had come quietly with your objections, I would have besought you to name a bridegroom for her more pleasing to you than yourself. You know why I cannot do that now.' Maud did not like to remind Rannulf of his obligation to Stephen, because such reminders, used too often, breed resentment; but she was determined to get Rannulf married to Catherine. 'Rannulf, Stephen has ever loved you and ever showed you kindness. What made you bespeak him so ill in open hall before all the court? You gave him sword-oath. It is your duty, even above others who have done homage, to uphold his honour. Naught now can save his honour but your yielding.'

Rannulf was silent still, for he was torn between the need to know how Soke had become conveniently free to be given to him and the fear that, once he knew, he would never be able to look Catherine or Maud in the eyes. Although he was very fond of Maud, he knew her to be capable of really evil acts in the defence of her husband and family.

'I know that Lady Catherine was married and that she had an infant son,' he burst out at last. 'I see that you have somehow disposed of the father and the husband. Did you destroy the child, too? Knowing this, am I to take the poor woman to wife? Have I been overhasty in my anger?'

'Merciful heavens!' Maud gasped, 'It is no wonder you were in a rage. But you are unjust. Soke died of his age – you know that. The husband and child are both dead too, but by no means of ours. I will swear that upon my husband's life! You must believe it.'

Rannulf sighed and sagged, more at ease, in his chair. What Maud swore on her life or honour might be doubtful; what she swore on Stephen's life was true. 'Dead of what?' he asked with only the mildest interest.

'The wasting fever. The whole keep was stricken; the whole countryside was sick with it in the south. I thought you must have heard even in Sleaford, the plague was so bad. It was God's will, not ours, Rannulf. More than that, you need have no fear that she carries her husband's seed either, for she was lightened of a seven-months' daughter, who did not live, only three months since – and that was after the husband was buried.'

'She has lost much. It will be bitter to her to be pressed into this new marriage so soon.'

Maud stared attentively at her guest's face, trying to read its expression. Was Rannulf expressing sympathy for the suffering of the woman, or was he merely worrying about her reaction to him under the circumstances? It did not matter. From the way the sentence was phrased, there could be no doubt that Rannulf now intended to accept the offer.

'Indeed,' Maud soothed, 'I have lost children of my own and I feel for her grief. Even so, there is no other way. The land must be guarded by a strong man. If she and the property had been taken by Bigod, worse might have befallen her than marriage with an honourable man – and she knows it. For her sorrow there can be no cure, but I speak from the heart when I tell you that it may be eased by giving her other children. You need not fear her spite – she has no spite in her, and too, a woman with such losses cleaves strongly to the father of her new young ones.'

Rannulf scowled, but Maud waited without doubt. 'Very well,' he growled. 'I will give you the manor and lands nearest to my western border that you have long craved as a bride-price for her, but nothing more. The lands are great, it is true, but Soke loved his books too well to care for the lands properly, and drained them, too, in Henry's cause. They are doubtless in bad condition and I will have much to do before I can wring a groat from them. Worse, if the vassals fight, they will cost me rather than pay me.'

'Just as you desire, my lord,' Maud agreed, meekly but triumphantly. 'I am sure we will not quarrel about terms, since it is our desire to please you, but let us leave these matters for the clerks in the morning.'

# Chapter 2

It had been a particularly mild winter, Catherine thought, shivering and drawing her furred cloak closer around her, but now, in March, it had begun to snow. She stopped pacing and leaned forward over the ramparts to watch the large flakes settle softly on the bare branches of a tree in the courtyard. Soon there was a ridge of white on each limb, for there was no wind at all to sweep the branches clean. It would be wonderful, her thoughts continued, if there were a wind that could sweep the mind and heart clean, instead of allowing past sorrows to cover all with a pale mantle. If she could but clear her soul of its burden of grief, perhaps she could understand what the queen was trying to tell her about Sir Rannulf. Even through the pain that dulled her mind, he had sounded a man of whom to be proud.

'Alas, Lady Catherine, what do you here all covered with snow?'

Turning her large eyes with their misty blue irises on the speaker, Catherine replied softly, 'I do but very little, only breathe the air and look upon the courtyard, Lady Warwick.'

Gundreda, Lady Warwick, looked with apparent compassion on the fair, slender woman before her. 'Your state is sad, no doubt, but there is no answer for it in death. You cannot fool the Lord, and to chill yourself in hopes to end your life is self-slaughter as much as to plant a knife in your breast.'

Catherine had a charming habit of looking up at people through a fringe of lashes which, although blonde, were long and thick enough almost to hide her eyes. She used the trick unconsciously on men and women alike, and this time it was of great value to her, for she saw something in Gundreda's face that stopped her speech. Since she had never once, not even in the greatest depth of her despair, thought of easing her

28

pain with death, she had been about to protest. Now she merely dropped her head a little lower.

Maud has slipped this once, Lady Warwick thought, having read Catherine's expression quite correctly. She does not need soothing; she needs awakening, and fear is the best source of attention. 'The queen,' she said gently, 'should not have told you how reluctant Sir Rannulf was to make the match. We spoke of that matter, she saying that since he had spoken against it before all the court you would be bound to hear of it, and I that it was needless to distress you over what you would soon enough understand. Perhaps, however, she was right – she is very wise and she felt that you needed to be warned. I could not see any reason to that either. Reluctant or not, I said to her, Sir Rannulf is an honourable man. I cannot believe he would harm the lady to take her lands unto himself.'

'He has the lands anyway,' Catherine forced out, a pang of fear even sharper than her grief pinning her attention on Gundreda's words. 'I am only a woman and there are no heirs. All is in the king's gift.'

Maud had told Catherine nothing of Rannulf's reluctance. On the contrary, she had emphasized only his habitually harsh voice and rough manners, hinting that these covered a generous heart and a warm nature. She had also told Catherine everything she knew about Lady Adelecia, explaining how unpleasant a wife that lady had been and that Sir Rannulf was, on that account, a trifle soured upon women. He needed careful handling, Maud had said over and over; he needed to be pampered and deferred to; he needed cheerful compliance without fretfulness, nagging, or whining. Catherine had heard with only half an ear, knowing herself not to be a fretful or whining woman, but now the words came back with an ominous ring.

'So it would seem,' Gundreda explained sharply, 'but do not talk like a silly woman. To insure the land to his blood, if you do not breed with him, you must die first. If he should die before you, which is in the course of nature because of his age, you will marry again and take your lands with you. I said he was an honourable man, but do not tempt him.'

'I must go in,' Catherine whispered, shuddering. 'Now I am indeed chilled.'

It was cruel to frighten Catherine, Lady Warwick thought, but she did it out of kindness and the hints could soon be wiped out by explanations. Moreover, Catherine might be useful. Her father's vassals might not be pleased with this forcible change in overlords. If they clung to Catherine and Catherine could be manipulated, it would be well to have her confidence.

In the great hall where those men who had not gone to hunt sat idling away the day with chess or dice, Robert, earl of Leicester, leaned forward and prodded his foster brother with a stubby forefinger.

'You are no eager bridegroom, I hear, even though you have seen the advantages of the match. Well, that is not so hard to understand, but that you should not even be curious enough to go look upon the woman – that passes understanding.'

'I will look sufficiently upon her when I have her to wife.'

'Perhaps even so indifferent a husband as you will not find that a burden. She is passing fair. I, loving you as I do, went to see.'

'And if she had been foul? What matter what she be since the lands are certainly hers and no other man has a claim to her?'

'Ah, but she is not foul – in no way. Beautiful, silent as a mute – which you will find a pleasant change – and heiress to Soke. Fortune seems to have turned her most favourable orbs upon you.' Leicester paused a moment and continued in a slightly altered voice. 'We have all been very fortunate of late, it seems to me. It was fortunate that you were beside Eustace at Devizes; it was fortunate that you came safe away; it was fortunate that young Henry took that so much to heart as to return to France. Surely we sit at the top of the Wheel. Mayhap we should begin to look for a soft spot upon which to fall when the goddess spins the Wheel again.'

'What?'

Rannulf had been studying the chessboard between himself and Leicester, giving only a small part of his attention to the commonplace gibes about his coming marriage, and the meaning of the last portion of Leicester's remarks shocked him when it penetrated.

'Why do you look so startled, Rannulf? Is it beyond chance that the young devil may return?'

'Beyond chance?' Rannulf asked slowly. 'Nay, of course he will return – unless he dies. Even that will matter little, for there is another spawn of the same breed. But what talk of falling is this? I climb to no heights. My feet are firmly upon the ground. Wherefore should I fall?'

'Have you never seen the ground cut away from below a great wall? Does it stand thereafter?'

A very faint flush darkened the master of Sleaford's weather-beaten complexion, giving a brighter gleam to the keen eyes. 'I am an old man, and very stupid, my lord of Leicester. If you would warn me that I have an enemy, speak out and name him, and if you have other matters in mind, speak out of those things also. Do you think that I will be overpowered with fear if I hear that one hates me or that I will run quickly bearing tales if—'

'Nay, nay, Rannulf, rise not so in your stirrups. If ever I knew a man with a more touchy pride! When I speak out, you growl for one reason, and when I go softly, you growl for another.' Robert of Leicester glanced carefully around them to be sure that no one was in hearing distance and spoke in a lowered voice. 'To speak out then, there is a portion of both in what I say. I have never seen in Eustace's eyes the glance he bestows upon you. Moreover—'

'Oh, he is a hot-headed young cub, and I sat somewhat firmly upon him throughout that last campaign. Just now, he loves me not. Stephen, too, can be angry, but not for long, and the son is like the father.'

'No!' There was real urgency in Leicester's voice, for he thought that Eustace's hatred was based upon more than the disagreements of the campaign.

'What means this, Robert?'

Leicester had a heavy body and a slow, deliberate manner of speech that deluded many people into thinking that his mind moved slowly too. It did not.

'Speak low. I know not whether he has cleverly concealed what he truly is by intention all these years or whether this fruitless battling without hope of decision has soured and

31

destroyed his true nature, but Eustace is not the man he was before Henry came. There is a bitterness under his smiles. Worse, he now seems the very opposite of that generous man Stephen and grudges every man his own livelihood. You have not been to court since he rode home from Devizes – you bury yourself at Sleaford in spite of my urgings of you to come here – and therefore you could not know of this, but he seizes whatever he can now, rightly and wrongly.'

'But wherefore? Stephen has never denied him aught; why should he take what is not his when he could have as much rightfully merely by asking?'

Leicester glanced around again. 'Because he does not wish his father to know how much he has. I have no proof, but I believe he plans to buy mercenaries secretly. I tell you, Rannulf, he will not keep to the old ways. He is as bad as Henry – and not as honest.'

'I am growing deaf,' Rannulf said. 'I did not hear that last remark at all. What you said of the prince – I hope you are wrong. I will not believe it without the evidence of my own eyes, certainly. What is more important to me is why you tell me things like this just now.'

'Have I had a chance to tell you anything sooner? Have I been such a bad friend to you all these years? Is it so strange that I should warn you when I see danger?'

'What danger that I need fear?' Rannulf laughed harshly. 'Not even Eustace would dare meddle with my lands – my vassals know me of old.'

'I never thought you a fool before. No, he will not meddle with the vassals of Sleaford, but what of those of Soke? You are suddenly doubly rich and burdened with men who owe you as yet no loyalty. Would that not attract a greedy man's attention, more especially when he believes he owes you a grudge? There is no harm in Stephen, but Eustace – he hates you, Rannulf, and if I were you, I would listen to what Hereford has to say – it is not about the Angevin.'

'Oh ho! The young firebrand, eh? I thought you too old to be caught by a scent of bad fish.'

'But what if it is not a scent of bad fish? He is hot-headed, but he is honest. I have never known him to lie and if he does

32

not speak treason, which I warrant you he will not to you, you should listen to him and judge what he says.'

'I always listen, but,' Rannulf's eyes were attracted by a flash of light and he realized that two of the young bucks who danced attendance on Maud's ladies were surprisingly close, 'your attention wanders from the game. You were not wont to be so easily caught. Your king is checked.'

Leicester caught the infinitesimal alteration in his companion's tone, looked at the board, and swiftly moved a knight. 'My man stands between,' he murmured meaningfully, 'and the church looks kindly from behind.'

Rannulf frowned. He hated these allusive conversations, but Leicester wanted to tell him something, and they could neither talk freely nor leave their game suddenly without giving their discreet audience too much to think about. Rannulf could see Leicester's bishop trained on the square to which he had just moved the knight, protecting it from Rannulf's rook, which also covered the square. However, it was also true that the churchmen of England favoured the Angevin cause.

'I would not put my keep in jeopardy too lightly,' Leicester continued, punning on the other name commonly given the rook – a castle.

Whatever Leicester was trying to say to him was unhealthy. Rannulf moved a pawn so that the queen behind it could overshadow the square upon which the knight stood. 'But when the men march out,' he said firmly, 'the queen still stands guard. It is best to play all games slowly, and strictly according to the rules.'


Ordinarily Stephen of Blois was extremely dilatory in matters of business, but the hard fighting of the past year had aroused him to unusual activity. The effects of this quickening of the blood still lingered sufficiently so that it was only a day after Maud brought him word that Rannulf had changed his mind and decided to marry the heiress of Soke that he summoned his scribes and dictated to them the letters that would announce the name of their new master to the late earl of Soke's vassals. He had just completed the complimentary opening when Eustace, who had been staring moodily into the fire –

a practice which was becoming unpleasantly frequent – raised his head to listen.

'To whom do you write, father?'

'The vassals of Soke.'

'Why?'

'To tell them that I invest the new earl a month from this day. I invite those who can to come to court to do their homage and instruct those who cannot come to meet the future Lord Rannulf meekly and do his bidding.'

Eustace scowled heavily, the expression marring his handsome face. He looked, at first glance, very much like his father, being tall, fair, and heavily built, but on closer examination his features were less prepossessing. The son's jaw was more brutal than the father's, his mouth thinner-lipped and held more rigidly. There was a still greater difference in the upper face. Stephen's forehead was broad and his balding had given it a height that could pass for nobility; his eyes were large, slightly protuberant, and their expression decidedly benign. All in all, Stephen looked to be what he was, a very kind and generous man with excellent intentions. With very similar features, Eustace looked no such thing. Perhaps it was the full head of blond hair, crisp and curly, which gave the broad forehead an unpleasant shallowness; perhaps it was the setting of the eyes that gave the appearance of cunning. Whatever it was, when the deceptive smile was absent, Eustace's countenance proclaimed that he was being consumed by not very pleasant emotions.

'Have you not done enough,' the young man snarled, 'in making him this offer? Let him make his own way with the vassals. Has he merited complaisance from you by his arrogant and disrespectful behaviour?'

Stephen laughed good-naturedly. 'If Rannulf Tefli spoke a respectful word to any man living, I would at once call my best physician to attend him – he would be sick unto death.' Then he grew more serious and a worried frown creased his brow. 'My son, he has merited any kindness I can bestow, any gift in my giving, for that he has preserved you to me.'

'Preserved me!' Eustace gasped, trying not to scream. 'He

34

has shamed me – all men heard me say I would take Devizes or die – and he has dishonoured you also. If it had not been for his cursed interference, I could have had the Angevin in my grip on the retreat from York or have trapped him in Dursley. Always he counselled caution and delay, and he was so cautious that we delayed until we missed our prize. I tell you he is a traitor and that his caution and delay were planned for the Angevin's benefit.'

'Nay, my child, I know your bitter disappointment, but that you did not take Henry was neither Rannulf's fault nor yours. Such things happen in war – yes, even three times. Come Eustace, I do not rest my opinion on his word alone – although I would take it above any man's in the land. All who were with you agree that he could have done no other way.'

'Cowards all!'

'Nay, Eustace, it is not true. They are all brave men, and Rannulf especially – I have fought with him and against him too, remember. I beg you to guard your tongue. Only think how comfortable is our present situation. The land is at peace; Hereford and Chester sit in the council—'

'To preach rebellion!'

There was the sorrow of hopelessness in Stephen's eyes, but he smiled again. 'While they are here, at least we know what they do. The last time I drove them from the court as traitors, they gave up all pretence and raised armies against us. You should not always look ahead to seek out trouble. Mayhap, if we look aside, speak softly, and are generous in our pardon of their treachery, this time they will not break faith.'

Eustace's lips parted to reply, but an instant later he shut them tightly. He was flooded with shame, with a misery beyond expression. Thus his father always was, hopeful without hope, seeing good in all men, fooled thereby, tricked, played upon, but never wiser. What joy it was to be son to the king of England – son to the king but not heir to the throne. Even that his father had thrown away, openly promising to make Henry the heir and secretly scheming – if anything that Stephen could do could be secret because he was too open to hide anything – to circumvent the promise. And all men knew it! What joy to be the son of him who might be the most feared and respected man in the land and who was, instead, its standing jest.

Eustace's eyes filled with tears. If he were to die, that butt of England's humour, that king who was no king, a strong hand with sufficient mercenaries could weld the realm into unity. It needed only to root out the founding stones of the rebellion – Chester, Hereford, and Gloucester. Now, while they were at court, it might be lightly done. A knife in a dark passage, an arrow on the hunting field, poison in a cup – and it would be over. But, dishonoured a thousand times over by breaking his word, his father called such thoughts dishonourable. None would dare call him dishonourable or anything else – if his father were dead.

Meanwhile, Stephen had signalled to the scribes to go. If it troubled Eustace to hear of these arrangements, there was no need to make them here and now. Just at this time the boy's blood was hot against Rannulf; it was foolish to torment him. Stephen studied his son's averted face in silence for a while, then rose and embraced him fondly.

'My beloved son, do not let your unease make you angry with me. If I have not always done well, I have always tried to do well.'

For a moment Eustace remained rigid in the embrace, but only a moment. His arms came up around his father's neck and he pressed the older man to him frantically, protectively, and broke into sobs.

'Alas, my son, why do you weep?'

'Because I am afraid, papa, afraid of myself. I have such thoughts! I do not know what evil thing possesses me. Papa, I do not wish to see you die before me!'

'My child,' Stephen soothed, smothering a sensation of shock, 'my child, it is the will of God, the course of nature, that fathers should die before their sons. If you love me, do not desire for me the greatest grief any man can know. Any other loss I can bear, but not the loss of my children. When your brother died – it was so long ago and my heart still bleeds for him – I thought that if I had to bear such grief again I could not live. Yet you are dearer far, Eustace—' Stephen tightened his grip and then relaxed it. 'What fools we are. Last

36

year we bade each other farewell full blithely and went to fight. Now, when we are at peace, we weep and speak of death. Come, we grow stale from too much sitting within.'

Maud, sitting among her women, listening and embroidering, felt it too. They were all stale from their winter confinement and a vast restlessness pervaded the entire court. Men rose suddenly from their seats to pace the hall; women laid down their needles and pushed open the shutters to stand shivering, staring out at the quickening grass. Low and seldom at first, but louder and more frequently as the last weeks of February passed and the first days of March came, was the sound of agricultural talk. Now the serfs would be breaking the earth as the ground thawed; now they would set the seed. Deep within the breasts of mail-clad warriors and befurred and bejewelled ladies stirred the basic love of the land.

· In itself the thing was good, but Maud knew it was also dangerous. The trouble was that the knights and ladies of the court were too far removed from true union with the soil. They were close enough to be caught up in the recurring tides of the seasons, but they were not country squires and housewives. These men and women would not be satisfied to oversee their serfs' work nor even play at joining the labour. They were no longer close enough to the land to obtain satisfaction from giving advice on what grain to plant or how often to freshen the cattle. Such bucolic joys could hold their attention for only a limited time. Then the restlessness, which was basically a frustrated desire to create — and Maud knew this because she had seen for years that the pregnant women alone were free of the feeling — would drive them to seek other cults. Maud knew these people; she knew that the outlet they would seek first because they knew it best was war. A neighbour's strip of land would appear greener, his cattle fatter, his serfs meeker — an insult would be thrown and men would be in arms.

The time of the first ploughing and planting was the worst. If she could hold the court together until the soft, listless days of April, the queen knew that the deep urgency to be up and doing would pass. Last year there had been no need for devices because Hereford had been gathering his armies to renew the civil war and the barons faithful to the king had more than enough to occupy their energies. This year the rebels were quiet, almost too quiet. Maud's eyes went blind although they seemed bent on her stitchery as she thought about holy days, fast days and feast days, any excuse for a great celebration which could promise sufficient excitement to keep the barons in London. There was Easter, of course, but the Church frowned on tournaments and would certainly object to that method of celebrating the event of Christ's rising. Nonetheless, the men needed to fight and the woman needed to see blood spilled. That alone would keep them quiet.

'Madam.' The soft voice of a lady-in-waiting broke Maud's chain of thought. 'Sir Rannulf desires a word with you.'

Now what, Maud wondered, as she hurried down to meet him. Perhaps she should have called a priest and had him marry Catherine immediately after he had agreed. He was not given to vacillation, but that worked both ways. Perhaps he was regretting having changed his original opinion. Her heart sank when she saw him pacing uneasily. Rannulf was a man who knew the value of rest because he had very little of it. He was not one to walk the floor unless he was deeply disturbed. His face, when he turned it to her, held a look of deep embarrassment, not grim determination.

'I scarcely came prepared for this eventuality,' he began irritably as soon as she was near enough to hear him.

'What eventuality?' Maud asked steadily, subduing a desire to cry out that she could face no more problems.

'My wedding,' he replied wryly, and Maud could have wept with relief.

'In what way are you unprepared, my lord? We stand as parents to the bride and will furnish the feast and all other matters. If you provide a willing heart and,' she added despairingly, 'a less black countenance, that will be all that is necessary.'

'Hmph,' Rannulf grunted. 'That is all I am like to provide. It came to me just before that all the garments I have are what I stand in. A pretty sight I will be, rust-stained and mud-splattered.'

'I never knew you were so vain – or so desirous of pleasing,' Maud laughed, unable to resist the temptation to prick a spot she had not previously known to be vulnerable.

'I hope I am neither, but I can see no reason to shame the poor woman who must marry me. She will doubtless hear enough from the court – if she has not already heard – of my great desire for this match. I need not drive home the point. Moreover, there is another matter. I have not even a seal ring upon my finger to offer as a bride-gift. In any case, I will need more than that and there is no time to obtain anything from the goldsmiths. Let me buy some trinket from you that she has not seen you wear. I would not have her think that you drove me to this against my will and that I will hold a grudge against her for it.'

Maud's expression softened and her warm smile lit up her eyes. 'Ah, my lord, I have found out your soft heart. How kind of you to think of these things.' Rannulf scowled and roughly shook off the hand she had laid on his arm, but the queen laughed, very well satisfied. 'Wait, I will bring down some things that I think fitting and you shall have your choice – and let there be no more talk of buying.'

'I do not like to incur such debts.'

But debts were just what Maud wished to load him with. 'You are incorrigible. May not one friend offer another a free gift for love? In that there can be no debt.'

It was surprising, Maud thought, as she searched hastily through her jewel boxes, to find so much consideration for a woman in Rannulf of Sleaford. She thought too about how she could add some magnificence to the wedding on such short notice and then almost choked with regret for having pushed Rannulf into celebrating it so soon. If only she had set it a few weeks off, that would have been all the excuse she needed for holding a great tourney.

She dared not suggest delay now; the smallest thing could reawaken all Rannulf's suspicions and expose Catherine to even more gossip than she had already heard. Moreover, to delay the marriage would delay Rannulf's investiture as the new earl. The vassals were reluctant enough to take an earl who was loyal to Stephen. To leave them longer in freedom might make them totally unwilling to obey such a master. The sooner – that was it!

When the vassals of Soke came to do homage to their new overlord, she could rightfully celebrate the event with a grand tourney. It would flatter the vassals that such an event was held in their honour and – yes, that would solve another problem too. Let Rannulf stand off a selected number of his new vassals in the lists – that would give the worst disaffected a chance to work off their ire and give them a healthy respect for him. Then let him lead the remainder in the mêlée. Any hard feelings remaining should melt into loyalty when they fought behind his banner.

# Chapter 3

'My lord, if you wish to bathe and eat, you must rise now.'
John, youngest son of Simon of Northampton, shook his master
gently.

'I am awake.'

'The queen bade me give you these garments, my lord, and
also ordered me straightly to tell you that the king's barber
waits to shave you and cut your hair.'

Rannulf burst into laughter. 'Very well, when I have bathed
you may send him to me, but if she hopes to mend my looks
thus, she will be sadly disappointed. There is nothing better
to be seen under the bristles.'

Sure of his prowess and courage, proud of his family, of his
reputation for integrity, and of the respect of all men, Rannulf
of Sleaford feared only one thing – women. A man could be
reasoned with or challenged fairly to fight, but what could be
done with a woman? Except for Maud, Rannulf knew them to
be utterly without the power to reason, and, although they
could easily be beaten into submission – he had sufficient experience of that with Adelecia – it made him so sick to strike
such weak and mewling things that his gain was not worth his
pain.

Rannulf surveyed himself with brooding eyes in the polished
silver mirror the barber held up for him. Here he was, about to
be married to a great lady, a lady whose lands and wealth
equalled or exceeded his own, a lady who, his friends told him,
was very beautiful, a lady whose father and husband had been
his enemies – and he had made it plain to all the world that he
desired neither her nor her lands. The barber, seeing the expression of impotent fury in his client's face, began to expostulate hesitantly, assuring him that he was trimmed and furbished
in the very latest fashion. Rannulf waved him irritably away.

No matter how distasteful to him, he would have to settle the fact that he was to be master in his own household at once. At the first sign of opposition, he would bring her to heel, and then perhaps – perhaps not. He remembered that when he beat Adelicia, no matter how many apologies and promises of amendment he wrung from her, she became worse and worse. Not that kindness had improved her behaviour; if he offered so much as a civil word, she would think she had won all and could go her own way. And this one was Soke's daughter, whose enmity to him was likely bred in the bone. A horrible and unaccustomed feeling of inadequacy shook him, only to be followed by a burst of laughter when he remembered how often he had faced death in battle without a shudder.

Lady Catherine did not need to be awakened. She had lain awake all night recalling her talk with Gundreda and trying to recall every word the queen had said about Sir Rannulf. Her mind was no longer dulled by grief, for it had been quickened by sharp pangs of fear. If Catherine could have preserved her son's life or her father's by the sacrifice of her own, she would have made that sacrifice without a moment's hesitation. They were dead now, however; no sacrifice could recall them, and she could do no more than pray for their souls and pay the priests to do likewise.

Gundreda had said nothing one could put a finger on, yet Catherine felt it was her life that was now threatened, and she discovered in herself a passionate desire to live. She walked to a shutter and opened it, fear giving sight to eyes that had been sorrow-blinded. There were the blue of the sky and the gilding the sun gave to the walls and roofs. Shaken free of her grief, she knew she desired to see the sun rise and set and take pleasure in its beauty; she desired to see the new corn spring from the earth, watch the fruit ripen, gather the harvest in the autumn, read and sew by the fire in winter.

The sounds behind her were those of the maids bringing in her bath. Catherine moved away from the window and closed the shutter. Perhaps she had read too much into Lady Warwick's words. But why had the queen urged her so straightly to do all to please her new husband? The master of Sleaford must be a dangerous man. And had not her father had some quarrel with him? Still, Catherine decided, seeking for calm as she stepped from the bath and dried herself, the matter could not be urgent. Surely Sir Rannulf would try for an heir out of her before he looked for other ways of securing her lands to himself. Suddenly she threw off the cloth she was using as a towel and looked at her body. She could not help but be pleased by it, and she felt that any man would also be pleased by it. Her pregnancies had not marked her nor destroyed the slender litheness of her waist and hips; the delicate, blue-veined skin of her full, firm breasts must be attractive. Clearly there was one way to save herself.

Laying aside all thought of the indifference towards him which she had intended to show, Catherine began to choose the outward instruments with which to trap her new husband into love. First, a thin woollen shift, bleached to perfect whiteness; next, an indigo tunic, its neckline and cuffs blazing with gold-thread embroidery to set off her fair complexion; last, a gown of paler misty blue that matched her eyes. Now to braid pearls into her moonlight hair, to bite her lips and pinch her cheeks; all must be done to bring forth her greatest beauty.

It was the path to safety, and Catherine never doubted she could tread it firmly. Even when she was brought to Rannulf's side and a quick glance showed that his face was set and cold, she did not falter. Her hands did not tremble, and her voice was low and sweet and steady as she repeated the marriage vows. The only thing she could not command was her complexion, and the pink she had pinched back into her cheeks faded until she became so pale that Rannulf took her arm to support her, fearing she would faint.

The priest was finished; the affirmative shouts of the crowd of noblemen and women who had witnessed the marriage were over; Rannulf had touched his wife's lips in the kiss of peace – they were mated. Now the grooms brought the horses forward, and Rannulf threw his wife up into the saddle to return to the White Tower for the wedding feast. He wondered if she could sit a horse in her present state.

'You are so pale, madam. Are you ill?'

Catherine looked down into the expressionless face turned up to her. 'No,' she murmured, quelling a desire to burst into

43

tears now that she knew herself to be irrevocably in this man's power, 'I am afraid.'

'Afraid? Of what? You have been a wife before.' Rannulf scowled, annoyed with himself because fear could do her no harm and him much good.

'I am afraid of you, my lord,' Catherine sighed, 'of the new things I must learn and the new life I must begin.'

Rannulf's scowl deepened. Perhaps it was good for her to be afraid, but he did not like it. Her voice was sweet as a child's; she did not whine or threaten, but spoke with a child's simplicity and looked with a child's simplicity for assurance.

'You need have no fear of me. I am not a boy to be impatient with an honest mistake or a little folly – and I have some knowledge of women.'

That last statement made Maud, who was coming to see what was delaying the bride and groom, turn away rapidly. She was convulsed with laughter for a moment, for it was perfectly plain to her that Rannulf had not the faintest understanding of women at all. As much as she disliked Lady Adelicia, it was necessary to admit that Rannulf's stupidity had caused most of the trouble, since his behaviour alternated irrationally between brutality and complete yielding. Look at him, Maud thought despairingly. Face to face with an oncoming army, he could decide matters of life and death. Now, face to face with one gentle woman, he must clear his throat as if to spit on her, look down at the ground, and scowl all the while as if the poor girl were his worst enemy. God grant her understanding or she will become another Adelicia, and I will have made him my enemy instead of binding him closer. She was about to touch her horse and go forward to relieve the situation when the wind rose and Catherine shivered. Maud pulled up her horse again as Rannulf spoke.

'Have you no furred cloak, madam?' He reached up to the clasp of his own. 'Here, take mine, and order one for yourself as soon as maybe. You are too frail to bear the chill wind.'

Surprise pierced the new shell of terror Rannulf's scowl had been building around Catherine. 'Nay, my lord, I am very strong.' A faint smile touched her pale lips. 'I have a furred cloak, but it was folly – and vanity – that made me leave it. It

44

is brown, you see, and would not be fitting with my gown.'

A laugh was startled from Rannulf. He did not doubt Catherine's statement that she was afraid, and it was ludicrous that in the midst of her fear she should concern herself with the colours of her cloak and gown. Amusement further tempered his general dislike of the female as he wrapped his cloak around her for Catherine looked very diminutive in the voluminous garment – like a child.

'Now you are justly served,' he said in a voice he might have used to reprimand his son, 'for surely mine suits you worse than yours could have done, no matter what colour. Can you ride, madam, or must I lead your horse?'

Maud was delighted with the turn the conversation had taken; nothing could be better than what Rannulf had said and done, and nothing more satisfactory than Catherine's surprised assurance that she could indeed ride. Catherine, after all, had not known Adelecia nor the ways she had of tormenting her husband, one of which was claiming illness and lack of trust in the grooms and making him lead her horse on foot. She was so pleased that she was just about to hasten away and leave them to themselves when Rannulf, true to form, ruined all.

'Good,' he replied. 'Find the queen and return with her. I have some business I must see to.'

Catherine was shocked. The queen had told her that Rannulf was an ill-mannered man and she knew he did not wish to marry her, but to be absent from his own wedding feast, no matter how unwelcome, was to be ill-mannered to an absolutely unparalleled degree. No affair could be so pressing. She did not have a chance to protest, however, for in that instant Rannulf turned his head, saw Maud, and, without waiting for a word with either woman, took the few steps to his horse, leaped into the saddle and rode away. Maud hastened up, revising her estimate of Catherine's sweetness and docility and cursing Rannulf of Sleaford under her breath. There was no way she could soothe Catherine, for the insult was beyond reason. All Maud could do for Rannulf now was to show Catherine that, although she was heiress to Soke, her public consequence as well as her private comfort depended upon her husband.

Rannulf had no intention of missing the wedding feast, for his errand took him only a few streets away. He expected, indeed, to catch up with his wife before she reached the Tower, and would have done so had not Maud hustled her away. He felt very virtuous, as a matter of fact, as he set spurs to his horse and careened down the muddy road, for his business was to determine whether he could offer his wife a home of her own in London. He had a house in the city, but he had not lived in it for some time and needed to know whether it was still habitable. If it was, he would write to Sleaford to have his clothing, bed, linens and other household items sent to him, and he and Catherine could live in comfort and privacy – things not to be obtained when lodging with the king – until his investiture as earl of Soke had taken place.

A brief visit assured him that the walls and roof of the place were sound and that such trifling damage as had been done could easily be repaired. When he realized, spurring even more hastily along the road that led to the castle, that he had missed Catherine, he was a little annoyed, but no comprehension of the apparent enormity of his behaviour disturbed him. He was sure that his bride would scarcely notice the absence of a groom so unwelcome in the press of well-wishers which must be surrounding her.

Accordingly, Rannulf did not hurry while he made his way to the head of the room. Catherine was not in the seat of honour. Well, there was no rule that she must remain seated, although it was customary. He would have liked to sit down himself, but it was also customary for the bride and groom to receive good wishes together. Rannulf turned his eyes on the crowd, seeking any large knot of persons which could indicate the presence of the bride. There was none near him, and he sighed and began to wander through the hall seeking her. Rannulf was very puzzled when he came across Catherine, who was sitting in a window seat.

'How now, madam,' he said mildly, 'What do you here? Why are you not at the top of the room?'

That was the last straw! Catherine was too well bred to shriek in public, but if a woman could be said to snarl, she did so. Her full lips drew back from her perfect teeth and her cheeks turned scarlet with the rush of her blood. Let him take what revenge he would. It was better to be literally destroyed than to die of shame.

'Because,' she spat, 'no one saw fit to take me there. Am I to push my way forward myself? Should I stop the passersby and bid them wish me well?'

The owner of a fine, full-fledged temper of his own, Rannulf could respect a round rejoinder. Apparently the woman – she did not look like a child now – could speak honestly what was in her mind. Rannulf did not understand why she was so angry with him, since he had nothing to do with the behaviour of the guests, but that thought could not hold his mind as he stared in amazement into Catherine's flushed face. He had been startled by her pale beauty when he first saw her, but he was dumb-founded by her passionate radiance now. An urgent sense of desire touched him, a sensation far different from his usual impersonal need for a woman.

'I had no opportunity to give these to you earlier,' he said finally, ignoring her outburst. 'Here is your bride-gift.'

He dropped the pouch gracelessly into her lap and stood somewhat bemused, waiting for her to open it. Catherine wanted to throw it back into his face, but again the fact that it was a public place restrained her behaviour. As she slowly un-tied the string which secured the mouth of the pouch, her fear returned. Rannulf of Sleaford was not the man, by the look of him or by reputation, to accept opposition meekly. Possibly his indifference to her temper meant that he did not intend to endure it long. As soon as possible she must repair the damage she had done and return to the role of cheerful and graceful compliance. The drawstring gave and the jewels slid into her lap. Catherine gasped, her temper and fear alike momentarily forgotten, for she had an inordinate love of beautiful things and a passion for finery. Rannulf, watching her, almost smiled. The leaping from tantrum to pleasure for a new toy was a child's trick which he understood. If she was always so easily dis-tracted, she would be no trouble to manage.

'I – I thank you, my lord,' she murmured, somewhat mollified. Perhaps it was this he went to get.

'You are welcome to them,' Rannulf replied. The jewels

47

were worth a goodly sum, but there were plenty in Sleaford keep which could be doled out to maintain peace.

The faint humour in his voice did not escape her, and her heart began to beat more quickly. Why should he not give her the best of everything? In the event of her death, it would all be his again. 'My lord,' Catherine said urgently.

If she wanted more, peace would not be cheap. 'What now do you want of me?' Rannulf snapped.

What little colour had remained in Catherine's face faded away. 'I only wished to beg you to pardon me for my hasty speech. What happened could be no fault of yours.'

Rannulf stared at his wife attentively. Certainly it was true that what had happened was no fault of his – he did not even know what had put her out of temper – but that a woman should set aside emotion for reason and, moreover, that she should admit herself wrong on the basis of reasoning, was astounding. He noticed that Catherine was very pale again and was sorry for her; he understood very well how hard it was to admit oneself at fault.

'Very well,' Rannulf said approvingly.

That nearly brought another burst of rage from Catherine, but he had led her away from the window seat and she was forced to return with civility the belated compliments she was now receiving. She smiled charmingly and extended a graceful hand to a young man whose fair handsomeness almost took her breath away. Roger of Hereford kissed her hand, murmured good wishes, and moved on to her husband whom he addressed more jovially.

'I do not need to wish you well – you are well. Who could believe that such a face would go with such a dower?'

'Your wife left nothing greatly to be desired on either score,' Rannulf replied good-naturedly. He was far better pleased with Catherine than he had expected and was perfectly willing to display his satisfaction.

'Ah, but my wife is not here. She was lightened of a daughter some weeks ago and is still confined.'

Rannulf's brows drew together. Childbirth was a serious and dangerous matter. 'We did not see eye to eye, but I remember the lady kindly. She does well, I hope.'

'Aye, and the girl is already a shrew like her mother – God bless them both. When I first held her in my arms, she struck me soundly on the mouth.'

'There speaks a new-made father,' Rannulf laughed, recalling his own feeling of pride in similar circumstances.

'But I am not a new-made father – at least, it is the third time. All I seem to get is women – not that I regret this one. I wanted a maiden this time for I have her already bound in marriage, but the next, I hope, will be a son. There is my brother Walter to succeed me, but my brother – but this is no time to speak of political matters.'

Hereford was ready to move on, but Rannulf stopped him. 'Why not?' he asked. He had no particular desire for Hereford to seek him out in private to discuss matters of state. It would only give Eustace another cause to howl about treachery. Far better for a rebel like Hereford to unburden himself of whatever he wanted to say in public.

'Very well. My brother is a case in point. Whenever he needs money, or is bored, or, for all I can tell, when what he has eaten does not sit well in his stomach, he goes out to ravage the land.'

Rannulf laughed. 'Are you asking me what to do, or asking me to make him mend his ways?'

'I can control my brother,' Hereford said impatiently. 'I did but use him as an example. Half the kingdom is made up of Walters. Say such a man attacked my land – what should I do?'

'Drive him off.' Rannulf looked annoyed and then laughed again. 'Bah, you are drunk already. What kind of a fool's question is that? You have held your lands very well against all threat, Hereford.'

'Yes, but why should I have that need? Why cannot a man rest in his own keep without listening hourly for the call to arms?'

'Another fool's question. Because that is life.'

'Nay, Sir Rannulf. Because that is England.' The men stared purposefully at each other, faintly hostile. 'What will you do,' Hereford continued, well knowing that they favoured his cause, 'if the vassals of Soke will not accept you?'

Rannulf slid a glance at his wife, his face black with fury,

49

and Catherine held her breath. 'Do you think I cannot beat them into submission? Those who do not submit, I will slay. There are enough younger sons among my own vassals to take the lands and serve me loyally.'

'Perhaps you can do as you say, but think of the cost. There should be no need for you to think of such matters. If the transfer of Soke to your hands is ordered by the king, there should be no chance of resistance. The law should be obeyed.'

Rannulf burst into mirthless laughter. 'If the sun were made of gold and I could reach it, I would surely be a rich man. Why do you frown? It is equally reasonable.'

'Aye, with the king we have, it is equally reasonable.'

'Do not talk treason to me, Hereford!'

'I have no intention of talking treason to any man, but tell me this. If all the earls in the land agreed that Soke was rightfully yours and would aid you to it, would any vassals then dare say you nay?'

There was a momentary silence. Rannulf's eyes dropped, and then he sighed. 'Aye, then,' he said regretfully, 'but you have the question of reaching the sun again. Men seek their own interest first.' So this was what had caught Leicester's attention. It was an attractive idea, but not new, and Rannulf's eyes held only sadness.

Catherine was fascinated. Her menfolk had left the fighting to their vassals and dealt with politics through account books. In any case, they had never talked of such matters in her presence. She was frightened by Rannulf's attitude towards her father's men, but interested enough to be annoyed when a touch on her hand drew her attention away. Lady Warwick was well pleased with the results of her interference. There was an aliveness in Catherine's face, and she decided to take the next step in her education of this very sheltered young woman. A moment or two passed in the expected platitudes while Lady Warwick listened to the men to be sure they were involved in a sufficiently interesting subject. She could see Catherine's attention wavering, although she was turned politely enough towards her, and she came to the point with deliberate bluntness.

'Now that you have had some talk with Sir Rannulf, what do you think of him?' Catherine glanced uneasily at Rannulf's back and Gundreda laughed. 'He will hear nothing. When men talk together they are deaf to women's voices. After all, of what can a woman speak besides cookery and children?'

'I cannot think anything, madam,' Catherine replied cautiously. 'I have scarcely exchanged twenty words with him in the hurry of this day, but the king and queen have no cause to use me ill and Sir Rannulf's reputation is as high as a man's can be.'

'Oh, yes,' Lady Warwick said with an odd smile. 'As I told you, I have known Rannulf of Sleaford for many years, and he is truly a man whose pride and honour go before all else.'

'Is that not a good thing?'

'Is it? My husband, too, is of that sort. Pride often goeth before a fall, and honour can lead to disgrace. You are young. You may live many years beyond this husband. Do not allow him to become your disaster.'

Catherine's fears returned at flood tide. 'You cannot mean that he would harm me to steal my lands,' Catherine forced herself to whisper.

It was time, Gundreda knew, to resolve Catherine's fear. Terror does not lead to clear thinking. 'Good God, no!' she exclaimed. 'Rannulf? He would as soon cut out his own heart and eat it. You need not have any fear of that, nor that he will yield a tittle of it to any man through force, but he might drain lands dry in this senseless war for the succession. He will breed with you – he gave his other wives sons. Through honour a man may lose his children's livelihood. See that the lands are still there to benefit your little ones.'

Lady Warwick's mouth twisted, and the bitterness of her voice showed that she was not merely offering impersonal advice. 'A pox take all kings,' she added, then smiled. 'But that is at a distance. A closer matter is that Rannulf is not the sweetest-tempered man in the world. I said he would not harm you, and he would not do so with intention, but he might well make a life a misery for you. A woman needs a refuge. When your father's vassals come to London, make a way to speak with them in private. Perhaps you can come to terms with them so that—' Her hand closed warningly over Catherine's. 'Come to my house, if you have your husband's

51

leave. I have a stitch to show you that makes all embroidery light work.'

Catherine was not surprised at the sudden change of subject because she too had been conscious of an alteration in the rhythm of the men's talk. Hereford laughed and Rannulf growled, not unpleasantly but as if he were being teased about something that amused him. Lady Warwick moved away, but others came, and although Catherine was tired out with tension and civility, she was happy to mouth platitudes about which she did not have to think. Her father's vassals! She had never given them a thought during the period in which she was frozen with grief, but they had loved her father and it was possible that they would not stand idly by and see her harmed. Whether they would risk their lives and property for her was impossible to guess, nor would she ask them to take that risk if there were any chance that she could find safety by other means. Lady Warwick seemed so sure that the master of Sleaford was worthy of trust. Catherine stole a glance at the face of the man who stood beside her. His face was hard and his mouth was bitter, but he did not look cruel and the attitude of the men who came to speak to him betokened trust and sometimes affection.

The stream of well-wishers was curtailed at last by the summons to dinner, and both bride and groom were grateful, although for different reasons. Catherine wanted peace to follow her own thoughts; Rannulf was bored by so much small talk for which he had no taste, and was pleased by the knowledge that in a few hours more he would have Catherine to himself. He thrust away a dish of eels, telling his bride to pass them along to Stephen who adored them, but he allowed his gaze to drift down from her face to her throat, as round as and whiter than any marble column. He responded to her polite attempts at conversation largely with monosyllabic grunts, but he was by no means ill-pleased with them and Catherine, who was keenly alive to his mood, was not discouraged by his lack of response.

The meal, by the standards of the participants, did not last long. All Maud's efforts could not make eating a real pleasure during Lent. No quantity of salt, herbs, and pepper could change fish and eggs to beef and venison, even though every fresh- and salt-water fish, shelled and scaled, was provided.

52

Roasted, baked, stewed, stuffed, or boiled – it was still fish. Worse than that, however, was the starvation for fresh vegetables that all men, of high station or low, suffered. It was not, of course, that the eating of vegetables was proscribed, but by March the supply of even those fruits and vegetables which could be stored was running out. What was served was woody and tasted of mould; even the fresh-baked bread was tainted with the musty odour of the dank bins in which the grain had been stored for months.

The one advantage to the brevity of the meal was that it allowed less time for drinking, too. Nearly everyone was still sober when the tables were cleared and stacked against the walls, and Stephen called for music from the minstrels so that his guests could dance with a grateful heart. He knew that a major danger of a feast at court was that the political opponents, drunk and belligerent, would literally come to blows. They would continue to drink throughout the evening anyway, but the energetic dances would keep them busy and work off the high spirits engendered by the wine.

Rannulf danced once with his wife, leading her out onto the floor only after he had been prodded thereto by Maud, who had been reduced to telling him in Catherine's hearing that the dancing could not begin without him. Thereafter, nothing could move him to dance again, although he permitted Catherine to be led away by any man who applied for her company. When Hereford came up to ask for Catherine's hand for the third time, therefore, she did not wait for her husband's approval. If he did not care with whom she danced, she would choose the best partner. Rannulf, however, stopped his talk and looked at the dancing couple with a scowl. Until now he had paid no attention to what Catherine did when the music ended. This time he made his way across to her, grasped her wrist possessively, and led her away.

'It is not wise to spend overmuch time in the company of the earl of Hereford,' he snapped when they were out of earshot.

Before she knew what she was doing, Catherine wrenched her hand free of Rannulf's hold. 'What harm could he do me or I permit in a room full of people?'

53

'I do not believe he would do you any harm,' Rannulf laughed. 'His wife would skin him alive if it came to her ears, and he fears her as he fears the devil, although he fears no living man. Nonetheless, he is a pardoned rebel and for my wife to favour his company can do neither your honour nor mine any good.'

Catherine was insulted to the point of speechlessness. It was bad enough to be lectured about associating with Hereford after Rannulf had done it himself, but her husband's disgustingly even-tempered reply proved he was not jealous. He did not want her, and he did not believe that any man could want her.

In this, Catherine was quite mistaken. Rannulf, although certainly not jealous, was far from immune to his wife's charms. He stood beside her watching the dancers with brooding eyes. He was too old for this sort of nonsense, he knew, but perhaps it would be pleasant to join them. It would be very pleasant to feel Catherine's hand on his and occasionally to place his hand on her hip. Still, dancing was an activity in which he scarcely excelled, and he had no desire to make a fool of himself like the old goats he was watching caper about. It came to him suddenly that he did not want to dance, he wanted to touch Catherine. Well, she was his wife. He did not need the excuse of dancing for that!

'Do you take pleasure in this?' Rannulf's glance indicated not only the merrymaking group but also his disapproval.

'Very little,' Catherine replied. Ordinarily that would have been a lie, but this evening it was perfectly true.

'I also.' Rannulf hesitated, trying to find a polite way to say what he wanted, and then merely extended his hand. 'Come, then, let us go.'

Catherine was in no doubt of what he meant but she was startled. 'Should we not tell the queen?' she asked, not because she was reluctant to go with him, but because her mind was on the bedding ceremony with which it was customary to conclude marriages.

In the absence of any real legal system, Catherine knew that the best guarantee that a bargain would be kept was the presence of a large number of eye-witnesses who could affirm that the participants had fulfilled their commitments. This led to the practice of marrying outside the doors of the church rather than before the altar – the out-doors being conducive to the presence of the largest number of witnesses. It also led to the practice of publicly bedding the bride and groom. The bride would be disrobed, as many ladies of suitable rank as were present attending her, and set naked upon the bed; the groom, following with his gentlemen attendants, would be similarly served. After the jokes and remarks that such a situation would normally call forth were exhausted, the couple was left alone to consummate the marriage. That, however, was not the end of the affair by any means. In the morning both male and female guests returned to strip the sheets from the bed and display the proof of the bride's virginity.

The system was very practical and Catherine had not the slightest objection to it. Simply, the public nudity of bride and groom offered proof that neither had any concealed defect or deformity, and the incontrovertible evidence of the maidenhood of the woman proved that she was not carrying any other man's child. Thus a great many repudiations of marriages on the grounds of bad faith were avoided. Rannulf had no objection to the system either and did not take Catherine's question amiss. After a moment of thought, however, he shrugged.

'I can scarcely expect you to be a maiden. I can see that you are whole nor, for a blemish, would I put you aside.' That carried the unfortunate inference to Catherine that he had married her for her dower, which was certainly true, and more, what was not true, that he intended to throw the fact into her face whenever he could. Unaware of the fact that he had insulted his wife yet again, Rannulf proceeded, equally unintentionally, to frighten her nearly out of her wits by adding thoughtfully, 'Since you have no power to repudiate me, having no family, I need not be concerned for that.'

Catherine, believing that her husband was threatening her when he was merely examining the aspects of conforming or not conforming to custom aloud, felt literally sick with fear. The room spun and she caught unconsciously at Rannulf's arm to steady herself, drawing his attention. Rannulf was mildly irritated at the conventionality of women. They could not deviate from the form in the least item, he thought, without believing that the world would come to an end. Nonetheless, if the bedding ceremony would make his wife happier, he was perfectly ready to go through it once again.

'If you wish,' he said irritably, 'I will summon the queen and we can proceed in the usual way. It was merely that in our case I thought the ceremony to be nonsense. Suit yourself, madam, I care not so long as we be quickly free of this throng.'

There was no more to be said; Rannulf had stated the case exactly. Catherine knew herself to be utterly helpless in her husband's hands. She had no powerful father or brother to support her cause for love or to repossess her dowry. At this moment there was no single human being in the land to whom she could look for succour. It was quite true that in their situation the bedding process was an empty ceremony. Above and beyond all, the path to safety lay in not irritating Rannulf of Sleaford.

'What you say is true, my lord,' Catherine murmured. 'If you will, let us go.'

Her docility received little open reward, for Rannulf grasped her ungently by the arm and propelled her through the nearest door. Once outside, his pace slowed and he glanced at Catherine with apparent uneasiness.

'Your maids will be still at the celebrations, I suppose. Do you need them? For me to fetch them would be no light task since I have never seen the creatures.'

'No, I can manage alone.'

A paragon, Rannulf thought. She can ride and undress herself. Through the mental scoffing, however, he was pleased at what he took for reasonableness, since he had not forgotten the flashes of temper, and understood that Maud had deliberately lied about or over-estimated Catherine's gentleness. He handled her more carefully now, however, and suited his pace to hers as they moved down the staircase and across the court to Rannulf's quarters. These were deserted, as was to be expected, since every servant was busy eating and drinking, playing rough games, or dancing, but Catherine was surprised to see that the room had not been readied in any particular way. For the first time in that long dreadful day, tears rose to her eyes at the proof of the depth of contempt in which her husband held her. She thanked God, however, for the freak of temper which had brought them to that place alone. At least she had been spared the humiliation of being sent with an escort of high-born ladies to that cold, dark, unswept chamber.

As soon as he came to the door, Rannulf realized the mistake he had made. Doubtless Maud had arranged a new apartment for the new-wedded pair, tastefully furnished and decorated, to which she had sent Catherine's possessions and possibly even her maids. There she would have led the bride and there Stephen would have escorted him. Under the circumstances it was reasonable that she should not have wasted the efforts of servants burdened with the preparation and serving of a great feast on cleaning and furbishing a room which would remain empty. It was too late to worry about that now.

Leaving his wife in the doorway, Rannulf groped about for flint and tinder, lighted a candle, threw brush into the hearth, and lit the fire. 'Come in,' he growled, and seeing that Catherine was trembling, 'here, drink this. It will warm you until the fire takes hold.'

Catherine accepted the goblet and sipped the strong, sweet wine, watching in surprise as Rannulf straightened the bed and threw the clothing he had worn the previous day onto a chest at the side. If he was proud, at least he was not too proud to do a menial's work when it was necessary. Perhaps in the press of his affairs he had forgotten to tell the servants to make ready or even had told them and they, wishing to enjoy themselves, had hoped but failed to return to the chamber before the bride and groom to prepare it. Certainly he seemed to be making an effort to remedy the oversight, and Catherine put down her wine and moved to help him. Between them, the place was quickly tidied and Rannulf threw more brush and then larger logs into the hearth so that the flames roared upward into the chimney and warmth seeped through the room.

He stood now with his back to the fire at one side of the fireplace, watching the play of the light on his wife as she folded the clothing he had carelessly thrown aside. It was none so ill. She was no complainer, nor did she scorn to lay her hand to any task that needed doing. And she was beautiful – very beautiful.

'If you undress here on the hearth, you will not be cold,' Rannulf said, undoing his belt and pulling off his gown. Whatever else needed to be done could wait. The woman was very beautiful, and she was his.

Obediently Catherine came. If there were any way in which she could gain a hold on this man, this was the way. She did not linger intentionally over her disrobing, but women's garments were somewhat more complicated than men's. There were the side laces to undo which held the bliaut tightly to the figure, and the fastenings of the long sleeves of the tunic which held the sleeve smooth so that one might see the shape of the feminine arm beneath. In the act of pulling her tunic over her head, Catherine's eyes fell upon her husband's body which was well-lit by the leaping flames. Unexpectedly, a quiver of passion ran through her. Before God, he was a fine figure of a man, heavily muscled but without an ounce of surplus fat, broad at the shoulder, narrow at the hip, with hard thighs which gleamed slightly under the fine coating of hair. Her first husband had not been ill-formed, but his flesh had been as smooth and soft as her own, lovely perhaps but ill-suited to a man. There was no softness about Rannulf of Sleaford; his skin was stretched tight over powerful musculature, and it was marred in many places by livid or ruddy scars. The sense of excitement grew; Catherine, almost unknowingly, took two steps towards her husband and touched the largest of the scars on his breast with fingers that were actually greedy. Could she but capture and hold him, this was a man to fulfill her pride.

'Are you ready?' Rannulf asked, and Catherine lifted her face to his in amazement, for his voice, miraculously, was very gentle. 'Come then,' he added softly, and lifted her in his arms so that she should not have to walk barefoot across the cold floor.

# Chapter 4

Catherine sat in the women's quarters of the White Tower not far from the queen, sewing and thinking about her husband. She had thought of little else in the two weeks that had passed since her marriage. He was a most peculiar and unpredictable man, but she no longer had much fear of him. Since she had fulfilled Maud's purpose, she was no longer held as a virtual prisoner. Free circulation in the court and some private talks with Lady Warwick had taught her much. It was very needful now to understand Rannulf's character for she understood something of the political situation and she was most anxious to be able to judge what he would do. He was often rude and crude, but it seemed to Catherine that the bad manners were assumed deliberately to hide something else. Too soft a heart? It would be well for her if it were so, since then his manners would be the least of her problems. It was difficult to understand a man who never offered a word of explanation for anything he did. The habit might be excused on the grounds that he was so accustomed to command that it did not seem necessary to him to explain himself. But he never allowed anyone else to explain anything either, and that prevented Catherine from judging his reactions. Take her request for money to buy cloth.

'Cloth!' Rannulf had roared, as he looked at the chests filled with Catherine's clothing.

Embarrassed, Catherine had tried to explain that the cloth was not for herself, but he had silenced her with a contemptuous gesture, unfastened a key from the group that he wore about his neck, and thrown it at her.

'So much as is in that chest is yours to use as you will. That, and no more,' he said coldly as he left her.

Catherine allowed a smile to develop. Perhaps she could get

some further response when she gave him the gowns she was sewing for him. So much apology as a softened glance in her direction would do her heart good.

A page made his way through the group of ladies and spoke to the queen. Maud lifted her head and smiled at the smiling Catherine. 'Your husband wants you, my dear, and that is a minor miracle. I never remember Rannulf sending for Adelecia in all the years he was married to her.'

Catherine dropped her work and hurried from the room. Although she did not fear that her husband would murder her, she had no desire to feel his heavy hand. Not that he had yet struck her, but waiting threw him into the foulest of humours and Catherine found Rannulf better company when he did not growl or bellow.

'Here is your cloak, madam. We are leaving.'

Never a word of greeting, Catherine thought with exasperation as she protested automatically. 'Leaving? But my work is above, and I have not bid the queen farewell.'

Rannulf scowled. 'You may return within the hour, or you may stay behind, for all I care. I thought you would wish to oversee the placing of your boxes.'

Catherine was even more exasperated. 'You mean we are moving to another house in London?'

'All women are idiots! Where would I go, when I must return within a few weeks to that accursed tourney and investiture?'

Mollified, Catherine realized that she had been rather foolish, but she had learned that excuses, like explanations, were not necessary. She merely took her cloak and followed Rannulf to their horses. She liked to ride with him, and one thing in particular gave her pleasure. Although there were always grooms present, Rannulf never failed to lift her into the saddle himself, as if he feared that someone else would not be sufficiently careful of her.

The journey was short, perhaps a quarter of a mile through the muddy streets, and Rannulf caught his wife to lift her down from the saddle, too. They were in the courtyard of a typical London house; they entered through the single door in the lower storey, which was constructed of stone. There were many other people in the courtyard who bowed and made way for Rannulf, mostly serfs who were carrying in loads of household articles. Catherine lifted her skirt as they walked over the hard-packed earth floor, her exasperation rapidly returning because the rushes which had once covered it were pounded to dust in most places and slimy with rot in others. At the far end of the single large room that made up the lower floor of the house, a staircase rose to the floor above. Here Rannulf stopped and turned to face into the room again.

'Hold your tongues and listen,' he bellowed, and then, scarcely waiting for the voices to die down, added, 'This is your new mistress, the Lady Catherine. Henceforward you will take your orders from her.' He gave the men a few moments to study her, then nudged her rudely. 'The women, I assume, are already above. Go up.'

The top floor was lighter and not as damp, being constructed of wood, but the walls were patched with mould and the floor was in the same repulsive condition. Catherine stared about, dismayed. She had been wrong – Rannulf was a pig! He not only dressed like an animal, apparently he lived like one too. Could he not have set the servants to clean the house before he brought her to it? Rannulf slammed the flat of his hand against the door frame to draw the attention of the women, about to introduce Catherine to them in the same graceful manner he had used below. Indeed, his lips had parted when a child's thin voice broke through the hubbub.

'Papa! Papa!'

A small form tore through the press of women and flung itself upon Rannulf. Catherine gasped. Was this a nobleman's child? Unkempt, dirty, dressed in little more than rags, the little boy was revolting – and all Catherine's starved maternity leaped to life so that she could scarcely refrain from grasping at him. Meanwhile, Richard had embraced his father as high as he could reach, squealing and wriggling with joy.

'What do you here? You disobedient little devil!'

The child cowered back at his father's voice; Rannulf raised his hand to strike; and Catherine leaped between the father and son, taking a stinging blow on the shoulder.

'How can you strike a child that runs to you in love?'

Catherine shrieked, dropping to her knees and clasping the filthy and trembling form to her breast.

There was an utter, paralysed silence. The maids stood mute, expecting their master to kill the woman who had opposed him or to beat her senseless. The child was too frightened even to whimper. Catherine, too, was frightened by what she had done, and Rannulf stared down at his wife and son in stunned, disbelieving amazement.

'How dare you?' he asked quietly. 'Do you know how dangerous the road from Sleaford to London is in this season? Do you know how many enemies I have along that road? The child could have lost his life or been taken for ransom a dozen times.'

'How should a babe know of such matters?' Catherine blazed, her eyes nearly purple with the reflected heat of her countenance. 'He is here, alive. Could you not tell him what he has done amiss? What will a blow teach him except that his father does not want him or does not love him. Who would take him for ransom anyway? A villein's child is better cared for.'

Rannulf nearly choked with rage and frustration. The only thing to do now was to tear the child from the woman and beat them both, but he could not. Without another word, he turned and left. Catherine remained on her knees, clinging to the little boy and trembling herself, wondering fearfully what would become of her. This time she had gone too far. She had shamed her husband before his servants. If ever she had a chance to win his love, now it was lost. He was not a forgiving man; he would never forgive this transgression of his rights over his own child. The little boy was struggling in her arms, crying, 'Papa, papa,' and at last broke into despairing sobs. Catherine could think of herself no longer.

It was fortunate for Lady Catherine that the house was in so wretched a condition and the child needed so much attention. The next five days passed swiftly, and as she tended to Richard and listened to him the bond between Rannulf and herself tightened. Oh, he might return and beat her. From what the maids and Richard said it was very likely – and richly she deserved a beating, she acknowledged. Nonetheless, she looked forward to his return. No man whose servants had such implicit trust in him and whose son adored him so passionately could be other than basically good. Bad-tempered, yes, but Catherine was getting an earful about Lady Adelecia and she admitted that Rannulf had reason to dislike women.

Besides, Catherine was growing concerned. Rannulf seemed to have disappeared off the face of the earth. When he did not return that first night, Catherine had assumed indignantly that he was comforting himself with some slut. She repressed her jealousy, telling herself that the man who could prefer a woman of greensleeves to herself was not worth jealousy. Nonetheless, when she returned to court to gather her work together and explain to the queen what had happened to her, she had asked discreet questions. She learned that Rannulf had not gone alone into the town; he had called his men-at-arms together and ridden away with the group. He had not gone to court a slut, but where he had gone no one could even guess.

One good thing had come of Catherine's quarrel with her husband. The maidservants and menservants regarded her with superstitious awe and leaped to obey her slightest wish. Catherine could not tell whether they were reacting to Rannulf's restraint towards her or to her own flash of temper. She took advantage of the situation, however, getting more work out of them in five days than Adelecia could have obtained in five months. Catherine was troubled, but too busy to be unhappy, and the days slipped by insensibly.

Rannulf's situation was less satisfactory. Incapable either of punishing Catherine or accepting what she had done, he had retreated to the keep of a minor vassal of his not far from London to nurse his grievance. The trouble was that his rage would not rise, and the grievance against himself, the more he thought about it, became more and more a virtue on Catherine's part. Rannulf never pretended to himself that Catherine saw anything attractive in him, although she was agreeable throughout the day and willing throughout the night. She had said she was afraid of him, and he believed her. Her behaviour was no more than a reasonable reaction to fear, and, in spite of an uncomfortable feeling that he wished she would yield him the same complaisance without the fear, Rannulf did not trust her enough to attempt to reduce her terror of him.

The wonder of it was that, putting her personal good aside, she had leaped to the defence of a defenceless child – his child, at that, not even hers. Adelecia had never defended Richard from his discipline, justified or unjustified, had not, indeed, paid any more attention to her son than if he were a stray dog. It was that which had changed Rannulf's dislike and disdain for his second wife into absolute loathing. That the woman seemed revolted by him and would not be a wife to him naturally enough made him dislike her, but that she would not be a mother to the child she had borne made him hate her.

How much Catherine's beauty and his steadily increasing desire for her contributed to his recognition of her courage and virtue, Rannulf was not certain. Having a keen sense of humour, however, he admitted freely that her physical charms clarified greatly the beauty of her character. In fact he would not have protracted his absence as long as he did except that – Rannulf smiled grimly thinking of his reputation for coolheaded courage – he was afraid to face his wife. For the life of him, Rannulf could not decide how to behave when he had to confront her.

It was fortunate that he resolved only to act in a manner suitable to Catherine's demeanour towards him because he had no previous experience whatsoever with anything that happened to him after he walked in his own door. First of all, he very nearly walked out again, almost believing that he had wandered into a stranger's house. The walls were newly whitewashed, the floor spread with clean rushes, although they were dry and scentless from long storage. In the large hearth a fire burned clear, unchoked by the ashes of previous fires. The benches and tables for eating were stacked neatly along the walls and beneath them lay clean straw pallets for the servants and men-at-arms to sleep on. Even the servants themselves seemed neater and cleaner. While Rannulf stood in the doorway taking in the changes and thinking that no keep or manor of his had had this appearance since his mother's death, he saw his third wife coming towards him.

Rannulf swallowed nervously and scowled. Catherine's face was red as fire and, thus far in his experience with her, a flushed face had always preceded some insubordination. She was beautiful, very beautiful, and had many virtues, but if he permitted any more willfulness on her part he would be no better than a slave to his own lust.

Catherine sank to her knees. 'I come to beg your pardon, my lord. I did great wrong to come between your son and yourself.' It was not easy to humble herself, for Catherine had great pride, but she had been wrong and, more than that, she wished to spare Richard the sight of her humiliation and punishment. The child was very passionate and had taken her to his heart. To tear him apart by the sight of the father he loved striking the woman he was learning to love would be cruel. 'Indeed,' she forced herself to add, 'I can offer no excuse except that my heart is sore for the loss of a babe, and—'

'Get up,' Rannulf snapped, every other feeling submerged in the violent revulsion he felt when he saw Catherine kneel to him.

'Nay, my lord, I do not expect that you will so lightly pardon me. Do with me what you will, but show a softer face to the child. I have explained how wrong he was to steal away with the servants and how much trouble and grief he could have brought upon you. Indeed, he is very sorry. He swears he will never do so again. Do not be angry with him any longer. He has been crying for you for days.'

'Get up!' Rannulf roared.

'Not until you pardon the child.'

The tone brought Rannulf somewhat to his senses. Whatever the meekness of the position, there was no meekness in that voice. 'A pox take you woman, I am not angry now.' The fury of his own voice penetrated his ears; his sense of humour was touched again, and he began to laugh. 'At least I was not angry when I came in, and would not be except for your silliness. For God's sake, if not for mine, get off the floor.' Catherine took the hand he extended and rose to her feet. 'We will come to the subject of my son when I desire to come to it. Tell me first, since we are here, what has happened to the house.'

'I had it cleaned,' Catherine said, and then the thought of the repulsive condition the place had been in and his lack of consideration in bringing her to it overwhelmed her. Her voice filled with contempt. 'I hope you did not desire us to live like pigs.'

Perhaps he had misjudged her; perhaps she was not afraid of him after all. Rannulf had to laugh again at her indignation, but all he said was, 'I care not how you live so long as the labour comes not upon me. Now, I am ready. Where is my son?'

Catherine's apprehension returned. 'Above, but—'

A gesture silenced her. She had no right, after all, to interfere, and she knew now that Rannulf would not be unduly harsh with the child. He paid no more attention to her, and Catherine followed him up the stairs hoping that Richard's behaviour would do her credit. She had worked hard with the boy. If Rannulf was pleased, all might yet be well. She watched her husband while he listened to Richard's apology, and her heart sank at the increasing rigidity of his expression. Rannulf, however, was not at all displeased. He was only striving, with growing difficulty, to prevent himself from laughing as he listened to the elaborate phrases which the child had obviously learned by rote. He did not wish to hurt the boy, nor to hurt his wife. Catherine had plainly taken great pains to teach Richard what she hoped would pacify his father's anger. There was a little pause, but Rannulf still could not speak because he was having trouble in controlling his mouth.

Richard raised his eyes to the stern countenance. 'Oh, please, papa, I am sorry. Truly I am sorry, but you said you would return at once and then the servants began to pack your clothes and I knew you were not coming back. Let me stay with you, papa, oh, please, do not send me away.'

That plea was completely natural, the child stuttering slightly in his earnestness, and Rannulf dropped his hand on the boy's head, all desire to laugh fading into tenderness. 'The labour of keeping you does not fall upon me, my child. Nor is it safe, perhaps to keep you in London where I have many enemies and one foot beyond these doors you are on a stranger's land—'

'You do not want me. You do not love me. You always go away from me or send me away from you.' Richard's eyes filled with tears.

'Let him stay, my lord,' Catherine pleaded. 'I will not let

66

him out from under my eye for a moment. No man shall harm him or take him – upon my life.'

'Well—'

'Thank you, papa, thank you!'

A wet and smacking kiss was pressed on Rannulf's hand, and he shook his head. Give a child or a woman the smallest sign that a decision was not absolute and irrevocable and they assumed that the decision would be remade in their favour. Rannulf could not, however, destroy the joy that had filled his son's face. They were at peace; the danger to the child was not acute, and for some reason Catherine's assurance that she would guard Richard imbued him with perfect confidence.

'You should thank the Lady Catherine, Richard,' he said yielding completely.

The boy capered away, gave his benefactress a rough hug, and jumped upon the bed, sending a pile of neatly folded linen flying. 'Oh,' he laughed, 'she does not mind. She likes to have me. She told me so.'

'If you make her pick up what she has just folded ten times a day, she will soon be sorry.'

Catherine moved to her husband's side, smiling at him with a genuine warmth. 'Truly it is a pleasure to have him. He is such a clever child. Only think, he learned all that long speech and did not forget a word of it, and I only told him three or four times over what to say.'

So she was not stupid at all! Rannulf burst into laughter. 'I thought you meant me to believe those were his words.'

'Nay, how could I be so foolish? A child does not speak so, and it would be an indifferent father who could not tell his own son's way.'

Rannulf's eyes narrowed. Stupid! Perhaps she was altogether too clever. She seemed to read him very well. 'And how is it known to you that I am not an indifferent father? What you saw of us together did not speak of great tenderness.'

'How not? You were only afraid for the child's welfare. Have I not beaten my own child with one hand while I clasped him to my bosom with the other after he had committed some dangerous folly. My lord, even at the moment I came between you, I knew I did wrong.' Rannulf continued to frown, not angrily but thoughtfully, and Catherine, feeling that he might have a distaste for her discussion of her past life, changed the subject. 'Now, my lord, will you bathe and change your garments? You are wet and muddied. Did you ride far?'

'Not five miles, but the roads are very bad. I wish, however,' Rannulf added caustically, 'that you would content yourself with making my child and my house models of cleanliness and propriety. I am not four years old to be told when to change my clothes.'

Looking sidelong under her lashes at him, Catherine thought that he was acting very little older. Still, if he wished to remain wet and dirty just because she had suggested that he change, it was his affair. In the future, she would know better how to manage. She would order the bath and lay out the clothing without question, and also, she decided, looking at her husband's face, she would employ a barber. A man should either grow a beard or shave, not walk around looking like a half-mown field. He was a well set-up man; he would look none so ill with those grey eyes and curly hair if he did but comb his disordered locks now and again.

Unobtrusively, Catherine put her scheme into practice. The bath and the barber appeared regularly; little by little, as she and the maids sewed them, new shirts, tunics and *chausses* took the place of worn-out underclothing. The rents and stains disappeared from Rannulf's gowns and surcoats and new ones, beautifully furred and embroidered, gradually filled a sadly depleted wardrobe. He noticed it – indeed, he was often the butt of sly jests about assuming finery to charm his new wife which sadly tried his temper – but again the situation was beyond his management. To send away a ready-prepared bath or refuse to don the garments handed to him seemed ridiculous, especially since there was no one to complain to but the maids who were only following orders. Slyly, Catherine disappeared each time the bath or the barber was summoned or when a new set of clothing was to be introduced, and as long as she did not mention the subject at other times, Rannulf was at a loss for a reason to do so.

Occupied by her husband's needs and demands, by the training of Richard who had come to her hands with the manners of a wild animal covering his sweet nature, Catherine drifted into contentment. She thought no more of independent use of her father's vassals, but she was troubled by the political situation. She felt the tension in the court and, although she liked Maud and Stephen well enough, she had no sympathy with Rannulf's commitment to their cause. She had no leaning towards the rebels either, and wished that her father had taken the wiser course of holding himself aloof from all intercourse with either side. Then, perhaps, Rannulf would not freeze or look so black at her when she suggested that peace was a better state than war.

Neither side had the right of the matter completely, Catherine judged. The rebels were wrong because they had no right to fight against God's anointed king, but the king was not right because he had not fulfilled his duty to the country. Catherine flushed slightly with irritation. A pox upon both sides, she thought, as long as the disease does not infect my family. The trouble was that she could not escape infection. Rannulf was bound to the king, and Lady Warwick said that his honour would not permit him to free himself from that tie. If anything disturbed the uneasy peace, doubtless Rannulf would drain her property as well as his own to support the king's war.

That notion annoyed Catherine, who not only felt that there were better uses for money but also knew her vassals would resent that use of their taxes. She did her best not to dwell on the subject for fear of quarrelling with Rannulf. The irritation, in spite of her efforts, was recurrent. After all, Rannulf himself had said once that the property was hers by inheritance and would go to her children. Why then should he be able to use it in a way of which she completely disapproved? She was sewing, puzzling the matter over in her mind once again when the page entered to tell her that Sir Giles Fortesque was below.

'Oh, he has doubtless come for Sir Rannulf's investiture, but he is an old friend. Send him up, I will speak with him since my lord is not here. It is not courteous to send him away without a greeting.'

She advanced with a smile and an extended hand towards a man of about her husband's age. Sir Giles had been chief of her father's vassals and she knew him well. To her surprise, for he had always treated her as if she were another daughter, Sir Giles bowed profoundly and kissed her hand.

'Why, how formal you are grown. Have you forgotten how you dandled me upon your knee?'

The man's leather face creased into smiles. 'Nay, I have not forgot, but one does not dandle the countess of Soke upon one's knee. I would not fail in respect to my lady, presuming on past familiarity.'

'I am countess of Soke since my husband is earl, but I hope I am still Catherine to you, Sir Giles.'

'You are countess of Soke, husband or no husband, to us, my lady. I cannot tell you how grieved and enraged I was when we learned you had been stolen from us. I am to blame for that, I fear, but not through neglect or ill intention. I was so sure that Bigod would try to seize you that I summoned the men to guard that border. Alas, I did not know the king could be roused to such early action, and by the time we turned to your rescue, Bigod was behind us. We were trapped between two fires.'

For a moment Catherine stood with wide eyes, then dropped her lids slowly until her lashes concealed the misty irises. 'You mean you would have kept me from the king – and from Bigod too?'

'If our lives and lands held, we would.'

Catherine searched the face before her from under her lashes, but there was nothing in it except anger and the honesty she had long respected. 'And what would you have done with me?' she asked slowly.

'Done with you?' Sir Giles was shocked, but he thought he understood the ignorance that prompted the question. The late earl sheltered his daughter too much. In marrying her to a weakling and shielding her from all knowledge of affairs, he had done her more harm than good. 'You are our lady,' he explained, 'and what you wished to do was for yourself to decide. We would have hoped that in time you would choose as husband a man worthy to wield the lands of Soke. Until that time, it was our duty to protect you and obey you.'

Catherine had not asked out of ignorance, and she was well

satisfied with the answer. 'Well, I have a husband. He is from home just now, but he will want to see you.'

'I do not wish to see him, however. At least not until I have spoken my mind to you and heard your orders.'

Catherine nodded her satisfaction and reseated herself. Rannulf was about to receive quite a shock.

'The man, we know, was none of your choosing, and that is bad. Also bad is the fact that your father loved Henry but was content to send him money, and I know Sir Rannulf rides constantly to war in the king's cause. We do not desire to have our lands overrun by Norfolk on the one side and by the king on the other. On the good side is that we know Sir Rannulf to be a just and honourable man who would faithfully judge between us, as your father did, and as faithfully succour us in time of need. Therefore, all except a few of us are agreed that the matter should be left to your judgment.'

Now Catherine was puzzled. 'But my judgment about what? I am married to Sir Rannulf already. What can there be left to judge?'

'The same thing, madam,' Sir Giles said, his face suddenly grim. 'We will accept this man as earl of Soke only if you are content to have him to husband. If you wish to be rid of him and have a man — perchance one of us — of your own choosing, we will kill him in the tourney.'

'No!' Catherine shrieked, leaping to her feet. 'He is a good man. Before God he is my husband, my troth is plighted to him. Through that marriage and the king's gift, he is your earl. I will not have him murdered by his own men to smirch my name, and yours also, forever.'

'Calm yourself, madam. I did not think you would be party to such a plan, but Sir Herbert Osborn bound me over to put it to you.'

'Sir Herbert offered for me once. Perhaps he thought to free me from Sir Rannulf to snatch me to himself.'

Catherine received a strange, considering glance, but she was too much distressed to think what it meant. 'Perhaps. But there are others of his mind. I must speak plain, my lady, even if I offend you. Dearly as I loved your father and just as he was, he did not oversee his barons closely. We are somewhat accustomed to our freedom – that is good, and even I would wish to keep it that way, except that with overmuch freedom comes trouble. There is a party among us now that seeks to oppress the others. Thus far I, and those who think as I do, have kept them in check with words alone, but I think that if a strong man does not take matters into his hands soon there will be fighting.'

A rich and completely satisfactory sensation of pride filled Catherine. 'There can be none stronger than Sir Rannulf,' she said firmly, and then with narrowing eyes, 'No doubt Sir Herbert leads that party also.'

'Aye, that is true.' Another thoughtful glance raked Catherine, but she had nothing to hide and ignored it.

'He was ever a maker of trouble. He caused my father much grief from time to time.' Catherine was about to tell Sir Giles to bring the problem to Sir Rannulf's attention and not trouble her with such matters when Lady Warwick's advice came to her mind. She no longer thought of needing her vassals' protection against her husband, but if she and the vassals stood together against involvement in the king's war, Rannulf might have to listen. 'Certainly,' she continued, 'the way things lie I would be a fool to align myself with one faction or the other among my own men, even if Sir Rannulf were not to my taste.'

Sir Giles nodded in agreement. She was quick to see that, whatever might have been good before, now an outsider was needed to keep the men from struggling among themselves. If he, himself, had not been married, there might have been a benefit in Catherine taking him because the men, whatever their faction, were accustomed to obeying him. Since that was not possible, it was indeed likely that Sir Rannulf was best, providing he did not interfere too much in the old, established order in the earldom.

Catherine, meanwhile, flushed with confidence because of the assurances of loyalty Sir Giles had given her, had decided that since the men believed they were hers, hers they would remain. 'Of Sir Rannulf,' she said with a certain asperity, a mistress' impatience with doubt in a servant, 'you have heard the truth. He is both strong and just. For all your decision to do this or that, it is lighter, with such a man, to say than to do

72

against his will. You had better leave him to me. Thus far we have no quarrel about the management of my lands or the disposition of my monies, so do as he bids you. On the matter of the war, I will tell him of your desire, to remain apart from it.' Suddenly she smiled, looking at once like the Catherine he loved as a daughter. 'Truly, I know little enough of the whys and wherefores of this madness that makes men tear each other apart. Do you wait on Sir Rannulf here about the prime tomorrow and hear what he has to say on the matter. Then, with your guidance I can decide what is best to do.'

The remainder of the conversation was of commonplaces, her health, that of Sir Giles and his family. Catherine called Richard from the room below where he was playing among the men-at-arms and introduced Rannulf's younger son to Sir Giles. The boy did her proud, his burnished hair neat, his clothing pretty and well-fitting, and his manner such a combination of innocence and childish dignity that stepmother and vassal had much ado to maintain their gravity. Catherine's devotion and the child's affection for her could not be mistaken, and Sir Giles saw that, whether she cared for the man or not, she was already irrevocably bound to him through his son.

Unfortunately the stimulation and excitement, the feeling of assurance that Catherine had in Sir Giles' presence, departed with him. When she thought over what she had done, she was appalled. It was simple enough to say to Sir Giles that she would tell Rannulf this or that, but what reason could she propose to Rannulf for her interference? Sir Giles might say that she was still his lady, but Catherine was sure that Rannulf would not see it that way, or, since he had said the money was hers, might acknowledge that the men were hers but had no right to follow the will of a fool of a woman. She could tell him of the plan to murder him. Surely that would be excuse enough for her to have spoken her mind. No, she could not. To do so would surely set him against her vassals, and if they owed her loyalty she must protect their interests. When Rannulf came in to dinner, she had still decided nothing, and she sought in vain throughout the meal for an opening that would not enrage his irascible temper.

'You are strangely silent, madam,' Rannulf said at last. It was not that Catherine was a chattering woman, but she had a well-bred way of making pleasant conversation at the table about things she knew would interest her husband. Having sought without result during the unusual silence that greeted his remark for something he could have done to annoy her, Rannulf turned on his son. 'Richard, have you distressed the Lady Catherine today? Do you have something to confess?'

The child's startled eyes proclaimed his innocence even before Catherine spoke. 'No, my lord, indeed he is very good. I – I do not feel very well today.'

Rannulf turned his eyes to his plate. It was now almost a month that they had been man and wife. Possibly she was breeding. The thought gave him no particular pleasure although he liked children. He had an heir in his eldest son Geoffrey and a guarantee in Richard. True, it would be well to have a man-child out of Catherine for the better security of the lands of Soke, but there was time enough for that. Women died in childbearing.

'Do you wish that I stay within this afternoon?'

Catherine looked at her husband. His head was lowered over his food and his voice was harsh and angry, but it always was, except in love-making. Still, what he said in conjunction with her remark could only be meant as an offer to help and comfort. Tears rose in her eyes at the thought of her intended duplicity. She knew he found her presence pleasant although he never spoke a fond word nor offered a caress. How could she have been so stupid as to endanger his growing attachment for her merely for the sake of a little power over her men? If she had been wiser and sent Sir Giles to him directly, her faith might have fixed his fondness on her more securely and in the end brought her more power, even if indirectly wielded. She had to think of some way out of the situation though, and to have Rannulf in the house would effectively paralyse her.

Catherine forced a smile. 'No, thank you. I am only a little listless.'

'Then I will take the boy that he may not plague you.' He caught his wife's anxious glance. 'I am only going to the armourer to see how goes my new hauberk. There will be much to interest him there. He will not plague me either.'

74

'Will you buy me a sword, papa? Oh, please! You said I might have one soon.'

'Not if you overset the table and your trencher. Sit still. Are you fed only upon rabbits that you jump so?'

'And not if you bang it upon the floor and spoil the edge as you did with your wooden one,' interjected Lady Catherine.

Rannulf looked from his wife to his son and bit his lips. There was a strong conspiracy here. He had heard nothing about the damaged sword. Doubtless she had provided the child with another or had one of the men-at-arms repair it. Or had she taken it from him? This was a good time to test out a small fear he had. Sometimes women who doted upon children would not permit a boy to grow into a man.

'Go,' the father said. 'Go and get your cloak and wait for me below. I see you will eat no more, nor permit us to finish our meal in peace.' When the boy was gone, he turned to Catherine. 'What say you, shall he have the sword?'

Catherine's heart sank further. To ask such a question of her betokened no little trust. 'Yes, he is more than four. It is time for him to learn how to care for it. But not too sharp an edge, my lord, or we will not have a stick of furniture left.' She smiled involuntarily. 'He duels mightily with the chairs and bed-curtains.'

Her husband laughed shortly, but his eyes were considering, and he tested further, glad of the natural opportunity to sound her on the management of male children. 'He does, eh? Then it is time for him to have a tutor in arms who can give him more steady attention than I can. I will look about me.'

He expected a protest at the threatened removal of the child from her influence, but Catherine nodded approval. Because of her first husband's gentleness and disinterest in the usual male pursuits, she had thought long and often on how her own son should be raised to make him more manly.

'It is not my place to tell you how to raise your sons, but I have thought so, and wished to speak to you of it. He is large and very forward for his age. For a tutor, too, it is time.'

'You see more of him than I. You always have my leave to speak your mind about the children – mine, and those I hope will be yours.' He cocked an eye at Catherine expectantly, but

75

she did not respond. Perhaps she had only pretended a desire for Richard's company in the beginning to impress him and now, still not wishing to harm the child, wanted to be free of him. 'Perhaps you find Richard more trouble than you expected,' Rannulf remarked to test this hypothesis. 'I can send him home if he is a burden to you.'

'Oh, no! I love him dearly, indeed I do. Do not take him from me completely.'

There could be no doubt about the sincerity of that plea. Rannulf gave up. Whatever was troubling his wife, she would have to settle it for herself or tell him outright. He could do no more for her than reassure her of his approval of her handling of Richard. 'Nay,' he said, 'if you do not desire to be free of him, I care not where he bides. I see you are to be trusted. You will put no woman's garments on him, nor give him a spinning wheel in place of a sword and shield. Good God,' Rannulf exclaimed as a loud crash and considerable laughter came up the stairwell, 'I had better go before he wreaks greater havoc. The men are fond of him and let him do anything.'

Richard was returned by a contingent of the men-at-arms in time for his supper and bed, but Rannulf did not come with him. As the usual hour for his return passed without sign of him, Catherine grew more and more nervous. Her guilty conscience kept telling her that he had met one of her father's vassals and heard from him what she had said to Sir Giles. Slender as was the actual possibility of such a chance meeting taking place, it seemed to Catherine that it would be in perfect conformity with her uniform bad fortune. She had to speak before Rannulf met Sir Giles in the morning – that meant this night – and if she confirmed any rumour he had heard of her desire to come between her men and himself – Catherine shuddered as she heard his step on the stair and shuddered again as he came in scowling horribly. She turned pale, knowing that her worst fear had been realized, but her lips and hands were steady and her eyes met his squarely.

'Sir Herbert Osborn was your father's vassal, was he not?'

No greeting, as usual, and a voice deadly quiet with fury, but the opening was not the one Catherine had feared. Unless

76

Catherine was conscious of some guilt, Rannulf's rages had no longer any power of really frightening her.

'Yes, my lord.'

'He has laid a complaint that I married you falsely against your will, and that you were promised to him. Woman, did you hold your tongue for fear and put this shame on me?'

Catherine's colour came rushing back. 'No. He lies. Neither by my word nor by my father's was any promise given him. He offered for me – so much is true – but I could not even think of such matters at the time. He was no favourite with my father either, and I cannot believe so kind a father would have promised me without my knowledge.'

'He says he has a letter bearing such a promise from your father. Moreover—' Rannulf was about to add that Sir Herbert said more than that. He said that Catherine had known of the promise and had been terrified into silence by the threat that he would be killed if she spoke.

'I cannot believe it!' Catherine cried, and then, incomprehensibly even to herself, she burst into tears.

It was the first time Rannulf had seen her cry, and it took a self-control made strong by many years of practice to allow him to maintain an apparent indifference. 'There is no need for this caterwauling,' he said repressively. 'I hope you speak the truth and that you have not dishonoured me and yourself by coming, promised to another man, to my bed. Be quiet, I say. What good will this do now?' He passed a hand across his face and came farther into the room, watching her strive to control herself. 'Very well. It is like enough that no more will come of this since the king and queen are surely my friends in the matter. Probably it will amount to nothing else than a challenge for swords as well as lances at the tourney. I will lesson him well, and he will hold his tongue.' In spite of all efforts, Catherine's tears still flowed and Rannulf was so wrenched with jealousy that he scarcely knew what he was saying. 'I would give much,' he burst out bitterly, 'to know whether you weep for the loss of the chance to have him to husband. For him you need not weep; I will not slay him unless he forces me to it.'

That brought her head up as if she had been hit, the tears

like clear pearls clinging to her cheeks. 'I would not weep for the loss of any man I have yet seen,' Catherine spat, but the shock to her pride did her good. Pig of a man, she thought, no one but he may have honour or worth. It will do him good to learn I am no cipher and that he must walk warily lest I outfox him. 'You asked me at dinner why I was so silent, and I said I was not well,' Catherine began, swallowing the last of her sobs and dashing the tears from her eyes. 'That was a lie. Now I will tell you.'

'You knew of this?' It was a bellow that brought a restless cry from Richard on the other side of the room screen. Catherine turned her back on her husband and went to quiet the child as if Rannulf was of no more importance than the meanest servant.

She eyed him coldly on her return. 'Not of the formal complaint, of course. No doubt care was taken that it should not come to my ears, but of talk among the vassals of Soke I did know. I had hoped that you would not need to hear of it for the sake of the men involved. Sir Giles Fortesque, chief of my father's vassals, came to me this morning to ask if I had been forced against my will into marriage. I told him that it was not true and that, since the king had given me to you, I was content.'

Rannulf turned to the sideboard to pour wine to soothe his throat which was aching strangely, but his hand shook so that the wine slopped over the goblet on to the floor. If any man had told him a month before that a woman's word could cause his throat to ache with unshed tears, could cause his hand to tremble so that he could not hold a cup of wine, he would have laughed – and struck him down.

'Was that all he said?'

'No,' Catherine replied, her path clear now. 'He asked me to tell you of Sir Herbert's faction, which does not wish to see a strong man made the earl of Soke – at least, not a strong man other than himself. He also begged me to tell you that as my father's men they had lived long at peace and to pray you not to press them into this thankless war.

'He comes to a woman for a strange purpose.'

'Some men,' Catherine said icily, 'are fond of their wives

78

and are moved by their prayers and entreaties. Then too, I am all that is left of my father, and Sir Giles was ever attached to him and to me. Perhaps he is thus blinded to my imperfections and thinks all men must look upon me with favour.'

The fragile golden stem of the goblet bent and twisted in Rannulf's hand. The next day he discovered that one of the leaves which was chased upon that stem had pierced his palm. Just then he felt no pain except that in his heart. How did a man show a woman his fondness without making himself a fool? He had done everything he knew how to do – given her the keys to his money-boxes, entrusted her with his son, not failed a night in her bed so that she might know there were no other women. If she desired words, he was lost. He had none and knew none. What did she want of him? It was a woman's form of sport to make a man confess his love when she felt nothing, that she might boast of it among her friends. Did she sound so fond that he must open his heart to make her sport?

'And you, no doubt, gave answer for me,' he said bitterly. 'Well, what did you say? Tell me, that I too may speak by rote as you taught my child.'

'I said that he should wait upon you at the prime tomorrow morning and that you would doubtless explain fully to him what you desired. And now, in truth, I am ill. I can speak with you and listen to your insults no more.'

She could have dealt with the vassal in no more proper or dutiful way. Filled with remorse for his sharp words, Rannulf lifted a hand towards his wife in an unconsciously pleading gesture, but Catherine had turned away to join her women. She did not return to their bed that night, and Rannulf spent the long hours until morning cursing marriage, cursing women, and, most bitterly of all, cursing his own hasty tongue.

# Chapter 5

The beginning of April was not the best time of the year to hold a tourney; the earth was still soft with rain and the grass had not yet formed a solid mat. Needs must, however, is a master that is obeyed, and the queen's purpose was best served by setting that date. Rannulf made no objection to the time because it could not be soon enough for him. If he was to be earl of Soke, the sooner he took homage of the men and proved his ability to rule them, the better. Leaderless barons were likely to take the bit between their teeth, and then it was no small labour to check-rein them into docility.

The day before the tourney, Robert of Leicester had come, surprisingly, to offer himself and some of his vassals to back Rannulf in the mêlée.

'What the devil do you mean by making an offer like that? I lead the vassals of Soke against all comers. If you want to fight, fight against us,' Rannulf paused and smiled, 'but not too hard.'

'I mean what I appear to mean. I do not believe the vassals of Soke are to be trusted. I think they will sooner run a lance through your back than through the opposing party.'

Rannulf was not shocked; it was not unknown to happen in spite of oaths of homage when vassals were desperate to be rid of an overlord. Usually, however, the overlord had to be completely insufferable before such drastic action was taken, and Rannulf knew himself to be well-liked by his own men and of good repute as an overlord in the world at large.

'What reason have you to so missay these men, Robert?'

'I have two good reasons, neither of which you will like, but it were better for you to credit them. The first is that they have long sided with Henry and take no pleasure in vassalage to a king's man. Second, you know your wife was promised to

Sir Herbert Osborn before the queen pressed her into marriage with you. Nay, there is no use scowling at me, you have seen her father's letter. Well, Osborn says at large that the father was unwilling and it was the woman who urged the match. Add but this, that the whole party speaks of the lady as the countess of Soke and makes no pretence but they will follow her will over yours. Rannulf, save your black looks for her or for her men, I am your friend. I have been much interested to see what the lady would do since the coming of her men, so I have watched. She has been closeted with their leader more than once – a little thing that perhaps you did not know.'

'You are wrong, Robert. I did know it.' Rannulf's face was an ugly mahogany colour, but he made an effort to control his temper. 'My wife herself told me of the matter and the second visit of Sir Giles was to me. Moreover, she has sworn that the letter is not genuine, seal or no seal, and that, even if it is, she knew nothing of it. She told Sir Giles as much, and he confirmed her words.'

'The witch,' Leicester said slowly, 'she has entrapped you already. Who would have thought that at your age you would be so easily enamoured by a pretty face?'

'I pray you, Robert, for the years we have been brothers, say no more. I stake my life that she is as virtuous as beautiful.'

'You fool! You *are* staking your life on it. Let my men fight behind your banner.'

'No!'

'Very well,' Leicester snarled, 'even if Catherine is a saint, the men of Soke are not to be trusted for a third reason. This you will not like either. But Eustace has been in close conference with Sir Herbert, and it is said that he will yield estates to Eustace for the title of Soke when you are dead, and hold of Eustace instead of Stephen.'

'Oh, God!'

'So, finally you see the light. I will send some thirty knights to you before dark. They—'

'No, no. This changes nothing for me. I know of Osborn's party against me. It was largely that which Sir Giles came to discuss with me, but I have watched Eustace close and I cannot doubt your words. This will break Stephen, and we will

81

be lost. If the boy turns against him, he will have no heart to fight to keep the kingdom.'

'So I think also, which is why I say you should guard yourself well. We will need every man in the days to come.'

Rannulf shuddered, unhearing. 'So loving-kind a father. Who could believe that a child so cosseted would turn like a serpent to sting what protected him? Nay, I missay the snake. Not even the venomous reptile is so unnatural. Only man destroys what loves him.'

'In the name of God, Rannulf, this is no time for philosophy on the ingratitude of children. When I want to hear a sermon, I will call a priest. If you will not have my men, what will you do about the mêlée?'

'Sir Herbert Osborn will not fight in the mêlée, and I hope that the chastisement visited upon him will somewhat cool the blood of those who follow his lead. I have thrown his lie in his teeth – Catherine swears that the letter could not have been truly from her father unless extorted by force.' Leicester snorted and Rannulf cast him a warning glance. 'I have challenged him to make the lie good upon my body.'

'Oh,' Leicester groaned, 'you are mad! Mad! Why I have maintained an affection for you all these years, I will never know. You have spoken with the Lord, perhaps, that you are so sure of success? Osborn is under thirty and a strong man – I have seen him.'

'Am I so old?'

'Plainly your mind is like a babe's, but your body is too old to play games with trial by combat.'

Rannulf looked startled but not angry. 'In truth, Robert, have you heard that I am less strong a fighter of late? That creeps on a man without his knowledge, and it might be that I have not seen what other men have and are too kind to speak of.'

'Nay, nay,' Leicester soothed, 'it is nothing of that kind. But it is one thing to fight on the field where a man may draw behind his vassals to breathe when he has need of breath, another to oppose a man more than ten years younger in single combat.'

Robert of Leicester was not the only one distressed by the trial by combat. Maud was, at the same moment, confronting her husband with a mixture of rage and despair.

'How could you allow this to take place? Who is this upstart Osborn that he has the right to challenge Rannulf of Sleaford?'

'He too is a baron, my dear, and not yet less in rank. Moreover, he did not issue the challenge – Rannulf did.'

'Did you say nothing? Did you not try to point out to Tefli that he only demeans himself and dishonours us by giving credit to the man's ravings by such a challenge?'

Stephen laughed. 'Did you ever try to reason with Rannulf when he was in a rage?'

'Yes, I have,' the queen snapped, 'and I have always found him to be a reasonable man, in spite of his hasty temper.'

'Not when his pride is touched. Another thing of even greater importance is that perhaps Sir Herbert has the right in the matter. It is no fault of ours, for the woman said nothing, but Eustace has examined the letter and says it certainly bears Soke's seal.'

'Eustace?' Maud faltered. 'Was it he that brought this before you?'

'Aye.'

'Oh – oh.' Maud seated herself beside her husband and took his hand in hers; but she looked into the flames before them with tear-blinded eyes.

She had striven so hard to keep her family free of the all-too-common power jealousies. Stephen had never been a problem; he loved his children well and tenderly, and was only too willing to give them anything they demanded. Never had he shown the faintest sign of fear that his son wished to succeed him before the natural event of his death. Six months ago Maud would have sworn that she had succeeded with her son also, but since this last campaign Eustace had changed. Was she now to choose between her husband and her son? Maud wondered. Her hand tightened convulsively on Stephen's, and he pulled loose so that he could put his arm around her shoulders.

'You trouble yourself too much with such matters, my love. Let Rannulf of Sleaford do his own fretting. He is no easy man to match on the field, and we have done as much as we can for him.'

'Yes,' Maud sighed. 'Oh, Stephen, I am so tired. I could almost wish—' She let her voice drift away, telling herself for the space of a few breaths that she would strive no more.

'Are you sick, Maud?' her husband asked anxiously.

There was now no return from the path she had chosen, for Stephen needed her. She shook her head at the question and found a smile. 'No, my beloved husband, I am just growing older – if you had not noticed. It is too bad that Eustace may not lead the party against Rannulf. It would greatly ease his heart to come to blows with him in proper person.'

'Not if he were beaten,' Stephen remarked, for once having a clearer understanding of his son's character than his wife did.

'You are right,' Maud sighed, recognizing the truth of this insight. 'Yet, my lord, we must find work for him. He is young and restless.'

About to protest, Stephen suddenly recalled his son's peculiar outburst when he was writing to the vassals of Soke. There had been others before and since, flashes of impatience and a spate of bitter words followed by tears or remorseful apologies. Absently, Stephen stroked his wife's arm and shoulder. Work in these times meant fighting; Eustace was a fine fighter, but there was always danger, and the father's heart fluttered with fear. Characteristically, knowing Maud was right, Stephen followed his emotions. Perhaps he could find a new estate to confiscate and send Eustace to put it in order and collect the rents. He had a suspicion that his son's accounts were not always faithful these days, but he cared little for that. Let the boy have the gold to play with – perhaps that would content him.

Had Maud followed his thoughts she would have protested. Eustace did not desire gold to play with, for he was not a gambler by nature. He was a man who desired a sure path to his goal, and he was as furious with Sir Herbert Osborn as his mother could have been, although their reasons were different.

In fact, earlier in the day in another part of the castle, Eustace had expressed his disapproval with considerable force. 'You have marred all by your wagging tongue, Osborn. Did you not realize that Tefli was not a man to take calmly a slur cast upon a woman belonging to him? He could not tamely accept what you spread abroad about her.'

'I cannot see, my lord, why you should be so angered. Is it not your desire to be rid of Sir Rannulf? Where is the difference if he fall in the mêlée or in single combat? It will be greatly to our advantage if I alone put him down. Surely then my claim to the woman and the earldom must be attended to.'

'Surely! Surely! Have you ever seen Sir Rannulf fight? Are you so sure you are the better man?'

'I do not wish to boast, but you have not seen me either, my lord. He is old. His powers, whatever they were, must be waning.'

Eustace shugged. Perhaps it was better thus. If Osborn won, he would be rid of Rannulf and Osborn would still need his support to obtain the earldom because he knew who wrote that letter and how Soke's seal had come upon it. On the other hand, if Osborn were killed, Eustace would be rid of an ally of very uncertain value.

'Very well,' he said at last, smoothing the frown from his face, 'It is too late to mend anyhow. We may as well arrange the battle as close as possible to suit our needs. Tefli will cry you first thing in the morning, no doubt, but do not answer then because you have the full day to reply. Let him run the jousts against the regular challengers of Soke first. If he is indeed failing, you will cut him down more easily.'

'Why not wait until after the mêlée?'

For a moment Eustace could not hide the contempt in his face. He could suggest such an action to another, but he knew with a mixture of shame and pride that he could never carry it out himself. Had he been able to challenge Rannulf personally, he would have met him when he was fresh and fought honestly to see who was the better man.

'It might continue until dark,' Eustace replied, masking his feelings as best he could because he knew he could not back out of the arrangement. 'You would then lose by default. Do you think they will stop the battle because you appear to answer a challenge? Come when the last course is run, but before Tefli has a chance to refresh himself. Remember, after the

85

battle is done, do not approach me. Make your claim and let me work in my own way to seek our ends.'

Lady Catherine lifted herself cautiously on her elbow and pulled the blue bed curtains aside so that the light of the night candle would penetrate the darkness. In the faint and fitful gleam she stared down at her sleeping husband. Relaxed, he looked more than ever like Richard, because the brown curls tumbled over his forehead and softened the hard planes of cheekbones and beaked nose. Catherine pulled the feather quilt upward to cover a bared shoulder, and Rannulf sighed softly and reached out for her. She presented an arm to his groping hand, not wishing him to wake; he did wake these last few nights if he could not find her in the bed beside him. Nonetheless, he had not offered a word of apology since their quarrel and he avoided any but the most necessary conversation.

Rannulf released her and turned again, pushing the covers off his arms. His hair now came more directly into the candle-light and Catherine saw with a contracting heart how much grey sprinkled the brown. Sections of flesh knotted into ugly scars from past wounds picked up the fitful gleam. Catherine made a little sound between a gasp and a sob and released the curtains hastily, gripped for the first time with knowledge of what the next day would bring. Neither her first husband nor her father had been fighting men; both had left that to vassals and men-at-arms. Now Catherine had time to regret the disappointment she had felt for their bookish, unmasculine ways. Now she could blame herself for the many prayers she had offered that her men might be of stiffer fibre. Now that her prayers had been answered, she knew she had been punished for her presumption. Catherine stole quietly from the bed to kneel at her prie-dieu.

Rannulf's hand moved the bed-curtain infinitesimally and let it go again. Once more she was on her knees, but for whom did she pray? Catherine returned to the bed and pressed her chilled body against her husband, who did not appear to have stirred at all. Rannulf struggled to keep his breathing in the smooth rhythm of sleep. Could even a woman be so deceitful as to pray for one man and cling to another?

Whatever Catherine's fears, she could not forbear a healthy mixture of pride with them, for Rannulf showed no qualms at all. He had, to the best of her knowledge, slept quietly through the night, and he woke in the morning at his usual time and in his usual way. He was no quicker or slower in washing or eating; he gave no special instructions to anyone. Catherine had to think twice to assure herself that this really was the day of the tourney and that Rannulf was not merely going out to hunt or to render his normal court attendance. At first she tried to match his sangfroid, but minute by minute her calm slipped away. By the time Rannulf was ready to dress, she had given up all pretence of casualness and she sent away the servants so that she could attend him herself. Rannulf accepted shirt, *chausses* and tunic from his wife's hands without comment. He knew very well that her behaviour was odd because she had never personally helped him to dress before.

'You know where you are to sit,' he burst out suddenly, unable to bear the silence between them any longer.

'Yes, my lord.'

'You may be asked to answer some questions in public. Do not act the fool. Hold up your head and answer readily and clearly.'

Catherine's pride pricked her. 'What shall I say, my lord?' she asked caustically.

There was a rather long pause. Through the fringe of her lashes, Catherine could see Rannulf's rigid countenance. No expression stirred it, but he closed his eyes suddenly as if to hide some inner pain.

'Say what is in your heart,' he replied harshly, and, after another pause, short this time, he added flatly, 'I hope you have told Richard nothing of this. He is not to come.'

Catherine was holding her husband's cross garters in her hands. She sank to her knees to put them on, grateful for the excuse to hide her suddenly brimming eyes and trembling hands. There was only one reason to keep Richard away; Rannulf did not want his son to be a witness if he should be hurt or killed. Catherine's excuse for concealment was short-lived, however. Before she had looped the first garter around his leg, Rannulf reached down and dragged her roughly to her feet.

'Get up,' he snarled. 'Have we no servants that you must kneel on the floor to dress me?'

The rejection of her service, the only tenderness she could show him, destroyed the remnant of Catherine's self-control. She dropped the garters and sobbed aloud.

'Are you a woman or a watering-pot?' Rannulf roared. 'Every time I see you or speak to you, streams pour from your eyes.'

Stung, Catherine whirled to face him, dashing the tears from her cheeks. 'One thing you may be sure of,' she spat, 'I will weep no more for you.'

Waiting with unusual patience to lift Catherine to the saddle, Rannulf was not at all ill-pleased. If she wept for him, then she prayed for him also. Good enough. Possibly she was rather cross with him just now – Rannulf smiled. How beautiful Catherine was when her face flushed with anger. Well, she would forgive him when he gave her the tourney gauds. For the first time in his life, Rannulf approved of the changing fashions that had introduced the practice of giving jewellery as tourney prizes. Previously he had resented it because, if he won, he had nothing to do with his prize but throw it into the jewel chest. Now he could give it to Catherine and watch her blush with pleasure and hear her murmur 'thank you' in that sweet, soft voice. He felt strong and certain; Leicester's warning was a piece of over-cautious nonsense.

With all his casualness, Rannulf was in very good time, early enough so that he and Catherine could stop and hear Mass at a church on the way and still arrive at the field before the heralds were done urging the late sleepers to hurry and make ready. A faint flush brightened Rannulf's complexion as he rode with his wife towards the lodges. He had not sought it and it could not increase his honour, but it would be pleasant to be earl of Soke. Stephen came across the barrier to clasp Rannulf's hand.

'They have all come,' he said, gesturing with a jerk of his head, 'except for a few of the very minor knights. If you make this a good day's work, you will have no further trouble with them.'

Rannulf glanced over towards the raised dais draped in

crimson cloth upon which the king would display him to his new vassals. The sun glittered on the gold-thread embroidery as the slight breeze stirred the drapery, and the red made a fine backdrop for the varicoloured surcoats of the men who stood before the platform. The vassals of Soke stood grouped together to the right of the dais. To the left stood the vassals who held keeps and manors of Rannulf's other properties. These too had to acknowledge him as earl of Soke and repeat their homage to him under that name, lest they revoke their fealty on the technicality that they had sworn to Sir Rannulf of Sleaford, not to the earl of Soke. Probably that was not necessary; Rannulf's men appreciated their overlord's qualities, but it was a good thing to repeat the oath of homage as often as possible.

'Is Osborn with them?'

Stephen frowned. 'I have not seen him.'

'No more than I expected.' Rannulf laughed harshly. 'He has no stomach to fight, only to spread foul rumours.'

The king shook his head. 'I hope you are right, but I would guard myself carefully.' There was a pause while both men surveyed the filling grounds, and finally Stephen nodded. 'Let your squire take your horse to the lists. The lords, as far as I can see, are assembled. Let us go.'

When necessary, Stephen of Blois had great dignity and a truly regal appearance. It was these, together with his un-doubted good nature and strong right arm, which had cozened the lords of England into believing he would make a good king. He now mounted the dais, a handsome and impressive figure magnificently clothed in blue, a jewelled circlet adorning his burnished helmet, and a cloak of royal purple trimmed with ermine thrown back over his shoulders. The heralds blew their trumpets, calling the field of folk to attention, and the nobles attendant upon the king drew closer to act as witnesses of the proceedings. From the lodges, the women watched, Catherine torn between pride, fear, and resentment and Maud deeply troubled.

Stephen spoke well, praising Sir Rannulf's justice, strength, and loyalty, giving his reasons for his choice of their new suzerain to the vassals of Soke. On the dais, a little to Stephen's right, Rannulf listened to his king, his eyes filled with bitterness. If Stephen were what he sounded like it would be a happy land. His glance ranged past his own vassals to the nobles witnessing the investiture – Leicester: was he about to change his coat? Hereford, Cornwall, Gloucester: a tight-knit group of hard and fast rebels, but among them the seeds of an idea that called to him. Chester, Lincoln, Peverel, Shrewsbury: men who cared for nothing but their own aggrandizement and riches, the curse of the kingdom. Warwick, Northampton: men like himself, loyal to the king, but unlike himself seemingly blind to Stephen's total inadequacy.

He shook himself free of his notions, mentally damning Hereford who had, by his insistent talk, put the ideas into his head, as Stephen called upon him to kneel. Raising his hands to grip the king's mechanically, he responded as mechanically with the standard oath of homage. He meant it and would keep it, but Stephen's reply, just as standard, rang hollow in his ears.

'. . . will guarantee to you the lands held of us, to you and to your heirs against every creature with all our power, to hold these lands in peace and quiet.'

A rush of unequalled bitterness filled Rannulf so that he nearly jerked his hands away, nearly turned his face so that he would not receive Stephen's kiss of peace upon his lips. What guarantee could Stephen offer to any man of anything? What power had Stephen? What peace and quiet had any man in the nation since he had become king?

Stephen felt the incipient movement and tightened his grip painfully; Rannulf relaxed and accepted the kiss. It was the barons' fault more than the king's. If they were not such greedy boars, if they were content to keep what they had and oversee their vassals, if they were willing to support the king without bribes and presents, the rebellion could have been put down completely at any time. If the barons did their duty, the king would be adequate, a pleasant figurehead for a smoothly running feudal state.

Having conquered his brief revulsion, Rannulf took the oath of fealty on the holy relics held out to him without further qualms and received from Stephen's own hands the lance bearing the gonfalon with the arms of Soke which was the symbol of his investiture as earl. The use of arms was a new fashion just coming into real popularity, although many men had used colours and symbols to identify themselves in tourney and battle for a long time. It was another of the new fashions of which Rannulf approved heartily, and he looked with pleasure at the gold waterfowl on a green ground, thinking that it could easily be added to his own dagger and chevrons.

The king's part was all but finished. He stepped forward, shoulder to shoulder with his vassal now as if to give physical evidence of his intention to support Rannulf. 'Vassals of Rannulf of Sleaford, will you do your lord homage as earl of Soke?'

'Fiat! Fiat!' roared the group to the left with honest enthusiasm. The higher their lord climbed, the greater their own importance.

'Vassals of Soke, will you have Sir Rannulf of Sleaford, husband of the only child of your late lord, as your present earl and undoubted suzerain?'

Momentarily there was a tense silence. Everyone knew that the testing of Sir Rannulf had been arranged with his concurrence, but it would be ill for those who stood out if he chose to take it ill. Even the men who were of Osborn's party originally were no longer so eager to oppose Rannulf. In a week at court they had learned much about the new earl, and no man of the group wished to bring his wrath or his power down upon their heads. Nonetheless the arrangement had been made.

Sir Giles cleared his throat. 'We hear your words, sire, and we know that Rannulf of Sleaford is a loyal vassal to you, but we are men who wish to be led by a man. Let Sir Rannulf prove with his body that he is worthy of our loyalty.'

'Sir Rannulf,' Stephen said formally, 'do you accept this challenge?'

'Bring forth my shield,' Rannulf called in his harsh voice. 'Let him who dares prove me touch it.'

The triangular, concave shield, bossed and bound in shining brass, was hung upon a post while the squires brought forward the destriers for the knights to mount. Slowly, led by Sir Giles, five of the vassals filed by, touching the shield with the butts of their spears. The king's herald pretended to take down the names although he already had a list. Of the men who appeared, none was Sir Herbert Osborn, however, and Rannulf, having examined the list, spoke quickly to the herald. The trumpets were blown again.

'My lords all,' the herald called. 'One of the vassals of the late earl of Soke is said to have spread infamy and spoken dishonour of the present earl. Sir Herbert Osborn, you are hereby appelled by Lord Rannulf, earl of Soke, to make good upon his body your words before the sun has set or acknowledge them as foul slanders.'

The cry was repeated over the field by the other heralds, but there was no reply. Rannulf knew Sir Herbert had been absent earlier, but he had hoped he would appear. He preferred, in spite of what Leicester said, to fight it out man to man instead of having to attack Osborn's keep and fight what amounted to a war against him. It was never profitable to war against one's own vassals because the land always suffered and, win or lose, the suzerain always lost by the damage to the property.

When a decent period of waiting proved that Sir Herbert was not going to take up the challenge, Rannulf picked his shield off the post and rode towards the defender's end of the field. Sir Giles was Rannulf's first opponent and, as he levelled his lance to rest, Rannulf had to fight a desire to hit hard enough to kill. He had no feeling of animosity towards Sir Giles at all; he rather liked him and knew his value as a sober and reliable chief vassal. The impulse to kill came solely from a desire to show off his fighting prowess to Catherine. He laughed low as he raised his shield almost to his eyes to cover his body. Catherine would scarcely be pleased if he wantonly killed a man she had long known and regarded as a true friend.

The heralds blew, the chief marshal called, 'In God's name, do your battle,' and Rannulf sighted carefully above the centre and slightly to the left on Sir Giles' shield. If the lance held, he would unseat his opponent; if the lance slipped off, it would go above Sir Giles' shoulder and do him no harm. The horses thundered across the turf, urged by the spurred heels of their riders, but the shock to a battle-hardened man was nothing.

Neither rider had thrown himself forward into the impact; neither wished to harm the other. Rannulf's lance splintered; Sir Giles' slipped off between the bosses of Rannulf's shield.

Two more encounters were equally formal and inconclusive, as both men intended them to be, and the watching crowd, sensing the restraint, was silent and disapproving. They had come to see serious jousting and a little blood spilled; this courteous mockery was not to their taste. The next opponent was a younger man, a claimant to a barony through inheritance but not yet invested. It would do him no harm to take a fall, Rannulf decided, and made short work of the young man on his first run. As the youthful knight arched over the croup of his horse, Rannulf wheeled past the royal lodge and brought his lance down and up in salute. The compliment might have been for the king and queen, but Rannulf meant it for Catherine. Unfortunately it did not reach her for she did not raise her eyes, but Rannulf was not much troubled.

The third course was a repetition of the second, but on the fourth, exhilarated by the way events seemed to be molding themselves to his desires, Rannulf made a mistake. His lance had held through two encounters and, even though it still balanced correctly, and showed no sign of strain, he should have changed it. He did not.

Wheeled on the end of the lists, Rannulf's destrier sprang forward without needing the touch of the spur. A quick glance showed the experienced fighter that this man carried his shield straight and well in over his body. Rannulf fixed on a middle point just right of centre so that when the impact took place the iron tip would slip exactly into the slightly concave centre of the shield and throw the horseman out of the saddle. About twenty-five feet from his opponent, Rannulf dug his spurs into his stallion. In the same instant that the beast leaped forward with renewed energy, the rider flung himself against the front pommel. He saw the lance tip hit just where he intended, heard the ominous creak of the wood before it splintered, and threw his left arm, bearing his own shield, up and out convulsively. His opponent's strike, uncushioned by the holding power of his own lance, made him reel in the saddle. Desperately, Rannulf dropped his broken lance butt, gripped his saddle pommel with

93

his right hand, and wrenched his horse over towards his opponent. The change in angle was sufficient. The lance tip slipped off through the bosses and slid over Rannulf's right shoulder, but the shaft struck him hard on the jaw below the ear. A frantic jerk upward of his shield struck the shaft higher and freed him totally. Rannulf bowed forward over his saddle pommel, safe, but dizzy and shaken.

Ten minutes to recover was all he needed, but he did not have two. The stallion, trained by long habit, turned without direction at the end of the field and trotted towards his own post. Habit, too, held Rannulf in his saddle; a man with his years of fighting experience would need to be more than half unconscious to lose his seat. Without a sound he took the new lance handed to him by his squire and fewtered it, but his eyes were glazed, and while habit still came to his aid and permitted him to hold the weapon steady, he could not see well enough to aim with any exactness. A second shock in which he was saved from being unhorsed only by the splintering of his opponent's lance dazed him still further. He managed to retain his seat even on the third encounter because the dizziness passed and he could control his body properly, but there was a weakness in his limbs and he ached with effort almost as he did after a hard day's fighting.

Now Rannulf had his ten-minute respite while the fifth jouster came on to the field and made ready. He waited quietly at his barrier, pressing his arms against his body to still their trembling and licking his dry lips. It seemed to him at the moment that he would gladly have given the whole earldom of Soke for a goblet of wine, and he knew he had only to tell John to bring it, but pride kept him still. No man would say of him that Rannulf of Sleaford needed refreshment after four encounters with the lance. Three more courses, that was all he needed to withstand; then he could rest. Briefly, Rannulf considered putting off the mêlée until the next day. Actually that was the normal procedure, the jousting in a tourney taking place on one day and the mêlée the following. However, since only five jousts had been planned, Rannulf himself had insisted that the entire event take place at once and be done with. The thought was only a passing one. The same pride which kept him from asking for a drink would not permit him to request an even greater concession.

The fifth jouster, to compound the trouble, was the strongest of all with a seat in the saddle so secure that unhorsing him would be well-nigh impossible. One pair of lances was fairly broken, and Rannulf, returning to his barrier, felt nauseous with fatigue. One little ray of hope lightened his trouble. The jouster opposing him apparently counted on his offence to protect him. He carried his shield poorly, tipped inward towards his body, a dangerous practice. Rannulf did not wish to kill or seriously injure one of his new vassals, his desire to show off having passed, but he was not sure he could take two more fair shocks from a rider of the strength of this one. He spurred his horse, which was also tiring, fewtered his spear, then with a fervent prayer that the beast would not stumble, wrenched him inward towards his opponent's horse at the last moment. His lance, caught on the inside of the jouster's shield, slipped through the bosses. Rannulf flung his body against it and, with a low cry of relief saw it slide through under the man's arm, tearing his mail and the flesh of his chest.

Rannulf reined his horse so sharply that the beast nearly sat on his own haunches, turned, and rode back to steady the bleeding knight with his own hands.

'How badly are you hurt?'

'Not – it is little more than a scratch.'

The face that looked into Rannulf's was not much older than that of Geoffrey, his eldest son. 'Is this a jest?' he roared, enraged and ashamed. 'Have they sent boys against me? Who are you?'

'I have my spurs,' the young man answered faintly. 'I am Sir André Fortesque, Sir Giles' youngest brother. Am I not a good jouster?'

'Would you be in the condition you are if you were a good jouster?' Rannulf said in exactly the same tone of exasperated fury he would have used to his own son. 'How comes it that your brother has not told you of the abominable way you hold your shield? I hope you have learned. Go to – can you ride?'

'Yes, I think I can. I am sorry I did so ill.' The young face became bitter with disappointment. 'I had hoped if I rode well

95

enough that you might find a place for me in your household. I am a great charge upon my brother, and if I do not find a place now that I am knighted—'

Rannulf laughed harshly. 'If you think you would win my favour by laying me in the dirt in front of all my vassals, you have peculiar notions.' He swung himself off his horse at the barrier and helped the young man down. 'Here, hold him. See that he receives the best care,' he said sharply to the herald at that end of the lists, and equally sharply to Sir André, 'Go nowhere. I would have a few words with you when this is over.' Then as André pushed back his helmet and his expression became more apparent, Rannulf said more kindly, 'You did none so ill. Except for your brother, who was holding back, you were the strongest jouster indeed. If you desire service – well, you are in no case to talk now.'

Remounting, Rannulf was again conscious of his weariness, but also of a strong sense of satisfaction. After a rest and some food and drink, all would be well. It was a necessary formality that he return to the barrier to stand forth in case of an additional challenge, but he had no expectation that anyone would look for trouble, especially after what had happened to Sir André.

The herald called once, repeating the challenge. Twice. Rannulf was just about to drop his rein and allow his mount to move forward as the third and last call rang out, when a large man in a grey surcoat lavishly embroidered with gold came to the opposite barrier. He leaned down from his destrier to speak to the herald.

'Lord Rannulf, hold,' the herald called. 'Sir Herbert Osborn is here to prove that you, not he, has lied. That the countess of Soke, your wife, is falsely wed to you, being first promised to him, and that she dare not avow this out of fear for her life at your hands.'

A gasp arose from the lodges. Stephen rose to his feet, a frown marring the usual good nature of his countenance. 'What brings you so late to answer this challenge, Sir Herbert?'

Osborn rode forward. 'Foul play, sire, and it does not need great thought to discover whose. My wine was drugged, and I could not be wakened. Had I been a lesser man, I would not have wakened at all.'

Another gasp passed through the lodges. One man would not survive this encounter, so much was clear. The crowd of common folk shrieked with excitement. This was what they had come for. Now they would see a duel in earnest; now there would be sword and mace play, and blood would truly flow. Sir André's mishap had just whetted their appetites, and they roared their enthusiasm for the coming show. Rannulf could not make a sound. He did not at first even feel angry, so impossible did it seem to him that anyone could accuse him of such a deed. Numb with surprise, he listened to the herald calling aloud the formal phrases of permitting God to decide the right of the quarrel until the enormity of the slander became clear.

'Have done,' he choked at last. 'Get him on the field before I burst.'

The slow-rising rage was of benefit to him for it gave strength to his tired body, but even spurs dug deep enough to draw blood could not revive his mount. Sir Herbert had not underestimated himself, although he had made a mistake in infuriating Rannulf, and the shock threw not Rannulf, but the tired horse. As the beast went down, Rannulf was still in the saddle. The crowd howled appreciation and excitement, but again long experience came to the rescue. Many horses had gone down under the master of Sleaford in considerably worse circumstances than faced him at present. By the time Osborn had wheeled his horse about, Rannulf was free, sword in hand.

The decision that faced Sir Herbert was not an easy one, and there was little time in which to think about it. If he stayed in the saddle, he would have an almost insuperable advantage over the heavily armed man on foot. On the other hand, it was an unchivalrous action which would make him odious to the men he wanted to convince to follow him, and an action which would be impossible to explain away. Sure he could beat his shaken opponent, he too leaped clear of the saddle, and the cry of approval, not from the crowd but from the lodges, showed that he had done right. They would be more likely to believe the tale of the drugged wine now.

The men approached each other warily, Osborn quite apparently carrying his weight of mail more easily than his older opponent. They circled, eyeing each other like hostile cats, and with the swiftness of a cat Osborn brought his sword across in a sidelong slash. It was stopped on Rannulf's blade with a clang that rang clear through the field while in the few seconds that the swords hung together, Rannulf thrust forward and upward with his shield, hoping to stun his adversary. The thrust was beaten back; the swords were free. Now Rannulf raised his weapon and brought it down. It caught on Osborn's shield, but sliding down struck his cheek. Even though the main force of the blow was spent, the flesh was laid bare to the bone. It was a small advantage since in the same moment Rannulf felt the searing heat of a blow on his hip and the less burning but more dangerous warmth of blood trickling down his thigh.

The battle continued, slash, thrust and parry, the combatants too evenly matched for much advantage on either side. In twenty minutes both were bleeding freely from several minor wounds and both were breathing heavily enough to back off mutually and lean, resting, on their swords. The lodges cheered, the men calling advice and the women urging their favourites to greater endeavour. Only the front bench was silent. Stephen was angry. He was not a very clever man, but he had known Rannulf too long to credit the ugly slur cast upon him. Somewhere in the back of his mind he knew there was something more than a simple rivalry for the earldom involved. Someone high up in the court must be behind Osborn or he would never have dared insult Rannulf.

Maud guessed far more than her husband of the truth of the situation, but she would say nothing. She could not even decide whom she desired to win this combat. Rannulf was an old friend and a loyal vassal. Maud knew the civil war was not over and knew too that Rannulf would be most valuable to her and her husband, but perhaps his destruction would ease Eustace's heart and wash away his restless dissatisfaction. Beside her Eustace bit his lip in equal indecision. He clung to his hatred of Rannulf, because Rannulf had shamed him and because he wanted to believe Rannulf a traitor. Still, it was a dreadful thing to see a man like Rannulf of Sleaford die at the hands of a cur like Osborn.

Catherine alone thought only of one man on the torn grass of the field. She prayed for her husband and feared for him because she loved him, but she was filled also with a bitter resentment because she was sure he did not love her. How strange, she thought, her eyes resting on the panting men, that she could not love her first man who had deeply adored her. Now that she had a man whom she considered worthy of her love, he did not care for her. It was a judgment upon her for her dissatisfaction and selfishness, but if he came alive out of this she would show him that she, too, would be indifferent. The bloodstained warriors moved towards each other, and Catherine resolutely closed her eyes and began to pray. *'Ave Maria, Gratia plena, Dominus tecum . . .'*

Less blindly angry now, Rannulf had considered his position carefully while he caught his breath. There was no point in deceiving himself; he was not strong enough to rush Osborn and bear him down. The man was his equal in strength and was fresher, but it was also plain that Osborn was not his equal in experience. For the next half hour Rannulf waged a strictly defensive battle, making no effort to hide his weariness, but allowing Osborn to exhaust himself in fruitless attempts to cut through his guard. He was losing blood, but not much and, although weaker, felt with satisfaction when Sir Herbert again withdrew to breathe, that he could have continued to fight longer without danger. A swift glance at the sun gave him more cause for satisfaction. It was too late now to start the mêlée; he would have the night to rest before he needed to exert himself again. Now when the lying cur attacked, he would take him.

Osborn, puzzled, furious, and a little frightened, stared at his drooping adversary. It seemed impossible from moment to moment that Sir Rannulf could parry another stroke. His shield hung lower and lower; his sword moved more and more slowly. Yet, each stroke *was* parried, and Osborn felt as if his head and chest would burst with the effort he was making. This must end it, he told himself; the man can barely stand upright. I need only try once more and the more swiftly the better. He drew one more deep, slightly shuddering breath, and charged.

Slowly Rannulf backed away. One mighty downward blow

he took on his raised shield. The sword rebounded, was turned swiftly in Osborn's hand and brought round in a slashing side-swipe. Rannulf countered with his sword, retreating again. Another blow and another were caught and fended off, but they were weaker. The grey eyes on either side of the shining nosepiece grew keener and more calculating; they were nowise glazed nor did they waver, Sir Herbert saw with a sudden choking sensation of panic. His strokes became wilder and, when Rannulf's hard lips parted in a merciless smile, be began to sob.

Once more Sir Herbert raised his sword above his head, but this time Rannulf did not content himself with guarding against the blow. This time he leaped forward, using his favourite thrust of the shield, trusting to being too close to his opponent for Osborn's stroke to touch him. At the same time he swung hard and low with his own sword. He felt metal bite metal and then cleave something softer; he heard Osborn's scream as the tendons of his thighs were cut and saw him topple.

Catherine heard the cry. Her eyes sprang open. She nearly screamed herself before she recognized the arms of Soke on the shield and the surcoat she herself had made for Rannulf. Terror washed over her again when she saw how much the cloth was bloodied, but as Rannulf easily lifted his sword and she realized he was not badly hurt, Catherine suffered another revulsion of feeling. Doubtless he had been enjoying himself while she had been near fainting with fear for him. Well, she could not help loving him, but he would never know it. If it killed her, she would not again display the love for which Rannulf had only contempt.

The battle was over. To strike the sword from Osborn's hand was the work of a moment, and in that moment Rannulf decided to pardon the slander upon himself and redeem his promise to Catherine by permitting Sir Herbert to live. There was no particular point in killing the man, if he was willing to admit that he had lied both about Catherine and the drugging. In all likelihood he would never fight again – cut tendons did not heal well and, in any case, Osborn's lands would be forfeit. Rannulf set his point at Sir Herbert's throat, preparatory to telling him to yield and confess his falsehood.

'Do not slay me, my lord,' Sir Herbert sobbed. 'I will confess all. It was the prince, Eustace, who set me to this deed. I did complain that I had offered for Lady Catherine and, though I thought she favoured me, her father would give me no answer. It was Eustace who bid me write that letter, and he who took the seal of Soke from the king's strongbox to seal it. I will tell the world, if you desire, that he—'

With a face as yellow as parchment, Rannulf drove home the blade, right through the mail, cutting the jugular. It took a frantic effort, and he laid the whole weight of his body behind the thrust to still the voice before the heralds could reach them and hear. The bright mail turned red; the bright blade turned red; the green grass turned red. Only the future was black as Rannulf of Sleaford denied mercy to a fallen opponent in loyalty to his king.

# Chapter 6

Mary, Rannulf's bastard daughter, sighed with relief as she took her seat before her spinning-wheel. She liked to spin. It was very pleasant to twist the soft fleece between one's fingers and listen to the hum of the wheel. It put all sorts of strange thoughts in one's head. Strange, pleasant thoughts, far removed from washing and fulling clothes, cleaning and airing beds and bed-furnishings, and endlessly polishing silver and gold plate.

Spinning still, Mary looked out through the open window over the fields of Sleaford which were fresh and green with the burgeoning life of May. It was two years exactly, no, there was an extra three weeks, since the Lady Catherine, countess of Soke, had come to be mistress of the forbidding keep at Sleaford. Now the wheel slowed as Mary looked around her at the women's quarters. She had grown used to them of late and hardly noticed, but they were nothing like what they had been in Lady Adelecia's time – nor in any other time, for that matter.

The entire keep had changed in the past two years, but one noticed it less than the change in the women's quarters because these, the least important, were the last to receive Catherine's attention. Casting her mind back, Mary remembered Lady Catherine's cry of consternation when she first entered her new home, remembered how she had stood, clinging to Richard as if the child alone kept her from running away. Mary remembered herself too as she was then and laughed. There had been a change in herself as great as the change in Sleaford. Then she had been a half-wild child of thirteen, snatching crusts of bread off the tables between the men-at-arms. She raised a hand to stroke the smooth braid that lay on her shoulder and jumped a trifle as she realized she had made a fault in her spinning. The wheel was stopped, the fault corrected, and the even hum began again. It was a great pleasure to have smooth clean hair instead of ragged and louse-infested tresses and a pretty, if plain, gown instead of filthy rags.

Only one thing had not changed at Sleaford – its master. Mary frowned and the wheel hummed faster. She had developed a fanatical devotion to Lady Catherine who, like an angel of heaven, had made all these changes and given her every blessing she enjoyed. It was the master who made Lady Catherine so sad. Every time he came home, which, praise God and the blessed saints, was not often, her ladyship drooped anew. She was never very lively, but Mary guessed that it was oppression of spirit that made her so subdued. When the effect of the master's infrequent visits had worn off, Lady Catherine could show flashes of great merriment if she were playing with Richard or herself. The wheel hummed even louder and the fleece flew through the nimble fingers. He was coming home again. That was why all the bedding was to be cleaned and aired and all the silver polished. That too, no doubt, was why Mary heard Lady Catherine weeping in the night, and why she sat so silent over her embroidery.

Catherine's mind too was on the past on this bright May morning, but she was not considering what had changed, only what had remained the same. In two long years she had come no closer to her husband's heart. If anything, they were more strangers to each other than they had been when they were first married. Despairingly, Catherine wondered why every effort she made to attach Rannulf only seemed to drive him further away. To the best of her ability she had patterned her behaviour on what she believed he desired. She cared for his children with great tenderness; she made his home comfortable; to him she maintained a manner courteous and respectful without any hint of affection.

Perhaps, she thought, bending the bright silk over and under to form the central knot of the flower she was embroidering into the neckline of Richard's tunic, she had not been careful enough. Perhaps her love had shown through from time to time and that was what disgusted him and drove him away. The movement of her needle was suspended for a moment while she fought back the tears which were obscuring her vision. She had tried so hard, even denying herself the pleasure of responding to his love-making, keeping herself cold and still when she desired nothing more than to render passion for passion. It was so hard not to betray oneself. How often she had stifled a sigh of pleasure or turned her face from his kisses to conceal her joy.

It was indifference he wanted, was it not? The ever-recurring hope that she had misread him caused a faint colour to bloom in her pale face, but the pink did not live long in her cheeks. There was always that rejection of her tenderness before the tourney to remember. Also, for a time after that, while she had still been furious with him and shown it by her coldness, Rannulf had seemed satisfied with her, even pleasant in his hard way. When she had been ready to forgive his rudeness and willing to smile on him, however, he had turned cold again. Then there was that night when her sadness had made her take a cup too much of wine, and she had – deliberately Catherine put that thought aside, but it was after that night that Rannulf had left Sleaford, and he had been away for months. Catherine's hand lay still on the embroidery frame as the slow tears trickled down. He had come so seldom to her bed after that – so seldom – and for almost a year now, not at all.

Lady Warwick touched her horse with her heel and left her husband to ride beside Lord Soke. 'I hope your wife expects us, my lord.'

'Yes,' Rannulf replied dully.

He is ageing fast like my own husband, Lady Warwick thought. How his face has fallen in! It is well that I should speak with the countess of Soke at this time. She may be a widow again before she thinks to be, and it will be well that her mind be given a proper direction.

'Surely the news is ill,' she continued in an effort to bring some life into her companion, 'but it is no more than was rumoured beforehand. Is there some reason I do not know of for your being so cast down?'

'Am I cast down? Nay, there is nothing the whole world does not know of. Henry is now duke of Normandy, count of Anjou, and having snatched the divorced wife of the king of France, will soon be count of Aquitaine and Poitou also. God, it seems, is never tired of showering good on that young man.'

'He is a most capable young man, from all I have heard.'

'Capable of making a bitch howl in bed,' Rannulf growled with such bitterness that Lady Warwick was startled. 'What is he capable of? Geoffrey the Fair – he was a good man, it is true – won Normandy for him. Having done so much, he did more – he took a fever and died, giving his son Anjou and Maine also. Now a woman hot with lust is about to give him Aquitaine and Poitou.'

'Nay, Lord Soke, there must be more to him than that. Hereford says—'

'Hereford! Hereford! He has dinned in my ears also till I am almost deaf with his talk. I believed him once an honest man. I believe so no longer. First he is a king's man—'

'You shall not missay him. He was never a king's man, never gave oath or did homage.'

Rannulf bit his lip, conscious that his personal unhappiness was making him unjust. It was true that Hereford had made a truce with the king, but he had done no more than that ever. He had never said he would forswear his rebel sympathies or his loyalty to Henry. The truth of the matter was that Rannulf envied that bright and beautiful young man the close understanding he had with his wife.

'One good thing, at least, has come of this,' Lady Warwick continued. 'Even you must admit that it will benefit everyone that Eustace should go to France.'

Again Rannulf made no reply. What she said was incontrovertible, for Eustace had grown worse and worse so that all men looked at him askance. Maud was being racked apart between her conflicting loves, and even Stephen, blindly fond, agreed that Eustace needed action. Still Rannulf would speak no word against the prince, not though Sir Herbert's death, useless as it was in retrospect, had precipitated his marital misery.

Catherine would never forgive him, he thought, staring between his horse's ears, deaf to Lady Warwick's voice. He had almost believed her when she swore she cared nothing for Osborn, but after he had killed the cur, she turned to ice. He had given her the tourney prize, hard-won, for he was sore all over with his wounds, and she had thanked him as if for an insult.

The only time since then that she offered him the slightest response of any kind was when she was light-headed with drink.

Unbearable. It was unbearable the way she endured his caress, cold and stiff. It was unbearable the way she turned her head to avoid his lips, her teeth gritted together. Better far to let her be, even though he ached so with desire for her that his stomach fluttered in her presence and he could not eat, even though no other woman could truly give him ease.

'—and I do not think it will be possible to turn him from that path.'

'Who?' Rannulf asked, realizing that he had missed what Lady Warwick said in his self-absorption.

'Leicester, of course. He has listened very attentively to the so-charming Hereford, and, what is more, Eustace has pricked him soundly.'

'I do not know what Leicester will do, and if I did, I would not discuss it with a woman, madam,' Rannulf snapped. 'To me it matters little what any man, even my foster brother, will do. I have lived so long in one pattern – do you think I can change now? Nor, though you are my guest and I owe you courtesy, does any man owe any woman so much as to talk of the doings of kings with her. You follow your lord's bidding, and all will be well – or, if it is not, no one can lay any blame upon a virtuous wife.'

Lady Warwick's face flamed. She should have known better than to try to speak sense to such a hidebound, stiff-necked, self-righteous boar. It was really for the best that she had urged her husband to press Rannulf to make his keep the place of the meeting of the barons. What was to be decided was who should go with Eustace to France and what force should be furnished. The problem presented no easy solutions. First of all, Eustace had managed to alienate even those men who were steadfastly loyal to his father through his greed and dealings with their vassals which bordered on the dishonourable. Second, although the great magnets of England were not happy about Henry's steady aggrandizement in France, by and large they were short-sighted men and would not recognize the implications this increase in power had for England. They could see little reason, they said, for wasting men and money in trying to wrest from Henry what, after all, was rightfully his and which cost them nothing.

Warwick, who was growing old, wished to settle the matter in a series of private conferences in London. This, his wife pointed out, was completely unsuitable for two reasons. One, Maud had spies everywhere in London and, through them, would hear of who had said what. Therefore, no one would speak his true mind for fear of her displeasure. Worse yet, any promise given in private could easily be violated. To that Warwick, who was an upright and honourable man, objected, but his wife laughed in his face, asking with derision how many fools like himself he thought there were.

The second reason Lady Warwick proffered for objecting to private meetings was that each man would suspect he was doing more than the others. It was a matter which should be talked over in an unrestricted atmosphere where everyone could hear what everyone else was offering – and hold him to it. Wearily Warwick agreed, suggesting that they hold the meeting in their own keep where, if his conscience must be troubled, at least his body would be comfortable. To this, Lady Warwick objected also. She did not present her private reasons for being opposed to the idea, which was simply that, if the conference produced insufficient support for Eustace, the holder of the conference might be blamed. She merely pointed out that their keep was so much on the border of the rebel territory that any great gathering there might be suspect. Sleaford was finally chosen as being the most out-of-the-way spot and the least likely to be sown with the queen's spies.

Rannulf was by no means enthusiastic about holding the meeting in his castle either, but since his reasons were personal, merely a disinclination to be at home, he yielded to what he felt was his duty. Now, riding home, he was bitterly sorry he had agreed. Matters never seemed so bad when he was away. Catherine's letters, although concerned solely with the children, estate problems, and household matters, were almost warm. It was only when he was actually in her presence, when he was forced to take her ice-cold hand in his and see her glance shrink away, that the full weight of his misery fell upon him.

Sir André Fortesque craved admittance to Lady Catherine's solar and was invited to enter. His eyes passed over his mistress with absent approval. Certainly she was a beautiful woman and when she took pains, as she had today, with strings of pearls braided into her moonlight hair and a bliaut of silvery-blue silk floating around her, she did almost look like the angel Mary called her. It was unfortunate she should be so pale and have so little vivacity.

'Madam, I can get no attention from Richard at all today. You know how he is about his father. He desires most earnestly to ride out to meet him. May we do so?'

Very faintly Catherine smiled. 'Yes, of course. But do not ride beyond the borders of the holding, and take some twenty or thirty men-at-arms. I suppose there really is no need, but his lordship does not like the boy to go unprotected.'

'Thank you, madam.'

'Wait, André. Richard makes good progress, does he not?'

'Indeed he does. He is as forward as any child of his age and more – but a devil.'

'I know. That is all high spirits and boyish pranks. Do not – do not tell his father of his mischief.'

'Some things may be overlooked, but what am I to say of the laming of the brown destrier? And the serfs assuredly will complain of the sheep that was slain.'

'I believe Richard will confess those matters himself – and it is better so. I reminded him last night, and he promised me he would not fail. We may wait out this day at least. If he does not keep his promise, it will be soon enough to betray him tomorrow.'

'Very well, you know I—' André's voice checked as Mary tripped in, also specially clad and looking very pretty. There, he thought, forgetting what he had been about to say, was true beauty. Perhaps the features were not so perfect, and assuredly Mary was less wondrous fair, but she had spirit and countenance, which was better.

'You what?'

'I – I – oh, yes, I love the boy. I would not wish to cause him any grief, but to spoil him with indulgence—' His eyes wandered away again and Mary blushed under his glance.

Catherine frowned slightly. 'I know you truly care for him, nor do I wish him spoiled. The real harm he has done must be confessed and, if our immediate punishments were not sufficient, he must bear what his father lays upon him. I merely wish the confession to come from him without urging. You had better take him now.' A rueful smile crossed her face again. 'If you do not, he will likely ride out by himself and truly enrage Lord Soke.'

Dismissed, Sir André went at once, but he looked back in the doorway, and Mary's eyes followed him. Catherine sighed. More trouble. She attended absently to her stepdaughter's message, noticing more the girl's confusion. What was to be done about this? The attraction between the pair was plain and had been growing steadily stronger in spite of all efforts to check it. Mary was ripe for marriage too, and should be given at once, but Rannulf had made no reply to her repeated messages on the subject. Catherine did not know whether he simply could not decide, whether he did not wish to dower the girl, or whether he was reluctant to acknowledge her publicly.

What increased the difficulty was that Sir André had not declared himself. True, he was the youngest of a number of sons and had nothing but the arms he bore and his horse. Therefore, under ordinary circumstances, he could not marry unless his father or his suzerain could find an heiress for him. Mary too had nothing in her own right, her mother having been a maidservant whom Rannulf had taken casually to his bed between his first two marriages. Still, if André had asked for Mary, she would have had a reason to go to Rannulf and demand some settlement of the girl's future.

If only she had some influence with her husband, the matter could be easily settled. She would gladly have parted with some of the revenues from Soke temporarily if Rannulf was straitened for money. There was nothing for it but to demand a settlement for Mary anyway. Once Mary had a portion, she was sure André could be brought to admit his desire for her, and the portion would not need to be given up at once. They could continue to live at Sleaford while André tutored Richard. Later, when the affairs of the country were more settled – if ever such a time came – André could be made castellan of one of Rannulf's or Catherine's properties.

Of the three minds at work on the same subject, Mary's was the least depressed. She had little faith in or affection for her father, but her dependence on Catherine's ability to bring about a miracle was enormous. She did not know how it would be or what would happen, but she was absolutely sure that Lady Catherine would give her her heart's desire.

Sir André had considerably less belief in miracles and had not even considered soliciting Catherine's help. He was in no doubt whatsoever about who was the master of Sleaford. If he was to make an offer for Mary, it had to be directly to Lord Soke, but he was not at all certain that he should even try. It was not that he did not love her, nor that he was greedy and wished to wait until he knew what her portion would be. What troubled Sir André was that he could not believe he had the slightest chance of success. True, Mary was a bastard, but she was acknowledged to be Lord Soke's daughter, and the earl of Soke could look higher than a mere penniless knight for the husband of even a bastard daughter. Many a petty baron would be willing to take her, even with a small dowry, for the assurance of Soke's good will and influence.

Richard, riding beside him, chattered and chattered, but André muttered 'yes' and 'no' only half hearing. He had better hold his tongue. If Lord Soke knew of his desire, he might dismiss him from service. Even if he could not have Mary, he could see her and speak to her here, and he had a true affection for his scapegrace charge. An ear-splitting shriek beside him woke him in time to spur his horse forward so that he reached Sir Rannulf only a few seconds after Richard did.

'Papa, Papa!'

The boy freed his feet from the stirrups and launched himself from his saddle into Rannulf's arms, neatly avoiding the hand Sir André stretched out to detain him.

'Richard, Richard!' his father mocked breathlessly, struggling to hold his reins, grasp his son, and keep his shield from knocking the child to the ground. 'Will you never learn to observe the smallest propriety towards me?' he scolded. 'You are too old for such tricks.'

'You have been away so long!'

'Yes, and if you strangle me, I shall soon be sorry I have returned.'

Richard giggled. 'But you are squeezing me too, papa, so I know you are glad to see me.'

Rannulf laughed. 'You disrespectful imp. I am squeezing you so that you will not fall off and be trodden underfoot. There now, my child, enough. André, put him back on his own horse. Richard, I want to present you to Lord and Lady Warwick.'

Sir André held his breath, but the boy said his piece in acknowledging the introduction very properly. Richard was well taught, but he was a very passionate child, and occasionally took an instant aversion to certain people. When that happened, he was neither to hold nor to bind and acted more boorishly than the worst-educated child of a serf. It was important to Sir André that Lord Soke approve of his training, so it was fortunate that Richard committed no solecism at all on their way back to the keep. As a matter of fact, he gave André good reason to be proud of him when, as the battlements came into view, the happy chatter died down and Richard looked thoughtfully at his father.

'Papa?'

'What now?'

'I have not always been so good a boy as I should.'

Rannulf took his lower lip between his teeth in a hard bite. 'If you have been brought to believe you did something amiss, I am surprised to see the castle still standing. Very well, I am prepared. What disaster have you wrought?'

'If you will permit, I would rather tell you in private.'

'Then you are a fool, and Sir André has not properly taught you tactics. If you anger me in private, I will doubtless beat you.'

Richard thought that over and turned clear eyes upon his father. 'I do not care for that,' he replied at last in a low voice. 'I had rather you beat me than you scolded me and shamed me before others.'

'Ride on ahead,' was Rannulf's only reply, 'and tell Lady Catherine that we are but a few minutes behind you.' As the boy started, he gestured to Sir André not to follow but to come closer. 'You have my gratitude. The boy is forming well.'

'I wish I deserved it, my lord, but what I have taught him you have not yet seen. The courage he was born with, and the manners and sense of honour, Lady Catherine has given him.'

There was, fortunately, no need to answer, since they were now crossing the drawbridge. Sick already with desire for what he could not have and a faint hope that his long absence might have caused an amelioration of her feeling towards him, Rannulf lingered in the bailey and court as long as possible. He saw to the disposition of the horses, visited his kennels and mews, and then, realizing that he was acting out of pure cowardice, made for the external wooden stairway that led into the great hall.

There he found Warwick already disarmed and ensconced in a chair by the hearth. Lady Warwick was in earnest conversation with his wife, but Catherine excused herself as soon as she saw him and came across to drop a deep curtsey and offer her hand. She was pale, far paler than she should be, and her icy hand trembled in his. If Rannulf had been younger, if he had had a less unhappy relationship with his previous wife, if he had not been buckled and armoured with pride, he would have burst into tears. As it was, his greeting to Catherine was as cold and formal as hers to him.

Across the wide hall, Lady Warwick watched, pursing her lips in thought. She could not hear what Rannulf and Catherine said, for the high-raftered, stone-walled room echoed with the bustle of the servants, nor could she see clearly their expressions in the dim light. There was, however, a stiffness in both bodies, a rigidity in the way their heads were held when their eyes met, which augured ill for a good understanding between them. She had, initially, counted on Catherine's influence with her husband, but in a way this was just as good. So long as the two were not indifferent to each other, she had some material to work on.

At first when Rannulf joined his guests the conversation was devoted to the improvements in Sleaford Castle, Catherine receiving the compliments bestowed upon her with becoming modesty. Rannulf, when applied to for his opinion, resentfully

112

grunted that it was all the same to him, and his wife's face reddened with chagrin. Shortly after, Mary came bearing goblets of wine and plates of sweet cakes. Catherine's soft lips hardened with determination. The ungrateful brute! This was a perfect opportunity to force his hand with regard to his daughter.

'Stay a moment, child,' she said softly. 'I would like to present my husband's natural daughter, Mary, to you, Lady Warwick. She has been a great comfort to me, and a great help in my labour in Sleaford.'

'What a pretty maid. Where have you hidden her all these years, Lord Soke?'

'She has always been in the keep,' Rannulf snarled. 'Lady Adelecia would take no pains with her, and I know nothing about the raising of daughters. It is one of my wife's virtues,' he added caustically, 'that she takes to her heart all stray lambs.'

'You should be grateful that she cares so well for your children,' Lady Warwick countered in a deliberately shocked voice, watching Catherine's colour deepen still more.

Rannulf snorted. 'Women! Carpets and children is all they can think of. Warwick, I expect that Leicester and Northampton will be here tomorrow. If you and I can settle what we think will be best, we can present a united front to them. Ride out with me where we will be free of this women's foolishness and we can talk at our ease.'

The gibe was directed at Lady Warwick, but it was Catherine who rose to her feet. 'We are in the way, Lady Warwick,' she said in a trembling voice. 'Let us withdraw to my solar. I would not have it said of me that I drove my husband from his own home.'

'Nonsense, my dear,' Warwick laughed 'I have no intention of leaving my wine or my comfortable chair just because Lord Soke has bad manners. I have known him for some thirty years, and have learned to put up with him. If you take Gundreda away, I will merely have to repeat the whole conversation to her to still her nagging, and I have no lust for such dull work. Besides, it is very pleasant to look at your sweet face, and I have no desire to lose that comfort when I am about to embark on what I know will be a very unpleasant discussion.'

'Mayhap,' Catherine said bitterly, 'my lord does not trust me to hear of these great matters.'

Rannulf's face twisted with pain because it was true. Often it flickered across his mind that Catherine's coldness was not owing to Osborn's death but to his refusal to give up active participation in the king's cause. As fast as the flickers of doubt came, he damped them out. Better to blame her for loving Osborn. It was a more curable ill than a love for the rebel cause. But he did feel remorse for his sharp remarks about her housewifery. To a certain degree he resented Catherine's care for his home and his children because he felt that she threw her duty in his face, caring for everything of his but himself. And now, when perhaps his long absence had blurred her memory of the past, his foul temper had destroyed all chance of a reconciliation.

Having paused for a moment to give Rannulf a chance to repair his blunder, Warwick shook his head. 'Sit down, Lady Soke. I assure you we shall say nothing that the whole world cannot hear. For myself, Soke, I would offer nothing, and I tell you that plainly, except that I see the necessity of ridding ourselves of Eustace.'

'You are right, my lord,' Lady Warwick concurred. 'He has made himself so odious to the barons that more of them listen daily to Hereford's preachings. If he does not soon go forth from this country, they will turn on Stephen to be rid of his son.'

'Now you go too far, Gundreda. Eustace has not behaved well. He has extorted money where he could and, worse, he has meddled with the vassals – I know he approached some of Leicester's men and some of mine too – but it is not senseless greed.'

Rannulf's head came up. 'What then, Warwick? Why is he changed from a most promising young man into a monster?'

'You do not read men well,' the older man replied. 'You speak what is in your mind openly for all to hear and you expect that others will do the same.'

'Well, and if a man has honest thoughts, what else need he do?'

'There are other things in the world besides one man's

114

honesty of purpose. Eustace might propose to rule the nation honestly, but he cannot well speak of it while Stephen is alive.'

'Why should he think of it before his father be dead?' Rannulf's grey eyes were angry and his gesture impatient. 'Oh, I read him well enough, but what does he gain? He flaunts his dishonesty in all men's faces and then is angered because they do not believe in him. What would things come to if all men behaved the same? What if my son were to cozen my vassals – no, make the case more like – my wife's vassals because he planned to rule them when I was dead '

Warwick smiled. 'You have not reduced your estates to the case that Stephen's are in.'

'That is not the point. It is not all Stephen's fault, as you well know.'

'It is the point, although I agree that it is not the king's fault. But Eustace, day by day, sees his patrimony dwindle and itches to manage it better himself. Above that lies the fear that there will be so little power in the king's hands when Stephen dies that it will be too late to hold even the loyal barons together except by force – so he gathers his forces. I do not say I believe this, Rannulf. This is what Leicester says, and I must admit, he is seldom wrong. Moreover, Eustace's succession is by no means certain. And that brings me to the other side of the case. I do not believe that it is a good thing to molest Henry, and Leicester agrees with me in this also. If we leave the Angevin alone, he might be content with what he has already.'

'No. That I know from the talk with Hereford. Henry says that England is his by right and he will have it. He is power-mad, and that much even Hereford does not deny, although he overlays the facts with honeyed words of peace.'

'Then it is mad to send forth our strength into France. Better we should keep our men here. I have given my fealty to Stephen, and I have sworn to him, personally, that I will support Eustace to succeed him. I am willing to do my duty to uphold my honour, but I am not clear in my mind what is best to do.'

The women had been silently listening, Catherine with such intentness, because she had heard nothing of this before, that her pain and shame receded. Lady Warwick was more interested in her and her husband than in the subject, having known the facts previously. What Rannulf said and how Catherine reacted would determine her approach to the subject later.

'I too have so sworn and mean to keep my oath,' Rannulf replied. 'It is clear to me, however, that nothing but good can come of giving full support to Eustace in France. It is always possible that he will defeat, or, by God's mercy, destroy Henry. Yes, I know there is another son, but he is younger, of less weight, and has little interest in England With Henry gone the way would be smooth. Also, while he is attacked in France, Henry cannot come here to trouble us.'

'You will hold by Eustace then?' Warwick asked slowly. 'I honour you, Soke, but I feel that I must warn you that Eustace appears to have an ineradicable hatred for you. Why it should be so, I cannot tell, for you have ever done well by him and spoken well of him. Still—'

'I know it,' Rannulf said shortly, his mouth grim.

Lady Warwick sighed imperceptibly. Her husband had solved one problem for her in presenting Eustace's enmity to Rannulf and therefore, probably to Rannulf's heirs, to Catherine's mind. Rannulf's acknowledgment of the enmity had put the seal of truth on Warwick's statement. All that was necessary now was to show the young woman, who was obviously totally ignorant on political matters, that her husband's position was disastrous to himself and his children.

For many years the Warwicks had been staunch supporters of Stephen of Blois, the earl by virtue of his hatred for Matilda the empress and his personal loyalty to the king, the countess because she believed her good, her children's good, and her husband's good was best served by attachment to the throne. Her conviction had been somewhat shaken by Henry's behaviour and victories during the campaign of 1149 and she had watched the developments and the shifting climate of the court with keen eyes since then.

Now Gundreda sensed unerringly the inevitable turn of the tide in favour of the Angevin Henry. Stephen was growing old; his charm and his good nature palled. Maud was weary; her eyes were still inscrutable, but more and more often there was

116

exhaustion and despair behind them instead of plans and expedients. Eustace was no longer a bright hope against the harsh rule of another despot; to some he was merely greedy and unscrupulous, to others merely a less-appealing despot. Most important of all, however, the barons were glutted with lawlessness. More and more they desired a king to whom they could bring their wrongs, whom they could call upon to defend their rights, who could do more than 'pray' a powerful neighbour to desist from molesting them.

There was no sense in wasting time and energy in arguing with her husband – so much Lady Warwick clearly understood. When Henry came again, as she expected he would, Gundreda of Warwick planned to yield her husband's property to Henry for the assurance that her children would inherit the estates and earldom of Warwick unmolested. Her intentions in bringing Catherine around to her way of thinking were simple. If sufficient strength were mustered to the Angevin party, her husband and the few other major nobles who were faithful to Stephen, like Rannulf, might be brought to yield peacefully. A man could do very little if his estates were already in enemy hands. Furthermore, Gundreda had a genuine liking for Catherine while she disliked Rannulf. It seemed only right to show the young woman a way to protect herself from the catastrophe her husband was about to bring upon her by the stubbornness and folly he named honour.

# Chapter 7

From a discussion of political generalities, which Catherine had found very interesting, Lord Soke and Lord Warwick drifted to particulars of men and arms, a subject she did not find nearly as fascinating. Lady Warwick, too, was indifferent to this aspect of the conversation at the present time. It did not really matter to her whether her lord furnished half- or full-strength forces for Eustace. She had no quarrel with fulfilling her obligations to Stephen as long as he remained king, all she wanted was assurance that Warwick should remain in the hands of her family with its full power no matter who was king. Therefore, when Catherine murmured an excuse and rose to see about some household chores, Lady Warwick followed her

By the evening of that day, in bits and pieces, but nonetheless clearly, Catherine was presented with the history of the past seventeen years. She learned of the oath of fealty which Henry Beauclerc, Henry I, had forced from his barons, making them accept his daughter, Empress Matilda, as queen after his death. She learned of the repudiation of that oath by the majority of the English nobility and the seating of Stephen of Blois on the throne. Once more the nobles swore, and once more there were repudiations, but this time England was torn apart by civil war. Sometimes the war had raged in bloody battles which had encompassed nearly the whole country; sometimes the fighting was localized while the true war was waged subtly at court. In 1141, the Empress' forces had been so successful as to mount her on the throne. There her behaviour was such that by 1142 she was in sore straits, only the western lords still faithful and the rest of England gladly swearing loyalty to Stephen again. By 1147 Matilda was convinced that she could make no headway, and she had retired to Anjou. In her stead had come her

118

young son, but his mother's image was too clear in men's minds, and he, too, had retreated to France a few months later.

The battle that defeated the young Henry in 1147 had been waged at court, but when he returned in 1149 with the fiery earl of Hereford leading his armies, the fields and streams had run red with blood again. That time there had been setbacks in his campaign, but no defeat. Actually, he had been dangerously close to success when, for no known reason, he had suddenly returned to France. The rest of the story, Lady Warwick said, was very recent history, and Catherine had doubtless heard of Henry's acquisition of Normandy, Anjou, Aquitaine, and Poitou, an acquisition that made him richer and more powerful than the king of France. With that power behind him, it was scarcely likely that the battle-weary nobles of England would care to contest his right to the throne when he came to claim it for the third time

'Will you see your vassals ruined, their estates sequestered because your husband stubbornly follows a lost cause – and the lost cause of a man who hates him and would destroy him even if he did gain power? Your men even favour Henry, as did your father. Why should they and you be punished?'

'You are so sure the cause is lost and that Eustace could not be reconciled?'

'Believe me. I have spent my life in the court and I can sense the temper of the lords. You do not need to believe me. Listen closely to what your lord and mine say and you will hear the tolling of the mourning bells in their voices. They know too, but their honour – a pox take all men of honour for the grief they bring to all about them – will not permit them to yield. Oh, the fall may be delayed – a few months or even a few years, but in the end it will be the same.'

The light evening meal of bread, cheese, cold meat, and wine was consumed by Catherine in thoughtful silence. In silence, too, she sat over her embroidery, so absorbed in her own thoughts that she did not even hear when the chaplain finished the tale he was reading aloud. Her husband, who had not addressed a single word to her since the scene of the morning, glanced at her in surprise, for it was not Catherine's way to

119

ignore her guests. At last, when she did not move, he summoned Mary to show Lord and Lady Warwick to their bed. He watched Catherine for some moments longer, gazing at the play of the flickering light of candles and torches on her fair hair, at the long delicate fingers, pearly white, as they plied the silver needle, at the rounded cheek and throat, whiter still than her hands.

'Madam, where is my cloak?'

Catherine's great blue eyes went wide with astonishment. 'Your cloak? Are you cold?'

'Of course I am not cold. I am going out – to the village.'

Instantly the flames of wrath mounted to Catherine's cheeks. 'Have you not mortified me sufficiently? Must you go into the village to seek a whore on the first night of your homecoming?'

'Hold your tongue! You should count yourself fortunate that I do not really wish to mortify you. I could take one of your maids to my bed and set you to wait upon us. Be satisfied that I am a patient man – for all that some call me hasty – and I have not sought to repay you in the false coin you have given me.'

'False coin?' Catherine gasped. 'In what have I failed you? Have I not been a dutiful wife? Have I cared ill for your children or your interests?'

Rannulf burst into bitter laughter. 'For such matters a man can hire a nurse or a bailiff, if he cares to.'

Catherine gasped again. To a remark such as that there could be but one meaning. 'If I have given you no heir to the lands and title of Soke, you can scarcely blame me. It is you who prefer the commonest slut—'

'They have their advantages.'

'To one who craves sin instead of decency, I can well believe it to be true!'

'What?'

Rannulf was stunned by the obvious explanation for Catherine's coldness which certainly had seemed to intensify as his own warmth increased. It was something he had overlooked, but it was entirely possible that she believed it sinful to enjoy the physical relationship between husband and wife. The priests were always preaching about the sin of lust, and there were many of them who insisted that it was almost as sinful to enjoy one's spouse as to commit adultery. If he could be sure that it was no personal revulsion she felt for him, he could be satisfied to accept her coldness while she was re-educated. Tomorrow, Rannulf thought, I will speak to her chaplain and speak with some point. If that priest will not listen, there will be a score of other hungry clerics who will be very anxious to take his place and do as they were told.

'You heard me very well,' Catherine was replying breathlessly. 'I need not lower myself by repeating what I am ashamed to have to say about my own husband. But I will not be blamed for what is no fault of mine. It is sufficient to know that nothing I can do can please you. Take anyone you like to—'

'Catherine, hold your tongue,' Rannulf said again, but this time quietly and with a hint of amusement in his voice. 'If anyone heard what you have said to me and what I have listened to without lifting your hide with my belt – buckle-end forward – that person would think I had gone mad.'

She was too angry to notice the humour. 'I pray you, do not hesitate for a moment. It needs only that to complete my happiness. My labour you scorn. My care for—'

'Mayhap if you were not so hungry for compliments you would receive more.'

Rannulf was teasing her, but Catherine did not even know he was capable of such light behaviour and, besides, was in no mood for a jest. 'Oh,' she choked, speechless with rage, 'oh!'

'That is already an improvement,' Rannulf laughed. 'A speechless woman is always better than a railing one. And, since you are so anxious to provide me with an heir, that, with God's help, may also be arranged – but only if you will continue to be still.'

'I did not say that I desired – you are foul-minded as well as foul-mouthed. I said I would not be blamed unjustly for what—'

Her husband laughed again, giddy with his sensation of relief, and Catherine felt that she would die of shame. It was bad enough that he did seem to prefer the village whore, but to be told that he believed her to have asked for his favours was unendurable. Her eyes filled with tears of impotent rage.

'If you spread that story about me, Rannulf, I – I will run away!'

'Run away? Where do you think you could go that I could not fetch you back? What story?'

'That I asked you—' Her face was crimson, her eyes averted, and tears sparkled on the long blonde lashes.

'Nay, Catherine,' Rannulf said pacifically, realizing that what he had meant as a jest had really hurt her. 'It was but a jape. Even if it were true, you should know me better than to think I would tell such a tale of my wife. I have other things to think about and to talk about when I am among my friends.'

Her colour receded, but she was still thoroughly angry. Naturally he did not think about her; she was the least important and the least valuable of his possessions. He had never wanted to marry her, and was too lazy and too arrogant to make sufficient efforts to attract any woman but a whore. Look at him! As dirty and ill-kempt as when she first met him, and he had made rags of the clothing she had left in London. It was no wonder Lady Adelecia had done nothing; probably she had given up in despair.

While Catherine fed her rage, Rannulf had propelled her ungently, but this time because he was in a hurry and not because he meant to be rough, up the stairs. He gave her a last push into the solar and stood in the doorway looking around the room. From a shadowy corner, Mary and two maids came into the light.

'Out,' Rannulf said briefly. 'Neither of us are crippled. We can do for ourselves.'

The maids fled at once, but Mary moved to her stepmother's side, conscious that Catherine was trembling. 'I will not leave you,' she whispered.

Catherine neither wanted nor needed protection, but she was far too distracted to choose her words with care. 'No, no,' she murmured in reply, 'do not enrage him.' And then, trying to collect herself because of Mary's look of horror, 'He will do me no hurt.'

'No,' Rannulf said, grimly amused and unconscious of the effect he was having on his daughter, 'I always beat my wives in public. Then no explanation of the bruises need be given.'

He pulled the screen closed behind his daughter, and watched avidly as Catherine struggled to unknot the laces of her bliaut. Then, thinking that his close attention might be embarrassing to her, he turned away and began to undress. When he had shed all of his own clothing, however, Catherine was still no further advanced in her disrobing. Her hands trembled pathetically, and Rannulf was sorry he had dismissed the woman for Catherine was plainly in no state to help herself. Her obvious distress destroyed his elation. It was clear enough that she did not really want him and yielded only to salve her pride.

'Shall I call your maids again?'

'No!' If he called, Mary would come and Mary disliked her father enough without crediting him with reducing his wife to hysteria. 'If you will but undo the laces for me, I can manage. I cannot see how they are tied.'

The silk was soft as cobwebs, and Catherine's tugging had pulled the knots tight. Rannulf bent his head under her lifted arm. Her scent, sweet and faint, of lilies and roses came to him. He swallowed nervously, keeping his hands from shaking only with great effort. What he would have liked to do was break the laces, but he did not wish to annoy or frighten Catherine further, and he knew she set great store by her clothes.

'At least you can see that I am no hand at this work.'

Catherine had been staring straight ahead, but the uncertain and embarrassed tone of that remark drew her eyes to her husband. With a pang she saw how much greyer his hair was, how the bones stood out in his thinning flesh. He was not dirty either, although his hair was uncut and he needed a shave. His body was as fair as hers and the skin was fresh and smooth where it was not knotted and discoloured by scars. Nor was his odour the sour smell of unwashed filth; faintly acrid it was, but only with the pungency of a healthy man. The knot gave and Catherine turned to present her other side. As she moved, her hand brushed Rannulf's shoulder and she felt with surprise that he, too, was trembling.

'Thank you,' she said when the other lace hung loose.

'A service I will be glad to perform at any time.' He meant

123

to mock, but the shaken note in his voice made him sound gallant.

'Then by your mercy,' Catherine said when she had pulled off the bliaut and dropped it on the floor, 'undo my tunic sleeves also.'

Her hands were icy cold. 'Are you still afraid of me, Catherine?'

'Only a little, when you are raging. Are you not to be feared then?'

'I am not angry now. Why are your hands so cold?' He finished with the sleeves and moved away. When Catherine was so close, he could not think. 'I have meant to tell you for long, but somehow I never did. I killed him of necessity, not of my own will or spite, for he spoke what could have harmed the king.'

'Who?' Catherine asked.

Rannulf faced her again. She had shed the tunic now and the light from a branch of candles behind her shone through the thin shift outlining her figure clearly. 'Osborn.'

His voice was shaking too, and so low that she could scarcely hear him. He does desire me, Catherine thought, and he is afraid. But of what? Totally absorbed by this revelation, Catherine made no reply. Indeed, she could not imagine why he should mention a thing two years dead and gone except if he were talking at random.

'If you hate me for that,' Rannulf said with a sudden return of bitterness in his voice, 'I can do nothing. I am not sorry. I would do it again today if needful.'

Catherine had bent slightly so that she could pull the shift over her head, but she straightened up with a start. 'Hate you for killing Osborn? I never gave it a thought. Why should I?' For the first time she realized that her husband believed she loved Sir Herbert and lied to him out of policy. Hurt, she lashed out. 'If I hate you, believe me, it is for reasons nearer to my heart than Sir Herbert ever was.'

Rannulf was appalled at what he believed was the beginning of an open confession of rebel sympathies. He would not listen to what would divide them forever. 'There is no need for you to endure me then, not even to salve your pride and save yourself mortification. Get you to bed. I can sleep by the fire.'

'No!' The protest was startled out of Catherine before she could control her tongue. 'Oh – I – oh.' Totally unnerved by the conflict between pride and desire, Catherine stretched pleading hands. 'Rannulf,' she whispered, 'I do desire children. I grieve still for my lost ones. I have Richard, but I want – I want a baby.'

Rannulf was so hurt by her clinging to a cause he hated that he was about to ask caustically whether she wanted *his* child, to remind her that he was old and she was young and there would doubtless be other opportunities for her with one of her dear rebels, but Catherine burst into tears and, fortunately, he held his tongue. Instead, he took her in his arms and held her against him, comforting her as he comforted his sons when they were little and bruised by life. He stroked the bright hair and kissed it.

'Catherine, if I can give you your desire in this or in any other matter, I will do it. You must know that you have only to ask me for anything. Do not weep.'

It was the work of a moment to carry her to bed, to strip her of the thin shift. To quiet her took longer, but Rannulf felt no impatience even though at first she wept harder in spite of all his attentions. Her crying had not quenched his desire, but he was in no hurry to satisfy it. Tonight, driven by the fierce longing that many women have for children, she was willing. There could be no doubt of it, because she clung to any part of him she could reach and, sobbing, returned the kisses he showered on her. Tonight he need not hurry to his climax so that she might be sooner free of him; he could savour his pleasure without a shadow.

The low rumble of a male voice made the earl of Soke open his eyes.

'Hush,' Mary said softly but intently, 'Lady Catherine is not here and my father is asleep.'

'No, I am awake.' Rannulf put aside the bed curtain and sat up. He was a little surprised at the embarrassed expression of chagrin on Sir André's face, but it was too unimportant a

125

matter and the expression was too fleeting to absorb him long. 'Do you want me?'

'Richard would like to speak to you, my lord.'

'Send him in then.'

Again Rannulf was surprised for his ebullient son came in very slowly and made no attempt to leap on the bed or climb up the curtains. He looked, indeed, so apprehensive that Rannulf groaned aloud with a mixture of humour and despair. 'Now what have you done?'

'I did not mean to do it, papa.'

'No, you never do,' Rannulf growled, struggling not to laugh, 'but do not make yourself sound lily-livered by offering excuses. Tell me what you have done and how you came to do it. Then take your punishment without whining.'

'I lamed Geoffrey's brown destrier and I shot two of the serfs' sheep. One died.'

Rannulf turned his back on his son. It was immediately apparent to him how Richard had come to commit the crimes he confessed, but his silence and his unresponsive back frightened the child. Richard stumbled through his explanation which, indeed, was so close to Rannulf's expectations that he was inwardly convulsed. Then by natural transition, Richard's fear changed to resentment.

'I cannot see why you are so cross. I have been punished already, for I was made to bring the sheep home on my own pony and butcher it like a common servant. And Lady Catherine took my favourite cloak-clasp to buy another sheep for the serf.'

Very well pleased that fear bred anger and not more fear in his son, Rannulf found his voice. 'And what of the horse?'

'Oh, I had to tend his injury myself and sleep in the stables applying fomentations and poultices. Mayhap,' the boy added in a small voice, 'I should be punished for the horse, for, truly, I did not mind working in the stables a bit. It was far more pleasant than learning to read and write and such-like with Father Philip.'

That was the finishing stroke. Rannulf hurried into speech knowing that if he listened to Richard any more he would laugh and irrevocably destroy the discipline his son badly needed. If only he was not so happy; if only he were not in such total sympathy with his son's feelings about education.

'Very well, we will say no more about the sheep, but for the horse, you shall bring me – written fairly in your own hand – an explanation of why it is unwise to attempt to ride a beast for which your tutor says you are not ready. When you have finished that,' Rannulf's voice shook and he paused to steady it, 'bring the writing to me and you will receive my pardon.'

It was just as well that the day started mirthfully for it did not continue so. Northampton and Leicester arrived as scheduled, but they brought more open disunity with them, rather than any spirit of co-operation. Leicester said plainly that he could do nothing. He did not deny that he thought it well to send Eustace to France, but since Louis of France was Eustace's brother-in-law and was the one most nearly concerned in Henry's possession of Normandy, he felt that Louis should provide Eustace with forces. Warwick agreed partially with this view of the matter, but held that they should send a token force to please Louis and Stephen. Northampton insisted vehemently that Eustace should receive full support. He held that Eustace was going as Stephen's deputy to fight against the claimant to the throne, not to support his brother-in-law. Rannulf held his peace.

His situation was difficult in the extreme. He believed firmly that as great a strength as could be gathered should be sent to Normandy with Eustace. He was not only ready to send his men but to go himself, except that Eustace had stated flatly that he would not have the earl of Soke with him. To send his men without himself at their head entailed many risks. They might not fight willingly for Eustace in a country in which they had no interest. His own vassals might do so simply because he ordered them to fight, but his wife's vassals certainly would not. They would resent being sent to war at all, and to send them all the way to Normandy without going himself would certainly provoke them to rebellion of one type or another. Eustace, too, was not to be trusted. Either he would push the hated earl of Soke's men into the most dangerous situations or he would endeavour to convince them to violate their oath of homage to Soke and become his own men.

Rannulf's silence did not go unnoticed. After dinner, Leicester turned upon him eyes reddened by sufficient wine to make tact unnecessary. 'You are unnaturally quiet, my dear brother and friend. Let us hear your voice.'

'My voice can but repeat what it ever has. Do you not remember the state of the barons under the first Henry?'

'I do – and not unkindly. At least then the churches we built were not burned before the ornamentation was finished.'

'You groaned loud enough that you were tethered to his heels like a dog. I tell you this Henry is another of the same cut.'

'We are not talking of Henry but of Eustace. Will you trust your vassals to his governance?'

'But it is Henry of whom we speak whenever we speak of Eustace. It is either one or the other of them. If Eustace conquers in Normandy, Henry will not come to England to trouble us.'

'That is what I say also, Leicester,' Northampton threw in. 'So strongly do I feel, that I would go myself if I were a stick of use, but I am so crippled that I cannot hold a sword in my hand.' He held out his hand, gnarled and twisted as evidence.

'I too am old, and I too would gladly go, but if we send the flower of our strength to France, what surety have we that Henry will not come when we are naked and unprotected? Nay, I do not side with Leicester,' Warwick added, 'and I agree that it would be well to keep Henry in Normandy, but might we not do it with a smaller force?'

'We might do it in many ways, Warwick. We might send money to buy mercenaries; we might send promises to the King of France – but I wonder why Soke did not answer my question. Out with it, Rannulf. What will you send with Eustace, and will you go yourself?'

'I cannot go,' Rannulf said slowly, flushing slightly, 'but I will send the full strength which I am pledged to give Stephen if that is what is asked of me. Wait, my lords, I have a proposal to make which may suit us all. Leicester has asked if I would trust my vassals to Eustace's governance, and there is merit in the question.'

'Oh, so he has been tampering with your men too,' Leicester said on a caustic note of satisfaction.

'Not that I know of, but I have heard others complain. What say you, my lords, to making up a force of younger sons?'

'But—'

'Wait, Simon,' Rannulf said to Northampton, 'I realize that such a force would cost heavily in gold for they cannot support themselves, but there are other benefits to be gathered. Our sworn vassals will be clear of Eustace's meddling. Those young men are strong and eager for battle – they will fight for the love of fighting alone. Some may win patrimonies in France, some will certainly die, so that, best of all, we will rid the country of them. You know they are the worst plague of all upon us. Out of ten penniless younger sons, nine gather the scum of the earth about them and go out to ravage the country-side for a livelihood.'

There was silence as eye met eye and the men began to add the benefit against the cost. 'Certainly it is a proposal to be considered most carefully,' Warwick said slowly. 'Let them plunder France instead of England.'

'I do not think the king or Eustace will welcome the substitution of that rabble for reliable fighting men,' Northampton protested, but there was consideration in his eyes.

'You have opened your mouth finally to some point, Rannulf,' Leicester added, 'and it may well answer, but I am curious about one matter. Why cannot you go to France?'

Rannulf reddened noticeably. 'You will have your jest, Robert, so have it. You well know that Eustace refused my attendance – he made no secret of it.'

'Aye, I know well, but you interest yourself so earnestly in his well-doing that I wondered if you did. Eustace is no friend to you and you will not soften him by any display of loyalty – remember that. He has called you traitor openly in the council.'

Between gritted teeth Rannulf grated, 'I will not be forsworn. I will not raise my hand against my liege lord's heir no matter what that ungrateful—'

'My lords!'

Every head snapped around because there were tears and

129

tragedy quivering in the young voice. There were tears and tragedy too on the dust-stained young face of a page of Stephen's household.

'The queen is dead!'

# Chapter 8

'Oh, God!' Warwick and Northampton breathed together.

'It is too soon. We are undone,' Leicester cried.

The flush of rage drained from Rannulf's face and the natural colour followed it, leaving his weatherbeaten complexion an ugly, pasty brown. 'How did she die?' he asked.

The page, a year or two older than Geoffrey, wiped the tears unashamedly from his face. 'She said she was tired and that she would go to Hedingham in Essex to rest. That was in the third week in April. When we came there, her ladies saw that she was not well, but she would not confess it nor send for the king. Then, it must have been the 28th day or 29th day of April, she could hide her sickness no longer and she sent for her confessor. He came in time so that she died shriven and at peace, but the king did not come in time and he is greatly distraught.'

The messenger was sent off to eat and rest, and the four men remained, staring at each other. To continue their discussion was fruitless, since every plan was now subject to drastic change. A little desultory conversation followed, praising the queen and regretting her loss, but each man truly desired to be alone so that he could think over the news in private and consider what was best for him to do. Leicester broke away first, saying he had to write to his wife, and Northampton rose too, seizing the same excuse with relief. The Warwicks soon followed, leaving Rannulf alone with Catherine. He did not look at her, but he felt her presence and felt, too, strangely removed from the event that had taken place. As long as Catherine sat with her beautiful eyes fixed upon him, Rannulf could not grieve for the queen nor even think clearly of the future. He was suddenly afraid of this woman with rebel sympathies who could so bedazzle him that he could think of nothing but his desire to be with her.

'Rannulf?'

'What?'

'What did Lord Leicester mean when he said you were undone? Why are you all so distressed? As long as the king still lives—' Rannulf frowned, and Catherine misunderstood the expression. 'I do not mean to pry into your affairs, my lord. You know I have never questioned you or complained of your management of my vassals. I do but wish to understand what is taking place.'

'Your vassals, eh?' A day previously Rannulf would have been enraged by her presumption. Today, in spite of his knowledge of how she might use the men, he merely raised his brows and said softly, 'They are mine until I am no more, lady. Do not forget it.'

Catherine dropped her eyes and flushed; she wanted no new quarrel with her husband. Rannulf kept his face expressionless with an effort. He remembered too well what she had said the night before, but he could not threaten her. If she turned to ice on him again— He would speak of the queen. That would distract her.

'The queen's death—'

Rannulf paused and looked at the mass of servants and retainers in the hall. They talked and they listened. What he planned to say to Catherine had better be said in the privacy of her solar. Upstairs, the maids had no need to be told a second time to make themselves scarce; they slipped from the room before their master spoke. The door was not quite shut, however, when someone scratched for admittance.

'Come then,' Rannulf growled. 'Who is it?'

A blond stripling opened the door cautiously. 'I am sorry to trouble you, father, but I must speak privately with you.'

'Very well, what is it Geoffrey?' He saw his son's eyes slide to Catherine. 'Yes, speak. There is no need to trouble yourself over Lady Catherine.' Perhaps that was not wise, but Rannulf was not concerned with absolute wisdom. Rebel or not, just now nothing was more important to him than that Catherine have no further cause to be angry.

'May I sit down?'

'Sit down.' Rannulf sighed resignedly, understanding from the request that the conference was to be an extended one. 'What trouble are you in now?'

'I am not in trouble, father, but I am very uneasy in my mind.'

'In your mind, eh? Well, is it a woman or money? Out with it quickly – which?'

'Neither.' Serious blue eyes gazed earnestly into Rannulf's grey ones. 'I have been listening to the talk today, and to a great deal of other talk in this past half-year. I know no one in the world who speaks the truth as you do, so I have come to you to have my questions answered. Why am I to hate Henry of Anjou?'

Rannulf blinked. 'Whoever told you to hate Henry? Did I?'

'You never told me to hate any man, but others say you hate him, and I can see for myself that you are unalterably opposed to him. Why?'

'I do not hate him,' Rannulf replied slowly. 'As for my opposition, that comes from two causes. The first you know. I have given my sword-oath to Stephen of Blois. Henry would wrest the throne from him and, of course, I must oppose that. The other cause is harder to explain, for it concerns the theory of governance. I believe that the barons should be able to share in deciding what will happen in the realm. Henry's grandfather – also Henry – believed that the king alone should decide. This Henry believes as his grandfather did, and I will not, if it be in my power to prevent it, have such a man as king.'

'But father, how can any man simply decide such a thing? Mayhap, the first Henry, through having governed so long, encroached little by little, stealing power until all lay in his hands. Surely this Henry, coming into a realm where the barons are established in their might, could not do the same. Another thing: has any man, baron or common, the right to say who will be king? Is that not a matter for God? Is not Henry of the true line?'

The patch of sunlight in which Rannulf was sitting shifted perceptibly before an answer came. Even then, it was not an answer to the problems that Geoffrey had propounded.

'What does this mean, my son?' Rannulf asked warily. 'Are you trying to tell me that you wish to be free of my rule? Do you really believe that the Angevin should rightfully be king or do you fear for your patrimony?'

The young man jumped as if he had been hit. 'No, father.' He went to kneel at Rannulf's feet. 'You know I do not mean that. You know that I would follow you landless and homeless even if I knew you to be wrong. I know you are right, but I do not understand and I wish to understand.'

Rannulf turned his face away from the searching eyes. Absently, he fondled his son's hair. 'You know far more than I do, if you know me to be right,' he said sadly. 'Only God is always right. All men err. I can give you no answer because I am not sure that there is an answer. Of a certainty the way we live, torn by constant strife, is not good. At least there was peace in the time of the first Henry – even if it was a little like the peace of the grave. Mayhap that peace is better than this unrest – I do not know. Whether it is man's right or God's right to choose a king, I know not either. But I do know that a king is only a man, and since all men err, the way of wisdom is that the king, too, be governable. My son, to think about these matters, so long as your thoughts lead you not into treachery or any other dishonourable action, can only be good.'

'Papa, only tell me what to think!'

Rannulf heard the child crying out to the all-wise father, rejecting the painful responsibility of manhood, rejecting the knowledge that the human father was not all-wise, not perfect. Body and soul, Rannulf responded to that cry. He remembered how he had held Geoffrey in his arms when his son was an infant, how he had taught him to ride and hold a sword, how he had answered all his questions – as he still did for Richard – about right and wrong with calm certainty. The impulse to answer now, to shield his child from the pain of manhood and the pain of decision, was so strong that his eyes stung with tears.

'I cannot tell you what to think. God have mercy on me, I do not know what to think myself. I can only tell you how to act because, right or wrong, I have given my oath, before God, to Stephen of Blois to be his man. For me, there is no other path. As long as Stephen lives, I am his man.'

134

Geoffrey lifted his head from his father's knees where he had allowed it to rest momentarily and his eyes were alight with adoration and gratitude. His appeal had been sincere, but within him was also the burgeoning pride of his growing adulthood. He cried out for security, but he also desired to be forced into freedom no matter how dangerous.

'That is good enough for me, father. It must be so if you have pledged your faith. May I ask something else?'

'You may ask anything.'

'Why does Eustace hate you? I have heard it whispered behind my back, and the earl of Leicester said it aloud today, that the prince has accused you of treachery. This must be a lie, but what is his reason for missaying you?'

'I do not know, other than he chooses to blame me for our defeats at Dursley and Devizes. Are you troubled by these whisperings, Geoffrey?'

'No. I have belaboured the few who dared whisper in my hearing in such a way that they do not speak at all now.' The blue eyes were clear and trusting. 'To me it does not matter, except that it goes against the grain to fight for one who befouls my father with lies.'

Rannulf's mouth twisted with pride and pain, but he could not command his voice to reply. Instead he kissed his son who, taking that as a dismissal, returned the salute heartily and left. Before Rannulf could move, Catherine had taken the place that Geoffrey had vacated. When she laid her hands on her husband's she could feel that he was shaking.

'I pray God,' she said softly, 'that I may bear you a son. Whether you are right or wrong in the king's matter, I do not know, but surely no man can be wiser in the handling of his children. No son could have a better father.'

Pulling his hands roughly from her grasp, Rannulf turned away. 'Could he not?' he asked bitterly. 'My pride and my honour may cost that boy his lands. Oh, God, what am I to do? Stephen loves me well, but I cannot pretend even to myself that he is other than a weak reed. Now that Maud is dead he will be blown hither and thither like the dead leaves of autumn with every breath of advice and rumour. Eustace— Now who is at the door?'

'I am, Rannulf,' Leicester replied. 'Forgive my intrusion in your women's chambers, but what I have to say to you needs walls with no ears. Why do you look so tired?'

'I fear I suffer more from my age and from my dismay than from any weariness.'

'Nonsense. My age is close to yours, and it troubles me no whit. I would say from looking at you that you are somewhat disordered with a superabundance of black and yellow bile, but that is no surprise after what you have endured these two years past. No, I thank you, Lady Soke, no wine. I am sorry for it, Rannulf, but I have come to add to your troubles.'

'Can you?' Rannulf asked, laughing wryly.

'Is this a time for laughter?'

'I cannot think why not. If I do not laugh, I must weep. Is it not better to laugh?' Rannulf accepted a goblet of wine handed him by Catherine. In the process their hands touched, and he was seized with an impatience for all matters of state. He turned to Leicester with deep concentration. 'Very well, you wish me to be grave – I am grave.'

'It is a grave matter enough. While Maud was alive there was good mixed with the ill of Stephen's reign, but Stephen must be ruled by someone. Eustace will try to fill his mother's place.'

Rannulf began to laugh again. 'What surprising news.'

'Has it come to your mind that Maud was patient with Stephen's waverings and Eustace might not be? Stephen might not long outlive his wife.'

There was no mistaking the implication that Stephen's death would not be natural and would come about through his son's doing. Rannulf was so revolted that he started out of his chair as if he could physically avoid the words Leicester had said.

'No!' Then his mind rejected the fantastic, and he laughed uneasily and sat down. 'Hey, Robert, mind your tongue. If you fright me again like that, I will die under your eyes. It is not kind to kill a brother with an unhealthy jest.'

'You fool,' Leicester said furiously, 'this time I will not let you be blind. If Eustace comes to the throne you may well die under my eyes – with your head on the block. That is no matter,' he continued caustically, 'for the way you use your head, you would be as well off without it as with it. But do you realize that Geoffrey's head and Richard's too must follow yours? Man, I do not ask you to abandon Stephen. I know you gave him sword-oath. But if he dies—'

Rannulf knew what was coming and interrupted Leicester before he could say it. 'And now that you have filled my mind with this filth – be it true or not – you must be satisfied. Will you leave me in peace?'

Leicester stood up, his normally equable temper aroused. 'I wash my hands of you. Go your own way to your own destruction. Think whether your promise, even an oath, lightly spoken in other times when affairs were far otherwise, is worth your estate, the destruction of your children, the loss of all you hold dear. I will tell you once in plain words, whether you will or nil, that there is much good in the Angevin. He has the right on his side and, as Hereford says, if the barons stand together we can keep his lust for power in check.' The anger passed and Leicester gripped Rannulf's shoulder. 'If you will not act wise, at least do not act the fool. Stay out of Eustace's way. Go not to court. Sit here on your own lands where no man can harm you – you will not have long to wait.'

The soft closing of the door brought no reaction from Rannulf other than that he allowed his head to drop into his hands. Catherine stood paralysed, slowly gathering to her the full acceptance of what Lady Warwick had told her, that Stephen's reign was doomed. She knew that a woman's pleas would have no influence with Rannulf so she was silent, retreating at last to the window where her embroidery frame stood.

The patch of sunlight moved slowly across the floor, touching the bright crimson cushions of an empty chair, touching the carved, curved bedposts, the blue bed curtains. It came to the edge of the room and reddened as it began to crawl up the wall. Then, as if the effort was too great, it faded slowly. Catherine tried to match an orange silk thread and found that she could not judge between two shades which she knew to be different. She laid down her needle, glanced towards Rannulf, who might have been carved from stone for all the movement he had made during the hours which had passed. It was useless to address any remark to him, she decided, and went down to make excuses for his absence at the evening meal. When she returned, he was still sitting where she had left him, unconscious that the fire was dead and the room dark as pitch.

'Rannulf,' Catherine said firmly, setting a branch of candles down on the small table she had moved to his elbow after lighting the fire again, 'I have brought you something to eat.'

Her husband closed his eyes and turned his head from the light. 'I have outlived my time. I cannot save the king I have sworn to. I am less than valueless to you and to my children. I can see no way out of this morass.'

Catherine's heart leaped. He was speaking to her as a person who could understand, and he saw the hopelessness of his position. 'But Lord Leicester told you of a safe path. Who could harm us or take us when we have our full strength on our own lands? If you cannot save the king, surely sitting still can do him no harm.'

'All women are fools,' Rannulf muttered wearily. 'Every man who withholds his support in such times is an active traitor. Do not speak to me of Leicester. Leicester and I live by different rules. The king once gave my life and these lands to me. Are both not truly his? I have wrestled with myself all of this long day, and I cannot throw off this knowledge. I must go when the summons comes. If I cannot live with honour, I cannot live at all.'

Catherine's little hope died unborn. Rannulf knew what was coming, but instead of avoiding disaster he was about to rush headlong into it. The dreadful vision of Richard murdered or, at best, in Sir André's position rose up to drive sharp spurs into Catherine's protective instinct. The child was dear as flesh of her flesh, and she could not bear the thought of his death or even of his eking out a precarious living by travelling from tourney to tourney or living on another man's bounty in a position of servitude. She could not permit that, but to argue or plead with Rannulf would not change his mind. Still worse, it might make him distrust her so that he would set a guard upon her that would hinder any future attempt to save the child. She could not leave Rannulf in his present despairing state either. His mind was like an ox on a treadmill, going round and round on the same path until it could travel no other way. If he was jolted from the path, he might yet find a new one.

'No doubt you know best what to do,' she said indifferently, 'but it cannot be done tonight nor yet tomorrow. Meanwhile, the soup I have troubled to bring you grows cold. Do eat it now, because I wish you to try on some clothing. I have measured three old gowns of yours and each is a different length so that I cannot tell where to place the hem of the new ones I have made.'

'Madam,' Rannulf roared, rage rapidly replacing despair, 'are you deaf? I have been telling you—'

'Certainly I am not deaf, but I will be if you shout so right into my ears.'

'How can you speak of – soup and new clothes when—'

'Even if the world were to end tomorrow, we must eat today. And I cannot see why you should be hungry or dressed in a gown either too long or too short.'

'God save me from women! Because of the death of one, I am to be destroyed, and because of the stupidity of another, I am to be driven mad first.'

'God save me from men,' Catherine retorted tartly. 'Will it help our state or the state of the realm if you are starved or ill-clothed? I would go naked on the king's highway myself if I believed it would do us good, but as it cannot, I am resolved to live with decency until it is beyond my power to do so.'

Colour returned to Rannulf's face with a rush. 'Are you calling me a coward?'

Wondering how far she dared enrage him, Catherine retreated a step or two. 'I would not dare,' she replied truthfully. 'But since you have determined on a course which you know to be disastrous, it seems to me that it were more fitting not to repine in public.'

'I shall take good care in the future to show you only a good face. I see that I was mistaken in my belief that we had come to better terms with each other so that in your presence at least I could be only what I am and no more.'

This turn of the conversation was totally unexpected, and the inference Rannulf had drawn from her remark was the last Catherine wished him to make. 'Indeed, my lord, you need put no face on for me – good or bad – for whatever you are or do I

139

am your chattel and I go your way.' That was not sufficient to soothe him, the look of personal hurt remained. 'I did but wish to prick you to anger,' Catherine confessed desperately, 'thinking it was better for you to rage than to despair. Trust in the Lord, Rannulf. Surely He will find a way to extricate us from this trouble.'

Rannulf was suddenly conscious of the warmth of the leaping flames, of the cheerful yellow glow of candlelight. He had a passing thought that the Lord would have little enough cause to extricate him from anything, since he had, from time to time, offended Him mightily. It made very little difference, because he was as flooded with pleasure by his wife's confession of anxiety for him as if he had discovered that the messenger's news and Leicester's deductions were both a nightmare.

'So you wished to prick me to heat, eh? Well, you have succeeded. Now let us see whether you enjoy the fruits of your victory.'

He spoke with a lowering frown, levered himself stiffly out of the chair, and advanced purposefully. Catherine backed away, surprised and frightened. She had heard so many tales of his violence towards Lady Adelecia. Judging from her own experience, Catherine would not have believed that a few sharp words could make Rannulf angry enough to hurt her, but he had endured much this day and it was not unusual for a man to relieve his frustrations by beating his wife. A few steps more brought her up against the bed and she could retreat no further.

'I will teach you to jape with me,' Rannulf said softly, and with battle-trained swiftness pushed her so unexpectedly that she toppled over backward.

'Rannulf, stop!' Catherine faltered as he bent over her.

'Thus are wives with overmuch sauciness punished.'

'Oh, Rannulf, stop,' Catherine whispered a few minutes later. 'You will tear my gown. Someone will come in.'

'You have a hundred gowns, and I will give you gold to buy a hundred more.'

'Rannulf—'

'I will cut the eyes and tongue out of anyone who opens that door.'

'Oh, Rannulf.'

140

# Chapter 9

The sun, which shone on the fields rich with the promise of abundant harvest, was a mockery to those who dwelt within the dark keep of Sleaford. Two tense days passed, days in which masters and guests alike avoided each other's eyes and endeavoured to kill foreboding with pleasure. They rode madly after their hawks; they played chess and gambled with the marked bones; they drank, laughed at the antics of minstrels and jongleurs, and listened with well-simulated attention to the tales of love and war that the chaplain read. Outdoors, however, all eyes turned repeatedly to the track that led south to Essex and London, and within, all ears were cocked for the hasty tread of a royal messenger.

To all, the courier's arrival was a relief. As they had expected, he bore a summons to appear to attend the queen's funeral, and unexpectedly one to attend the king's council. Rannulf, having read the messages aloud, shrugged.

'We are summoned within the fortnight. I suppose we may rest here a while longer and ride together direct to Feversham.'

'Nay, Soke,' Warwick said hastily, 'I have matters to attend to at home. I must ride to Warwick first.'

'And I to Northampton to bring my wife and son to Feversham.'

Rannulf looked from one to the other. Both were making excuses to dissociate themselves from him. Warwick had planned to stay at Sleaford for several weeks and had received no message from his lands; what then could be so urgent to draw him home? Northampton's eldest son, Simon, was a man full grown, perfectly capable of coming himself and escorting his mother anywhere in England.

'Perhaps,' Rannulf said coldly, 'you would like me to withdraw my son from your service, Northampton? Are you not afraid that he will carry my taint?'

'Do not talk nonsense,' the old man replied, although he had the grace to look somewhat self-conscious. 'I have a great regard for Geoffrey.'

Rannulf was about to remark caustically that he was sure Northampton's regard for Geoffrey was in direct proportion to his hope of controlling the property through the young man after his father's death or disgrace. He restrained himself, however, realizing that someone would have to help Geoffrey, and Northampton was honest and honourable, even if he did not wish to be dragged into Rannulf's personal feud with Eustace.

'And you, Robert, you must go back to Leicester to escort your wife also, no doubt.'

'Aye, I must,' Leicester laughed, but his eyes were hard and cold. 'You will not take out your spleen on me, Rannulf. You are more than welcome to ride with me home and from there to Feversham.'

'I thank you for your gracious kindness, but I will not so burden you.'

The sarcasm drew no more than another laugh from Leicester, this time a somewhat more genuine one, but as soon as he was free he sought Rannulf out. Soke was discussing the final arrangements for his departure, but he stopped mid-sentence when Leicester came in view and turned a face of stone with blank grey eyes on him.

'You cannot freeze me, Rannulf, I have known you too long. You should not go at all. Nay, be still. I know you were fond of Maud and would wish to do her honour, but hard on the burying comes the council, and that you must avoid.'

'I have no intention of avoiding it.'

For a moment Leicester stood silent, a rich colour dyeing his face. Then the colour faded and he laid his hand on Rannulf's arm. 'Fool! I do not think there are ten like you in the world. If you must go, then I beg you in all sincerity that you come first to Leicester with me so that we may ride to Feversham together.'

'No.'

142

Again Leicester flushed with rage. 'You are the most pig-headed— Whom do you spite but yourself and your family by this behaviour? There is a chance that proof of our continuing bond may do you good.'

'Even now I need no man's charity,' Rannulf replied harshly. He raised his eyes to Leicester's face and the set look softened. 'Nay, Robert, it can do me no good. I must stand or fall alone. My heart is heavy enough. Think how I must feel if you should be involved in my troubles.'

'God keep you, Rannulf,' Leicester sighed, and surprised his foster-brother by embracing and kissing him warmly.

In the women's quarters an even more unusual embrace was being given and received. Mary pulled her lips free of Sir André's, her eyes filled with tears. 'I should not have permitted that. Now you will think I am such another as my mother was.'

'Nay, dear heart,' the young man murmured. 'I know nothing of your mother except that she must have been a woman of virtue. Had she not been a maid and forced into the earl's bed, he would not have acknowledged you as his daughter. If there is a fault in one kiss, the fault is mine.'

'But you did not need to force me,' Mary whispered.

'Thank God for that. You do love me, do you not, Mary? Sweet love, do not hang your head. Let me see your eyes. Let my heart live on the knowledge of your love.'

'What can my love matter when my father is master here? What do you want of me?'

'You know I desire you for my wife. I love you. You cannot believe I would wish to dishonour you.'

'I do not know what to believe,' she sighed. 'If you are true, why did you not offer for me? His lordship has no value for a bastard daughter. He would give me to a beggar on the road or a serf of the domain.'

'Mary, you know not whereof you speak. You are young and – and very lovely. There will be offers enough.' The young voice was suddenly bitter. 'What would we live on? Where? How? I have nothing but my horse and arms.' She sobbed and he caught her into his arms again, kissing her eyes and cheeks and hair.

'Mary!'

They sprang apart. Mary gave one glance at Catherine's face, uttered a low cry, and fled. Sir André sank to one knee, crimson with shame.

'What does this mean? Is this the way you repay my husband's kindness?'

'Madam, forgive me. I did her no harm. I love her.'

'Do you think it no harm to put such thoughts into a girl's mind? Have you her father's permission – or even any hope of such permission – to court her?' Catherine was furious, more furious with herself for allowing matters to get to the state they were in than she was with André. 'What if her father should contract her elsewhere? You say you love her. Is it love to fix her affections dishonestly so that she will not be able to give them to her chosen husband and will live in torment?'

The young head bent beneath the rebuke. 'It was the hopelessness that drove me. Just to touch her, only once— Madam, you do not know what it is to see a thing so dearly desired so very close and know you cannot grasp it.'

But Catherine did know and she responded to André's pain. 'Do you wish to marry her?' she asked more gently.

'Wish! What would I not give—' A harsh laugh followed. 'What have I got?'

'Nothing, of course, and Mary has nothing also, but Lord Soke is not a greedy man and is tender of his children. This, however, is no time to speak to him about anything. If you behave with propriety in the future, I will do what I can for you.' Catherine heard the door open and lowered her voice to finish what she had to say – the maids if they heard would spread the matter all over the keep. 'I offer you no hope – you must understand that – and you will have to wait a long time, but— Oh, my lord, how you startled me.'

'Did I?' Rannulf's eyes moved from the kneeling man to his wife's crimson complexion. 'The message we have awaited has come.'

'Oh!' Catherine's gesture sent André from the room. 'Was there aught of note in it?'

'A summons to council as well as to attend the funeral.'

They were both speaking somewhat at random, Catherine's

144

mind leaping from the complication of André and Mary to fear for Rannulf and back again. Rannulf's mind did not leap. From an initial, agonizing shock of jealousy he recovered immediately because his belief in Catherine's virtue was absolute. The receding sensation left a small core of uneasiness. There was something she was keeping from him deliberately. Rannulf now had what he had assured himself he would be content with – the knowledge that his wife did not hate him and that she welcomed his caresses. Having achieved that distant good, once desired as passionately as a saint desires heaven, Rannulf found it without value. Like most mortals, he had asked for a finger and, having received it, discovered that what he truly wanted was the whole arm. He wanted, in fact, what he would not give to Catherine, complete trust and faith.

'When must you leave?' she asked anxiously.

'Straight away. I came only to tell you I would go as soon as my men are ready.'

'So soon? Surely the few hours cannot be of significance. Go tomorrow.'

There were many reasons for keeping Rannulf another day, both emotional and practical, but although Catherine sincerely loved her husband, the practical reasons were paramount at the moment. If she had a little time, she might be able to convince him to take André with him without the necessity of betraying Mary. It would be an excellent thing all around for André to go. True, Richard was an imp and not easy to handle, but his need was less desperate than Mary's – anyone could tutor Richard for a while. With André gone, temptation would be removed from Mary. Furthermore, André in the keep of Sleaford could win neither advancement nor particular notice. If he were with Rannulf, Catherine was sure that her husband would grow to appreciate him. If worse came to worst and Rannulf was unjustly accused and needed to fight his way home, André might be of great value. He was strong, young, and skilled in the use of arms. Certainly he would exert himself to the uttermost to protect Rannulf because he was grateful to his lord for his position, because Rannulf was his beloved's father, and because he might, through impressing the father with his strength and devotion, win the daughter as a reward.

Searching his wife's lovely face, Rannulf was even further disturbed. There was sincerity in her voice; she did not wish him to go – so much was plain. There was also a certain abstraction which brought deep doubt of her motives for wishing to keep him.

'Do you have some particular reason, Catherine, for wanting me to stay? I thought it would be best for me to reach the king as soon as possible. In his first sorrow he might well cling to an old, familiar friend, and if I am there the tongues which wag against me will have less freedom.'

'Then you must go, of course. If it is for your good to go, I would not keep you for any purpose of mine.' Rannulf turned away. 'Oh,' Catherine cried, catching hold of him, 'you cannot mean now, this very instant.'

There was satisfaction in that. Whatever her reason, it was honey-sweet to have her cling to him. 'The sooner we go, the less need to ride in the dark. I will arm, and then I must go.' But he made no move towards his armour, holding Catherine close and resting his cheek against her hair.

Catherine decided to make her request without reason. If Rannulf suspected the affection between Mary and André, so much the better; it would be less of a surprise to him when the offer was made. She hurried into speech, the realization that he was really going pushing practical matters from her mind. Catherine wanted to use her final moments with her husband for kisses and a fond parting, not for discussion of other people's affairs.

'Rannulf, I have a favour to beg of you before you go.'

He released her, shed his gown, and began to lift his mail shirt before he replied. Catherine came to help with the stiff hauberk. 'A favour?' His voice was muffled by the mail.

'Yes. I pray you, take André Fortesque with you. I will find another tutor for Richard. He is brave and strong and loyal. Every man of that kind must be of value to you at such a time.'

Rannulf's initial expression was concealed, but when he had pushed his head through the neck-hole he searched Catherine's face as he laced the hood. Did she wish to set a spy on him? The misty blue eyes that looked up into his were so unshadowed that Rannulf was immediately ashamed of the thought. More likely

146

she had discovered that André was in love with her and wished to remove him from temptation.

'If you desire it, I will take him.'

Voluntarily, for the first time, Catherine walked into her husband's arms. 'You are so kind to me, Rannulf.' Her voice quivered. 'You do not even ask me why I desire this, but give it freely.'

So much gratitude for so small a thing was suspicious. But for what could Catherine need a spy? Her face was turned up to his in mute invitation, and so much passion was evident in her when their lips met that Rannulf was enlightened. She was jealous – jealous of him. Oh, God, what fools women were; what silly fancies controlled them. He did not laugh or expostulate, for that would hurt her. He merely kissed away the tears which were now forcing their way from under closed lids. More tears; more kisses; the minutes flew by.

'Catherine, I must go. I need not tell you to care for the children.'

'Where shall I send to you in case of need?'

'I wish I knew. I will go direct to Feversham, but after that, I know not where I may be.'

'Rannulf, I pray you, write to me often. Do not leave me to eat out my heart with worry.'

'I will write.' He lifted his arms to loosen hers from about his neck, fighting the frightening desire to change his mind and stay. Rannulf had done many hard things, but at the moment this seemed to be harder than all the others. 'Do not cling to me so, my love.' He was unconscious of using the endearment, hardly conscious of what he was saying at all. 'You must send me forth, or I will never find the strength to go.'

It was a parting to keep the heart warm through a long, sad ride. For a man in love, it was a parting to lighten the heaviest load of worry. All other doubts and dissatisfactions could be submerged in the memory of clinging arms and lips, and if Rannulf's face was drawn with anxiety when he entered the presence of the king, his eyes still held more peace than they had for two years past.

Stephen, sitting by a window with blank, unseeing eyes bent

147

on the pea blossoms in the abbey garden, did not hear the squire announce the earl of Soke, did not turn his head until Rannulf's hand fell lightly upon his shoulder.

'My lord, I am come to you.'

Rannulf was prepared for anger, for coldness, for recriminations, but sympathy warmed his normally hard voice. Stephen had loved Maud, and Rannulf, in love himself, could feel the king's grief sincerely. That sympathy and sincerity touched emotions rubbed raw with sorrow, and the one reaction Rannulf was not prepared for left him wordless and embarrassed. Stephen burst into tears and flung himself physically on his liege man.

'I am alone,' he wept, 'all alone. She was the only one who loved me and she is gone.'

The reaction was not unusual, nor was it shameful for a man to weep for his grief, but Rannulf was not one to indulge himself with such behaviour. He had no close friends who had yet needed to call upon him to comfort them, and he did not consider using the methods he employed with his children to soothe his king. As a result he stood silent, very much at a loss.

'Thank God,' Stephen choked after a few minutes of unrestrained sobbing. 'You, at least, do not mouth platitudes and texts at me. She is with God, these accursed priests tell me. I know she is with God. Was she not the best woman in the world? But she is not with me – and I need her.'

'We have all suffered a great loss in the queen,' Rannulf said quietly, 'and we all need her, my lord. I would not presume to try to comfort you in any way. Indeed, my own heart is too heavy to offer platitudes, and texts I know none.'

'You were ever dear to her. She spoke well of you always.'

Rannulf nodded. The queen had been a good friend to him when it was possible for her. In the last two years, certainly, she had countered Eustace's plans to discredit him when she could. Suddenly Rannulf realized that his moment of trial might not be, as he thought, over. If Eustace had not come with his father or had not yet arrived, he would have had no chance to poison Stephen's mind.

'Is your son not with you?' Rannulf asked as Stephen seemed about to sink into abstraction.

'Yes, he is here,' the king replied resentfully. 'I have been greatly deceived in him. He never loved her, nor me. He has no time to sit with me. All he thinks of is the campaign in France and he spends all day – the very day he received news of his mother's death was the same – talking of money and arms and men.'

'Aye, and it is a better thing to do than to sit weeping in a corner.'

Both men, who had just sat down, turned sharply towards the new voice which came from the doorway. In his first glance at Eustace's face, Rannulf saw that the king's judgment was, as usual, at fault. Eustace's red-rimmed eyes told of tears shed through sleepless nights and the deep-etched lines on his young face of a bitterness even deeper than his grief.

'Are weak tears a fitting epitaph for a great woman? She did not simply die, I say. She was slain!'

'What?' Rannulf gasped, leaping to his feet.

'The Angevin killed her as surely as if he had come here and sunk a knife into her breast. I say my mother was murdered.' Eustace's voice, beyond control, shook, and he stopped speaking and bit his lip.

Stephen dropped his head into his hands and began to sob again. 'If anyone murdered her, I did. She laboured harder in my cause than the meanest serf of my lands, and I gave her no rest. She was overworn. I saw she was overworn, but still I brought my troubles to her.'

Eustace's face twisted with agony for he knew how much he had torn his mother's heart and destroyed her peace in the last two years. His guilt shrieked aloud in his mind, but he could give it no voice nor find relief in self-blame and confession as his father could.

'We all did our parts,' he said quickly, 'for she alone never failed. All of us failed her. The plans she made, the wisdom she taught us, we cast aside. Let us at least give her soul peace. Let us destroy the Angevin. Let that be our atonement for her years of struggle.'

'Can you think of nothing but killing? Can you not mourn your own mother with decency?'

'It is not a matter of decency,' Eustace shrieked. 'I will be revenged on those who hurt her.'

'Kill me then,' Stephen screamed in reply. 'I hurt her most. It is mine to say whether you will go to France. See who will give you aid without my word.'

Rannulf walked to the window to be out of the way, his heart beating sickly. It was unbelievable that they should already be at each other's throats. As the shock of hearing a son so contest his father's will wore off, however, Rannulf's sickness began to abate. This quarrel was not born of hate but of love. Stephen did not want Eustace to go into danger in France. True the love might be one-sided, but Eustace could not be planning any harm to his father if he intended to go to France. He knew how seldom an absent landlord succeeded peacefully to his estate, and, if he wished to rule England, he must expect his father to live until his return. Whatever Stephen's desires, Rannulf thought, Eustace had to go to France. For the country it was good, and for Rannulf personally it was salvation. Eustace was a bold and reckless fighter, as Rannulf knew. Without proper guidance, perhaps he would not return from France.

'Well, Soke, surely you have something to say to this. No doubt you, too, think me unfilial and counsel delay. It would well suit your secret purposes.'

Rannulf turned slowly. 'I have not, nor ever had, any secret purposes, Eustace. Pardon me, my liege, but I have ever spoken my mind honestly, and I must say I do not think your son unfilial or hasty. These are perilous times, perilous hours even, and the queen was ever one to set the general good over her own convenience.'

'Then she is to be scorned and overlooked even in her death?' Stephen cried.

'Nay, my lord, she was never scorned nor overlooked, even by her enemies. All men respected her. No man to whom I have spoken felt there was aught amiss with summoning the council to sit after her obsequies.'

'No doubt you spoke to some purpose, whether or not you call it secret,' Eustace snapped, more infuriated by Rannulf's support than he would have been by his opposition. 'I can guess what that purpose was. You would saddle me with land-hungry, gain-mad younger sons instead of giving me a true vassal's levy. Was not that your purpose, oh loyal friend?'

So someone had already sent news of the conference at Sleaford to Eustace. A spy set into the household? Leicester, Warwick, or Northampton? It made little difference since Rannulf had intended to bring the matter into open council. With the support of Leicester, Warwick and Northampton, he hoped that concurrence in his suggestion could be obtained from the other major magnates of the country and from Stephen. Eustace would then have been forced to agree or take nothing. All that displeased Rannulf about the premature disclosure was that he needed to argue the pros and cons of the plan alone with a hostile and unreasonable young man and that the argument might make Stephen hostile too.

'There was never any secret about the matter,' he began. 'Nor do I believe it a drawback that young men who are, as you say, land-hungry and gain-mad should be employed in such an enterprise. In Normandy, that which makes them our scourge would change them into our blessing, for they would fight most earnestly to get from the Angevin what they cannot have here. Think, Eustace, it is a cheap price to pay for loyalty – someone else's land. Let them keep what they win. It is no loss to you.'

'No loss except that of my army. Once their maws are filled they will drop away and I will be left naked.'

'Not so. When they have a little, they will fight for more. Even if it were true, however, you will sooner be left naked with an army of unwilling vassals whose hearts and minds are on their own lands across the narrow sea. They are bound to serve only forty days in an offensive war, as well you know. The hour their service was ended, they would leave you.'

'Am I not defending their lands by fighting him who would take them away, even on a foreign shore?'

Rannulf laughed harshly. 'You will never convince them of that, more especially as none, including myself, believe that Henry desires to strip us of our land even here. He—'

'Traitor! Will you announce before my father's face and in the teeth of his grief that you are—'

'Why not?' Stephen asked with biting bitterness. 'None cares for me. The part of your mother's health which I did not destroy by labour, you destroyed by raising dissension among

151

the men she struggled to hold together. You will go to France and die there. I will die of grief. Why should Soke not look to the Angevin?'

It was so close to the truth that Rannulf turned pale. The quarrel continued to rage around him. but he could not speak because the contents of his stomach were sour in his mouth and he dared not part his lips. It would be more honest to change his coat openly, to deny his sword-oath and turn rebel. And brand his sons as children of a turncoat? Some could bear it, those who had been raised on talk of expediency, but he knew only the pride of honour. Better to damn his own soul than to destroy their spirit. It was not his choice anyway, Rannulf knew as he listened. Whether he helped or hindered, Eustace would bend his father to his will and go to France.

# Chapter 10

The king sat upon the dais, his eyes red and his face blotched with weeping; his expression, however, was not one of grief but one of absolute fury. Three weeks had passed since Maud had been buried and the court had moved from Feversham to London. Three weeks had passed and those he had waited for had not arrived—neither at Feversham nor at London. For three interminable weeks his rage had mounted. It was not often that the good-natured Stephen developed a lasting, burning rage. When he did, however, he was lost to reason and the barons standing in the hall regarded him with caution and anxiety. To a man, they knew what had caused his fury; their anxiety was stimulated only by the question of what he would do about it. They were not long in doubt for, without any preliminary other than a sharp gesture, the king's chancellor began to call the roll of the barons and name for each the days of service and number of armed knights owed the king for war.

The roll was long, every man present answering to his name and confirming or denying the terms mentioned. In the present temper of the king, no man denied, although some grumbled softly and there was a good deal of shifting from foot to foot. Eye met eye, and, as the chancellor's voice droned on, broken by the sharp answers, the mass separated imperceptibly into groups, groups allied by blood, friendship, or homage ties as if the men were already on the field and were grouping their banners for battle.

What was most notable was not the unanimity of affirmative replies but the dead silence and growing tension each time the name of an absent baron was called. Ordinarily, more than half of such absences would be accounted for by a bellow from the crowd with explanations such as, 'His wife was brought to bed, I am to answer for him,' or 'I passed him on the road, he

153

will be here anon,' or 'There is sickness in his house,' 'He is on pilgrimage,' 'He is at war.' Now there was nothing, only a hardening of bleak countenances, a tightening of bonded groups, or an uneasy shifting of eyes.

'William, duke of Gloucester,' the chancellor called.

'Reginald, earl of Cornwall.'

There was no reply but a low gasp from an unidentified member of the listening crowd.

'Rannulf, earl of Chester.'

'Roger, earl of Hereford.'

'Traitors!' Stephen screamed, leaping to his feet and breaking the silence he had maintained up to that moment. 'They are traitors and I will bear their treachery no longer. Hitherto I have sought peace with my barons, now they will taste war. Call up your men. I will ravage their lands and take their keeps. I will hang their bodies upon gibbets and set their heads upon stakes so that the world may know that the king of England may be scorned no longer.'

A sigh fluttered through the room, but it was no sigh of pleasure. The blood and famine of 1149 would be renewed, and there was no certainty that the king would triumph, for the power of the rebel lords was a match for his. Beneath the sigh there was even a low growl of resentment. The barons were tired of the king's war, tired of the blood-letting which brought them nothing but more blood-letting. A war of their own with a neighbour had sense; that might bring a new field, a new town, a new wood into their hands or gold into their purses. A war against a single rebel or a group of no particular power might bring some gain from sequestered and redistributed estates, but to fight against so large and powerful a group, to provoke them to unity by attacking them, could bring nothing.

'What you say is true, my lord, but it is not the matter that we were summoned to discuss.' The harsh voice grated across the renewed, half-rebellious silence, and another sigh stirred the attentive men. Many eyes turned with approval to the stolid figure standing a little forward of the main grouping of men. 'You are angry, and justly so, but let us settle who we are to fight. No man can be in more than one place at one time.

154

Are we to go to Normandy, or are we to make war here in England?'

Surprise alone had kept the king silent long enough for the earl of Soke to finish his speech. Now a roar of relief and approval so intense that it penetrated even Stephen's blind fury shook the black-smoked rafters of the room.

'Fool!' Leicester hissed, coming to stand beside Rannulf. 'Why Eustace troubles himself to try to harm you, I do not know. You will destroy yourself without any man's help.'

'I cannot permit this madness without a protest. If Eustace goes to France, there may yet be hope for all,' Rannulf replied under the noise.

'Did you think I intended to permit it? There are other ways to manage Stephen. Could you not wait for the rage to pass?'

'And let him make such plans in full council so that Hereford and Cornwall would hear of them? Do you think Roger of Hereford will sit quietly waiting for us to come to attack him?'

Leicester ground his teeth, but what Rannulf said was true. Doubtless there were rebel spies among the assembled barons and a definite plan of attack might spark a new full-scale rebellion even if that plan were cancelled later. The noise was dying down and Leicester stepped farther forward, bellowing for silence. The quick mind in the big, slow body rapidly revised plans in the few seconds before it was quiet enough to speak normally. In many ways, what Rannulf had done was the best possible thing for everyone but himself.

'My lord, I wish to add, to what the earl of Soke said, this piece of news. No insult was intended to you or to your late queen by the earl of Chester. He is sick unto death. You know how Hereford is bound to him by tie upon tie. Truly, let us settle the question of Normandy and let the council choose some trusty messenger of high degree to go to Hereford and the others and learn their minds before we commit an injustice.'

There was an ugly light in Stephen's eyes, for the news was no news to him, but in dying Maud seemed to have bequeathed him some measure of her control and he answered quietly. 'What need to ask the council to choose? Plainly the earl of Soke is best fitted for this work. We know his loyalty and all men respect his truth. Even Hereford will trust him. What say my barons to this?'

Another roar of approval clinched the matter. No man wished for so hopeless or thankless a task, and it was a relief to have it settled quickly with Stephen alone to bear the resentment the suggestion might cause. Not a muscle of Rannulf's face quivered, but his eyelids dropped to conceal his eyes. He had brought it upon himself and could not complain. No amount of persuasion could convince Hereford to supply men or money for the king's campaign against Henry. It was no secret that Hereford had done homage to Henry and not only his personal profit but his honour was involved in the hope of an Angevin succession.

Nonetheless, it might be possible to bring Hereford to court and induce him to offer condolences on Maud's death. Stephen was easily moved and might be temporarily satisfied with that much. Then if the plan of sending only money and young men to Normandy could be carried through, the threat of retention of Stephen's full strength in England might keep the rebels quiet while they waited on the outcome of the fighting in France. If Eustace died there—

Perhaps all would be well even if Eustace did not die. If he conquered Henry and his self-esteem was thus restored, perhaps he would recover his past good nature. It was a very slim chance, but it was the only one they had as far as Rannulf could see. If Stephen provoked Hereford and his allies, the country would be wasted to no purpose at all, and if Stephen should die in the fighting, the worst would befall at once. Rannulf was prepared to throw himself into the breach again to put forward his notion of a knight errant army, realizing that Stephen was already so angry with him that he could not make himself more detestable. Leicester, however, took the words from his mouth.

Robert of Leicester genuinely loved Rannulf as a brother and valued him as a friend, but that was not his reason for making the proposal. Thus far in the eighteen years of civil war he had managed to maintain almost perfect neutrality, twisting, shifting and making excuses, devoting himself to building churches, giving Stephen money from time to time when he could no longer avoid it, but never calling up his vassals to fight. In his own fashion he had been loyal to the king, always giving him excellent counsel, but he had also kept open a line of communications with the rebels. They wooed him constantly, hoping to win his wealth and power to their cause, so that between their hope and Stephen's trust, Leicester's lands and his vassals' keeps had remained inviolate through the long years of strife.

In this crisis, it was plain that soft words and shifting promises would not be sufficient. If Stephen called him and his vassals to war, he would either have to go or break with the king, and he was not yet ready for the latter action. On the other hand, if Rannulf's plan was adopted, he would need do no more than he had done in the past. Someone had to make the proposal, and Leicester was afraid that if Rannulf did so Stephen would reject it out of spite without consideration. He spoke and listened to Eustace's rude rejection of the offer with a scowl. Robert of Leicester was not accustomed to swallowing insults from men young enough to be his son – but just now it was dangerous to answer as he would have liked.

'Be still,' Stephen snarled at his heir. 'I am still king, and I think the earl of Leicester's plan has much merit.'

A more controlled murmur of approval followed the king's statement. Leicester and Soke exchanged glances which spoke volumes although neither permitted his face to assume any expression.

'Let the council depart,' Stephen continued, 'to discuss this matter as it seems best to them. Tomorrow morning, by the prime, let us meet here again, that I may have the considered advice of my loyal liege men. If it seems good to you that it should be so, we will set the time for the men and tithes to be ready. If this plan is not to your liking, see that another giving me no less than my due is ready in its place.'

They were only too ready to go. Another day's grace had been given them. That was valuable in itself, and the idea had, as the king said, merit. Many a man was already sighing with relief, thinking that he would soon be rid of an expensive, unwanted, and dangerous younger son, or brother, or cousin – some land-hungry young man who was a drain on his coffers

157

and who, perhaps, plotted his death or overthrow to steal his lands. The war in Normandy would be a drain on the coffers too , but it was better than going to Normandy oneself or fighting in England where one's own lands might be ravaged when one was away. Moreover, a man could always lie about money, and demands from Normandy would come slowly, the distance being great. Truly the earl of Leicester was wise, and his proposal had great merit.

The great hall was deserted and Stephen looked, by habit, at the chair beside him for his wife's approving glance. The chair was empty; tears rose to mist his vision, but through the mist the outraged expression of Eustace's face showed clearly. Stephen lifted a placating hand.

'My son, do not be angry.'

'Do not be angry!' Eustace gasped.

'Nay, I am angry myself, and that is how I was tricked out of the immediate muster I planned to have. One thing I have discovered, however, is that my soft heart has led me astray again. Rannulf of Soke *is* a traitor. But for him, I would have had them following and approving like sheep.'

Eustace had gasped with rage a moment past; now he gasped with surprise. His father nodded at him encouragingly. 'Aye,' he continued, 'your mother always trusted him and so did I, but this time you have seen more clearly than either of us what lay in his heart. Still, nothing is lost, only delayed a few weeks, and in the end he worked more good for us and ill for himself than he planned. Listen, my son, we will have two full armies out of them yet.'

'Two?'

Eustace could scarcely believe his ears or his eyes. The features were his father's, but the hushed secretive voice, the sly, angry eyes belonged to someone he did not know. A deep sensation of revulsion made him feel as if his bowels were weak. Even if this stranger accomplished what he desired, he did not want to know him. He wanted his own father, cheerful, perhaps foolishly trusting, but essentially good, unselfish, and well meaning.

'Aye, two, and as much more as we need. You will take the young men and the gold – as much gold as we can wring from them. With the gold you will buy more men, good, mercenary troops, and Louis of France will give you great aid for he still loves the woman who is now Henry's wife, or if not, he loves her lands. Therefore he hates Henry bitterly. Let the young wolves free on the Angevin lands; pay them nothing and feed them nothing. Let them wrest more from their kin in England if they have need, or wrest it from Henry, or die. Any way it falls, we profit. Meanwhile, I will let Rannulf appeal to Hereford. If he fails, I have just cause to call up my vassals. If he succeeds and brings the rebels to court, they will fall alive into my hands. Again, either way we profit.'

'And what if Soke goes over to them completely? Have you thought of that?'

'It is you who should have thought of that and not insulted him,' Stephen spat. Then, more calmly, 'No, he will not do that, for Simon of Northampton is at court and Soke's eldest cub is with him. The old boar will not twitch a whisker while the young pig lies in my grasp.'

'Well,' Eustace replied ungraciously, 'I suppose you are right.'

He turned away sick at heart. He was furious with Stephen and furious with himself. He had what he wanted; his father, if he continued this new pattern, would no longer be the dupe and jest of the barons of England – but was it worth it?

'Stay, Eustace,' Stephen cried suddenly, gripping his son's arm. 'Have you nothing more to say?'

'What is there to say? You have planned all better than I could.'

'Oh, God,' Stephen choked, dropping his son's arm and burying his face in his hands. 'I have said those things, but I do not believe them. If what I plan is right, I were better dead, and if I am wrong, I will be dead. Aye, that is best of all, to lie in peace beside your mother.'

'You will have peace in this life.'

'I do not know – perhaps—'

The anger and assurance had faded from Stephen's face. He looked old and tired and glanced again, uncertainly, at the empty chair beside him. Eustace strove for reassuring words but found none. He too looked at Maud's empty seat and, although he did not tremble visibly, he could feel a shaking hollowness within his body. Making a hasty excuse, he fled from the dim chill hall into the bright warm sunlight, but the noise and bustle of the bailey brought no comfort. Wherever he walked conversations were suddenly suspended, eyes shifted, or greetings were over-hearty.

'Have a care where you walk, my lord.'

That harsh voice was unmistakable as was the fine grey stallion reined back upon its haunches. Eustace looked up into the thin, hard face past the mouth with its tight-drawn unhappy lips, and into clear grey eyes. They did not shift, but returned his glance squarely, and Eustace had to fight the temptation to scream insults or strike out because the glance was filled only with bitter amusement.

'It is you who should have a care!'

The amusement faded from Rannulf's eyes as he watched Eustace storm past him. He eased his reins and touched his mount gently with his spurred heels. Behaviour that was funny in a child like Richard, or even in an ordinary spoiled young man, was not funny at all when it was indulged in by the heir to the throne at a critical moment. God only knew to what imprudences this unreasonable hatred and envy would drive Eustace. To send this furious, hag-ridden youth to Normandy would at least permit him to vent his spleen where it might do some good. Certainly to prevent him from going was disaster. Rannulf shrugged his heavy shoulders; he knew he could do no more than he had done, and resignation had taken the place of despair. At least there was a flicker of hope in the present situation.

A week passed and then another. Rannulf threw himself with immense energy into the task of gathering and outfitting the army that was to accompany Eustace to France. No man, no matter how supicious, could claim that he was not exerting himself in the king's interest, and such success attended his continual harassment of the barons of England in the rapid accumulation of men and money for the expedition, that even Eustace could not cavil that he had not as yet set off for Hereford. Rannulf was, as a matter of fact, in the grip of a surge of optimism. If Henry could be destroyed in Normandy and

Eustace could ease his heart and restore his confidence with that victory, all might yet be well.

With everything in excellent trim in London, Rannulf took another fortnight to ride south to stir up the lords of the Cinque Ports so that sufficient shipping would be available for the men and supplies. The Cinque Ports were doubtful and moved slowly; Rannulf soothed their doubts and quickened their interest with gold. Ships were out of repair or busy with trade in the good weather of summer; Rannulf hastened repairs and guaranteed against loss with more gold.

Now his coffers were nearly empty. To return to Sleaford in order to wring more from his people was impossible. It would wake all Eustace's suspicions and, worse, what he had done here might be undone in his absence. Some wives, like Gundreda of Warwick, took the burden of collecting money on themselves. Probably Catherine was incapable of getting everything that was owed to him, but if she could send something the fleet could be readied. He wrote, telling her how much he wanted and describing methods for obtaining the sum. To his surprise exactly what he asked for arrived – and much sooner than he had expected. Rannulf was too busy to consider the meaning of this efficiency, but he accepted its results gratefully.

More sweat-soaked couriers arrived on exhausted horses at Sleaford demanding gold and more gold. Desperately Catherine squeezed the serfs, made bold demands of the churches and the merchants, and finally took to her horse to drain her own lands to satisfy the demands. Rannulf's serfs and vassals groaned, but paid; Catherine's paid also, but they growled.

'This is not our war, madam,' Sir Giles Fortesque protested. 'We have paid our dues and no man has attacked us that we should pay more for the defence of our lands.'

The blue eyes that he had always known so softly misty were now opaque and hard. 'It is every man's war. If Henry comes again with the wealth and power that is now behind him, you will need to decide whether to violate your oath to my husband and fight for the Angevin or violate your belief and fight against him. For now, all men's safety lies in keeping him locked in France.'

The voice was gentle still, but the utterance was very firm and the vassal suddenly noticed that Lady Catherine's softly rounded chin was attached to a remarkably determined jaw. He wondered how he had missed that characteristic previously, and realized that he seldom looked at anything but the broad white brow and large eyes. Also his lady pushed back her hair because of the heat, and the lines of cheekbone and jaw showed clear, unobscured by the heavy braids. Nonetheless, it was not that alone. Her carriage was different, her hands were roughened and tanned from much handling of reins, and a vital force emanated from her. It was Sir Giles' duty to obey her, but it was also his duty as leader of her vassals to reason with her for their benefit.

'And if we pay? There are still rebels in the land. What if we are called to war to attack them? Will we not have paid double?'

The soft, red lips, so womanly, so appealing, tightened perceptibly. 'Have you any complaint against me or against my husband in the management of your affairs? Has aught been done or asked of you that was not to your best interests?'

'No, my lady, but—'

'Then you should trust me. This demand, too, is in your best interests. If you pay, you will not be called to war, except it be a matter of life or death.'

Sir Giles bowed his head. 'As you will, my lady. I will ride with the sun tomorrow to do your bidding.'

'I will be grateful for your company,' Catherine said sweetly, and Sir Giles bowed his head again in recognition that her ladyship intended to leave nothing to chance. She would make her demand personally of the vassals, reaffirming their loyalty to her as she picked their purses.

In spite of her promise to ride with the sun, Catherine sat up late that night writing a letter that she would not trust to her scribe. First she relayed the good news that the money Rannulf had demanded would be forthcoming within the period he had specified, and the better news that she had managed to obtain it as an extra levy, not a borrowing against future rents. After that she sat for a time with wrinkled brow, wondering

162

how to tell him most soothingly of the promises she had given Sir Giles.

'My dear husband,' she wrote, 'I have been guilty of sweetening you with good tidings first, but you have lived too long to think that any good comes without need for payment. You have told me in the past, however, that I must never borrow money.' Catherine's pen hesitated. Rannulf had forbidden her to borrow, but that had been for personal things and had nothing to do with the present situation. He would consider her as empty-headed as a sheep for not knowing the difference. Well, it was better so. 'Therefore I could not ask the sum as a loan. I spoke much of the king's necessity, but they questioned me so straightly that I had great need to give them some assurance that this was not a plot to wring them doubly dry. I dared, in this necessity, to promise the vassals of Soke that they would not be called to war except it be a matter of our own defence or safety. They took my word as yours, but I knew not what else to say, having no orders from you. If I have done wrong, I pray you to forgive me out of your own indulgence, which has always been so great, and out of the knowledge that I desire only to do what is best for you and to be always your dutiful wife, Catherine, countess of Soke.'

He would despise her for an idiot. Catherine's lips trembled. Then her mouth hardened. She would not permit Richard to become a beggar, not laughing Richard with his generous heart, nor even Geoffrey whom she knew so little but already loved because he was so like his father.

If Catherine was not quite the same woman as she had been when Rannulf married her, her husband seemed equally changed in Robert of Leicester's eyes. That worried gentleman had arrived in Rannulf's house not half an hour after Soke had entered it himself on his return from the south. In whatever state of fatigue or irritation Leicester had expected to find his friend, he had not anticipated that he would discover him consumed with laughter.

'May I ask,' he queried caustically, 'what you find to be so merry about in times like these?'

A dust-smeared countenance with eyes heavy from lack of sleep was turned to him. 'Women,' Rannulf replied, laughing even more heartily, 'are extremely disobedient and untrustworthy creatures – God bless them.'

'You are mad!'

'Very likely,' Rannulf replied without heat. 'At least you are said to be a wise man and you have been telling me that for years. André, bring some wine to cool the earl of Leicester.'

'I do not want wine,' Leicester snapped. 'You pass all understanding. For two years, while all went well with us, you were not fit to be spoken to. Now, when the rudder of the ship is gone, the helmsman mad with greed and self-interest, the captain lunatic, and the crew rebellious, nothing can exceed your constant good humour.' He paused and regarded Soke searchingly. 'Do you know something I do not, Rannulf?'

'Nay, Robert. I do not see things as black as you paint them. All goes well with regard to Eustace's departure. If he is as forward as it seems he would be when I left, another few days should see him hence. When the gadfly is gone, I hope Stephen will be more manageable. If all goes well in France, and I can but bring Hereford to mouth platitudes—'

'In France! With Louis and Eustace pitted against the Angevin? He will grind their bones between his teeth for the first course and swallow us whole for the second.'

Rannulf laughed no longer. 'If that is true,' he answered with a recurrence of his sick feeling, 'then Eustace may not return.' He could not go further with that thought and added quickly, 'Perhaps I have been wrong all my life and what is needful is an iron hand to rule men who cannot rule themselves.'

'So you see at last that a firm guide keeps all straight. Tell me, Rannulf, if—'

'No! Do not break my peace, Robert. Stephen is my king. Let us pray that Eustace's mind and temper will be healed by victory. At least do not speak treason to me—'

'Faugh! I wish to speak reason, not treason, but if you are so sensitive, let us confine ourselves to the trouble in hand and leave the future to itself. I came to tell you that Stephen wakes again from his long stillness. He has been very active in Eustace's business of late and has been asking for you, desiring

164

to know what your answer from Hereford is. I sent you word. Did you not receive it?'

'Of course I received it. Do you think it is my practice to ride day and night without sleep for pleasure? Well, I am ready. I have not the word he desires, but I have other news that will gladden his heart. The Cinque Ports are fitted and ready. Eustace may march tomorrow if he chooses.'

'So soon?'

'I have applied much golden grease to make all run smooth,' Rannulf said drily.

'In this case it is well, but you do agree with me that in the matter of Hereford we desire not smooth running towards war but another truce?'

'If you mean you wish to keep Stephen from attacking Hereford – yes, I agree with that.'

'Then for God's sake, do not lose your temper because of Hereford's hasty words. He will have plenty to say that you do not agree with. If you return here in a passion, it will be none so easy to find another excuse to prevent Stephen from calling up the vassals.'

Suddenly and incomprehensibly Rannulf began to laugh again. 'You will need some excuse,' he choked, 'but I, who have a foolish and disobedient wife who loses my letters and cannot remember what I said in them, I am already excused.' He thrust Catherine's letter into Leicester's hand. 'The countess of Soke, instead of borrowing against next year's rents, as I bade her, has levied an extra tax on her vassals, promising them in return that they would not be called to war except in defence of my person or their own lands.'

'And you find such behaviour a source of merriment?'

Leicester's amazement, which was based upon the change in Rannulf's attitude towards women rather than on any objection to what Catherine had done, was misunderstood. 'You always seem to doubt Catherine's actions. Why should I not find this a source of merriment, even if she did forget what I told her? It admirably suits my purposes. The money was spent in the king's service, and Stephen has the choice of accepting that in lieu of service from the vassals of Soke, accepting the personal service of the vassals of Sleaford alone, or commanding me to use the vassals of Sleaford to fight the vassals of Soke and bring them to obedience to me in disregard of my lady's word. Or, he might repay me the gold to return to them, but you know how likely that is. Where has Catherine acted ill?'

Leicester had been reading the letter while Rannulf spoke. 'Nowhere,' he said, and after a thoughtful pause, 'she has done well – very well indeed.'

# Chapter 11

In the fresh bloom of early summer, before the ripeness of the full season brought a sense of decadence to it, the countryside seemed like a Garden of Eden. The sun was warm, the breeze cool; large white clouds decorated a deep blue sky, and shade delicately dappled the winding road. A gentle lowing from a small herd of cattle waiting patiently for their afternoon milking added a deliciously mournful note to the regular clip-clop of the horses' hooves on the hard-packed earth. To crown the picturesqueness of the scene, several wisps of smoke from a small village hidden by a stand of trees curled upward through the clear air.

Rannulf looked about him, for once really seeing the countryside instead of just noting the weather. Why could it not always be thus? Why was it necessary to see the green fields smoking black, to see the cattle wallowing in their own blood, to see the peaceful wisps of smoke changed to a raging inferno of flames that would devour the village and the wood? He jerked his mind away, because those thoughts were leading steadily to treason. True, he could speak to Hereford of the peace, could urge him to maintain it by agreeing to those demands of the king which were reasonable. Unfortunately, there were unreasonable demands also which Rannulf was bound to state but which his conscience must prohibit him from urging even if his reason did not assure him that no sane man would agree.

The situation was impossible, and war was inevitable in Stephen's present mood. Of course, Leicester was doing what he could, but the king was strangely adamant, and the plea for peace to Hereford was a waste of time. It was the king who would break the peace this time, not the rebels. The whole world was upside-down. Why go at all? Why not make one last desperate effort to wipe out the rebellious barons? Because their chance would be better later. Earnestly Rannulf searched his heart. It was true that their chance would be better if Louis and Eustace were successful, but it would be far worse if the attack in Normandy failed. No, he was riding to Hereford because he, personally, desired peace with such fervency that he no longer cared much how that peace was achieved. He was putting himself to this labour, snatching at a few days' delay, hoping for a miracle.

What ails me, Rannulf wondered, his eyes following the stain of smoke that gave the clear blue sky the mistiness of Catherine's eyes. I am growing old, he decided. It was impossible to blame this longing to lay down his arms upon ill-health. True, he remembered that once or twice when he had been wounded very badly and had lain long abed recovering, he had been taken by these sickly fancies. But his health was at its best now. In spite of his worries, his food had savour, firm flesh covered his bones again, and he was full of energy. Only it was the wrong kind of energy. He could see himself hawking, hunting, teaching Richard, playing at single-stick with Geoffrey, even breaking horses or lending a shoulder to the uprooting of a stubborn stump. He could see anything except war. He was tired of death. He must be getting old.

Old or young, this was the beginning of the end of delay. There across the valley, on the rise of ground beyond, stood Hereford keep. Rannulf pulled up his horse and sent Sir André ahead as messenger while he and his men followed very slowly. Midway into the valley Fortesque returned with the news that Hereford would not receive them. Then this was not the beginning of the end, but the end. Rannulf cast his eyes again over the rich fields and woods and upward to that single stain of smoke which made a patch of sky misty. Then, resolutely, he spurred his horse forward.

'He must receive me,' he said stubbornly, and his men, with wondering eyes, followed.

The earl of Soke, in the opinion of his men, was the best leader in England. He was both brave and cautious, leading in battle with such ferocity that he cleared a path for his troops to follow, but never taking them where no path could be hewn or where there was no road back. From Hereford keep, however, there was no road at all – neither back nor forward. Such a small band could not besiege the great keep of Hereford nor assault it. To encamp before it and arouse its master and the townsfolk to resentment was tantamount to self-slaughter. The men need not have troubled themselves; neither siege nor assault was in Rannulf's mind. When they had made their way past the tight-shut gates of the town of Hereford, up the winding road to the foot of the eminence upon which the keep sat, Rannulf bade his men dismount and wait.

'I will go forward from here alone. Hereford must receive me.'

'No, my lord.'

Rannulf turned his head to the young voice. Not since his father's death, when he had shaken off his tutor, had a man of his flatly contradicted any statement he made in a military matter. Fortesque blanched at the cold anger of his lord's expression, and tried to explain himself.

'You cannot go alone into Hereford's power. They could shoot you from the castle walls and claim innocence in saying they did not recognize you. Tell me what to say – I will go.'

Rannulf wondered if that scene between Catherine and André could have been misread by him. Had his wife commended him to the young man's care because she though him ageing? Whatever his reason, it was certain that young Fortesque was in earnest.

'Sir André, you are a young man of most peculiar notions. When you first wished to recommend yourself to me, you tried to overthrow me in a tourney. Now, perhaps, you think to show your devotion by risking yourself in my stead. That is commendable, but unwise and unnecessary, and your manner – flouting my command – is offensive. If you think me a fool or an old dotard – keep it to yourself. Give me credit for being old enough, and not too old, to know my own mind.'

The reprimand was harsh, but the eyes were considering and even kind. André blushed under the lash of the sarcasm, but he was not resentful, recognizing the fact that he had been impulsive and foolish. There was no reason for Hereford to make any attempt on Lord Soke. It was merely that Sir André was frightened by the notion of going all alone into the power of one's enemy, and he transferred those feelings to his master. His offer had not been made solely out of love, although his respect and admiration for the earl of Soke grew steadily with every day he spent with him, but out of the desire to prove himself brave and loyal. He wished to impress the father of the girl he loved with his value. Now André watched the figure of the earl dwindle as he rode to the edge of the moat alone. He transferred his gaze to the silent keep with its raised drawbridge and imagined the vigilant eyes of the men who watched the lonely figure through the deep, narrow arrow-slits in the walls.

'Hereford, come out, I wish to speak to you,' Rannulf bellowed across the murky water. He had guessed right; Hereford himself was on the walls. A figure moved out upon the battlements near the main tower, the sun glinting on golden hair.

'I have nothing to say to you, Soke. Nothing to say to any man who comes from Stephen of Blois.'

'Then you are more a fool than ever I thought you, Hereford. Do you fear one single man that you must bide armoured and shut up behind your walls?'

'Neither single man nor all the forces of the man who calls himself king do I fear. You are the fool, not I, to come upon a thankless, fruitless errand.'

'If I am such a fool, why guard yourself so carefully from me? What harm can I do?'

'I never thought you to be a maker of trouble, Soke. Why should you be the one to be sent with the king's writ, except that they wish to use you as a scapegoat? You cannot enforce the writ to bring me to court. In mercy to yourself, go and shut yourself into your own keep.'

Rannulf laughed without mirth. 'I have no writ from the king, although I do come from him. Must I bellow at you across this water all day, or will you let me in?'

There was a pause, then Rannulf saw the mailed figure on the battlements make a sharp gesture and the drawbridge groaned slowly downward. Alone, Rannulf rode across. Alone, he dismounted in the bailey. Equally alone, the slight, upright figure of the earl of Hereford came across to him.

'Your men?' Hereford asked.

'Let them bide. Too much mixing might lead to words – though they care less than nothing one way or the other, as yours do, no doubt.'

'Enter then.'

Within the keep the hospitality offered was gracious, if not warm. If it had been ten times as cold, however, Rannulf would not have noticed for he was so much struck with the building to which he was taken that he had eyes for nothing else. The thick, carefully guarded walls and eight great towers of Hereford keep, Rannulf passed without a flicker of interest other than that aroused by tactical considerations. Sleaford was as strong or stronger, although not as large. It was the only weak thing in Hereford keep, the manor house built as living quarters for the earl's family, which drew his attention and held it. A house within the walls of the keep itself and, therefore, safe. A comfortable house, warm and light and dry, whose walls did not seep moisture from the earth filling which was ever wet. Catherine would love such a house.

Thus far Rannulf had made no answer to several icily polite inquiries about his trip that Lady Hereford had put to him. Her large amber eyes grew brighter, golden flames of wrath leaping within them for she knew Rannulf of old and knew his opinion of women. He could be rude as he liked and think what he liked of women – but not in her house. Roger of Hereford's expression grew wary; he understood all to well the burning eyes and the two spots of bright colour his wife's cheeks displayed. It would be amusing to see how Rannulf reacted when a real woman he could not lay hands upon lit into him, but it was far more important to hear what his unwelcome guest had to say and be rid of him.

'Elizabeth.'

The gentle note of warning in Hereford's voice pierced Rannulf's abstraction as nothing else could. His glance flickered from the earl, whose expression expressed nothing, to the magnificent flaming countenance of his hostess. There was nothing in the warning to concern himself, Rannulf decided. Lady Hereford was merely about to fly into a rage about something. She was always flying into rages – and very beautiful she

171

looked when she did, he thought indulgently. He had started to look back at the walls to judge, if he could, what kind of masonry had been used to point the stone when it occurred to him that Hereford might be embarrassed by his presence at a quarrel. Catherine, he knew with the stirring of warmth which always came with her name, would never misbehave in such a way.

'I would like to look around,' Rannulf said abruptly. Permission to do so would serve two purposes; it would remove him from the scene so that husband and wife could have their battle out, and it would give him a chance to fix the details of construction of the manor house in his mind.

Hereford's mouth dropped open with surprise. He knew Soke to be a brave man, but to enter an enemy keep alone and boldly ask to inspect it so that one might know best where to attack was not bravery but insanity.

'You expect me to show you—'

'You need not come,' Rannulf said indifferently. 'I can see what I want for myself.'

'I have no doubt that you can,' Lady Hereford replied in dangerously gentle tones, the sarcasm of which passed right over Rannulf's head.

'Yes. It does not seem a different structure.'

'It does not!' Hereford snapped. 'Yet I think it could well withstand all that Stephen of Blois could muster against it were there no traitors within.'

'Surely not,' Rannulf exclaimed, 'unless your masons have discovered some secret unknown to all others. A few blows with a good catapult must certainly destroy these thin walls.'

'Thin! Why they are twelve feet—' An expression of puzzlement replaced the outrage in Hereford's face.

'Nonsense,' was the rude reply. 'Anyone not blind can see that the windows are less than a foot recessed.'

Lady Hereford caught it first and burst out laughing. 'You mean you wish to look around the manor house?'

'Yes,' Rannulf looked surprised. 'What could I have meant else? You could not think me mad enough or uncourteous enough to expect to examine your keep with matters as they are between us.'

Now Hereford was laughing as heartily as his wife. 'You must forgive me, Rannulf. After this trip here and your coming alone into my power, I can believe you mad enough for anything.'

'Nonsense,' Rannulf repeated. 'Perhaps my hopes are not high for making accord between you and the king, but even faint hopes are better than nothing. And, with regard to my personal safety, you have proven yourself to be an honourable man. You would no more do me hurt or keep me against my will than I would you, if you came to my keep.'

'I will not gainsay you,' Hereford said slowly, realizing that what might not be generally true was certainly true for Rannulf, earl of Soke. 'Well, then, let me show you what you like and tell you what I can. I know little enough, for the house was built in my father's time and my mother is no longer with us.'

Rannulf shook his head regretfully. 'It does not matter. I had some thought to build such a place for my wife. Catherine loves beautiful things – but I will build nothing if it comes to war and if it does not, I will have time enough to ask my questions. The king desires to know, Hereford, why you did not come to pay your respects when the queen was buried.'

Hereford laughed again, but with a cold and bitter undertone to the sound. Before he could speak, his wife laid a hand on his arm. She knew that Rannulf had been fond of Maud, quite aside from his duty to her as queen, and she had warmed towards him when she realized that he loved his wife enough to expend a large sum in building a house just to please her. Since it could do no good for her husband to offend Rannulf by telling him outright that they were glad Maud was dead, let him give other reasons which were equally true. Although Lady Hereford was braced for war and would face it as courageously as she faced every other trial of her life, she no longer desired a quick victory at any cost. With the passage of the years she had grown more patient, more wary, as the circle of those really dear to her who could be hurt by war expanded.

'Lord Soke, why do you ask a question to which you know the answer already?' Lady Hereford asked in gently reproving tones. 'You must know that he did not attend the burial for

173

two reasons. My father was sick unto death – praise God he is so greatly recovered now that he needs us no longer – and it was needful for Roger to be there to guard the lands for my brothers who are so young. Even you could not desire the lands of Chester to fall into Lincoln's power or perhaps others still worse. Also, it was no secret that Stephen was to call a muster of the vassals to attack Henry – God knows why, for Henry has offended no man in England by taking what his father bequeathed to him and what came to him in his wife's name.'

Hereford, too, was not anxious for war although ready for it. He had decided that he could do nothing to stop the attack on Henry in Normandy. Even if he prevented Eustace from setting out for France by beginning hostilities in England, Louis would attack alone. That would be sufficient to tie Henry to Normandy for some time, at least until he was certain that his vassals were loyal and would resist the French king even if he were not present to spur them on. In council with the other pro-Angevin lords, Hereford had discussed the probable result of Eustace's mission. The decision had been against interference, the general opinion being that, considering Eustace's and Louis's dispositions, they would soon be at each other's throats. The rebels hoped that the dissension that would arise might make the combined attack less effective than either alone might be.

Aside from these considerations, there were others even more basic and practical. An attack on Stephen of Blois in Henry's absence would be futile. One could not put an absent king on such an uneasy throne. Furthermore, Hereford had sworn, not long since, to lead no more lost causes. He was not ill-pleased, under the circumstances, to catch a definite gleam of satisfaction in Rannulf's eyes. If soft words alone could keep the peace, Hereford was well prepared to follow his wife's lead.

'I thought, Lord Soke, that it would cause less trouble if I absented myself rather than refusing openly what Stephen has no right to demand. Neither I nor my father before me recognized his right to the throne. Neither I nor my father swore fealty to Stephen of Blois. Whatever right he has to demand service of his own vassals, he has no right to demand anything of me. Nonetheless, I did not desire to argue such matters in

174

the moment of his grief nor to provoke him to particular anger.'

'So much then you would be willing to say – that your father-in-law's illness kept you, and that you intended no disrespect to Maud's memory?' Rannulf asked, ignoring a good part of what Hereford had said.

Lord and Lady Hereford exchanged glances, studied Rannulf's face, and exchanged glances again. 'I might be willing,' Hereford conceded warily, and then added impulsively, 'I will fight if I must, but I have little lust to it.'

'So we all feel. There has been too much fighting, too much blood, too much death, and too much famine.'

Both listeners turned amazed eyes on Rannulf, but he was looking beyond them through the open window at the green fields and clear sky.

'This is a new manner and a new way of thinking that you have, Soke,' Hereford said suspiciously.

'No, why?' the older man replied. 'If you find it surprising that I, who am a man of war, come to you on a mission of peace, you have but to look at the difference in the circumstances. On the other occasions when we crossed swords, Lord Hereford, you bore the sword and held it at my throat. I could not with honour sue for peace. It was needful to defend my king and what else was mine. Now it is the king who threatens war, and it is no shame for me to come and ask you to make what submission is reasonable to avert a war that will hurt all and help none. There is no difference in me.'

Doubtless, Lady Hereford thought, the man believes what he says, but it is not the truth for all that. Some woman, and Maud being dead it could not be she, was exerting a powerful influence on this harsh and bitter man. She knew nothing of Rannulf's wife but conceived a great desire to meet the lady who could have softened so hard and stubborn a character. Without anger, Elizabeth listened to Rannulf who was now relating the exact terms of the submission the king required and then swiftly stemming Hereford's angry negative with an upheld hand.

'Many of these matters are impossible for you to promise or to perform,' Soke said, 'and had I not sworn to name them, I would not have risked inflaming your hasty temper. If you will look below the words, however, you will see that something or nearly all can be done with both honour and safety.'

'What can I do with honour and safety?'

'You cannot, of course, cede your keeps, but you can take oath that you will not use them for war unless you are attacked.'

'You fight for your overlord. What if my overlord should come and demand my service? What am I to do then? Which oath must I break?'

'Henry of Anjou will not come this year – let the truce be until the new year.'

'So much I might chance,' Hereford admitted grudgingly.

'Then, you cannot take oath to keep your allies from attack, but you can take oath that you will do your uttermost to prevent them from this action.'

'You might, Roger,' Lady Hereford said softly. 'My father will do nothing yet awhile – he is still so weak. Gloucester will never begin to fight on his own, and the others all wait upon your move.'

I can consider it, at least.'

'The other matters may be similarly agreed upon.'

Hereford bit his lip. He hated to make any concessions at all to the king whom he despised and scorned, but to waste his strength in a useless battle was even more hateful. To his mind, there could be no doubt that Henry would swiftly defeat Louis and Eustace in Normandy. Then the Angevin would come to England to claim his own. It was true that there might be some profit in exhausting Stephen by war before Henry came, but the effort would also exhaust his own forces. Then, too, Leicester and some other great neutrals were wavering ever closer and closer to Henry's cause. To disturb them, possibly to force them into action on Stephen's behalf, would be most unwise. If a small sacrifice in pride would keep the peace until Henry was free to join them, it would be well worth it.

'There is much in what you say, Soke, but affairs of this weight cannot be decided in an hour. Call in your men, and let us consider more particularly what can be done that will satisfy both the king and my necessity.'

As the days passed and point after point of an acceptable

176

agreement was hammered out, a spirit of genuine optimism began to infect both the earl of Hereford and the earl of Soke. When the blue eyes met the grey, there was now confidence and respect where suspicion and caution had previously reigned. Rannulf saw that Roger of Hereford really wished to compose a pact of which he could keep both the spirit and the letter. Hereford recognized that Soke was as anxious as he to avoid ambiguous phrasing or vague commitments that could cause claims of violation where no violation was intended. For men of short temper and sharp tongues, both showed great restraint in dealing with each other and, although angry words were exchanged often enough, at no time was the conference in danger of breaking up.

The agreement was exceedingly detailed; even minute points, such as what type of raid or the numbers of men involved in a raid that could or could not be cited as a violation of the pact, were considered. This was necessary, for it was inconceivable that all hostilities could be brought to a halt. Private quarrels would continue unabated; indeed, neither man thought or desired that they should stop. It was every man's right to settle his personal quarrels by force. All that was necessary was to decide what level of quarrel merited interference by an overlord and what that overlord could do for the defence of his vassal without violating the treaty of peace.

'I believe,' Rannulf said, frowning thoughtfully at the innocent cleric who was writing down what had been decided, 'that if the battle is not carried outside of the lands of the vassals concerned, either in offence or defence, that the overlord may be said to be blamelessly performing his duty in succouring his man.'

Hereford considered that. 'You mean that if Salford, who is Oxford's vassal, should attack Evesham, who is my man, I could go to Evesham's aid if the battle was kept within Evesham's or Salford's property?'

'Aye. To restrict either overlord to the defence only of his own vassal's land would be unworkable. You could attack Salford, but not, for instance, Evenlode.'

'But I would need to pass through Evenlode. It would be almost impossible— Yes? What do you want?'

177

The page so addressed backed away. Hereford was usually very good-natured, but he could land a stinging blow when interrupted inopportunely. 'There is a messenger below for the earl of Soke.'

'From whom?' Rannulf asked sharply, and then, before the page could answer, he turned to Hereford, his eyes shadowed. 'If he be from the king, I will not receive him here. It will be safer for us both if I were outside the walls.'

The flash of concern died out of Hereford's eyes. Even if the king had sent a writ, Rannulf had sense enough to see that he would only be trapped himself if he accepted it. He nodded to the page.

'From Leicester, my lord, so he says.'

Rannulf rose eagerly to his feet. 'Robert must have succeeded with him then. Let us see what he says. We will have to try to finish this matter today so that I can set out at once to obtain his approval before someone can shift his mind for him.'

He seized on the scroll bearing Leicester's seal and broke the wax impatiently with a grim smile. A quick jerk unrolled the parchment and Rannulf's eyes fell on the words hungrily. Now he would need only bring Hereford's signed agreement to the king and he could go home again, home to his wife and his children. Hereford, watching, saw the eagerness, even the life, drain out of Rannulf's face as he read and his own heart sank. It was all useless; they were too late.

As if he had read Hereford's mind, Rannulf groaned, 'Useless – all useless. Maud's death has unsettled his reason. Hereford, I must go at once. Leicester writes that he could do nothing – worse than nothing. Stephen is on the march.'

'He planned it from the beginning,' Hereford snarled.

'No,' Rannulf denied instinctively, 'he is a good man, and—' His voice died away and he shrugged. 'He has been different since Maud's death, more— Hereford, there is still one chance to bring him to our way of thinking. Come with me and speak with him yourself. You know how easily Stephen is moved by soft words. Perhaps face to face—'

So firm was Hereford's confidence in Rannulf's honour that he felt not a flicker of anger or suspicion. 'I could not chance it. Even a fool like Stephen could not fail to grasp such an opportunity to have me at his mercy.'

'Nay, I will ride before and have his safe-conduct for you to come and to go.'

'Can any man trust Stephen's safe-conduct?'

A touch of colour came into Rannulf's face. This was the hardest part of being Stephen's vassal – the knowledge that, well-meaning or not, your overlord's word was worth nothing. Desperately he offered the only thing he had left to offer.

'I will be your hostage. Upon my honour, you will go out of court as free as you come in, even if I must raise my men and fight to free you.'

Hereford's blue eyes caught and held Rannulf's. Although nearly twenty years lay between them, the blue eyes were, in this moment, older and wiser, bitterer and more cynical, than the grey. Seldom had an opportunity more golden fallen into the earl of Hereford's hands. All he needed to do was to agree. There could be no doubt that the safe-conduct would be offered; less doubt that it would be violated; and still less that Rannulf, earl of Soke, would, indeed, raise his vassals and fight against the king for Hereford's freedom. Then Rannulf would be lost to Stephen as a supporter. He could not, in all probability, be brought to join Henry's cause even then, but he would be forced to stand aloof. Leicester was more than half-convinced to break with Stephen already. The loss of Soke's powerful support for Stephen of Blois would probably be the deciding factor to drive Leicester into Henry's camp. Northampton was old, Warwick was also old and his wife, like Leicester, would jump to whichever side seemed strongest.

The struggle was bitter, but brief, and Hereford laughed aloud. 'Nay, it is too late for that. It was too late the day Maud died, but you and I, deluded by our dreams, did not wish to see. Go then in peace, until we meet in war, and remember that the earl of Hereford, though bespattered by filth, was not yet so sunk in the mire that he set advantage above honour.'

# Chapter 12

The day upon which the earl of Soke rode away from Hereford Castle was as perfect as that upon which he had arrived. This time, however, Rannulf saw neither the blue skies nor the green fields. There was now no time for consideration of such trifles nor for vain regrets. He had desired peace so fervently that it had been like a physical ache within him. Yet, if it was not to be, it was not; and the quickest road now to that goal was a hard enough and successful enough war. Accordingly, that part of Rannulf's mind that was not wondering where the king had gone and the quickest way to find him was taken up with the problem of where to notify his vassals to meet him.

At home, his heart cried, go home. The men will come quickest to Sleaford which they know best. Aye, replied the hard voice of duty, and then you will be farthest from the king. Go to Oxford. The heart cried out again, but hopelessly, for Oxford was of all places the most logical. It was the favourite stronghold of Stephen and Eustace outside of London, the place where the king was likeliest to be if he was not already in action. It was on the direct road to London from Hereford and on the direct road from Sleaford towards the Angevin strongholds of Devizes and Wallingford in the south. Leicester had given no hint of where Stephen would go – it was possible that Stephen himself had not yet decided – but whether the king planned to attack Gloucester or Hereford or the southern fortresses, he would certainly pass through or stop at Oxford.

They moved fast and openly as they were on Hereford's domain, riding due east so that they could avoid passing too close to Gloucester. It was possible that Leicester's messenger had outstripped those whom the rebel spies had sent from court, or it was possible that the spies would wait to discover where Stephen meant to launch his attack, but it would be foolish to count too heavily on that possibility and chance being taken prisoner. Better to ride hard to Winchcombe, rest a while there, and continue on to Oxford through the night.

It was easy to decide once the longings of the heart had been subdued, but there were discomforts to be endured in the accomplishment. They were no longer riding at a foot-pace with every reason for delay, so that the faint breeze could cool the armour upon which the sun blazed. There was now no time to idle through the streams they forded, dismounting to drink themselves and allowing the horses to fill their bellies. A full belly makes a slow mount, and the cursing men dragged up their horses' heads and drove spurs into the lathered beasts, hating the sparkling, chuckling waters that were beyond their reach.

Rannulf alone was impervious to heat and thirst, not because his body was any different or any harder than those of his men, but because he alone had things other than his body to concern himself with. The men of his household guard were free mercenaries, serfs of his land in whom he had recognized a spirit and willingness to fight, or the younger sons and brothers of his lesser vassals to whom he gave employment. They rode when and where he told them; they fought when and where he told them; most of them cared for nothing except the rewards they won from their master for their service. Sometimes to the highborn members of his troop, Rannulf would explain why he undertook a certain action – largely for the sake of having someone to talk to – but none of them would dare ask for an explanation that Rannulf did not offer voluntarily. Their safety was in his hands, and he had never failed to guard it well in the past; therefore, the men had nothing to think about beyond the heat of the sun, their thirst and fatigue, and where and when they would stop to rest.

The path of safety having been considered and chosen, Rannulf was free to think of other matters. What had happened at court while he was gone? What had spurred Stephen to action? Why had Leicester failed to move him, and how much unrest among the barons had Leicester caused in attempting to force the king to change his mind? Leicester's hurried note had answered none of these questions.

The men and horses rested at Winchcombe, filling their stomachs, slaking their thirst, and snatching a few hours of sleep in preparation for the long night ride that they faced. Rannulf, just as he had been unconscious of discomfort, was unmindful of the amenities their refuge offered. He ate and drank, it was true, but only because the food was set before him. He could not send out summonses to his vassals to request the forty days' service for an offensive war before he knew positively where to tell them to meet him, or before he knew positively from the king himself that there would be war. Rannulf wrote only to Robert and to Catherine, and it took every minute of his time in Winchcombe to compose his letters. Leicester was easy. Rannulf thanked him for his warning, told him that he would be at Oxford the following day, and asked for a full explanation of what had happened. He sat for hours, however, wondering how to explain to Catherine just what he wanted of her.

She was to tell her vassals nothing, yet she was to manage so that they would be in readiness to march to war on a few days' notice. She was to assure them that he had every intention of backing her promise to them that they would not be called to war, yet she was to word her assurances so that, if their strength would bring victory, Rannulf could summon them nonetheless. She was to arrange the strengthening of all castles and fortifications fronting on the lands of the earl of Norfolk, but in such a way that Norfolk would have no cause to suspect that any attack would be launched against him. She was to wring what more money was possible from the land, but on no account to borrow against the future because still more money would be needed for next year. She was to levy an excess tax upon all merchants travelling to Rannulf's domains, but not to make the tax so exorbitant that trade would be brought to a halt.

When Catherine first received the letter and had skimmed through it, looking more for a personal message or a sign in Rannulf's handwriting of his state of mind and health, she giggled faintly. He was explaining everything so minutely because he thought her an idiot that he ended by following every command with a negative and every statement with a qualification. Catherine patted the parchment fondly, realizing that her husband loved her all the more for thinking her a fool.

Tenderly, almost as if it were part of Rannulf himself, Catherine unrolled the parchment again and set herself to read between the lines. As the real sense of the missive came across to her, the fresh colour faded from her cheeks. Here there was no matter for laughter at all, not even in the qualifications and contradictions. Although Rannulf did not state specifically that the period of truce was over and war had broken out, that fact was plain. Once she had prayed for a man of action; now she had one. Catherine pressed a hand to her side, for her heart was fluttering with fear.

'Madam, what is it?'

Mary, ever watchful, was beside her. Catherine swallowed. 'Nothing that need concern you, my child.'

She could control her voice, could even force her lips to smile, but her will could not bring back the bloom to her cheeks. Mary's eyes flicked to the close-written sheet, to the broken seal which displayed the dagger and chevrons of the Master of Sleaford.

'He is coming home?' Nothing else, to Mary's mind, was a matter of sufficient weight to drive the colour from her stepmother's face.

'You should speak more respectfully of your father, Mary. You should call him "father" or "my lord" or by his title.'

The words were an automatic response to Mary's reluctant designation of Rannulf as 'he'. She rarely spoke of him in any other way and, in spite of all of Catherine's efforts, Mary, docile in everything else, persisted in fearing and disliking her father. Catherine was not really thinking of that, not really thinking about Mary at all, or she would have realized that there was more hope than fear in the girl's question. Mary, too, had an interest in Soke's return. Catherine had forgotten that, forgotten everything in the wave of longing that her stepdaughter's question awoke.

'No,' she added, 'I fear it will be long before I know the comfort of his presence again.'

'Have you bad news, madam? Is there danger of an attack on the keep?'

Mary was brightly excited; she had never seen a siege or a battle. Rannulf's major seat was too strong and too far out of the main path of the fighting in the civil war to have been the subject of assault. Norfolk was the only major magnate in the immediate area who could hope for any personal gain from attacking Sleaford, and thus far he had sufficient troubles of his own and too much respect for Rannulf to make the effort of overrunning the lands of Soke to get at someone who showed no signs of beginning hostilities.

'No, no,' Catherine comforted quickly and instinctively, 'we are safe, quite safe, but—' She cut that off. There was no sense in alarming the child. Mary might not care for her father, but she would understand that Rannulf's sudden death might leave them in a desperate situation. If Geoffrey could control the vassals all might be well, but they would be absolutely at his mercy. If he could not, their state would be worse. Without the earl's strength to protect them, the two young sons would be targets for assassination and the women, particularly the daughter who had no vassals of her own as Catherine did, prey for the strongest man who could seize her. Even if the vassals were faithful and would protect the boys, a bastard daughter was no concern of theirs.

Mary's line of thought was completely different. She had a new and absorbing passion to which everything else was subsidiary. 'Mary have mercy,' she gasped under her breath, and then, tremblingly, 'Has there been fighting? Has – have any of the men come to harm?' Catherine had forbidden her to speak of André until her father's permission could be obtained, and that was the nearest she dared come to asking about him.

'No fighting – yet. Pray for them. Pray for your father. Pray for them all.'

It was well that Mary should do so, for Catherine knew that she would have little time for that duty and comfort. Mary returned to her spinning wheel and Catherine bent her eyes and her mind on her instructions. Twice more she read the letter, feeling herself more incapable, more frightened with each reading. How was she to do all these things and yet prevent her own men from becoming involved? She rolled the parchment again, very slowly, very deliberately, forcing steadi-

184

ness on her fingers as if that could steady her trembling spirit. She tried to think quietly of what was most necessary, most efficient to do first. But her brain would not concentrate on the tasks before her; it only sought the image of Rannulf. Help me, my husband, she called to him across the miles, tell me what to do, what to think.

And Catherine looked across the room to the patch of blue that showed at the stone-framed window, but there was no strength she could draw from the strong stone walls or the clear peaceful sky. Her eyes wandered to her stepdaughter where she sat at her spinning, her lips moving silently in prayer, and Catherine envied Mary her simple fear. If that were all she had to fear, for the physical safety of the man she loved, she too could pray and give thanks. If she could only read the awkwardly written lines and bow her head and obey, it would be so easy. She and Rannulf were not alone, however, and Catherine's slender body trembled under the weight of her responsibility, for upon her lay the burden of Geoffrey and Mary and Richard and the vassals who called her countess and trusted her. Rannulf had said she must care for the children, but to care for the children it might be necessary to betray what Rannulf thought his interests were. Catherine felt torn in two between the needs of the children and the needs of the father.

The panic caught her and shook her as a large dog shakes a captured rat, but Catherine was only small and helpless in the same way a rat is. She could only be pursued so far, then she turned at bay to fight. That point was reached after she had decided she could not bear the burden placed upon her and bent, weeping, over a reply to Rannulf. She had written a full sheet of passionate expostulation, liberally spotted with teardrops; she had even rolled and sealed the missive when she realized there was nowhere to send it. Rannulf might be anywhere in England by now, and a messenger sent to follow his track might be weeks in finding him. Meanwhile, he would have depended upon the business he set her to being completed. There was no help to be had from her husband. Catherine was alone, and alone she must decide what to do.

Push away the terrors of the future. Pretend that there were

185

no larger problems than the strict fulfilment of Rannulf's instructions. Well, then, it was best to do the easiest first. By far the matter of money was easiest. Little was to be had from Rannulf's serfs and nothing from his vassals, who would be called to fight and would need to support themselves and their men through their period of service. Her own serfs could be squeezed and would be, but she dare ask nothing from her vassals either because of her promise. In any event the serfs did not yield much, even when one stripped them bare – but there were others. The town merchants as well as the travelling merchants would pay, and she could easily demand one-third of their goods from the users. That would net a round sum, if she could get to all those in the large towns simultaneously. If they were approached one at a time, one warned the others and they had time to hide their goods and money. So far so good, but to strike them all at once over a far-flung territory needed a large force, and Sleaford itself had only enough men-at-arms within it to defend the keep adequately.

Suddenly Catherine smiled, her fears of inadequacy dropping away as solutions for her problems fell into place. It was very simple. She would call up her vassals to collect the gold for her. They would be glad enough to do it because some of the money would probably find its way into their purses instead of hers, but that was a small price to pay for having them spread all over the territory. Catherine drew a deep breath and bent over her embroidery. She would be obeying her husband's literal word – having told the vassals nothing and yet having them under arms. And she would have accomplished her own purpose equally well at the same time because, although already armed, it would take weeks, not days, to collect them into a force which could be used to aid the king. Perhaps the few weeks' delay would be enough to change the need for them, but if they should be summoned, the delay would certainly give Catherine a chance to invent new causes for delay.

Delay would save her, if anything could save her from coming into conflict with her husband's will, because Catherine had decided long since in her own heart that the vassals of Soke would never fight either for Stephen of Blois or Henry, now Duke of Normandy. No matter which side won, Rannulf would lose, for the Angevin would no doubt want vengeance against those who held out to the last against him, and Stephen's heir had already shown himself to be a monster of ingratitude. If the vassals of Soke remained neutral, however, Henry would have no cause to quarrel with them, and even Eustace would not interfere with them because he knew the value of the protection they afforded against Norfolk. That Rannulf understood this was plain; that he would do his best to keep Catherine's vassals free of the fighting was also plain. Rannulf, however, was honour-bound to bring all his forces to Stephen's aid if ordered to do so, and Catherine knew that if he was pressed to that duty he would, indeed, try to obey the king's command.

A genuine and honourable reason for delay in the vassals' answer to the call to arms would be invaluable, for during the period of delay the problem might resolve itself. If not — Catherine's hand remained poised over her work as a shudder passed through her body, but her mind did not jib as her hand had. If not, she would have to order her vassals to disobey Rannulf's command. He will beat me witless, Catherine thought, but she did not fear that. Her shudder was a response to the thought of Rannulf's emotional reaction to such behaviour. It was a thing to cause the stoutest heart to quail, a thing to wake a loving wife screaming in the night. Could she bear losing her husband for the sake of his children, Catherine wondered. It was unthinkable, and Catherine, who was not given to indulging herself with the imaginary terrors she had created, pushed the thought away. It would never come to that. She would find a way.

The earl of Leicester had smiled too when he read through Soke's letter, but not because it revealed anything amusing about Rannulf's character. Leicester smiled with relief because one of the men he had known so long was acting true to form. Robert of Leicester had too much experience to expect perfect consistency of behaviour from any man, but Stephen's apparent change of character from extreme malleability to extreme determination had thrown many of his plans into disorder and given him an unwelcome and unusual sense of insecurity. Rannulf himself had added to this insecurity by giving evidence of a strange and unnatural levity in the face of remarkably serious circumstances. He, at least, had returned to normal in so far as Leicester could judge from a letter.

There was relief in being able to answer his foster-brother openly and honestly also, for as yet Leicester had nothing to conceal. He had tried hard to turn Stephen from his purpose of making war on the rebels, not because he was anxious to gain any advantage for Henry, but because he wished to spare himself useless expense and the country fruitless agony. To his mind it was inevitable that the Angevin would come to the throne unless God intervened by snatching him out of the world. All Robert of Leicester desired was to keep first himself, then if possible the kingdom, free of a major war until Henry could mount the throne in peace. Leicester gave no consideration to the thought that Eustace could succeed his father. Before the battles of 1149 there had been that possibility, but Eustace's behaviour since that time had fixed an active hatred for him even in the hearts of Stephen's most ardent supporters. Very few of them would feel driven by their honour to back Eustace if they were forced to choose between him and Henry of Anjou.

Leicester had no personal objection to Henry becoming king. He had endured a tyrant and found it distasteful; therefore, he had lent his support to Stephen of Blois. Under that king's reign Leicester had seen the effect of a weak king in anarchy and had found that even more distasteful than tyranny. For many years he had striven to bring the barons together and had seen, too, that they were more likely to combine against too great an encroachment of their liberty than to moderate that too great liberty for themselves. Aye, he thought, smiling at the unrolled scroll before him which displayed the strong, awkward handwriting of a man more used to the sword than the pen, you and I, dear brother, desire the same thing. You, however, had the dreams of a child and, when your dreams were broken, you could not pick up the shattered pieces and build anew because the structure would be cracked and imperfect. Rannulf, Rannulf, I have built churches and I know – a cracked dream is better than none at all.

A low chuckle shook the heavy, stolid body. Leicester was

imagining Rannulf's expression if he heard such poetic language from himself or if he were told that he was no more than a romantic dreamer – Rannulf, who prided himself on his bitter cynicism. Well, it was amusing but such notions brought a man no farther along the path he must walk. Leicester pushed the scroll slightly aside and drew parchment and quill towards him to tell Rannulf the only two pieces of news he had. The first item was scarcely news, merely that there had been no turning Stephen from his purpose, even though the solid opposition of the barons to taking action had restrained him for the few weeks Rannulf had spent in Hereford's keep. The real piece of news was the item that had precipitated the march to the west. Information had come to England that Louis of France had taken Neuf-Marché from Henry's adherents and, more, had instantly yielded it to Eustace for the better furthering of their combined assault on Normandy.

'From this cause,' the pen traced the words slowly while the mind sought a felicitous way to make a point Rannulf would not want to believe, 'the lords took heart, especially Northampton, and they at once acceded to the king's demands. It is their belief that, if Louis could do so much alone, he and Eustace together will conquer rapidly. I beg you to look with greater caution upon this event, remembering that the keep was strong but the master was absent from it. Surely if Henry discounted Louis' prowess, as he might with great justice, this will make him both angry and cautious. Moreover, he will certainly come himself to combat the double force now pitted against him. Bethink you also, my dear Rannulf, how a cart may well move forward better when hitched to a weak and silly ass alone than when a galled, stubborn ox and a silly ass both pull, but at different times and in different ways.'

The note of warning was presented to blind eyes. By the time Leicester's letter reached Rannulf, the latter was deeply absorbed by the promise of a highly successful campaign. Never had he seen Stephen display such energy and decision except in the final few months of the war against Henry in 1149. Beyond that, the information Leicester sent him faded into insignificance, for Stephen greeted Rannulf with open arms and showed him a letter from Eustace praising Rannulf's plan and efficiency. The letter, indeed, breathed so much of the Eustace who had existed before the campaign of 1149 that Rannulf's highest hopes seemed about to be exceeded. Everything was going well. If Rannulf had any cause for dissatisfaction, it was with what he regarded as his own weakness in deviating from his normal policy that the best defence is a good offence. What weakness had afflicted him and caused him to desire peace so ardently he did not understand, but it was past now. He should have known that it was better to destroy enemies than compound with them, no matter how attractive their ideas or their persons.

Rannulf pushed apart the flaps of the tent which was his home on the field and made his way to the king's pavilion. The summonses to his vassals were ready to be sent, lacking only the place and date on which their duty would begin, and that information he needed from Stephen now. The king's guards scarcely glanced at him, for the earl of Soke was one who had access to the king whenever he desired it, but a young man squatting in the shadows leaped to his feet.

'Father!'

With immence reluctance, Rannulf turned towards the voice. Nothing, he told himself, could be wiser than the practice of fostering. Northampton was fond of Geoffrey, but not with the gripping, protective love of the father who had steadied his son's first steps and who still saw in the boyish lineaments the infant that needed protection from everything. For him, the father of the flesh, it was agony even to know surely that his son would be among the fighting forces; how then could he lead him or send him into battle? Northampton cared enough for Geoffrey, having had him in his charge from the time he was eight or nine years old, not to send him into excessive danger, but his heart was not wrung with the memory of infant kisses and infant tears.

'How long have you been in camp? Are you hurt? Are you well?'

'I have just come with a message to Northampton from his eldest son. I am very well, papa. And you?'

'I am never ill,' Rannulf replied, smiling at the indifference in his son's voice. It was not that the boy did not love him, but thus far Geoffrey seemed to believe him invulnerable. Rannulf was very willing to encourage the belief. There was no reason for the child to suffer, fearing for him. 'I am camped yonder,' Rannulf pointed. 'If you have your master's leave, come and spend the night with me.'

The boy nodded and Rannulf smiled, patted his shoulder fondly, and again made to enter the king's tent. Geoffrey plucked at his sleeve; then, incomprehensibly, took his hand and pulled him away into an open field. Whatever protest Rannulf was about to make died at the expression of anxiety on Geoffrey's face. When they were well away, behind the tethered horses, Geoffrey faced his father.

'Papa, may I say something to you that I would say to no other man?'

'You may say anything to me.'

Geoffrey continued to look worried. 'I do not wish to betray my foster brother, but there is something I am sure you should know.'

Now Rannulf looked worried. If Northampton's eldest son was planning or engaged in some mischief, it would be very useful to know of it, but not at the cost of Geoffrey's honour. Right or wrong, a fosterling owed loyalty to his foster family. He might, in an emergency of conflicting interests, give notice and leave them, but he might not betray them. To encourage Geoffrey to tell tales of them might set a dangerous precedent. On the other hand, it was acknowledged that the bond of blood was a tie of even greater importance.

'What you have to say,' Rannulf temporized, 'would it bring danger to the house of Northampton or dishonour?'

Geoffrey thought it over. 'Not danger. It is not of such great moment, being but a straw showing which way the wind blows. Nor can I say that what I have to tell is shameful – honourable it is not.'

Rannulf bit his lip. 'We are one flesh and blood – speak then – but remember that when you speak to me it is as if you were alone. To speak to any other on such a matter—'

'You need not fear me. You know that Northampton has written to his son to gather the vassals and hold them in readiness? Well, I have just come with the reply – that he is presently too sick to obey his father's command. Indeed, when I received the letter from him he was laid upon his bed, but – but, papa, he is not sick.'

'Are you sure?'

'I am no leech, but the day the letter came he was hawking and I with him – I will swear he was not sick then. Nor did he have the heavy eyes, the complexion, or the listless manner of a fevered man or a man in pain when I received his commands.'

'Does Northampton know?'

'That I cannot tell. Certainly I did not speak of it to him, but there was more than one letter in the packet I carried.'

It meant nothing but a few days' or a few weeks' delay. A vague apprehension passed through Rannulf and dissipated almost simultaneously. He shook his head at his son, warned him again to silence, and told him the matter had no significance. That Geoffrey continued to look troubled did not disturb him. Earnest youngsters mistook caution for more serious matters frequently, and Rannulf's more sanguine hopes received confirmation from the good cheer with which he was welcomed by both Stephen and Northampton. The story was told to him again, and Rannulf judged that Northampton took the excuse, if it was an excuse and not the truth, as genuine.

'It is unfortunate,' the old man said, 'but the indisposition is not serious and I am sure he will be ready soon.'

'In a way,' Stephen put it firmly, 'it is not unfortunate at all. Not the illness of your son Simon, but the delay. I wish to clear the small keeps that could distract us by raiding before we attempt Wallingford. For that I have forces enough already under arms and for scorching the earth so that Wallingford can gain no sustenance during this harvest. It will do us more good to have the forces a month from now.'

'And what of my men, my lord?' Rannulf asked.

'As close as possible to the day that Northampton's forces are gathered. There is no need for haste because the news from France is good. I have fair hopes that Louis and my boy will crush the Angevin there. If so, the men who hold by him will yield, having nothing for which to fight. In any case, Henry will not come here, for he cannot afford to lose Normandy.' Both vassals nodded in agreement. Stephen had many faults, but when aroused he had always been capable in military matters. 'As soon as I have cleared the ground,' the king continued, 'we will fall upon them. Warwick's men and the others who are already here will have but a few weeks more to serve. Nonetheless, we will have our full force to fling at them in one or two assaults.'

'Aye,' Rannulf said with satisfaction. 'And even if the assault fails and their term of service is over, we will still have forces enough to besiege them. If they cannot harvest crops and store food, they will not long be able to resist us.'

'You have it. Do not forget also that the little victories which precede the assault of Wallingford will reassure many who are cautious and hold back. With each success they will come to swell the ranks.'

Rannulf scowled. 'It is not well to trust overmuch to such men. True, they come to join the victor, but at the first failure they fade away.'

In reply Stephen smiled, but Rannulf's scowl deepened. These days there was something in the king's smile that he did not like. If Stephen noticed his vassal's uneasiness, he neither commented nor changed his expression. 'Who knows better than I?' he asked. 'I do not think they will have cause to leave me this time, but I do not intend to be at their mercy either. That is why I wish to be very sure that your men, Soke, and yours, Northampton, are the best – the best-equipped, the best-trained, the staunchest-hearted. Your troops will be my hard core and that is why I ask you, Northampton, to wait patiently on your son's well-doing so that he may go himself to each vassal and hand-pick the men. You, Soke, I ask to return to Sleaford and do the same.'

Rannulf was stricken mute with joy. He had come to Oxford greatly against his desire to perform his duty, and his virtue's reward was that he was being sent home for a month. Nearly a month, his conscience corrected, and there will be little time to idle, but behind an expression held rigid by his fear of exposing his happiness his emotions danced and sang. He would take Catherine with him when he went to summon his vassals. They would ride together through the hot summer days and lie together through the sweet summer nights.

'You do not approve of this plan, Soke?' Stephen asked, misunderstanding the cause of Rannulf's silence. He smiled again, and this time the expression was warm and natural. 'You bloody old devil, you do not wish to miss the fighting!'

'No!' Rannulf exclaimed, conscious of a terrible revulsion of feeling.

He did not wish to fight. He was not afraid nor unwilling, but he did not wish to fall upon the small keeps which were defenceless in the face of the army Stephen had mustered. It was true that the lords or castellans of these minor castles had rebel sympathies, true that they had harboured or aided Henry in the revolt of 1149, but for more than two years they had done nothing to offend any man. They had kept the truce. Worse even was the notion of scorching the earth, of killing the serfs who tilled the soil and setting torches to the ungarnered crops. Stephen's military strategy was excellent, and Rannulf should have approved it. Instead, he was shaken by the notion that it was a sin to destroy wantonly what God had caused to spring from the earth, insensate cruelty to kill those creatures who, like the unthinking, obedient beasts, merely performed their natural functions in sowing, tilling, and harvesting.

Nonsense. This time he would not yield to the promptings of weakness or age. 'I mean yes, I do approve it,' he said a little too loudly, and flushed under Stephen's startled eyes.

# Chapter 13

Sir André Fortesque touched his brown destrier again with the spur, and the horse corrected its stagger and forged on ahead. He would not last much longer, however, without some rest. Anxiously, André fixed his eyes on the grey mount of his master just ahead. If only Rannulf's horse would fail, he would stop and rest the beasts. The strain of grey chargers that Rannulf bred in his own stables, vicious animals which could be half-broken at best, was now showing its mettle. While every other mount was moving painfully with hanging head, that devil had strength sufficient to lash out at another horse which came too close.

The destrier stopped, trembling, and André thought he would kill it if he urged it forward again. Yet he could not be left behind. Whatever had happened at Sleaford keep which necessitated this mad race northward, he had to know. The life of the horse was unimportant, although it was the only thing of value that he owned aside from his arms and armour. What was important was that if the beast gave out he could never make Sleaford on foot. His heart was in Sleaford; the only two people in the whole world that wanted him and needed him were there, and if danger were there, he must be there too.

'My lord,' he called desperately as his horse staggered a step forward and stopped again.

Rannulf pulled up his reins and turned his head. 'What?'

André dismounted, nearly falling in the process. They had ridden so long that his legs were numb. 'My lord, we have lost at least a third of the men because their horses could not keep the pace and now my own mount is failing. If you go forward, you will soon go forward alone.'

A single glance proved André to be speaking the truth. The men, too, looked at their master with dumb, pleading eyes.

They could doze in the saddle a little, but it was no way to rest, and the dried meat and grain in their saddlebags were even less satisfactory when snatched at in dry handfuls than when boiled together and eaten as a stew.

'Very well.' Rannulf glanced around and heard the trickle of water in a patch of woodland off to the right. 'This place is as good as another. We can stop for a few hours, at least until it is cooler.'

He moved off into the shade of the trees, dismounted, and signalled one of the men to take his horse to the stream to drink. As he pushed off his helmet and unlaced his mail hood to push that back and allow what breeze there was to cool his head, his eyes fell on André forcing his wineskin into his horse's mouth and trying to make the beast drink. Rannulf walked closer and watched, judging the condition of the animal quickly.

'You would do better to let him rest. In any case, do not trouble yourself. I will furnish you with a better mount if this fails.'

'Thank you, my lord. If he will but take me to Sleaford, I will be content.'

The young man's anxiety was so apparent that Rannulf was pricked by curiosity again. 'And why are you so anxious to reach Sleaford?'

The guilt of an unconfessed desire, of a stolen kiss, crimsoned Fortesque's complexion and made him shift his eyes under Rannulf's steady gaze. Mary was his overlord's daughter and should have been as inviolable as his own sister. Rannulf, watching the telltale discomfort, was rather amused. He had no distrust of the young vassal to whom he was becoming very attached and wondered when André would confess the purpose Catherine had when she sent him with her husband. The time was not yet, but it was coming. He listened to Sir André mumble something about his duty, kept himself from smiling with an effort, and walked away. Then he slaked his thirst at the stream and dropped to the grassy verge that bordered it.

André watched his overlord, cursing himself for a coward. Why had he not spoken? The moment was very opportune because Soke seemed calm, even strangely contented, despite his great haste to be at home. At least he would have cleared his conscience by speaking out, André thought miserably. Yes, cleared his conscience at the risk of being dismissed from his lord's service, and his lord was dear to him, almost as dear as his love. He would not only be separated irrevocably from Mary but reduced again into a pensioner on his brother's generosity.

Not that Giles was ungenerous or would not receive him kindly, but in Giles' keep there was no chance at all for him to lift himself to a state where he could hope to ask for Mary. If he stayed with Soke, particularly in view of the coming war, he might either serve his master so well as to be rewarded with money and advancement, or he might take a valuable prisoner for ransom. André sat down beside his horse, thirsty but reluctant to approach the stream because Soke was there. He wiped the mouthpiece of his wineskin, drank that, and closed his eyes. He might do even greater things – save his lord's life, take a keep by his own efforts. Sweet dreams to dally with, and possible as long as active service was before him.

The moon was misted although the evening was soft and lovely, and it would likely rain on the morrow. Catherine leaned on the battlements looking out across the peaceful fields and wondered if Rannulf would have sense enough to change his clothing if he got wet. She smiled into the night, conscious of her foolishness, but when the equally foolish longing to have him beside her to look also at the moon entered her mind, she did not resist it. Perhaps the war would soon be over and he would be free to return home in peace. She sighed. They had had peace, and they had wasted it in bitter misunderstandings. Catherine sighed again. True, she longed for her husband, but it was just as well that they could not be together again until this war was over. Convinced as she was that her actions were for the best, Catherine was equally convinced that Rannulf would not agree with her and knew that in his presence her conscience would trouble her. What if he asked what she had done or wished to speak to her men himself?

A figure moved, a darker shadow in the darkness of the battlements. Catherine waited peacefully, for no matter how dark or how stealthy-seeming the walk, there was no living soul in Sleaford that wished her harm. 'Yes?' she questioned softly.

'Richard is abed and all the maids also. Is there aught more you would have me do, my lady?'

'No, Mary my love. Get you to your bed also.'

A good girl, Catherine thought, a clever girl, and a glutton for work. She had been permitting Mary to manage the keep almost completely, partly as training for her own future as a wife, partly because Catherine intended to be away for several months inspecting and fortifying the keeps which bordered the earl of Norfolk's land. It seemed the simplest way to fulfil Rannulf's instructions. The training of men, stocking of food-stuffs, and furbishing of gear would all seem natural enough if the countess of Soke were inspecting her property. And, if the countess came alone, even Norfolk would not think that Soke's vassals were making ready to attack. The only thing wrong with the arrangements, Catherine thought still smiling, was that they left her too idle. That was why she tormented herself and longed too much for Rannulf. When she was ready to go and was absorbed in her new labours, she would not suffer these vapours. Catherine looked once more on the misty moon and quiet fields, shook her head, and took herself off to bed.

A touch brought her from the peaceful depths to the border of consciousness, a touch on her lips. It was very pleasant, like a physical manifestation of her dream, the hard masculine mouth on hers, the prick of an unshaven face against her smooth skin. For the span of time that might encompass a deep breath, Catherine gave herself up to the kiss. Then her eyes snapped open in horror, and all at once she wrenched her mouth away, screamed for help, and employed her well-sharpened nails like talons to rake the face and throat of the man bending over her. One scream alone passed her lips before a hand of steel closed over her mouth. Catherine fought in deadly, desperate earnest, writhing her lips back to bite the hand, kicking and clawing, blind and deaf with terror.

'Catherine, for God's sake, do not cry out and struggle so. Your women will think I am murdering you. Catherine!'

The struggles stopped as suddenly as they had begun. Cautiously the muffling hand was withdrawn from her lips.

'Rannulf?'

'Aye,' he laughed softly, 'and may I be damned if I ever try to wake you with a kiss again. In future I shall stand well off before I speak.'

'What are you doing here?' Her eyes strained into the darkness. 'You are not hurt?'

'Not hurt!' he gasped with mock indignation .'I have been mauled about as if I had tried to embrace a she-bear. Next time I come upon you suddenly, I will come fully armed. Do I dare try again?' He bent over her once more.

No cold hand was offered him, no averted eyes, no stiff, formal words of welcome. The arms were warm and around his neck, the eyes closed over tears of joy, and the lips offered as loving and informal a greeting as any man could wish. But not for long; fear followed joy. Catherine unclasped her hands from her husband's neck to run them anxiously over his body, pulled her lips free to question him.

'You are not wounded? Not sick? Oh, Rannulf, light the candles. I will not believe you are whole until I see with my own eyes. Why are you come? What is wrong?'

'Nothing is wrong,' he soothed, still laughing. 'Nothing. I am perfectly well and unhurt. I cannot see how I could have been hurt since I have not yet drawn my sword.'

He struck the flint, nonetheless, breathed upon the sparks which flew into the tinder, and lighted candles from the tiny flame. When he saw how anxiously Catherine was examining him, he laughed again. 'I always used to consider you a very calm woman, Catherine – and a peaceful one also. You are changing all my views at once. Nay, in truth, all is well. I have only come home to call up my vassals.'

Fortunately in her struggles to rid herself of the tangled bed-clothes and sit upright, Catherine's face was shadowed and Rannulf did not see her new expression of terror. Was this all she was to have, the one kiss, before they were locked in a struggle of wills from which their marriage could not emerge unscathed?

'All of them?' she whispered.

He took the breathlessness as a natural result of her physical struggle, the low tone as a mark of intimacy, and his answer was as low as her question as he seated himself beside her on the bed.

'No. Praise God, the king laid no specific commands upon me. Those who have paid in lieu of service, I will not disturb unless I must. It would be no easy thing for me to find the gold to return to them, and I certainly do not wish to pass the debt on to cancel next year's rents at this time. I may well need money next year, and just now there is no pressing need for men.'

Catherine did not need to mask her sigh of relief, only to explain it. 'Then I am glad you are here, Rannulf – so glad.'

He had leaned towards her, but pulled away, frowning at her words. 'Is there trouble here? Do not the servants and the men obey you?'

'May I not be glad for my own sake? Must I regard you only as a curer of ills?'

It was worth the effort, all of it – the crazy ride pressing on day and night, the dead horses and exhausted men. He had saved two days at least, and those two days wrested out of time by his own strength were his to do with as he pleased. Rannulf could have sung and danced, capered like an idiot. He had not mistaken the warmth of Catherine's farewell, nor had she re-assumed her armour of indifference in the months they had been parted. He said nothing, equally afraid he would say too much or too little, and simply took Catherine back into his arms. She was willing, so willing that Rannulf soon detached his lips so that he could get into bed. His breathing was uneven, and he sighed trying to steady it.

'Oh dear,' Catherine said in a distracted tone, fumbling around the bed for her robe, 'You must be so hungry and thirsty. How could I have forgotten?'

'I am, but that can wait,' Rannulf replied, lying down and opening his arms.

'You are too tired to eat.' Catherine's voice was redolent with self-accusation. 'Sleep, my lord, while I go and rouse the maids so that there will be food for you when you wake.'

Rannulf glanced sharply at his wife, wondering if she could mean to put him off. It was ridiculous. She would not have kissed him with her heart on her lips one moment to turn to ice

200

the next. He put a hand on her shoulder and pulled her towards him impatiently.

'Catherine, you are a more reasonable woman than any I have ever known – except Maud, perhaps – but you can also be silly beyond measure. I can wait to sleep also. Just now there is something more important to me.'

'Oh,' Catherine said faintly, 'what is it?' He had heard what she had done and guessed her intentions, she feared, her sense of guilt making her misread perfectly obvious actions.

Rannulf lay for a moment, watching the way Catherine's hair glowed gold and then faded to silver in the flickering candle-light. Guiltily, she turned her face under his gaze, and he was both amused and enchanted, thinking she was suffering a sudden spurt of modesty. Smiling, he pulled her face towards him, a finger under her chin.

'How now, Catherine, we have been man and wife for more than two years. Why do you hide your face from me? Is what I desire repugnant to you?'

Catherine did not answer. Even guilt could not now cloud her realization of what was more important than sleep or food to Rannulf. She blushed rosily, conscious of her stupidity, thereby confirming her husband's opinion that she was embarrassed. Very satisfied, Rannulf laughed softly.

'Must I woo you as if you were maiden-shy?'

Catherine turned into his arms, laughing also. 'You need not, but it can do no harm.'

It was a grey morning, misty with rain as Catherine expected, and both she and her husband slept late. At that, Catherine was the first to wake, conscious of more than normal warmth in the bed and of a sag in the hair-and-feather-stuffed mattresses that tilted her downward. Cautiously she gathered her hair together and pulled it gently from under Rannulf's arm. Then she drew the bed curtain aside to let in some light and lifted her head. The light was of little value, as was her change in position; all she could see was the back of a tangled head of curls, a broad, scarred shoulder, and the swelling biceps of one arm. Drowsily and happily, Catherine lay down again to think about getting up, but the second change in position disturbed Rannulf who, still asleep, moved also, seeking the pressure of her body against his. Seconds later he jerked awake at her mingled giggle and cry of consternation.

'What is the matter, Catherine?'

'Your poor face! Oh, Rannulf, I scratched you unmercifully.'

He smiled and stretched. 'You do not have to tell me. I can feel it. What the castlefolk will say I shudder to think. You have made me a fine laughing-stock before my servants. There is some consolation, however, in knowing that you would not yield tamely to a ravisher.'

'Did you think I would before this?'

'No. Yet you look as if a strong breeze would blow you away. For all of that I have a growing feeling that you yield tamely nothing you do not wish to yield, Catherine.'

They had been speaking lightly, delighting in the warmth and relaxation between them which had outlasted their love-making. Rannulf frowned slightly as he heard and comprehended his own words, however. There had been more truth in them than jest. Catherine, whose guilty conscience flinched, still managed to laugh as she turned away to pull on a robe.

'Then you must have extra pleasure in the knowledge that I yield tamely to you.'

Rannulf put out a hand to detain his wife, frowning harder as he sought for words. 'There is nothing in my life that has given me equal pleasure,' he said awkwardly at last.

Catherine's eyes filled with tears. For Rannulf that was probably equivalent to a passionate declaration of love. 'Thank you, my lord,' she murmured, 'those are the sweetest words you have ever given me.'

'I am no hand at compliments,' Rannulf replied defensively.

He was uneasy, shying away from emotion. Catherine understood and hurried to his aid, smiling mischievously at him. 'Oh, no, not at all. It is a matter of proper understanding. Whenever you do not knock me down, I know you are satisfied, and when you do not call me an idiot, I understand you to be uncommonly pleased with me. And when—'

'Catherine, when have I ever knocked you down! Men punish saucy wives, Catherine.'

'Yes, I remember quite clearly that you told me as much before, when you were last at home. You inflicted a most severe chastisement upon me, but again I found that it was merely a question of how one looked at a thing. Being merely a woman, I was foolish enough to take that punishment also as a compliment. In any case, it gave me no distaste for being saucy.'

Rannulf's bewildered expression indicated plainly enough that he did not remember the incident to which she referred, but Catherine did not intend to explain. She slipped past the screen into the women's quarters where her husband was most unlikely to follow, and almost stumbled over Mary who was restraining Richard. Until he heard voices, the boy had been content to wait quietly until Rannulf woke because he understood that his father had ridden far and was tired. Now, however, he was straining and wriggling in Mary's arms and needed only Catherine's smiling nod to break free of his half-sister's grip. A boyish shriek of joy and a loud, anguished grunt from Rannulf gave evidence of a happy reunion. Listening to the childish voice, shrill with excitement, and the deeper masculine tones quickened by love and pleasure, Catherine could have found it in her heart to pray that life would stop for all of them in this one happy moment.

Neither time nor life does stop upon command, and Catherine wakened to this fact with a shock when she realized she had been waiting some minutes and the women had not brought her water for washing. A sharp question to Mary, a couple of slaps which landed with a more resounding crack than one would have expected from so delicate-seeming a hand and arm, and the maidservants got over their excitement and returned to their duties.

To restore order among the servants was simple, but Catherine received an even greater surprise when she returned to her bedchamber and found Rannulf still abed. For Rannulf to lie abed after the sun was up was unprecedented. Richard was asking and he was answering questions, but ordinarily he would have done so while dressing and then taken the boy with him while he went over the keep to see that all was in order, inspected the men-at-arms who had remained behind, visited the armoury, the smithy, the stables, the kennels, and the mews. It was excellent training for his son, and the men expected it. For the lord of the manor to show disinterest about the smallest detail of castle life was the first spot of a growing rot which destroyed that life completely.

The devotion of the many castle servants to their duty was integral to the smooth functioning of the keep as a self-sufficient community. Since the servants were paid in no way except by occasional gifts and their easier lives and greatly increased social status over the field serfs, and since each position, whether armourer, executioner, or huntsman, was virtually hereditary, a word of praise from the master for work well done or blame and punishment for work ill done was all the incentive available. That, and the great joy of passionate and uninhibited argument with their lord when his opinion and theirs differed about the best way to manage their special sphere. The master by no means won all, or even any, of these arguments.

Rannulf might have the right of life or death over his servants, but by long custom, he had no right to deprive them of their positions. For a sufficiently serious infraction of his trust, he might order a man to be killed or maimed, but since the man's son, or nephew, or cousin, or uncle would then inherit the position, severe or unmerited punishment was a double-edged sword. It was one of the few sure ways to destroy his own influence over his servants and the safety and comfort of his home.

Far worse, however, was any attempt to interfere with the hereditary status of each servant. Many masters were cruel and unreasonable; servants accepted this as the will of God to try them. Usually they still did their work faithfully while they prayed for their master's early demise. After all, if one master was a devil, the next might be a saint, and their sons or their sons' sons would reap the benefit of their patience and forbearance. If the hope of that benefit were taken from them, the fabric of their lives would be torn and all endeavour would be worthless.

Never had Rannulf failed in the minutest fufilment of that duty. He knew each of the men who were the chiefs of the various aspects of castle life since childhood. He knew their wives and their children and which of their sons showed the most promise. He laid his hand to the bellows or the hammer in the smithy; he walked with his farrier when a promising mare was in foal; he selected puppies or held a sick hunting dog on his lap while his kennelman dosed or treated it; he put his shoulder to the uprooting of stumps with his forester and tracked game with his huntsmen.

Most of all, he joyed in the verbal battles with old and faithful servants, descending to the vernacular and to their level of expostulation with grim pleasure, bearing unflinchingly with the language for which he would have killed an equal. Few men in the kingdom, king, duke, or earl – other than his foster brother Leicester – dared call Rannulf a fool, yet his servants informed him trenchantly that he was an unripe gapeseed, a mutton-headed ass, a gaping cod, without fear and without restraint. Rannulf bore all, but not meekly; he returned the compliments in even less-elegant language.

To see Rannulf, then, with his hands behind his head and half-closed eyes while he replied to Richard's questions was a shock to Catherine. Skilfully ridding herself of the boy by sending him on a short errand, she attempted to renew her examination of her husband for wounds or illness. He defended himself with laughter, protesting that nothing but old age and indolence ailed him. At last, seeing that Catherine was really troubled, Rannulf admitted how he had hurried to be at home, thereby saving himself the time for this lazy pleasure.

'You wish to be rid of me,' he complained. 'You wish to make the bed and attend to your women's duties without the burden of a lazy husband to mar your efficiency. Therefore you would drive me out to labour at dawn.'

'Dawn!' Catherine protested. 'It is nigh time for dinner, and you are lying abed like a slug. Your poor men have been indeed labouring since dawn, and some of them all night from what I hear, cleaning and making all ready for your eyes. Do have mercy on them, Rannulf. The past two years they have had far too much of woman's governance. Get up now, my lord, do. It would be too unkind to deny your servants altogether, but I am very glad you have some time to spend on pleasure. I, too, have naught to do.'

She explained about leaving more and more of the work of the keep in Mary's hands and added, 'She is a very good girl,

Rannulf, hard-working, obedient, and of a sweet temper. She deserves well of you.'

'I suppose so, but if her temper is sweet, she has caught it from you. Certainly it came not from her mother nor from me.'

Catherine refrained from pointing out that Mary's mother had reason enough to be short of temper, merely thanking Rannulf for his compliment and bringing his clothing to the bed. She called past the screen for water for washing and, after watching her husband scrub himself in silence, decided to try his mellow mood a little further.

'She is fifteen, Rannulf.'

'Who?'

'Mary.'

'Oh, yes,' he said indifferently.

'It is time she was married.'

'There is time enough for that. She cannot be unhappy here with you, she is useful to you, and, in all truth, I have nothing to spare for her just now, neither land nor gold.'

Catherine knew that to be true and resented it. Everything seemed to be swallowed up by the fruitless, senseless war. She knew she should have been satisfied with the knowledge that Rannulf intended to dower his daughter, but the very fact that he had reminded her that all his resources were presently committed to war increased her sense of urgency. If anything happened to Rannulf, Mary's position would be desperate. Doubtless Rannulf had lands and possessions given him or won in war that were not entailed upon his eldest son. Most of these, of course, would go to enrich Richard's portion, adding to Adelecia's dower, which belonged to her son. Nonetheless, Rannulf could, if he chose, give some part of the free property as a gift to his daughter who, being illegitimate, had nothing by right. If he died before disposing otherwise of his property, it would all, except for Adelecia's dower, go to Geoffrey. Catherine did not really know Geoffrey. Perhaps he would wish to be generous to his half-sister, but once the property passed into his hands, custom would bind him to pass it on to his own heirs. He might find money to give her, but certainly if the war continued there would be little left for him to find.

'It cannot be done at once, I know,' Catherine persisted,

'but you could promise something definite, and if you have no particular man in mind for her—'

'I have more to consider than a silly girl's marriage,' Rannulf snapped irritably, aware that he had really opened his mouth to agree to anything Catherine suggested. Momentarily he was frightened by her power over him, but as he realized he had resisted it successfully, he regained confidence. 'Do you think of nothing but the children?' he asked. 'I have wrested two short days from a hard duty. Is it wrong to wish to give myself to pleasure without thought for two days?'

'Of course not, Rannulf.' Catherine crossed to where he was moodily looking out a window. How cruel she was to him. He was so duty-bound that it was a sin to spoil his brief pleasure.

'Look,' Rannulf said suddenly, pushing away his fear, 'the sky is clearing. What say you, my lady, can you spare the afternoon to come hawking with me? Shall we ride away from our duty and our labour to indulge ourselves in guilty pleasure?'

Catherine giggled partly at the notion of so innocent an amusement being called a guilty pleasure and partly with the sudden realization that Rannulf would not know a guilty pleasure if one bit him. Not that he had not tried them all. Catherine herself had never seen her husband more than slightly heated with wine, but there were tales of past carouses. He gambled, yes, and took some pleasure in it; only the vice had so little hold upon him that there could be no guilt involved. Nor had Catherine forgotten the women. There, if you wished, was guilt, but pleasure? That was the meat of the matter. Rannulf was so made that when he felt guilt, he could feel no pleasure. Even sadder, Catherine thought, glancing quickly at him, he had not called hawking a guilty pleasure entirely in jest. Any amusement indulged in merely for pleasure gave Rannulf a sense of guilt.

'Oh, yes,' Catherine sighed, sliding her arm around Rannulf's waist, 'let us go and be guilty together.' Without turning to look at her, as if he were afraid to acknowledge to himself what he was doing, Rannulf pulled Catherine still closer and, after a short, silent pause, pressed his lips to her hair. 'Rannulf,' Catherine added urgently, 'do you have only the two days? Is there no way to stretch the time?'

Again the twinge of fear that he would yield and stay. 'I dare not,' Rannulf said. 'I have sent the summons out, but I am commanded to hand-pick the men who follow my vassals and, in truth, I believe much will depend upon their quality. If you wish,' he continued as if the idea were new to him, 'we may stretch the time of being together. You may travel with me to my vassals' keeps.' He had planned to take her, but that she should come by her own desire was sweeter yet.

A fool only, Catherine thought, walks wide-eyed into the maw of danger. Every hour in her husband's company carried the threat of the exposure of her plans and the clash of wills to follow. On the other hand, he had never been so soft to her. Perhaps now if she pleaded with him to withdraw from the king's war he would listen. Catherine snuggled closer to the hard body beside her as if she would seek shelter within it.

'Thank you, Rannulf. I do desire to come.'

She had thanked him for what he would have demanded of her. Rannulf understood at last the strange juxtaposition of the ideas in the 23rd Psalm – Yea, though I walk through the valley of the shadow of death, Thou anointest my head with oil; my cup runneth over.

The rod and the staff, however, were not missing. Sometimes subtly, sometimes directly, but always mixed with an outpouring of love that disarmed Rannulf completely, Catherine pleaded expediency. In terms of her own fears, she pointed out how naked his lands would be when he had stripped them of their best fighters. She told him of her recurring nightmare, in which his vassals turned on him to be free of the unceasing, hopeless war, and murdered Richard and Geoffrey so that there would be no heirs of his name to take revenge. She clung and she kissed and she wept.

Rannulf soothed her. He explained how the victories in France were healing Eustace's bitterness; how the rebels were shaken by those victories; how Stephen might at last be king of a peaceful realm. And each time he voiced these convictions, the optimism he had felt faded. Leicester's warnings, dismissed previously, burned in his brain, and Catherine's nightmare took such hold upon him that he scarcely dared close his eyes at night.

Never had Rannulf suffered such torment. He had often been bitterly unhappy in his personal life. Now, lapped in love, dazed – glutted – with emotional satisfaction, he found the scaffolding of his life collapsing. The music of Catherine's voice was no happy contrast to the clamour of war he would soon hear. The rich green fields were no invitation to make desolation elsewhere. And nights of love do not well prepare a man to go and look upon death.

# Chapter 14

Like a carved figure of obsidian touched with silver, the horseman sat in the moonlight. Before him, dropping away from the crest of the low hill, stretched the once-fertile fields around Wallingford. Even the night could not hide their ravishment. Nothing. Empty. There was a darker shadow which might be a single mud wall of a serf's hut still standing. Here, closer, was a tree, gnarled, stark, obscene without leaves in the late summer, writhing as if it still felt the fire that had stripped it.

A faint shudder disturbed the stillness of the horseman, and the moonlight flickered, a pale, cold flame without warmth or comfort, on the polished helmet. Another fitful gleam, light without light, showed faintly as a metal-sewn gauntlet moved the reins. The horse, dull-shining now in movement, went down towards that scorched nothingness, and behind, out of the shadows, came other horsemen whose accoutrements shone palely and faded. The silence was broken, but not by the voices of men. No command for silence had been given, for there was no danger in the empty fields for these horsemen, but their leader's burden lay upon them and they were weary.

For some time the dull thud of hooves unmuffled by any green blade on that blackened earth made a monotonous music. Then, across the emptiness, hanging threateningly above it, rose the black towers of Wallingford keep, and on the near side of the river before it the men could see the campfires of the besiegers – red eyes that gazed hungrily at the great stone walls. Each man saw something different in those fires. To most they were the cheerful heralds of comfort, telling of food and drink and sleep. To André Fortesque they were leaping beacons of hope. To Rannulf they were the final touch to a nightmare, the fires of hell glowing red in a burnt and desolate land.

A quicker beat; a galloping messenger came towards them.

Although they could not see the raised hand of their leader, the troop pulled to a halt.

'Who rides by night?'

The moonlight gleamed on a horn raised to blast a warning.

'Rannulf, earl of Soke.' He rode forward alone, pushing back his helm and unlacing his mail hood. 'Do you know me?'

'Aye, my lord.' It was one of Stephen's squires, and the horn was lowered. 'You have been looked for, and I rode out to take you to your place in the camp.'

Within the ring of fires, the squire led them to an empty area not far from the king's own pavilion. Rannulf dismounted, silent still. There was no need to give orders, for his men were well-picked, experienced soldiers. He need only wait, and his little village of tents and fires would spring up within the camp city. Fortesque's voice came clear, giving orders to the household guard, who would be placed closest to Rannulf's tent. John of Northampton was giving orders too, interlarded with a good kick to a slow-moving servant now and again. In a little while, Rannulf knew he could disarm and his cot would be ready.

Rannulf's armour was gone, the night was mild, and a soft woollen coverlet shielded him from the damp. Still his body was no lighter, and even heavy winter furs could not have warmed his inner cold. Softly, softer than a sighing breath, Rannulf groaned. Who would believe that the love of a good woman could bring such pain? Her fear and helplessness unsettled his very soul. And even here, there was room for doubt. Fear or rebel sympathy? Which drove Catherine to infect him with doubt? It was as if she instilled poison with her kisses. He could not doubt her love for him, but he had not slept through any night except the first that he had spent at home. He dreamed ever of a peaceful land and the love that was his to take and have at will, and he woke ever with an oppression of guilt as if such dreams were treason.

This was the price of his honour, this restless wrestling with endless doubt. Eyelids swollen and polished by sleeplessness lifted slowly and fell. There was the dawn The Lord was merciful even to weak sinners, for in this coming day the planning and fighting would begin and he would have such burdens

211

to occupy his mind and tire his body that he would dream no more of peace. He would sleep as a man slept after the labour of war.

'My lord.'

Rannulf pulled his shoulder from the hand that shook it and groaned.

'My lord, it is full morning and the king desires your presence.'

Unwillingly, heavy lids were opened. It was true enough; the sun was blazing through the drawn tent flaps. Squinting against the light and trying to move slowly so as to ease his aching head, Rannulf levered himself upright.

'Wine,' he croaked, and a goblet was thrust into his hand already filled.

John was learning that if his lord was not up and stirring before dawn these days, he needed an eye-opener to get him started. Soke looked awful, with swollen, red-rimmed eyes, crevices etched into his drawn cheeks, and his grim mouth so set that the lips had disappeared into an invisible line. Nonetheless, once he had donned his armour, he became less sluggish, and his stride was steady and determined when he entered the king's quarters.

'You are late in coming to us, Soke,' Stephen said.

'I am two days before my promised time. How am I late?'

'I mean this morning. Did you wish to avoid the council?'

'I knew not one was to be held. I came late in the night and had words with none. Then I slept late in the morning. Why should I wish to avoid council? What goes forward?'

'The taking of Wallingford. What think you of our labours thus far? You have ridden over the land. Are we ready to move on the keep?'

What Rannulf thought had better be kept to himself. He shrugged his shoulders and moved towards an empty stool. Sharply Stephen repeated his question.

'If you wish to know, I think that when you take Wallingford, you too will starve – so well have your labours been performed. And, if you are not ready to take the keep now, you will never be ready. There is nothing here except the keep left to destroy.'

'You approved this plan a month since. Now you return, having had none of the labour, to cavil at its outcome.'

Rannulf's eyes narrowed. 'You sent me hence and told me what day to return. You asked my opinion, and I have given it. These are not my lands. If you are content with what is done, then I must also be content. What is done cannot now be mended by talk in any case. Let us plan forward, not look back. Is this a council or a wake?'

'You are, as I said, late,' Stephen snapped. 'For your part, how would you go about taking Wallingford?'

An aching head and heart do not make for patience and soft answers in a man of hasty temper. 'If I must do your thinking as well as your fighting, I am in bad case,' Rannulf snarled in reply.

'Soke!' Northampton protested.

Stephen laughed, Rannulf's exasperation seeming to have restored his good humour. 'I once said that if Rannulf said a respectful word to any man, I should call my best physician to attend him. I am glad to know you to be in good health, Soke, but I still desire that you answer my question.'

'There are only two ways to take Wallingford, across the bridge over the Thames or by mustering an army from the west. Or, of course, by crossing the river above or below the keep in boats to attack from the west.'

'And which of these methods would you employ?'

'What, am I a child being tested in tactics? Oh, very well,' Rannulf sighed, as though humouring an idiot, 'all, if I had men and time. I have not seen the western side of the keep, and I cannot say whether there is any hope of scaling the walls, but to try would be to draw some defenders from the bridge – and the bridge must be taken.'

'Then we are all agreed,' Stephen said approvingly, 'for your judgment falls in with ours. Warwick tells us there is little hope of taking the keep from the west. He has been encamped there.'

Rannulf's tired eyes moved to the older man who nodded, adding, 'We have made some small sorties to give them something to think about, but I believe it hopeless. Truly, I think any assault is hopeless. We will have to starve them out. But while they hold the bridge, we cannot keep them from the river, and while they have the river, supplies may be readily brought in.'

'The use of boats is also hopeless,' Northampton put in. 'The waters are too low for large ships, too swift for smaller crafts to cross without much drifting and the banks are well defended. We could not muster sufficient force in boats to do aught but die.'

'Yet we will try that path also,' Stephen said. 'We have gathered boats for the purpose up and down the river.'

Rannulf shuddered. He could swim and enjoyed doing so in the quiet pools of the Slea, but the Thames at this point was a swift and angry river, beginning to swell already with the late summer rains. For a man in armour there was nothing but a certain watery death if he should be tipped from the boat, a helpless death in which he could not save himself nor deal a blow for his own protection and revenge. The banks, too, from the quick glance he had given them, were steep and unfriendly, a trap for a heavily armed man. Perhaps there had been a ford here once, but either the river itself had scoured a deeper bed or the defenders of the keep and town had dug out the banks after the bridge was built.

'You do not like that path to Wallingford, I see,' Stephen continued with a faint note of contempt. 'Very well, you will not be asked to take it.'

Colour surged into Rannulf's face. 'I did not say I would not take that path. True, my men have come to fight, not to drown, but yours is the ordering of the battle. If it is your will that good, mounted, and mailed knights be cast helpless into the water and, even if they reach the bank, need to fight afoot under the weight of their armour – order, and it shall be done.'

Stephen frowned and looked anxiously into his liege man's face, then slid his eyes away as if he were ashamed of something. 'Nay, the least of the footmen with leather jerkins silvered over to look like mail will be sent by that path. If they are cast over, they will have a chance to swim, and if they come to the bank in safety, they will be light enough to fight.' His glance returned to Rannulf, anxious, even pleading, torn with uncertainty. 'Thus are the men disposed, Rannulf. Warwick holds the west, de Tracy the south – that is entirely hopeless but we have set his small force there to see that none escape over the walls to call for succour or to bring in food. Peverel sits upon the north, many men but with little heart. Something has broken the faith of Peverel's men in their leader. They will hold the land, but not much more can be hoped from them. Northampton and I lie here before the bridge with those few men sent by Essex and Ferrers, and now you have come. A man does best what he does willingly. What part would you play in this game?'

The flush had already faded from Rannulf's face. He had been pale when he entered the tent, and no man could see whether he became paler. His eyes closed, possibly to hide some expression, but equally possibly because he could hold the swollen lids open no longer. In the tent, in spite of the distant sounds of the army of men going about their business, it was so quiet that Stephen's great vassals could hear each other breathe. The silence stretched until every man there longed to break it with a scream.

There were several paths Rannulf could take, all honourable. He could cast the responsibility of decision back where it belonged by telling Stephen again to command him. He could ask a day or two of grace to survey the field of battle so that he might choose where his men would be employed to their best advantage. He could say that he and his men would follow Stephen wherever he led them.

' I suppose,' he said at last, very slowly, 'that it must be my part to take the bridge.'

The tension relaxed as if a rope had been cut with an axe blow. Warwick nodded approval, Northampton sighed and shifted uneasily on his stool, and Stephen dropped his head into his hands.

'You have had heavy labour here already,' Rannulf continued, 'while my men are fresh, and—'

'Have you seen the bridge?' Stephen cried as if the words were wrung out of him.

'Barely,' Rannulf replied, 'but it would make no difference

215

if it were the gate to hell. Cross it we must and hold it we must. Either that or take up our tents and crawl back to our keeps.'

'There are towers and gates on the Wallingford side. All the span is within bowshot of those defences and it is scarce wide enough for four horsemen abreast.'

There was no change that anyone could see in Rannulf's expression. 'When has a bridge been otherwise?' he asked calmly.

'The gates open outward,' Stephen continued in an agonized voice, not knowing himself whether he wished Rannulf to reconsider his decision or whether he intended to fix his vassal's purpose by making him ashamed to go back on his word. 'If you tried to batter them down, the defenders need only open them suddenly to sweep you all into the river.'

'That, too, I expected,' Rannulf answered evenly. Then, suddenly, he smiled. 'You need not fear for me, I will look close.'

Equally suddenly Stephen dropped his head into his hands and began to sob. 'I should never have broken the peace. I should never have begun this madness.'

'We will give you all the aid we can,' Warwick said firmly, paying not the slightest attention to the king's outburst. 'Some hours before you ride out, I will throw every man I have into an assault on the wall. De Tracy will second me with whatever force he has, and Peverel's men will at least make a sufficient show so that they will not dare leave that quarter undefended either. To the best of our ability, we will continue until dark or until we have some sign that you have succeeded.' He did not need to add – or failed. Every man understood what was left unsaid.

'For my part,' Northampton added, 'I will make sure that the boats keep moving, filled with footmen. You must not expect much from them, they are largely rabble, but each boat-load will have at least one steady man-at-arms who will try to rally them and drive them against the towers and against the defences of the banks and the road that leads from the keep to the bridge. Thus, some of the tower archers will need to look behind them and not be free to let loose at you. Also, not knowing what force we intend to send across and believing, I hope, that better men will follow the weaker, they will not dare strip

216

defenders from the road or banks to swell the forces in the tower or behind the gates.'

Rannulf nodded his thanks to both. 'So I hoped. Is there aught to wait for?'

An uneasy, unhappy frown crossed Northampton's face. 'Not unless you wish to wait for Simon, my son. Most of the men have arrived and he, himself, should have been here a week since with the rest. I do know what delays him now, but I can send to him again urging haste.'

'There is no need,' Rannulf replied, swallowing a queasy sensation. 'We do not lack for men – at least, not to make this assault. When it is over,' he added heavily, 'then you may indeed need to send for him.' He paused, thinking of the coming losses, then continued briskly, 'Very well, if you can be ready in time, Warwick, I cannot see that any day will be better than the morrow. What say you?'

Warwick nodded and rose. 'I will ride at once. It is many miles to a safe ford and many more through back paths to my camp. Thank God, however, hearing is easier than going or seeing. At the dawn, I will let blow the trumpets for the assault as also will de Tracy and Peverel. You will hear us. If aught fails, do you reply with the sound for retreat. If all is well, keep silence until you need to urge your own men forward.'

'Good enough.'

'Wait.' Stephen had wiped his face and looked up. 'Where is the need for such haste? Let your men rest a few days, Rannulf, and do you take some rest yourself. You do not look well.'

Impatiently, Rannulf shook his head. 'The need for haste is in the scorched fields. Men do not gain stomach for fighting by camping in a desolation nor by eating camp rations. Also, they will hear, somehow, what is before them. It is not well to let them sit still and consider overlong on such a subject. They have come to fight and know it. They are hot for it now. It is unwise to let the blood cool.'

By nightfall, although he knew he was facing almost certain death, Rannulf felt much better. For one thing, even death was better than doubt. He did not wish to die, but if he must, it was good to die sword in hand. Somewhere John of Northampton had found a chicken and had it broiled over the coals for his master. Rannulf sat on a camp stool tearing at it hungrily, happily, his mind busy with what he had discovered about the bridge and what he would tell his men.

There were certain hopeful aspects about the construction. The side walls were unusually high so that it would be possible to make a shield wall for men to crawl under to the very edge of the towers. While the defenders were occupied with attackers in the middle of the bridge, some men might find a way with metal pins and leather ropes to climb around the towers and come behind the gates. Also, the arches of the bridge were braced above the waterline with crossbars. If men could be set on those crossbars, especially on the down-river side, they might use grappling hooks to rescue from the water such knights as were thrown over.

One other path to the far shore had come to light in Rannulf's careful inspection. The bridge was low to the water, but not so low, the river not being at flood, that some men lying down in boats might not pass under it in safety almost to the foot of the towers. Then, if the ropes and pins of the climbers held, those in the boats might be drawn up to lie hidden right against the base of the towers, where they might well be invisible to the defenders. Possibly, by fixing stakes and ropes to the towers themselves or to the banks shielded by them, a considerable force might be assembled hanging in the water to burst out suddenly and open the gates. Certainly the task was not hopeless. It would cost many lives, but it could be done.

'Now what, at such an hour, do you find to smile about, Soke?'

Rannulf looked up into Northampton's worried face. 'If a man sees a path to victory, even an uncertain and dangerous path, is that not reason enough to smile?'

The old man rubbed his gnarled, aching hands together, and John ran in to give him a stool to sit on and kiss him in greeting. Northampton stroked his son's cheek and patted his shoulder, and Rannulf stood up suddenly, his throat constricted with grief and remorse. He had forgotten that his squire was as like to die as he was. John's father had come to bid his son farewell.

'I will go out and stretch my legs,' he said huskily.

'No, Rannulf, I have come to speak to you. What I have to say to John can be briefly said, and they are words that all men may hear. Bear yourself like a man, my son.'

'I will not fail you, father, nor my lord either.'

'No, I do not think you will. Go, child, my talk with Soke concerns no one but himself.' Northampton passed a hand over his face, and Rannulf waited his convenience with averted eyes. He would have no more to say to Geoffrey, but he would not care to have any man see him after he had spoken. 'I think Stephen is mad,' the old man muttered wearily after a moment.

Respecting the anguish which had called forth the words, Rannulf held his peace. Actually, he did not agree, even though he had little expectation of enjoying the victory he hoped his men would win. It was better to die thus than to live tearing at your own gut or, like Northampton, so crippled that you needed to watch your sons go out to fight when you could not go yourself.

As if he had read Rannulf's mind, Northampton shook his head. 'No, not for trying to take Wallingford. There is sense enough in this action, but— Perhaps I do great wrong to speak to you of this now. Indeed, I have thought about it most of the day and my mind is still not clear. Nonetheless, we have known each other long, Rannulf, and fostered each other's sons. Do you know – did you realize that Stephen intended from the first to prod you into taking this desperate work in hand?'

'I suppose I knew – yes. Why he should think he needed to prod me into it, I cannot tell. Mayhap the poison Eustace instilled into his ears regarding me has seeped at last into his brain. It makes no difference. I was fittest for the task, and it must be done.'

'It is not you alone. He looks askance at us all from time to time and no longer really trusts any man. Then he repents and flutters like a leaf in the wind again. That is why I said I think he is mad. He has spent this day first crying out that you offered to take the bridge only with intent to fail and then he weeps aloud for fear you will be lost to us.'

'I cannot see that he is much changed from what he was,' Rannulf shrugged, 'except for his suspicion. So long as he does not permit his madness to interfere with his military action, it is of no account. I think he is still unsettled by Maud's death.' He sighed. 'We could use her steadying hand just now.'

'Well, you have been warned, although I do not know to what purpose. Even if he shows himself to be mad as a hornet – what can we do? I came to speak of another matter also. Where will you place yourself tomorrow?'

Rannulf looked surprised and offended. 'At the head of my men. What sort of a question is that? What would you have me do, shout for them to charge while I remain safe behind their wall of shields?'

'No, I thought you would lead them. It has ever been your way. Therefore must I come to my next question. What would you have me do with Geoffrey?'

Geoffrey?' Now, even in the dim firelight, Northampton could see that Rannulf had gone white. 'That is a cruel question, Simon, heartless even in the light of the pain you bear. Shall I make my son less than a man by bidding you hide him in safety, or shall I bid you send him where the fighting is fiercest to prove his valour and take his death?'

'Rannulf, control yourself. I know the purpose of fostering as well as you do.' The old man shook his head reprovingly. 'That is not what I meant, as you would understand quickly enough if you allowed your head to work instead of your bowels. This day I have kept him so busied that he had no time to seek you out nor question what your part in the assault would be. What I wish to know is whether I should send him elsewhere tomorrow – not to protect him, my forces will not be engaged unless you are successful and we can move forward over the bridge. But if he remains here, I cannot keep him from seeing what takes place.'

The question had been cleverly phrased, but Rannulf understood what Northampton was really asking. Did he or did he not want Geoffrey to watch him die? He started to tell Northampton to send the boy away, then checked himself, for there were other matters to consider than his desire to protect his son from such an experience. The likelihood that Geoffrey would actually see the strokes or the arrow that felled him would be small, and from that point of view it would be little worse than hearing of his death and suspecting that he had been sent away to spare his witnessing it. More important was the danger that Geoffrey would be so grieved that he would throw his own life away seeking revenge. That, however, Northampton should be able to prevent and might be true whether or not he saw the battle.

'Let him stay,' Rannulf said at last. 'It will be well for him to be here to rally the vassals – if any remain to be rallied.' He paused to steady his voice and continued, 'I cannot believe that Stephen, mad or not, has become such a monster that he would send a child to be slaughtered. Yet, if that be the case and my men are beaten back, it will be Geoffrey's duty to try to finish what I could not.' Rannulf bit his lip. 'Oh, God, until this moment I have not feared my death in this venture.'

'You need not fear it for that reason. Stephen will be more like to call you back than to send Geoffrey forth. In any case, I am not mad and I am still Geoffrey's master. If the boy can lead your vassals in such a way as will profit him, well and good. The sooner they learn to respect him the better. He will lead no lost causes at any man's bidding, even at the king's, while under vow to serve me. Content yourself. Well, I have said my say. If there is time on the morrow, send John to me that I may bless him.' The old man stood up, looking past Rannulf into the darkness. 'What joy it is to be a father in these times! If your son does not turn against you, looking sidelong towards your enemy, then you must send him forth to die without knowing whether the cause be worthwhile.'

Rannulf stood, too, grieved for Northampton, but so relieved by the knowledge that Geoffrey would be safe that he could not truly offer sympathy or even comprehend the implications of what had been said to him. When the torch which lighted his visitor back to his own quarters grew faint, Rannulf moved eagerly to the smaller tent to his right.

'André, summon my vassals, and do you come also. To-morrow there will be more to our labour than to charge straight ahead and bear down those who oppose us. We will have need of much planning if even a tithe of us are to escape with our lives.'

André leaped to obey with alacrity. Nothing could please

him better than a bitter battle in which he might win his lord's favour. No hopeless battle either, as rumour had predicted, or the earl would scarcely look so well pleased. Lord Soke might say grave words, might look heavy-eyed still, but he now had a spring to his step and an eager note to his harsh voice. There would be much blood spilled, but there must be good hope of victory.

# Chapter 15

No sun affronted sleepy eyes when John of Northampton presented his lord with a brimming goblet in the dawning of the day. Rannulf drank, but this morning only to warm himself, for a grey mist hung over the field, damping the clothes laid ready and chilling the body. He was rested and at peace; all that needed doing was done. Each of his vassals and each band of foot soldiers knew what part he had to play and, though each understood how high the bridge would cost in blood and life, each seemed to be imbued with Rannulf's conviction that it could and would be taken.

From Geoffrey, whom he had awakened in the night, he had received a promise that Richard would be cared for and Catherine protected until she decided what she wished to do with her life. Rannulf had been sorry to waken the fear he saw in his son's eyes, but it was well to prepare him and, if by any chance his life were spared, it would merely deepen Geoffrey's conviction of his invulnerability. His last visit had been to a priest. It had been long since Rannulf had confessed himself, and he was surprised at the lightening of his heart when he had at last, after much prompting, poured out not only the sins he recognized as sins but the doubts and fears that tormented him. For those too, he had been absolved, and he had returned to his bed to sleep very peacefully until John touched him.

Now he looked out on the shrouded figures of his men with mingled satisfaction and mild regret. For his military purposes, the weather was ideal – he had counted on some mist, of course, but was being blessed with an unexpected density. There were minor drawbacks – boats would doubtless go astray, men slip in the greasy wet, and anyone who needed to use his eyes at a distance, like the fishers on the crossbars of the bridge, would be hampered. Still, the fog – if it continued as thick as it was

223

at the moment – would hinder the defenders far more than the attackers. The archers of the towers in particular would be virtually blinded and their accuracy reduced almost to nothing. The trouble was, Rannulf thought, looking up into grey nothingness and smiling at his own foolishness, that he had wished to bid the sun farewell.

Very vaguely, muffled by the mist, came the sound of horns. Again they called, more loudly, from the left, and after a while even more faintly than the first calls, the signal for attack came from the right. Warwick had been as good as his word, and Rannulf smiled his grim satisfaction. The original plan had been to wait until some of the defenders were drawn from the bridge to other parts of the walls. The trouble was that the men of Wallingford knew the value of the bridge as well as their attackers. They might not fall into the snare and – worse – the heavy fog might thin. Rannulf smiled more broadly. They would not wait; they would attack now.

John nudged Sir André who stood beside him. 'This will be a bloody battle.'

'So I learned at the council last night. Were you listening in secret? I thought you had duties elsewhere.'

'I do not need to listen, I know my master. Look you how his lordship smiles. I have fought with him before and seen that smile before. He has forgotten even what he fights for. What he desires now is blood and killing. Pray God the bridge does not fall too quickly. If he is not sated, he will lead us on to assault the keep itself.'

Rannulf turned towards them, and it was plain he had not heard their talk although they were close behind him. He was deaf and blind to everything besides his own feeling of release. He could strike out now – not at Catherine who was blameless of his pain even if her sympathies were rebel – but at enemies who had been thrust upon him so that he could not be said to have sought the battle. When Adelecia had been his wife, he could not have fighting enough, and now, again, the blood raced through his body and pounded in his ears.

'André, bid the heralds summon the men to attack. I do not wish to lose this mist. Bring my horse when you return.'

John was right, André thought as he set off on his errand.

His master's eyes, normally quiet and considering although keen, held leaping points of light that cried aloud of the fever in the brain. Well, the bloodier the better. The fewer men who remained, the greater his importance to his lord would be.

'John,' Rannulf continued gaily, 'do not let your hot blood tempt you forward. You are to cling at all costs behind my left shoulder. This is no battle in which a wall of vassals will be behind me, for we will fight in narrow space, man upon man, with enemies behind as well as before. Be faithful, for if I believe you there, I will not guard myself. Do not fail me out of eagerness.'

'If I can keep pace with you, my lord. Do not outrun me.'

Rannulf laughed. 'Outride you, I might. Outrun you, I will not, for nigh on twenty years and some little girth burden my legs. Back to back then, John. It will not be the first time.'

'Nor the last either, my lord.'

Rannulf looked up into the swirling mist and drew a deep, happy breath. 'Mayhap not, after all. Nonetheless, John, I charge you, as you love me, if I fall do not try to revenge me. Win free and go to Geoffrey. He will have great need of you.'

A puzzled frown wrinkled the squire's brow. 'Of course, I would do that in any case, but will he not be – aie!' John barely leaped aside in time as the newly arrived stallion lashed out. 'The devil take your horses, my lord. How many times have I given him favours from my own plate, and thus he greets me.'

The mist was thicker and thicker as they rode towards the river, until man followed man by dim shadows and muffled sound alone. Somewhere to the right there were men's voices, the grating sound of wood drawn over stone, and fitful splashes as boats were launched. Northampton was at work. Rannulf shook his head. Fog was most welcome, but this was a trifle too much of a good thing. If any of those boats reached the opposite shore anywhere within striking distance of Wallingford, it would be a miracle. Even for his own purposes, the mist was too dense. If he did not know that John rode to his left hand and André to his right, he could not have recognized them. Perhaps it would be well to wait a time after all. Just now a man could not tell friend from foe and was as likely to launch a blow at a comrade-in-arms as at an enemy.

Behind him, a light laugh from one of the younger vassals drew Rannulf's ear. 'No doubt,' the youthful voice said in reply to some question, 'the Lord God favours our cause. This mist will destroy every arbalest they have better than fire or sword. Nonetheless, we are like to need to crawl on our hands and knees to find that accursed bridge.'

No, Rannulf decided, they would not wait. From this and other remarks it was plain that the men's spirits were as high as his own. Better to chance an odd blow going astray here or there, a man falling into the river, than to permit the enthusiasm to falter. If it were as thick on the other side as here and they made no sound, they could walk right up to the gates and knock on them before they were seen. Knock on them!

'John,' Rannulf called.

'My lord?'

'Ride back to your father – try not to fall into the river while you are about it – and tell him to send me a small battering ram if one is prepared.'

'Yes, my lord.'

'André.'

'Yes, my lord?'

'We will not need the shield wall if the fog holds, but go and tell the men who are to set the spikes that they are not to begin until they hear the first stroke of the ram. Belike that sound will drown all others and they should be able to come right around the towers without being seen or heard. It will be safe enough to use the ram,' Rannulf laughed. 'It will not hurt the gate, but the noise makes for fear and they will not be able to see to shoot so it cannot hurt us either. Mayhap they will open the gate to drive us off. Let some footmen wait in readiness with grappling hooks. Mayhap it will not be so easy to close as to open.'

A horseman approached gropingly. 'I thought I would never find my way back,' John muttered. 'The wain is ready, but where is it to go? Do you know where the bridge is, my lord?'

Rannulf's tension vented itself in a guttural laugh which was nearly a giggle. 'Nay, no more than you, but forward we

226

all go. If you hear a loud splash, you will know I have fallen into the river. Do not fail to pull me out – then we can work our way along the bank until we find it. Go back, John, and bid the grooms and kitchen hands to form along our path to direct the other knights and men-at-arms – and the wain also.' John disappeared from view for a moment, reappeared with surprising swiftness, and shortly vague shadows formed to Rannulf's right. He laughed again, touched his horse with his spurs, and moved forward noting with satisfaction that the hooves were almost silent on the wet grass. They might just as well find the bridge before they left the horses, which they would not need until the gates were opened.

They did not actually fall into the river, although it was a near thing. Straining ears at last caught the sound of a shoe grinding on a stone and the creak of leather harness. Rannulf stopped and touched André to stop him. John slid from his horse, dropped his shield, and drew his knife. They waited tensely, the men silent behind them, and Rannulf found himself fighting the desire to follow John, resenting the fact that any man should taste blood before himself. The silence was only minutely disturbed by a soft, choking cry. Rannulf drew his sword. If John had failed and that cry was his, the warning to the defenders of the bridge would come now.

'Sorry, my lord,' a peculiarly muffled voice murmured, 'my hand slipped from his mouth in the last moment. You are too far north. The bridge is below us.'

'John?' Rannulf questioned. 'Are you hurt?'

'No, my lord.' The voice was still muffled and husky and was now at a little distance. 'Dismount and follow, my lord. I know where we are.'

Could it be the enemy man-at-arms? No, he would be wearing the ordinary armour of metal plates sewn to leather and Rannulf knew that he had heard the harsh whisper of mail when the owner of the voice moved. Beyond that, there was a distinctly familiar quality about the voice under its peculiar muffling. Merely, it did not sound like John. God, the mist was driving him mad. Rannulf trod cautiously in the wake of the shadow before him, his feet aware of the soft earth and rank grass of a riverbank which he could not see. Now, however, he could hear the water, and almost at once, the change in the river's voice as its free flow was impeded by the supports of the bridge. If a man loses his eyes, his ears become clever, Rannulf thought, and immediately stopped thinking at all. Where a dim, leading figure had been, now there were two locked together, struggling.

Suppressing his usual hoarse war-cry, Rannulf leaped, his dagger already clear of its sheath. He had to loosen the hand-hold of his shield to grab the leather-clad form, but he knew the shield would cling by its arm strap. It was the work of a moment to drag off the helm, slit the leather throat-guard. Rannulf heard the scrape of his knife as it slid across his squire's mailed glove and saw the blood pulse out, dark but strangely colourless in the enveloping greyness. There was not much noise, the thud of their feet and the sound of the man's body as it fell, the rasp of their slightly quickened breathing. It was enough, however, to warn nervous listeners. From ahead came the cry, 'Ware! Arms!' and Rannulf was free of the restraint he had imposed upon himself.

'*Je combattrais!*'

The mist muffled both the warning and Rannulf's fighting motto, so that defenders and attackers alike were surprised to come upon each other seconds later. Rannulf had nothing but his knife in hand when he was suddenly faced by a half-dozen shadowy figures. He hurriedly sheathed one weapon and drew the other as his young squire leaped before him, sword drawn, to engage the men-at-arms until his master should be ready. Before the blades had clashed twice, Rannulf was ready by his side and behind them the battle cry was echoed from a hundred other throats. One man went down before Rannulf's first swing; the others broke and ran when they realized that it was a full-scale attack and no small scouting party which they had to face.

'Do not lose them,' Rannulf called to the squire who was a good deal fleeter of foot than he was. 'And do not go on to the bridge alone.'

His caution was unnecessary. A few steps more brought Rannulf himself to the hard earth of the road while his squire's form was still visible. He turned right, calling his motto to

228

guide his men. The ring of steel on steel drew him forward, but by the time he came to his squire's shoulder, the defenders of the bridge had disengaged again and were running, their feet pounding on the bare planks.

'*A moi!*' Rannulf called desperately.

If they opened the gates to save the guards, perhaps he and his men could force an entrance. For him to do so alone with John beside him was suicide, but ten or twenty men might be able to hold off the defenders long enough to reopen the portals and let still more men in. It was a desperate chance and would necessitate a complete change in plans without opportunity to tell his men of the change, but it was worth trying.

'Go back,' he said, his eyes straining ahead. 'Bid the men be silent and come quickly.'

The form beside him vanished, and Rannulf moved forward slowly, trying to step on planks that would not groan and betray his presence. The running stopped; Rannulf could hear the men pounding on the gates, calling for admittance. Knowing he was mad but unable to resist, he ran too, biting at the leather strap of his shield. Perhaps he could cast it under the gate and delay the closing. The pounding and voices were closer now. Perhaps they would not open the gates and would sacrifice the few men to caution.

Like a threefold sign from heaven, the strap on Rannulf's shield gave way, the grating of bars being lifted came to his ears, and below him the sound of fighting drifted from the bank, men calling that boats were coming ashore. Trembling with eagerness, Rannulf slowed his stride. He must not come upon them before the gates were opened. He tried not to breathe, fearing that he would miss the sound of the hinges. They would open barely enough for a man to slip through. Rannulf knew that his one chance would be to kill or stun the last man to enter, hoping the body would block the gate, add his shield to the body, leap through himself, and attack those who tried to move the corpse.

He loosened the shield still more and it sagged, the handgrip pressing painfully into his palm. Praise God! That blackness in the grey must be the gates, and there were the clustered shadows of the waiting men. A step; they had not turned, had not heard him. Rannulf raised his sword, moved to the left because they were opening the right gate. Now!

The forward leap gave impetus to his downward stroke. The blade hit true. Rannulf thrust his victim forward, cast down his shield, and leaped on to the body. They would need to kill him as well as drag the corpse away before the gates would shut. Time had no meaning; sound had no meaning; numbers had no meaning. Half-shielded, half-hampered by the oak walls on either side of him, Rannulf cried out for help and fought. Beneath his feet the body moved and the gate, drawn by many willing hands pulling on the great iron rings, thrust against his right shoulder. Irresistibly, Rannulf tipped forward, knew he was falling, knew he would die if he fell.

An anguished grunt was torn from Rannulf's lungs, then another, and another. He tried to call out, but his voice was choked with laughter. His vassals, leaping through the breach to keep the gates open and to protect him, were treading on him. No doubt they were treading on him as lightly as possible, but treading on him they were, and they were no featherweights. Five, perhaps six, had passed and formed a shield wall behind which the others could press forward after the bodies blocking the path had been removed.

'Let me up,' Rannulf gasped, for one man stood astride him so that no enemy could suddenly seize his body if the shield wall broke.

The young voice, no longer disguised and therefore instantly recognizable, tremulous with relief, cried out, 'He is alive!' And then, 'Papa, are you hurt?'

Rannulf leaped to his feet, more invigorated by rage than he could have been by a clear victory. 'What do you here?' he roared, but the desperate battle taking place in front of him brought the realization that if he stopped for explanations they might well all be dead before he received them. He had never lost his grip on his sword, for his sword hand would never open while he lived once it clutched the hilt of his weapon, but his shield was gone and there was no moment in which to seek it. Men pressed in behind him as grappling hooks gradually pulled the gate wider in spite of the efforts of the defenders to draw it shut.

'A shield,' he called, and a small, round footman's shield was thrust into his hands. 'Just wait,' he growled at Geoffrey as he pushed to the front of the battling men, 'if we come alive from this mêlée, I will make you sorry you did not die in it.'

Time flowed again, brief and interminable, endless and too short. Rannulf lost count of the strokes, of the men who fell and those who replaced them. He had one fixed determination, that the gates must remain open until they could be destroyed or the defenders of them subdued. Now the care with which he had laid his plans the previous night was working against him. Fearing that Stephen would recall his men or alter his dispositions in one of his moods of vacillation, Rannulf had ordered the leaders of his forces to accept orders from none but John or himself. Where John was, he could not imagine, so his only hope was to break free of the fighting group himself. In that way alone could he arrange that horses be brought forward to mount the knights now fighting afoot and hampered by their heavy gear and order the foot soldiers held in reserve to do the work the knights were now doing. Northampton's vassals could be called into action also, and with that weight of men, perhaps they could fight their way from between the towers which would become a death trap as soon as the mist lifted sufficiently for the archers to regain some accuracy.

Rannulf's duty was clear, but it was not easy to force himself to do it. The lust of battle was upon him, and to drag himself, unwearied and unsated, from the field was bitterly hard. He was not mentally adjusted to such a thing; there had always been John to send before. Moreover, the men who held that narrow space were his own vassals and his own household guard. They were accustomed to following him and if he broke away they might do so also, not through fear but through the habit of doing blindly as he did. Sir John de Vere, chief of his vassals, was far to his left defending the other gate. The only other man whom the vassals would follow was Geoffrey, who held John of Northampton's place and was fighting well. Could he leave Geoffrey alone to face the swelling forces that opposed them?

The fog was a curse and a salvation at once. Had it not obscured all, Rannulf's forces would have done as he desired automatically, seeing that the gates had been forced. Still, without the fog, they could never have been forced so easily and the few men who passed them would have been readily picked off by the archers above. Furiously, Rannulf used the point of metal which protruded from the centre of the footman's shield to thrust away one attacker as he slashed at another. Any moment now the sound of battle and the horn blasts from the towers would call forth the horsemen of Wallingford. If his own men were not mounted, they would be ridden down. As if to add point to that fear, a vassal to Rannulf's right uttered a choking cry and fell back with a feathered shaft protruding from his shoulder.

There was no longer time to yield to impulses of fear or desire. Geoffrey had thrust himself where he did not belong and now must bear the consequences. A quick glance showed that far more of the towers were visible, clearly visible. The mist was lifting. Rannulf jerked himself back and thrust Geoffrey forward.

'Hold the men to their work,' he cried, 'I must call up the full battle and find us mounts.' Then, bellowing at the top of his lungs. 'Follow Geoffrey of Sleaford.'

'*Je combattrais! Je combattrais!*' The young voice called the rallying cry above the clangour and cries of battle, and the men drew together and moved forward a step as if to prove they understood.

As Rannulf backed, someone pushed past to fill the space he had left, and Rannulf recognized André. 'Guard him,' he gasped.

'With my life,' Fortesque replied shortly.

Perhaps the forces Rannulf gathered could have been arranged better; perhaps his instructions to the men could have been clearer. Driven by so violent a craving to return to the field of battle that he could barely think, Rannulf did not not care. Mounted and leading a horse for Geoffrey, with his own reserve troops bringing mounts for the other knights, he galloped back without waiting for Stephen's or Northampton's men. He had sent a message to both saying the gates were breached. Let them come or not as they pleased.

'My lord!' The voice was desperate and Rannulf pulled up a bit. 'My lord, why did you desert me?' John was nearly in tears between his fear and his hurt pride. 'I have been seeking you high and low. I rode back to give orders to the men as you bade me, and when I returned, you were gone.'

Rannulf signalled him alongside, laughing grimly. 'I thought you were beside me. That devil's spawn that I thought before to have been an obedient son took your place. God knows where he came by such wilfulness. It comes not from me, and I would not have dreamed that the pale nothing who was his mother had such blood in her. Pray God he still lives. I will teach him so to diddle me.'

'I thought it was by your order,' John gasped. 'He came late to your tent last night and said he would ride with us. I never guessed—'

His sentence was broken off as they almost rode into the wain carrying the battering ram, the men with it patiently waiting for the order to attack the gates which had never come. Ahead through the steadily thinning fog, the bridge was vaguely discernible.

'Follow the troop,' Rannulf ordered. 'The gates are open, but you will be of more use to us in forcing the tower doors.'

Swift as he had been, Rannulf found that he had nearly been away too long. His men had been forced back and broken into two groups, but the main objective had not yet been lost. The gates still stood wide. Before each of them, backed against the oak, bloody and exhausted, the vassals and household retainers fought on. Mute but eloquent testimony to their grim devotion were the dead and wounded that lay between the spot where Rannulf had left them and where they now stood.

'Mount Geoffrey and see that he comes to no hurt,' Rannulf cried. He did not permit himself to look for his son, merely passed the reins of the riderless horse to John and spurred his own horse forward. His battle cry rang out, harsh and compelling, promising rest and protection – a breathing space in battle – for those who had so faithfully obeyed him. Swift redemption of the promise came in the thunder of hooves across the bridge as the second group of vassals rode to support their lord. Those who could of the initial group would fight again when they were rested and mounted; Rannulf alone could not withdraw until a man of sufficient rank came to replace him.

It was a long, bloody day. The defenders of Wallingford bridge, no less than those who attacked them, understood what was at stake. Their devotion and courage were phenomenal, and even Rannulf's lust for blood was more than sated before the towers fell. His memory of the battle was strangely rhythmical, the strokes of his sword seeming tied in some mysterious way to the strokes of the battering ram. Those dull thuds, a beat spelling out inevitable doom, were no lightener of the spirit, even to him who had begun their relentless movement. And when the splintered wood of the tower doors was torn from the hinges, the rhythm of death did not cease. The archers would not yield; they threw down their crossbows and fought Rannulf's men step by step, a body for every step of those bastions of safety which had become bloody sepulchres.

Few prisoners were taken; the defenders fought back and died. Nor did the fall of the towers break the courage of the men of Wallingford keep. Again and again they poured forth from the castle itself, at times pushing Rannulf's weary troops back to the very gates, at times being themselves driven to take refuge within their own walls. Again and again the earl of Soke rallied his forces, becoming, as the battle progressed, so covered with his own blood and that of others that, except for his harsh voice, no man would have known him.

The light was falling in the faint mist which had persisted throughout the day when the knights of Wallingford keep rode out for the last time. Now even Rannulf's voice was gone and he was reeling in the saddle from fatigue and loss of blood. Northampton's men had come and had fought ably for Rannulf, knowing their lord could not lead them. Had they not, the bridge and the strip of land before it could not have been held. Warwick, de Tracy and Peverel had done and were doing what they had promised also. Stephen alone had not appeared to relieve his hard-pressed vassals. Nonetheless Rannulf formed his battle line, riding up and down before it so that the men might see that he was still leading, still fighting, even if he could not cry out to encourage them any longer.

'Our swords,' he croaked. 'We will not yield what we have won so hardly.'

They formed, exhausted but determined, knowing the men of

Wallingford were as weary as they were, knowing it was the last charge. If they could hold the position until the light failed fresh troops would carry the burden the next day and there would be no need to take the bridge again. They formed and they would have fought, but when the sounds and cries of Stephen, at last at the head of his own troops, came across the bridge, some unashamedly wept with relief. Rannulf was too weary even for that. He let his sword arm drop and bent limply over the saddle bow. Consciousness receded as the will relaxed, making the sound of battle no more than a nightmare noise in the back of the mind. Consciousness did not recede far enough; not blackness but terror engulfed him. Not once since he had thrust him forward to lead the men, not once in that long day, had Rannulf seen his son or heard his voice. Consciousness returned; Rannulf could not even faint or die until he knew what had happened to his child.

'Where is the earl?'

Slowly Rannulf lifted himself upright, squared his shoulders, and forced his face into rigid blankness. 'Here,' he whispered hoarsely.

He could barely make out the man under the coating of mud and blood, but he knew the voice. 'Geoffrey is with John of Northampton. He is very badly hurt. Can you come, my lord?'

In the pause that followed André Fortesque staggered, and Rannulf reached across his left thigh, from which blood dripped slowly, to steady the young man. 'Take my stirrup,' he said as firmly as his cracked voice allowed, 'and lead on.'

They went very slowly, André barely managing to put one foot before the other. Still at one moment it seemed too fast, far too fast, and in the next Rannulf felt as if he would set spurs to his horse and ride André down to end his agony of suspense. It was nearly dark now, and the two young men were in the shadow of the gate, one slight figure stretched on the planks, the other leaning against the oak for support. Thus it was in such a land, in a place where men endlessly tore each other to bits, that the old outlived the young. The drooping head of the standing man, unhelmed and with the mail hood thrust back, lifted at the sound of their advance. Rannulf's hand trembled so violently that the reins quivered on his stallion's neck and

235

the beast laid back his ears uncertainly. Surely under the matting of dirt and sweat, surely that hair was Geoffrey's gold, not John's black. Rannulf tried to swing from his saddle, but his injured leg failed and he fell heavily, André, on the right of his horse, unable to help him.

'Papa!'

'Naught ails me but a little blood-letting and a hurt leg. Give me your arm that I may come to John. Does he live?'

'Aye, and I have staunched the blood as well as may be. But he does not wake, and I fear—'

Rannulf sank down beside his squire, his breathing as laboured as that of the ashen-faced young man. Hardened in war, he still winced at the blood-soaked rags that stopped gaping wounds in side and shoulder. It was one thing to deal such hurts to your enemies, another to look upon them on a young man almost as dear as your own child. Hope, however, there was. John's breathing was strong and Rannulf found his pulse readily.

'André.' No response but a soft groan. 'André!' Rannulf called more peremptorily.

Fortesque made an effort to heave himself off the ground and collapsed again.

'Let him be,' Geoffrey begged softly. 'He saved us both. My horse was broached and John leaped down to give me his. In that moment he was struck and a crowd of footmen drove the beast away. I stood above him as long as I might, but they were very many and I went down too. I was not hurt, papa. I believe someone struck me on the head. When I came to myself, Fortesque had pulled us both to the tower wall – how I know not for there was not another man of ours in my sight. From the dead around us, he must have held off an army. They must have seen your arms, papa, and thought I was you.'

Or known they could make me dance like a puppet on a string for my son's life, Rannulf thought, but of that he would not speak. 'Mount my horse, Geoffrey, and bring help for John. And put on your hood and helm! Have you no sense at all? There are still arrows flying about and a man here and there who can wield a sword. A head with an ache is better to bear than a head with a hole in it.'

In the distance the battle noise reached a new crescendo and Rannulf briefly lifted his head to listen. Cries of 'no quarter' drifted back faintly. No quarter for whom? Had Stephen lost what had cost him so much to win? Rannulf's eyes, half-blinded with tears he would not shed, dropped to John's still form. He had taken the bridge for Stephen; he had fulfilled his pledge and he would do no more. Shocked by the thought, Rannulf's hand instinctively moved to his sword hilt, then dropped away. It made little difference since, crippled as he was, he could not return to the fighting. He looked at his left leg, wondering how badly he was hurt. It had stopped bleeding again, but it felt strangely dead and would not bear his weight. Well, it was his own fault. He had been in too much haste to take a proper shield or even to tear one from an enemy and had used that cursed footman's bauble which could not protect his leg. Now he would be rightly served if— A low moan cut across his thoughts. Rannulf bent low as John's eyes fluttered open.

'It is all finished, John,' he said very firmly. 'There is no call to arms. The battle is done. We hold the gates. Geoffrey is safe and I am safe. Your charge is well fulfilled. Now it is time for all to rest.'

Whether or not John understood the words was impossible to say. The face of his master and the voice of authority was enough. He closed his eyes again and made no move until Geoffrey returned with the men and litters – two litters. Rannulf scowled.

'For whom is that second carrying case?'

'You cannot walk, papa, and I am sure you should not—'

'I did not intend to walk. If you can pry yourself from the back of my mount, I will not need to do so.'

'Papa, you should not ride either,' Geoffrey said, dismounting nonetheless.

'Whelp!' Rannulf snorted, but not unkindly. 'Do you want to frighten to death what remains of my vassals? All they need now is to see me carried in a litter and come to believe that I will not be able to rule them or succour the families of those who are dead or dying. Fool! Get me up on that horse.'

The pang of agony which seared his leg as he was lifted to

237

the saddle was comforting, although the wound spurted blood again. That was normal; it was better to endure pain than to feel the limb dead and senseless.

'How badly are you hurt?' Rannulf asked his son.

'Not at all, I think. I am bruised and battered all over, and a little dizzy still from that stroke on the head. Between Sir André and John, however, no man could come at me, and I scarcely was given a chance to land a blow. Papa, if I am so straitly guarded, how can I ever—'

'Hold your tongue! I have a few words to say to you which will fully explain, but this is not the time or place – others need our care. Get yourself a horse and gather together my men. For them this battle is finished. They are to return to camp and take their ease.'

Several of the leeches who travelled with Rannulf's forces were already in attendance in his tent, and the next interval was painful but satisfactory to him. No real damage, the physicians assured him, had been done to his leg. The cut was very deep and would take long to heal, but if he took the proper care all would go well. It was easier to believe them – physicians often lied – in that when the large gash was treated and bandaged, the leg settled down into a steady throbbing occasionally heightened by a stabbing pain which Rannulf, no novice at battle wounds, accepted as normal. The rest of his wounds were superficial; myriad bruises and nicks, none of which would trouble him after a few days. John's condition, too, was judged as desperate but not hopeless. No vital organ had been touched, and if his body was strong enough to fight off the fever and putrefaction which would certainly occur in the case of such large wounds, he would live. He was young; one could hope, but Rannulf knew that his service was lost for many, many months. André would be more than ever needed to reorganize the decimated household guard. There was no help for it; since he must have someone of perfect trustworthiness at his back, someone known to the vassals who could bear messages and orders, Geoffrey would have to come and serve him until John recovered or until another squire could be adequately trained.

Rannulf dispatched a messenger to Northampton with news of his son and a request for Geoffrey to attend him as soon as he could be conveniently freed from his duties. He sat up in bed and tried his leg tentatively, shook his head once more at his own carelessness, and ordered a crutch to be made at once. Then he ate, dry bread and dried meat, standard army supplies which were all that was available after the ravaging of the land, drank half a small skin of sour wine, and lay down to sleep. No amount of pain could combat the combined effect of deep satisfaction and physical exhaustion; Rannulf was immediately unconscious. He nearly slept the sun around also, waking in the afternoon of the next day to find his group alone upon the camping ground. The remainder of the army had moved during the night and the early part of the day, settling firmly into the area between Wallingford keep and the bridge. More cause for satisfaction. Stephen had kept what he had won and the men of Wallingford were well and truly penned inside the castle.

That was the first piece of news that Rannulf had from André Fortesque, who was up and about although each movement he made brought grimaces of pain. He had no wounds of any note, he told his lord, proud of the skill which protected him and others; he had merely been battered into total collapse. John of Northampton was no better, he replied to Rannulf's anxious questions, but none could say he was worse either. Geoffrey had not yet arrived and was presumably busy in Northampton's service, not belatedly showing injuries, because André had heard that he had come in the night to inquire of how his father went on.

'Very well, tell one of the servants to send him to find me as soon as he comes. Now, give me that crutch and your arm also to steady me upon my feet.' Rannulf was about to thank André for his service and tell him that a reward would be forthcoming, but the young man interrupted him.

'You do not mean to rise, my lord! You will bleed again.'

'Then bleed I must,' Rannulf said grimly. André was too young and inexperienced to be given a castle as a reward for saving Geoffrey's life; he did not yet know the duty of a leader. I will give him money, a horse, and new armour, Rannulf decided – and I will teach him. When he is ready, I will give him a keep to hold for me and a portion to buy him a wife.

'I must see what case my men are in,' Rannulf said deliberately, beginning the lessons. 'I must send news to the keeps of those who are slain so that the heirs may do me homage, and give what comfort I can to those who are like to die. There are some younger men, in particular, who have no heirs or only young sons. For those I must take especial thought if they be dead or sore wounded.'

André was silenced. There were joys in a great estate, but there were also burdens. A victorious lord could not, it appeared, even enjoy the rest he deserved. He went from tent to tent with his master, watching Rannulf grow more haggard as the tale of casualties grew, seeing that he did not spare himself even when blood began to seep again through the bandage on his leg and stain his surcoat. Not even when his sad duty was done, however, did he return to his tent. He moved to a spot from which he could see across the river to the tents of his allies camped before the walls of Wallingford. There was no triumph in his face.

'They are brave men,' he said to André at last in his harsh voice, flat now with fatigue. 'For the hurt they have done me, I cannot love them. Yet I do not hate them either. They fight for what they believe right, and I cannot but feel that it is hard that they must die by thirst and starvation. It is better to die in the field with a sword in hand.'

'Father—'

Geoffrey had found them. With a gesture, Rannulf dismissed André. He was going to give Geoffrey a lesson of a similar type to the one taught André, but on a different level.

'What I have to say to you, Geoffrey, may best be said here where there are none to listen. If you were not too old to beat, I would use my belt buckle on you until I could lift my arm no longer. As it is, you are nigh a man – and I must hurt you more than a beating to make you understand.'

'But papa—'

'You are about to say that you did not die, and thus all is well. Is it? How many commandments that I and Simon of Northampton have laboured to teach you have you broken? Are you not puffed with pride, pleased above all with your own wisdom in flouting our orders?'

Rich colour stained the fair skin, but the blue eyes met the cold grey ones squarely. 'No man gave me an order that I flouted. You say I am nigh a man, yet you shield me like a child, denying me my birthright which is to stand beside you and defend my name.'

No expression moved the iron countenance of the father, grey with sorrow and rigid with pain. 'You deserted the duties Northampton laid upon you to satisfy your lust for praise.'

'No,' Geoffrey flashed. 'What he bade me to do was done before I came to you. Nor did I neglect to ask whether he had orders for me to be carried out upon the day of battle. I had my freedom from my master.'

'One small splinter of the shaft is thus removed, but one small splinter alone. You are proud of your cleverness, are you not – coward!'

Geoffrey's face went white, blazed, and went white again. 'What right have you to use such language to me? Did I not do my part as well as I might? Is it a fault in me that you command your men to guard me as if I had no skill to defend myself?'

'I have the right of proof,' Rannulf replied in measured tones. 'I said naught and meant naught against your courage in arms, but there are other, higher, forms of courage – and that you have not. Oh, you are most brave to ride forth in attack or withstand a charge, but you have not that strength of spirit which is needed to bear the burdens of your station. Coward, I say again, did you ever think what would be if we both fell?'

Now the boy was trembling from head to foot, but he still held his father's eyes. 'Do you call me so? Then what are you, who, for what you call love, would make me less than a man so that you need not bear the grief of my loss?'

His passion beat and broke against the older man's stolidity. Here was the crux of the matter, the point Rannulf needed to pound home. 'To fight together in fair battle is one matter – I have begged your release from Northampton to do just that. The taking of this bridge was no such battle. You, above all men, must learn to distinguish what is utterly hopeless from what is nigh hopeless but must be done. When a thing is nigh hopeless, provision must be made to lessen the foreknown evil. This I tried to do, and you all but destroyed my work.'

'It did not turn out evil.'

'That was none of your doing, but God's – and God gives his help to those who try, in honour, to help themselves. I bid you think again what would have befallen. Our vassals would have been leaderless, to be preyed upon by any man who so willed, to destroy themselves by fighting one against the other for supremacy. Thus you would have, at one stroke, violated their trust in their lord to bring them succour against their enemies and to judge justly between them, keeping or making the peace. Further, you would have violated my oath to my overlord to bring the vassals to his aid.'

Rannulf drew breath, pushed away his growing need to lie down and rest, and plodded on. 'Your brother, your own flesh and blood, would have been left – a child of six – defenceless against those who would destroy him or seize him to have his inheritance. Thus you would have violated the bond of blood that commands you to protect your own. Twofold is that sin, for your sister – little of account as she is – would also have suffered. Would you desire to see her thrust into the arms of some filthy serf or destroyed utterly so that none could say my line could breed through her? You say I gave you no order. Did I not bid you protect your brother and the woman? Could you do that when you were dead? What would you not have cast aside to fulfill your folly and your pride.'

No longer did Geoffrey's eyes hold his father's. He had turned his head aside, almost as though Rannulf had struck him in the face.

'Protect you!' Rannulf said finally, bitterness filling the hitherto passionless voice. 'If I could protect you, it would be from bearing that burden while you are yet so young, not from a quick, clean death. There are ways and ways to die. A man may die inside his body, and that is the only death that is everlasting with no hope of redemption.'

The silence that fell when Rannulf's harsh voice ceased was, surprisingly, without tension. Rannulf studied his son attentively and was well satisfied with what he saw. Geoffrey's colour had returned to normal and his brows were contracted in a frown which spelled thought. At last a long shudder shook

242

him, and he moved his head so that his eyes met his father's again.

'Nay, I am a fool, but not a coward, father. Merely, I did not think at all, in spite of the many times you have described my duty to me. Nor do I think I desired praise for my courage and hardiness. In honesty, I thought not of that either. I am guilty still, it is true. I do not seek to shirk your blame, but rather count me guilty of that fear for which I blamed you. When you came to me and spoke as if your death were a certain thing, I had not courage to face that loss.'

'Sooner or later you will need to face that loss. I am not young and all men must die. Think on it, and do not permit your passions again to lead you astray.' Rannulf turned away.

'Papa, wait! You have spoken largely of my duties to my blood and to my overlord. Should he not guard my brother for me if I have done my duty properly? Even separately we both might die – what then?'

This was a turn Rannulf had hoped the conversation would not take. 'Because other men are weak is no reason for you to fail,' was the only answer he could make. He shrugged his shoulders with bitter contempt and beckoned Geoffrey to him. 'Help me back to my bed. I have strength for no more.'

# Chapter 16

Two men faced each other in one of the dark, dank wall chambers of Gloucester castle. There was little comfort in the room, since its floor was of damp earth and moisture beaded the rough plank ceiling and trickled down the stone walls. What light there was flickered unsteadily from two resinous torches which added their smoke to the dark they were supposed to dissipate. Surroundings less appropriate to the two elegantly clad gentlemen who were within would be hard to find, but one most necessary item was provided here that they could find nowhere else – privacy. When the oaken door of that chamber was closed, even the loudest shrieks of agony were no more than a dull murmur in the great hall outside.

William of Gloucester, clad in the silks appropriate for the late-summer weather outdoors, shivered in the bone-chilling damp but congratulated himself for this foresight. Hereford was, as he had expected, enraged beyond all self-control and was, indeed, shrieking at the top of his lungs. Lord Gloucester listened indifferently, not really hearing because it did not matter what Hereford said. In the end he would have to take William's path; there was no longer any other to tread. The volume of sound cut off suddenly, and Gloucester raised his eyes languidly to Hereford's flushed face.

'You have done everything you can – I agree,' William said in his silken purr. 'You have harassed Stephen's forces constantly and, while even a yard before their gates was their own, you sent supplies and men into Wallingford. What good has this brought us? No strength of arms can dislodge Stephen now, and in a few weeks more he will have Wallingford.'

'No! They will never open to him.'

'Perhaps not, although I have heard that it is not so easy to die of hunger and thirst. Nonetheless, soon they will be too feeble to man the walls, and Stephen's men will take what they wish by assault. Do you think they have sat idle all this time? What siege engine have they not built and made ready?'

'If you had joined me or sent your men out at least, it would not have come to this.'

'Perhaps that too, but I do not believe it. And I do believe that it is useless and senseless to waste our strength to gain what can be had more easily in other ways.'

'By lying and dishonourable practices!' Hereford sneered, but William only laughed softly, and Hereford bit his lips, ready to burst with frustration.

'You have written to Henry?' William asked finally, except for his laugh, seeming not to have heard Hereford's insult.

'Yes, but I have not sent the letter. What is the sense in crying for help where no help is? Henry's heart is first in France, and even if it were not he has sufficient to occupy him where he is.'

Gloucester's eyes dropped as if he were considering what Hereford said. He was not, for the matter needed no consideration. He was wondering, instead, whether he dared set one of his servants to search through Hereford's possessions and find that letter. With a few lines of his own added to it, it might not be nearly as useless as Hereford thought. William had information from France that Hereford had not yet heard and which, if William could arrange it, Hereford would not hear for some time. Louis and Eustace were already quarrelling, and Henry's forces were moving forward steadily. Very soon now, if nothing unexpected occurred to disturb the trend of events, Henry would be free to come to England.

Unfortunately, William of Gloucester knew that it would not be soon enough to save Wallingford if the pressure on that keep were not relieved. To drive Stephen off by force of arms was nearly impossible. Hereford had tried and tried again. The king's forces were too strong and too firmly entrenched. For a moment, as he sat with lowered eyes, William wondered why he bothered with either side in this stupid rebellion. Certainly not because his father, Robert of Gloucester, had been committed to it heart and soul. He had little affection and no respect for his late father, a man of direct nature and honourable purposes. Another Hereford in fact, just as pig-headed and just as stupid, unable to see his own advantage through the haze of his 'honour'. Nor was it for personal advantage that William schemed. True, if Henry came to the throne he would be rewarded and he liked gold, but he was rich enough. It amuses me, William thought – it amuses me to make them move about like puppets. He raised deceptively sleepy eyes in which no man could read aught. He would set his new little mute boy to find that letter. Once he had that request for help in Hereford's own hand – Henry loved Hereford almost as much as he loved his blood kin – his purpose would be all but accomplished.

'If you have not sent to Henry for help, Roger, I cannot see why you are so hot against my proposal. Look you, the count of Meulan is a robber baron, even if he is Leicester's twin brother, and is as much an enemy to Stephen as he will be to Henry when Henry comes to the throne. In this case, it matters not whether a man be for or against the king. The destruction of Waleran of Meulan would be a most laudable act. You owe your protection to William of Beauchamp. You are close-tied to his family, and he has a right to your help. If you go to fight Waleran and free Beauchamp, which you are bound in honour to do, Wallingford will fall into Stephen's hands in a week or two and be lost as Faringdon was lost.'

'Oh, God!' Hereford groaned miserably. 'Do you need to remind me? Why do you think I have come crawling to you for help? Would I do so if my need were not tearing me apart?'

'And I have refused my help. Nay, Roger, it is no good to curse me. I do not do it for spite, nor to hurt you, nor to hurt the Angevin cause. Not even because I wish to hold my men and my gold safe – I have risked both before and I will do so again. But I risk only when there can be some gain in the risk. There is no sense in beginning to rage again. You will need to listen to me in the end. Consider instead that, if you attack Waleran alone, you will anger Robert of Leicester. We have spent much time and effort in cozening Leicester, and he is nearly promised to us. If Stephen joins us in fighting Waleran, the blame can be divided – and perhaps unequally so that another wedge may be forced between Leicester and the king.'

Mute and trembling, Hereford stared at Gloucester with fascinated eyes. He loathed and feared this man whom he could break in two between his hands, loathed him because he hated his dishonesty, feared him because he knew that in the end he would be forced to dance to his piping. There was nothing openly dishonourable about William's suggestion. Hereford knew there was much precedent for two enemies making a truce while they attacked a third party dangerous to both of them. This was what William wanted; that he should suggest to Stephen that they join forces to destroy Waleran of Meulan. He would not be asking Stephen to abandon the siege of Wallingford, only to send what extra forces he had to help in driving Leicester's brother from Worcester castle. That keep belonged rightfully to William de Beauchamp, who was now a prisoner in his own stronghold.

Every instinct Hereford had, however, cried out that William had some deeper deception in mind than easing the siege on Wallingford. If a large portion of Stephen's forces were drawn off to Worcester, the men of Wallingford might win free by their own efforts, but if Stephen helped Beauchamp, might not his loyalties be shaken?

'Well,' Gloucester prodded, 'will you see Beauchamp murdered by Waleran? Will you see Wallingford fall into Stephen's hands? Will you see us lose Leicester just as he was about to give his strength to Henry? Or, will you abate one jot of your overweening pride, write as I ask you, and let my courier go to the king?'

'I must think,' Hereford said desperately, playing for time. 'I could not believe you would deny me help. I have never considered the effects of such an act.'

'By all means, take your own time.' Steel rang under William's soft purr. 'But while you are thinking, Stephen's men may be climbing Wallingford's walls or William de Beauchamp may be stretched on the rack. For me – there is no hurry.'

'William, if you plan by this to betray me – or, more important, Henry—'

Gloucester laughed, not his usual contemptuous snicker but a true guffaw of amusement. 'Strangely enough, I plan neither. If you were not such a pig-headed ass, you would have done just this the day after Soke – bless him, how I miss him, he is as easy to draw as you used to be – crossed the bridge. As it is, you have allowed Stephen's forces to become too firmly entrenched. They may try the assault anyway.'

It was true enough. Hereford's bright head dropped. In the past years he had swallowed bitter draught after bitter draught, but this was the bitterest of all. To need to write to his enemy, pleading for help, offering, even if only by indirection, a desire for conciliation between them. Could he force his hand to it? He must. It would be the greatest wrong to permit Beauchamp to die, Leicester to swing back to the king, or Wallingford to fall, only to salve his own pride. In the end it might come to nothing anyway. Stephen might have the wit to refuse the proffered truce, in which case Hereford felt he would have a strong arguing point with Gloucester.

A grizzled head bent low over a delicate, white hand, freshly ungloved. 'It is so good of you to receive me again,' Catherine said gently, and the old warrior fumbled out some complimentary phrases one would have thought he had long forgotten. Catherine blushed delicately with pleasure, and Sir Giles Fortesque was torn between a desire to laugh and a vast uneasiness. The slyness of women! Thus she cozened them all – some of them men who had knocked the teeth out of their wives. She cozened her way into their keeps – not that any man had a right to keep his overlord or his overlord's deputy out – but the custom was weak by default in the earldom of Soke, where for long the previous master had allowed the men to do as they pleased. Had Soke himself come, there would have been angry looks and possibly dangerous words.

'My husband,' Catherine was continuing, 'was so grieved that he could not join me in this second visit either.'

Sir Giles' lips twitched. Visit! She called it a visit; she asked to see nothing; but somehow she cozened her way into every nook and cranny, every tower and storeroom in the keep. Then she wrote half the night. Sir Giles did not know for certain what Lady Catherine wrote, but he had seen the results of that writing right here.

When they had first 'visited' this holding, there had been

men in plenty, but the defensive engines were old or outworn and few. Catherine had commented that she thought the baron very wise to keep his new engines of war safe under cover. He had mumbled some indefinite reply to which Catherine said brightly that, since he was so careful of them, she would have sent to him one of the newest trenchbuts. That it had arrived there could be no doubt because now, a bare month later, four similar instruments stood side by side on the walls. Three of them, quite obviously, had been newly constructed on the spot.

'Oh,' Catherine had exclaimed, smiling seraphically, 'I see I had no need to send one, you had them all the time and just wished to pretend that you liked the old style better.'

Why should it work? Why did they melt like overheated wax? Did none of them have wives and daughters? None so wondrous fair, perhaps, but there was something else too. Catherine saw what others did not. Time and again Sir Giles had watched men wince under the lash of what seemed to him a perfectly innocent statement on a subject he had never dreamed that man sensitive about. He had seen them wince and flush, and then melt still further at the application of some, to him, equally incomprehensible salve of flattery. Certainly she played no similar tricks on him – or did she? What did it matter, he thought, swallowing his uneasiness, when her aim had his fullest approval and was being accomplished apace. By the end of harvest, every keep that faced Hugh Bigod's earldom would be fully provisioned, fully armed, and fully manned. That was important, not what tricks Catherine played, and it was nearly done.

'My lady,' Giles said when they were alone, 'you have made these lands more secure than ever they were in your father's time. You know I tried often to bring this about, and I was very much disheartened when the new earl did not bend himself to the task in the first days of your marriage. Lady, what threatens us?'

The mask of maidenly amiability and curiosity was displaced, and the face of an anxious, tired woman appeared. 'You know as much as I, Sir Giles. Why do you call me "Lady"? May I not be Catherine to you?'

'Catherine in love, if you desire, but you are a child no

longer, and I must call you "Lady" when my judgment leans upon yours.'

No more than Rannulf, did Sir Giles love to be ruled by a woman. Perhaps the Catherine of his old memory, the maiden in her father's house or the young bride of a gentle husband, would have trod amiss. Perhaps not, for the inner person does not change and only responds to outer circumstance. This Catherine was neither frightened by knowing that her vassals leaned on her decision nor worried that she could not hold them to whatever duty she wished them to perform. In this case it would be best to tell Sir Giles the absolute truth.

'Do not credit me with more than I deserve, Sir Giles. This tightening of our defences was no plan of mine delayed until my husband was too busy elsewhere to notice what I did.' Her smile changed to a soft laugh at the curious mixture of disappointment and relief on his face. 'What I do, I do by Lord Soke's direction, and I must say that his judgment and mine have ever been one on the management of these lands.'

'On all matters, Catherine?'

A suddenly piercing anxiety wiped the laugh from her lips and pinched the full mouth. 'Thus far,' she replied cautiously, knowing quite well what was worrying Sir Giles. 'It is plain to me that Lord Soke does not desire to draw the men of the earldom into this war. It is also plain that to his way of thinking it may be necessary – before the end.'

'To *his* way of thinking,' Sir Giles repeated with a slightly different emphasis, 'and to yours?'

Catherine did not wish to answer that question. There was still a chance that it would not require an answer. 'How, after these years, does your duty bind you, Sir Giles?'

'To you,' was the prompt reply. 'As long as you live, Lady, we are sworn through you. Mind you, Catherine, I have no word to say against your husband. He is a worthy man and a good lord. Had he been born to the honour, I would have followed gladly where he led, for honour's sake, although my head tells me this war is senseless. I hope to follow his son with an undivided loyalty – or, perhaps, I should say that my sons will follow his.'

Sir Giles stopped abruptly, troubled by the tears that filled

Catherine's eyes. She was disappointed, he thought, in not breeding, but how could a wife conceive when her husband was forever at court or at war. Or perhaps—It was no business of his, yet she was dear to him, and she had no mother, no father, no brother. That question about where his duty lay, did that refer to the war alone?

'Catherine,' he said gently, 'if you need protection, every man of this holding will stand behind you. You have a home in Bourne or in my keep whenever you desire it.'

'How kind you are,' Catherine said, but the tears were gone and a wry smile succeeded them. 'Indeed, it is Rannulf's fault that I am sad, but not for desire to fly from him. I would fly to him if I could. May the plague take the king and the duke also, aye, and all their heirs on either side.'

'Alas, Catherine, leave us at least one,' Sir Giles laughed in return. 'Someone must needs be king, and it will be worse if there is no clear line to follow. I take it that you do not regret the decision you made in London some years since.'

'In no way. If it were not for this war, I would love Stephen well for choosing so well for me in the matter of a husband. This talk of a clear line to follow and the loyalty of the men puts me in mind of something that needs saying. Here, alone with you, I am free of any coercion, am I not?'

'Most certainly.'

'Then I would make arrangement that if anything befall me before a blood heir be vouchsafed the earl of Soke and myself, that you follow the earl as my true heir, or, failing him, his heirs. Nay,' she laughed, 'I did not think to vanish into thin air, and I am young and strong, but life is as God wills. I would not like to think of my vassals struggling among themselves for supremacy. I would take oath of them to make all plain.'

'You have great faith in your lord.' Sir Giles frowned. 'If this comes to his ears – which it will – he will be free to handle you as he pleases. He has two sons already, and I know he did not seek a third wife. I have said he is a good man, but to place such temptation in any man's path is not right. To leave yourself thus naked to your husband's whim is not wise, Catherine.'

A blush and a confident trill of laughter was all the answer he received. Plainly Catherine did not fear nakedness would be any temptation to her husband to dispense with her company. Sir Giles wished he knew Rannulf better, wished he knew the elder son better. Probably Catherine had judged right with respect to her husband for she understood and could manage men, but sons were too often unlike their fathers. If it had been the younger boy, Sir Giles would have been easier in his mind. Catherine had brought Richard along with her so that the vassals would get to know him, and quite plainly he adored his stepmother. Richard would never be a danger to Catherine, but he was not Soke's heir either. Sir Giles opened his mouth to urge caution again, but was interrupted.

'One last matter,' Catherine said more seriously. 'Would you be content to make a blood bond with my husband?'

Now Sir Giles was thoroughly distressed. What Catherine was trying to do was totally beyond him, but he was certain that whatever her influence on her husband she could never convince him to pledge either of his sons to the daughter of a mere baron.

'What are you up to, Catherine?' he questioned sharply. 'If you think I will be any party to pledging a child behind his father's back for any profit, you are wrong. Beyond that, my willingness is not in point. Soke can look as high as he likes for daughters-in-law.'

'I was not thinking of the sons. Rannulf will choose well for them – as he does well for them in many things. My lord has also a bastard daughter, a sweet girl whom I have put in the way of becoming a good woman. Rannulf sees her not and sets no store by her content. He will give her something – someday – but she grows ripe for wedding and, because he has not pledged her and she had no person on whom to set her affection, she has given her heart to André. Now, if you would be willing to settle some small sum upon him, I hope—'

'Settle something upon him! I would sooner settle him! André! How could he dare?' Sir Giles gasped. 'How could he have dared cast his eyes on his overlord's daughter? Good God, that my brother should so shame his upbringing. The ungrateful devil!'

'They are young, and it is my fault also. I should have watched her more closely. Sir Giles, it is foolish to regret the harm that is done. If you will approach my lord with the offer, I believe he will be willing to consider the matter at least. I tell you he sets no store by the girl, and—'

'And nothing. What am I to say? Am I to suggest that I had the temerity to look so high for my penniless brother? I have children, Catherine — what can I give him? Or am I to suggest to the earl of Soke that his girl is so depraved that she would not be trustworthy were my brother denied her?'

Catherine laughed at his heat while she sighed at his reluctance. 'The sad fact is that she is not over-trustworthy in this. She has a grudge against her father, not at all unmerited, that makes her long to disobey him. If she could find another protector, I would not put it beyond her to urge him to take her without her father's consent.'

Sir Giles shook his head, his eyes dark with anger. 'If my brother so dishonours his name and his house, I will hunt him down myself. Let him go to make confession to your lord, and whatever punishment is visited upon him, I will applaud it. I will lift no hand to help him steal what he has no right to.'

How I hate men of honour, Catherine thought, looking after Sir Giles as he walked away. For honour he will destroy the brother he loves. It is fortunate that women are more wise than honourable. I will plead André's cause without concern for honour, thereby making two young people happy, giving my lord a strong and loyal son-in-law, and providing a blood connection of influence for Sir Giles. Where is the wrong in this pleading?

André, however, was pleading his own cause, all the better for not thinking of it once. No son could have been more tender and devoted, more impervious to insults and blows while nursing the irascible earl. He and Geoffrey had formed a strong conspiracy to keep Rannulf abed, forbidding all visitors for days and screening carefully the bits of news that were passed on to him. Both would have liked to carry Rannulf off to Oxford or some other safe keep, for his wound festered badly and would not heal, but Rannulf would not agree nor would the king, to whom Geoffrey had appealed, override Rannulf's order with his own.

All too soon the situation was taken out of their hands, Rannulf being summoned to the king's council. Soke grumbled so much at the order, wondering peevishly what a council could be needed for in the middle of a nearly successful siege, that Geoffrey and André had hopes he would refuse to go out of pure perversity. However, when Geoffrey, hoping to encourage that spirit in him, urged that a king's summons must be obeyed to ward off ill consequences, Rannulf turned on his son.

'If I followed my own inclinations and my own advantage, I would be sitting at home in my own keep and guarding my own lands. God knows,' he said all the more bitterly because of his uncertainty, 'that if a few more men were willing to do their duty without regard to their own good or ill consequences, we would not be snarling and snapping and leaping at each other's throats.'

Rannulf's generally ugly mood was by no means improved by his trip to Stephen's tent, for he stubbornly refused to be carried in a litter. The distance was short, but for a man who had spent most of the preceding two weeks on his back, it was exhausting to walk even so far and the movement caused the half-healed wound to open in several places. He replied, therefore, with ill-natured grunts to those men who were unwise enough to greet him, and settled himself as comfortably as possible to listen to the business in hand.

'As you know,' Stephen began, 'I have received offers of a new truce from the earl of Hereford.'

'I did not know,' Rannulf muttered irritably to himself, 'nor was I aware that he had broken the truce and could offer a new one.'

'You do not call his constant attacks on us a violation of the truce?' Stephen asked sharply.

Rannulf laughed. 'Truth, it seems, is not a matter of fact, but a choice of words. I would have said that Hereford was defending his allies against our attacks.' He gestured indifference. 'Say what you like.'

'Hereford,' Stephen continued, allowing his eyes to dwell on the earl of Soke, 'proposes that our forces be united to wrest Worcester keep from Waleran de Meulan and destroy him.'

A severe pang made Rannulf bite his underlip hard. 'In the name of God,' he growled, 'surely you did not need to call a council to refuse so mad a proposition. Come to the root of the matter so I can get back to my bed.'

'What is mad about the proposition?' Stephen asked stiffly. 'I did not think it mad, nor did the rest of the council. You alone seem to know better. You have changed your tune strangely, Soke. But a few short months since, you urged us most straightly to keep the truce with Hereford. You even went to his keep to discuss the matter. Did you discover something there you do not choose to tell us? At that time you said Hereford was a truth-teller and an oath-keeper. Have you discovered different?'

Rannulf, aware that Stephen's attitude towards him had altered strangely but hoping it was mere irritability, ignored most of what the king said. He looked around the circle of seated men. 'Did you all, indeed, agree to this?'

'Why not?' Northampton asked.

'Why not?' Rannulf roared, at the end of his patience. 'Waleran is Leicester's twin brother. Is it safe to infuriate Robert at this time by attacking de Meulan when he has not offended us? If that is not sufficient reason, we are almost successful here. Why should we raise the siege and run off on some hare-brained plan of an enemy's choosing?'

'Calm yourself, Soke,' Simon replied without heat. 'We will thrust the blame for the attack on Waleran on to Hereford, naturally. Also, we said nothing of raising the siege. You know how we have been bedevilled by Hereford's attacks. Because of them, we did not dare assault Wallingford, leaving our backs naked. Let Hereford but take his men off to Worcester, and we will use the chance to assault Wallingford.'

'With what force? More than promises will have to be given to Hereford before he will draw his men away. Do you realize that the terms of service of many of the men here are drawing to a close?'

'Money will be found to pay the men to stay here longer,' Stephen put in, 'and we will be rid of Waleran who is a curse of the worst sort.'

The mention of money brought an expression of uneasiness

to many of the faces of the council. Northampton frowned. 'It is getting less and less easy to find gold, my lord. Let us borrow the time from next year's service. If we can but put down the rebels firmly once, there will be no need for fighting men next year. Besides, it will not matter even if they do not stay. So much of our strength has been taken up in guarding our rear from Hereford that scarce a tithe of difference will be made by what we send to Worcester.'

A younger voice added eagerly, 'It is true that Waleran is in Worcester keep. So much we have made sure of, and also that William Beauchamp is his prisoner.'

'Then let Hereford go to Beauchamp's aid alone,' Rannulf snapped. 'Then we will be sure he, not we, enrages Leicester, and we will be eased of his annoyance as well as if we lent him aid. He is bound to help Beauchamp for his honour's sake.'

There was a restless murmur from the younger men, and Rannulf rubbed his head which ached with fever. His hand was so cold on his own forehead that he shuddered. The impatience of Stephen's younger vassals was comprehensible to him; a siege was weary, dreary work. It was depressing to think of the brave men within the keep, of their women and children, starving and thirsty. Besides, the lands around Wallingford had been so ravaged that food was scarce for the besiegers also, and even the sport of raiding was withdrawn. That the younger men should desire action was understandable. What was incomprehensible was that men like Northampton and Warwick seemed to agree with the young hotheads. Rannulf wondered if his illness and his ever-growing desire to be free of this war were clouding his mind, and he addressed himself to Warwick who had been silent throughout the previous exchange.

'You, too, agree to this? But wherefore? Where is our profit? We divide our forces, send them to another siege or exhaust them with another hard battle – for what purpose?'

'So that all men may see that Hereford had need to come to the king for help,' Stephen snapped before Warwick could open his mouth. 'They can see also that even the worst rebel receives that help when it is humbly asked. Will that not shake Hereford's supporters? Do you not see profit in that? Or do you see it too clearly? You were eager enough to have me offer clemency to Hereford before he asked it, thereby, perhaps, showing that we feared him. Now that he sues humbly, you oppose the making of terms. Perhaps you are unwilling for all men to perceive the rebel's weakness.'

The reasoning was good and Hereford was an honourable man; in spite of this Rannulf's body was braced as if to face an unseen danger. Stephen had all but accused him of treason. Rannulf met his lord's eyes steadily, but he was heartsick. There was a trap here somewhere, he could feel it, almost smell it as one could sometimes smell men hidden in ambush, and he dared not argue because Stephen in this mood would only become more obstinate.

Northampton looked uneasily from the king to his friend. 'My lord, there is no harm in a just caution. The earl of Soke is right to question, and it is better to be sure his fears are groundless than to quarrel among ourselves. Rannulf, we are all in agreement that it would be expedient to accept Hereford's submission. We do not intend to send more than a token force to support him. Indeed, we are come together now to take thought for the best disposition of our forces to accomplish our purpose.'

A general murmur of approval drove home to Rannulf the hopelessness of his position. The argument of who should go and who should stay rose and fell around him unheeded, until, at last, a question asked directly aroused him.

'Since I cannot stand against the full council, nor yet bring myself to agree with it,' Rannulf replied wearily, 'I must seek to salve my conscience as best I may.' He turned to Stephen, and the memory of years of kindness, of unasked favours freely bestowed, of genuine affection, made him purposely blind to the look of fear and suspicion in his overlord's face. 'Do not ask me to decide what is best on a matter of which I disapprove. Give me orders, and I will obey.'

The weary weeks dragged into months, the warm rains of September yielding to the bright, nipping days of October. Time proved to Rannulf, who had been told that since he favoured the siege of Wallingford he could abide there, that his instinct had been right. Worcester did not fall to assault,

257

even though Stephen drew more and more men from Wallingford, and in the end, Wallingford did not fall either. The forces were spread too thin; time and again breaches were made in the encircling camps of the besiegers and supplies were brought into the keep. Not much, perhaps, and not often, but enough to keep life in the bodies of the defenders. At last it became a moot question whether the besieged or the besiegers would die first of starvation. No good was to be got from the ravaged land, and what supplies were sent from other counties went to the king at Worcester.

Nothing went well. Rannulf's health was not much improved for he had an intermittent fever and the thigh wound still drained, although most of his strength had returned. Far more important was that the news Rannulf had from Leicester concerning the campaign in France grew steadily worse. Henry, as if merely stimulated by the defeat at Neuf-Marché, ravaged the valley between the rivers Isca and Andelle, took and burned the castles of Baskerville, Chitrey, and Stirpiney. With hardly a pause for breath, he added Brueboles and Ville to the score of keeps destroyed and then besieged and conquered Mount Sorel, bringing to heel his brother Geoffrey who had joined Eustace and Louis in a fit of dissatisfaction.

With his customary indulgence to those he loved, Henry promptly forgave Geoffrey and enlisted him in his own service. Together they turned upon Louis, who was attacking in Normandy, driving him off before he could complete the destruction of Bourg Reguliar.

'That is all the matter of fact which I have to recount,' Leicester wrote, 'but I have heard rumours as strong as these facts. It is said that Louis will compound with Henry in spite of Eustace's will and that Henry, who in the flush of his successes might profitably refuse a truce, will accept the terms. I have heard that he will do this because Hereford has sent letters and messengers plainly stating that if Henry does not come now, he will have nothing to come to – all matters moving themselves to consort to Stephen's will. This does not sound like Hereford's way, but he may be desperate, and his actions tend to confirm it, in that he has withdrawn the major part of his forces from the action at Worcester. So much as this I have written to Stephen, begging him to leave Waleran to his own devices and leave me to manage him and bring him to depart from Worcester in peace. Whether he will act upon it, God alone knows. For the love I bear you, I add this: in spite of the near-success of most of Stephen's ventures, the temper of the barons is very bad. The tenacity of Henry's desire to have the English throne, added to the increase of his power from marriage with the Poitevin she-wolf, has convinced many that there will be no peace until his desire is satisfied. If Henry comes, it will be necessary to take him or kill him *at once* in one great battle. Should he withstand or defeat Stephen even once, there will be a rush to his standard. Take heed, Rannulf, and God keep you.'

Rannulf was torn as he had never been torn before. If he thought he had reached the ultimate in pain when Catherine had shaken his confidence in war, he now knew better. In a way, it mattered very little to him what happened, for he was a loser, whether Henry came to the throne or Stephen held it. These new defeats would turn Eustace into a ravening wolf, and if Louis made truce and Henry came to England, Eustace would follow. That Rannulf knew he could still follow Leicester's advice, go back to his lands and remain quiet, merely intensified his agony. He had not realized, until he lost it, how much Stephen's love had meant to him. In spite of the king's weakness, possibly even because of it, he loved that kind and foolish man. Kind and foolish and so bitterly lonely now that Maud was dead. Rannulf's hand tightened on another scroll of parchment which he had held all the time that he was reading Leicester's letter.

That one held much better news, but did nothing to improve Rannulf's spirits. Catherine's letter reported that the earl of Norfolk lay quiet on his northern border, that the castles fronting that border had been stuffed and garnished for war without his taking offence, that Richard was well and all things ran smoothly on his lands. Little space was spent on these facts, and yet the letter was long. It was filled with fond inquiries about his health, gentle protests at his long absence, and tender questions about the possibility of his return.

It would not matter if he went for a little while. Nothing

could or would happen now at Wallingford. But, though he longed for Catherine as a man on fire longs for cold water, Rannulf dared not visit his wife. She would soothe him, but she would also weep and plead. She would hold Richard before his eyes and fill him with her fears – which were all the more horrible now because they were more real. Rannulf did not believe he had strength enough to resist either Catherine or those fears, yet he could not let Stephen go down to defeat alone like a lonely child crying in the dark. That was why Stephen could not recover from Maud's death – because he was a frightened child who would never grow up, a frightened child who spoke cruel words because he was frightened. When two children cry for a father's help, to which does he go?

He goes to the child whose need is greatest and most immediate. Catherine was frightened, but she was competent enough to manage his lands as long as no emergency threatened. Even if worse came to worst and he was lost to her through death or imprisonment, Geoffrey would protect her – he had given his oath on it. Slowly Rannulf drew pen and parchment to him to ask to be summoned to Stephen's side. Perhaps he could win the king to trust and love again. Even the darkness of a final defeat is not so fearful when hand locks in hand and a voice whispers courage.

# Chapter 17

Henry of Anjou, even more squat and bull-necked than his companions remembered him, looked with well-hidden dismay at Roger of Hereford. To William of Gloucester, who examined them both with a detached amusement, Henry had changed very little in other ways. He still dressed like the least of his own mercenaries; he was, if anything, even more physically and vocally restless, talking incessantly and fidgeting constantly with everything movable in the chamber. He laughed as readily, often on so slight an excuse that one might have thought him simple. For all of that, there was a poise and power in him that gave William pause and would surely give determination and confidence to the barons who came to support him.

'Do you mean, Roger, that you will not hold by your oath to support me? I cannot believe that!' There was a humourous asperity in Henry's voice, almost a parent's impatience with a well-meaning but wrong-headed child.

'No, my lord, I do not mean that, as well you know. But what I said in Devizes some years since, I still mean also. I will not lead your army.'

'I remember as well as you what you said in Devizes. You said you would lead no more lost hopes. Do you fear the failure of this venture?'

'No,' Hereford replied quietly. 'This time you will have it, which is why I think it no shame to do as you order without thrusting myself forward.'

'Thrusting yourself forward! Roger, what ails you? You summoned me hence. I could have swallowed half of Louis' realm and brought him to his knees except that you told me my people here were in the last extremity. I abandoned a winning war. I indebted myself to the moneylenders to the tune of half my revenues so that I might come well-armed and in haste. Have I not fulfilled my promise to return? Was it not worth the few years to come again with this show of power?'

It was useless to try to explain that he had not summoned Henry, Hereford thought. Not only useless but dangerous, because that summoning was wise and well-judged. He should have done it of his own free will, as he should have offered the truce to Stephen of his own free will. Honour accomplished nothing. Had William not been dishonourable, Wallingford and Worcester would both have been lost. Now Worcester was Beauchamp's again – not through his efforts, not through the blood he had shed, but because William and Robert of Leicester had induced Waleran de Meulan to take gold and leave the keep as soon as Stephen had abandoned the siege. Possibly William and Robert could have done it before the truce was made with Stephen. That would have been the honourable course, but then Wallingford would have fallen. It was all wise and expedient, but Hereford's soul was sick. Since he was sure Henry's cause would now prosper with or without him, he would perform his obligations without seeking to go beyond them.

Hereford met the puzzled exasperation in the grey eyes of the man who would certainly be the next king. 'Partly it is that show of power I do not like. I will not lend myself to leading foreign knights in the looting of my own land.'

'Roger, you will drive me mad. You know how uncertain of faith and temper most of the English barons are. Except for you, William, and Cornwall, they wait to see who will win before they do aught. Had I come naked and alone – as I have tried before – half would have leaped into Stephen's embrace and the other half remained aloof. If they see me already strong, they will come to me. I swear to you that I will send the troops I have brought back to France as soon as my position here is secure. Now are you content? I do not swear lightly.'

'You did not let me finish.' Henry's charm, his genuine affection and desire to please, were having their irresistible effect on Hereford's own affectionate disposition. He thawed appreciably and though his disgust at the situation did not decrease, he absolved Henry of responsibility for it. 'The other more important matter is that you do not need me, not as a leader in your enterprise. Henry, you are a man now, not a boy. It would be better to stand alone at the head of your vassals with no man your equal.'

For the first time William's voice entered the conversation. 'About that, my lord, Roger is right, as he is also about the foreign knights. Perhaps it was wise to bring them as a show of force, but it will be wiser still to send them off as soon as may be. The grandfathers of these English barons won their land by conquest – therefore these men have no love for invading armies. Since the case is thus, let us take some major stronghold of the king's. If he marches upon us and we defeat him, you will have all but accomplished your purpose, for few besides the very old men now hold by him.'

'Take a stronghold! Let us go to relieve Wallingford. They have suffered enough.'

Henry shook his head. 'William is right in this, Roger. Wallingford is now in little danger. The few troops still besieging them are worn out and indifferent. We will gain little by lifting that siege completely.'

Hereford opened his mouth again to protest, and then shut it. What William and Henry said made good sense. Honour alone directed that Wallingford, so long faithful, should be relieved and rewarded, and honour was an outmoded and useless commodity. Swallowing the physical nausea engendered by his mental turmoil, Roger of Hereford applied himself to the discussion of which city it would be most profitable to take.

It would have been so easy, Rannulf thought, listening in a detached way to the military arguments around him, to call his men together and go home. No one really wanted him here. To Northampton and Warwick, possibly, his opinion was still of value, but since Eustace had arrived he dared not open his mouth in council. Whatever he approved the king would turn against, and whatever he argued against immediately became the bright hope of the realm. He had tried before Eustace's return to win Stephen's confidence, and there he had erred greatly. Had he not seen the terror and longing in Stephen's eyes then, he could have gone as soon as those eyes and the heart, too, were shuttered against him. Rannulf knew he was turning bitter and spiteful under the treatment he was receiving, that he was doing the king more harm than good by his presence, but now that the plans were made it would really be treason to withdraw without Stephen's permission.

During the council meeting none spoke to Rannulf and few dared look at him. When it was over, however, and the king had retired, Northampton drew Rannulf into the hearth. Soke smiled encouragingly over the old man's shoulder at a flushed and visibly trembling Geoffrey.

'Thank God,' Northampton began, 'you keep your head, Rannulf.'

'Come now,' Soke replied smiling wryly, 'surely Stephen is not so lunatic yet that he will demand that.'

Northampton frowned. 'You make the most untimely jests. I meant only to compliment you upon the restraint of your temper for your looks were black enough and I expected moment by moment that you would burst into speech.'

'No, for whatever I say only makes matters worse.'

'You remember what I told you the night before you took the bridge at Wallingford.' Northampton shook his head significantly. 'Nonetheless, he must soon see his error with regard to you. Continue only to have patience. Stay, that is not what I wanted to speak of really,' he added as Rannulf shrugged cynically and prepared to move away. 'I do not understand why you were not pleased with what went forward. Do you disbelieve Jordan? After all, he is the castellan of Malmesbury and must know what is happening there.'

Rannulf laughed mirthlessly again. 'Of course not. What Henry does is logical enough and to attack Malmesbury is a matter of great profit to him and to Gloucester. I have no quarrel with the march to save Malmesbury, but believing what you do, are you still content to see Eustace go to Norfolk instead of coming with us?'

'What else can be done? It is certainly necessary to save Malmesbury, which is our one strong point near Gloucester's lands, but if Stephen moves so far west, Norfolk will take the chance to attack. Someone must withstand him also.'

'If Stephen were not mad,' Rannulf gestured dismissal of

Northampton's cautious glance around, 'he would send me to face Bigod, for it is plain that men fight best to protect their own. Then he and Eustace together could go against Henry. Failing that, he should hold Bigod himself, and let the young cubs oppose each other. Aside from the fact that a defeat would then not have such generally disastrous results, Eustace has recent experience of the Angevin's ways. It does not matter that he was beaten before,' he snapped, stilling the protest he saw coming. 'That will but lend rage to strengthen Eustace's purpose and, moreover, the prince is on his own ground now. In any case, anything would be better than leaving this to Stephen's vacillation.'

'Nay, Rannulf, in your hurt you wrong him. He will not turn aside now. His purpose must be firm.'

'As it was before Wallingford, eh?' Rannulf rejoined bitterly, and then, surprised by Northampton's agonized expression, he turned to see the king directly behind him with Jordan of Malmesbury.

For a frozen instant no one moved or spoke until Geoffrey, pushing rather rudely past Northampton to stand shoulder to shoulder with his father, broke the tableau. Rannulf faced his master with no change in expression, but he put a hand surreptitiously on his son's arm.

'I never claimed my judgment to be perfect,' Stephen blustered angrily, 'but it was not I who made the agreement. My wise council pressed me into it, you not least of all, Soke, by your talk of Hereford's trustworthiness. Ever I have bad advice and ever am I blamed for the ill result. Even when I go my own way and find success, I have no good of it. Then my barons nod at each other and clap each other on the back for their wisdom in acceding to the king's demands.'

There was a hysterical note of self-pity in the voice, and Rannulf frowned and cast an anxious glance at Jordan who looked more and more worried by the moment. What Stephen was doing among his major vassals, men who knew him well and long, was bad enough, but to expose his weakness constantly to men who were not accustomed to his ways was to lose badly needed supporters.

'Is not your criticism a trifle ill-directed, Soke?' Stephen continued with a sudden assumption of dignity. 'You speak largely enough of standing firm to a purpose, but I do not see that you have offered any help to forward that purpose.'

'My men have served their time, and more than their time,' Rannulf replied, his grating voice covering the indignant gasp Geoffrey gave. 'However, I assure you that I will summon them again. There is no term of service for a defensive war, and Henry will no doubt attack.'

'Very clever,' Stephen snapped, 'you will wait until he launches his attack, send from the very gates of Malmesbury across the length and breadth of all England. That way you will be sure that your vassals come too late.'

Rannulf's grip tightened excruciatingly on Geoffrey's quivering arm. He was barely able to control his own temper, but he dared not remind Stephen of what he had already done for him in Jordan's presence. Evidence of such ingratitude might well destroy what small faith the master of Malmesbury still had in his king.

'Do not missay me, my lord, my patience is not without limit. I have done you good service through the years, and—'

'And you would like to rest on that. To speak of your patience has an ugly sound of threat, Soke.' The new voice, sharp and angry, was Eustace's. He had arrived hard upon Henry's heels, and he had already managed to set half the vassals into a rage by his accusations. 'I say that we need every man we can muster. When that weak-livered brother-in-law of mine made peace with Henry, the Angevin fiend flew back to Barbefleur and took ship. He had an army ready in wait there. What do you think he has come for – to go on pilgrimage for his sins? It is time to summon the vassals and over time. I say that any man who does not respond to that call is a traitor.'

Perhaps it was useless, but Rannulf had to try. 'I do not deny you. As little as I like the cast of things, I know what you say is true. But, my lord,' he said, turning to Stephen, 'my men are weary and have no heart to fight in a strange place no matter how just the cause. Let me go and withstand Bigod. You know they will give their all to defend their own lands.'

The fitness of the request could not be doubted. Warwick and Northampton were willing to fight in the west because the only direction in which Henry could move with profit was east, and their lands lay in his path. Rannulf's men had more to fear from Norfolk, being well out of the way of the Angevin's probable advance, and would resent being drawn away from their own property when there was danger of Bigod's striking at them. Even Jordan, anxious for the safety of his own keep and town, could understand and nod approvingly. Stephen frowned doubtfully, his military good sense fighting against the suspicion which had been planted in him.

'You have shown yourself so consistently wise in matters of war,' Eustace snarled, having his own reasons to keep Rannulf away from his earldom, 'that we cannot spare you. Perhaps some compromise might be had. I understand that the men of Soke, your wife's vassals, have as yet done naught to aid their king – summon them. And, so that your lands be not left defenceless, let your son come with me. Surely your vassals will follow him.'

Had such a proposition been made in 1149 and had Geoffrey been old enough then, Rannulf would have agreed. At this moment he did not doubt that to let Geoffrey go would be tantamount to murdering him. Directly or indirectly, Eustace would see that the boy did not live a week, and, in addition to the satisfaction of his revenge, Rannulf's vassals would fall into Eustace's power. There was no need for even one word of denial. Eloquently, Rannulf's hand dropped from his belt and fell to his sword hilt.

'Geoffrey is not free to go,' Northampton interposed bleakly, knowing Rannulf too well and being too fond of Geoffrey himself to hope for acceptance of such a plan. Outwardly it had sufficient merit to place Rannulf in an even more unfavourable light when he rejected it as he must. 'My son who was Rannulf's squire was hurt nigh unto death when Soke took Wallingford bridge. I have given him Geoffrey to do John's service.'

Eustace was a brave man, but he knew when he had gone too far. Rannulf regarded him with a cold hostility which no threat or insult against himself had been able to engender, his hand still resting suggestively on his sword. Northampton was also angry, and the blaze of hate that made Geoffrey's blue eyes

267

incandescent could not be misread. Judging others by his own background, Eustace decided that Geoffrey would be no safe vassal to carry with him. One who bore such hatred could slip a knife between his sleeping lord's ribs or change sides in the middle of a crucial battle before he could be controlled or eliminated.

'If you say you need Geoffrey, of course I will not wrest him from you. Naturally your convenience must come before the welfare of the country,' Eustace spat at Soke.

Rannulf whitened and bit his lips; even Northampton's old face showed a touch of colour. Stephen, aroused almost too late, now became alarmed. Eustace's tongue was alienating vassal after vassal, and Northampton was far too powerful to be freely insulted.

'Eustace!' he protested. Then, 'You must pardon him, Simon, and you also, Rannulf. These are bitter days for us and make us all do and say things we do not mean. Part of Eustace's suggestion, however, is most meet and fitting. We gave you Soke that you might be stronger in our defence, Rannulf. You have used it to enrich your coffers without adding one sword to our force. We had better left the lady to her own choice for all the benefit Soke has brought us. If, as you say, your own vassals are weary of their king's service, it is time to press your wife's men into action.'

Had Rannulf been twenty years younger, he would have burst into tears of frustration and chagrin. Had not a stranger been present, he would have told Stephen what he thought of him in no uncertain terms. As it was, Stephen's injustice left him choking. Men were not all that made a war, and the earldom of Soke had been squeezed unmercifully to pay for Eustace's expedition to France and the fruitless siege of Wallingford. He bit back his angry self-justification, his hand clenching on his sword hilt.

'If the men who hold Sleaford are reluctant to leave that land when Bigod stirs, think how much less eager will be those whose keeps face his borders.' So far Rannulf had controlled his boiling emotions, but the stubborn refusal to listen to reason that was mirrored in Stephen's face tore that control from him. 'I tell you they will be less than useless, not only because their hearts will be on their own lands but because they have never taken part in this war before. In fact, they are not to be trusted against Henry. You well know, my lord, their sympathy is for the opposite cause.' Jordan or no Jordan, that warning had to be given.

All pretence of civility now left Stephen. 'Did you swear sword-oath to me?' he shrieked. 'Are you my man or will you declare yourself openly a traitor? If you are grown too feeble to control your men, another must be found who can do so. I command you to summon the vassals of Soke to my defence — and woe betide you if they come not.'

A stillness like death had fallen in that portion of the great hall while vassal and servant alike awaited for Rannulf's reaction. White-faced, torn between his love and his contempt for the man to whom he had given it, Rannulf stood mute in the flickering light of the blazing hearth.

'How dare you speak so to one who all but laid down his life in your cause only a few months since!'

The young voice, trembling with fury, spurred Rannulf into action as nothing else could. Swiftly, he blocked Geoffrey's leap at the king's throat, and, forgetting all in his need to protect his child, said aloud the only thing which could calm the boy. 'He is mad, my son!'

With the words, a frightened conviction came into Jordan's face, fear filled Stephen's eyes, and Eustace looked both angry and satisfied. Desperately, Rannulf tried to pass the words off as a momentary display of his usual habit of allowing his tongue to run away with him.

'Nonetheless,' Rannulf continued, seeming to recover himself, 'a king's command to an homage-bound vassal must be obeyed. Bring me pen and parchment, and I will send to the countess of Soke and bid her order her vassals to come to me.'

The letter was written there and then given to Stephen to read so that he might be sure it contained nothing but the summons. Rannulf even suggested that a royal messenger be sent instead of one of his own men. 'I would not wish to be suspected of sending my wife a message by word of mouth. There, my letter is sealed — do with it what you will.'

There was some chance that Stephen would never send the

summons now that he was assured of having his own way. There was also a chance that Catherine, whose sympathies were with Henry, would refuse outright to act on the orders. What was likeliest of all was that Catherine would be confused and terrified by such an order. She knew nothing of summoning men and had never received an order from Rannulf before without the minutest instructions on how to carry it out. In addition, although he had ordered her to gather the vassals, he had not written a word of needing them in haste nor given a specific point at which to gather them. Perhaps she would have sense enough to write for more specific instructions. Perhaps she would try to fumble along as best she might. In any case there would be a delay. If that delay lasted long enough, it might be possible for Rannulf to countermand the order entirely. Not that Rannulf intended to cheat Stephen out of the service he owed. Even now he could not do that. He had given sword-oath and he would fulfil his obligations – but in his own way.

Stephen and Eustace departed to discuss what best use could be made of Rannulf's letter. Jordan appeared to go with them and then melted into the shadows behind the fireplace. Northampton watched until the king and his son were out of hearing and then turned to Rannulf.

'Thank God you still hold by us. I swear I do not know if I could have done the same under equal provocation.'

'One does not lose one's patience with a man made half mad by overgreat burdens, nor with a mooning youngster – at least I do not for long. But perhaps I have suffered more from my children than you have from yours,' Rannulf replied with a glance at Geoffrey.

'I am sorry, papa. I know I should have held my tongue, but when I heard him abuse you, I—'

Rannulf smiled wryly. 'It did no harm to let them know we cling together or that there is fire in the cub also. And that brings me to my thanks to you, Simon, for saving me the denial I would have needed to give Eustace.'

Northampton gestured wearily. 'Nothing. I am sorry I cannot do more.'

'You should not even do so much again. Nay, I do not

suggest this for your safety, although it is good to know it will be increased. What I wish to prevent is the weakening of your influence with the king. Anyone who is connected with me in opinion or love will be suspect – of what I am damned if I know, but suspect nonetheless – and there must be some influence on Stephen besides that of Eustace.'

What Rannulf said was true, but the earl of Northampton was now so aroused that he hated to give the appearance of weak-kneed yielding to Stephen's vagaries. They decided, after some talk, that the good to come was more important than appearances. Rannulf remained staring into the flames after Northampton had gone. A movement in the shadows at the other side of the hearth caught the corner of his eye and he looked up, but no one seemed to be there and Geoffrey, beside him, moved impatiently. Rannulf chewed his lip. They would need to fight at Malmesbury, and if Catherine acted as he hoped she would, he would have only his personal guard with him. That would not be sufficient. Geoffrey and he were alone in the hearth; the other petty nobles who ordinarily gathered around a great man to draw his attention were now fearful of contamination with Soke's taint and kept their distance.

'When you have finished your duties, ride to the abbey over the hill and buy me parchment, pens, and ink. I have some letters to write. The Lady Catherine is a very timid woman,' he added smiling faintly. 'I hope she will be so frightened by what I have written that she does not act at all or only writes to ask me what I mean. If she does that, the vassals of Soke will come too late, if they come at all. Still, I would not cheat the king of the duty I owe him—'

'He does not deserve your loyalty. What benefit is it to us if he wins?'

'Probably it is of benefit to no man any more,' Rannulf's voice faltered, 'but I gave him sword-oath once, and for fifteen long years he gave me love. When I am sick and mad, will you desert me and let me die alone?'

Geoffrey shook his head in angry denial; he could not conceive of such weakness in the father he knew.

'I cannot leave him, but remember that you owe Stephen nothing and neither of us is bound to Eustace. When I am dead, you are free to follow your own path. Meanwhile, I wish to gather a force of younger sons and brothers from my vassals. There should be enough to give us a pretty band of young men to lead. I will have to pay them, since they owe me no service, but it will be cheap at the price to know that our lands are guarded against both Bigod and Eustace by having our own vassals in their own keeps. Here is a piece of gold to give to the monks.'

Jordan, still shadowed, nodded to himself and moved away quietly. The earl of Soke was far from a traitor; he was a man tried beyond bearing by a bad or – maybe worse – a mad overlord.

'My lady,' Mary said, coming into the solar where Catherine was embroidering by the fire, 'there is a royal messenger below.'

The needle remained poised above the cloth while every bit of pretty colour faded from Catherine's face. Even her hair, which had gleamed gold in the ruddy firelight, seemed to become wan, dulling to silver. She put a hand on her frame and attempted to stand, but her legs would not support her. Rannulf was dead! There could be no other reason for a royal messenger to come to her house.

'Send him here,' she whispered.

It would be better that no one see her until she had mastered her first shock of grief. If she were to hold these lands for Rannulf's children and save herself and Mary from being snatched into hasty marriages, she would need to give the appearance of confidence. The seal she broke was a blob of wax, its device invisible to her tear-blinded eyes, but the sprawling, uncertain hand made her gasp. Hastily, making no attempt to decipher what was written, Catherine looked at the bottom of the scroll. Thank God, there was his name, no half-written letter finished by another hand to say that he would write no more. In her first relief she could do no more than press the senseless parchment alternately to her breast and her lips. If she had not lost him, nothing else mattered.

Rannulf's device very nearly cost him his aim, for when Catherine finally read what was written, her grief and despair

272

were not much inferior to what she had felt at first. What difference did it make how you lost your husband? Would his death divide them any more surely than her refusal to obey him in so important a matter? Caught in the fresh memory of her agony of loss, Catherine's first impulse was to throw all else away and yield to Rannulf's demand.

The sensation did not last long. Catherine had been over the pros and cons of this question too many times in the past long months, and the incompleteness of Rannulf's order soon added to her confidence. He wished her to write for further instructions and thereby gain a delay. That, however, was not sufficient. The earldom of Soke, at whatever cost to herself, must not join this war. Besides, she need not fear a permanent separation, Catherine decided. Rannulf loved her dearly. He would be very angry for a time, but when he came to consider the advantages of her resistance his reason would be powerfully impelled by his passion to find justification for forgiving her.

How to refuse was the immediate problem. Should she write begging pardon in advance, a meek letter of explanation? What explanation could she offer in a letter? She dared not admit that she was hedging against a rebel victory in case the letter should fall into hands other than Rannulf's. For the sake of her husband's safety, it would be best to act like an irresponsible woman who merely wished to exercise her own power in his absence. At first that might make Rannulf even more furious, but in the period which must intervene between his receipt of the letter and his meeting with her, he would surely come to understand her behaviour.

By morning she had constructed a small masterpiece of featherbrained nonsense containing, among other things, the idiotic statement that a husband should request politely, not demand in a cold official order, the service of his wife's vassals. That should infuriate not only Rannulf but every other man who laid eyes upon it. If there were repercussions, they would be verbal criticisms of herself, and Rannulf would be the recipient of sympathy rather than suspicion. Any man who had a wife who could make such a lunatic statement deserved pity, not punishment. Catherine's next step was to refuse to deliver this missive to the royal courier. When he asked her for a reply, she said only that she had been grossly insulted and she would not be hurried. At last, but not until he threatened to leave without an answer, Catherine delivered her letter to him with an angry pout and a pettish command that it be given into Rannulf's hand alone.

'And you may tell my husband,' she added, compounding the felony, 'that I am not a servant and am not to be ordered about like one.'

# Chapter 18

The earl of Soke received the answer to his letter in unlooked-for publicity. As Catherine suspected, the messenger had not gone to her husband directly but to the prince, his own master, and now Eustace came with the messenger to see Rannulf's reaction. His fury at being refused the service of the vassals was much mitigated by the manner of the refusal, but he was still suspicious that Rannulf had somehow contacted his wife and prearranged the reply. Certainly, Eustace realized, Rannulf had not arranged the time of the reply, because he appeared at his call, a ridiculous figure in a hastily donned shirt, clutching a naked sword.

'The messenger has returned from Sleaford,' Eustace said.

Rannulf dropped his sword point to the ground and rubbed sleepy eyes, wondering where Geoffrey was. 'For that you shriek my name at the door of my tent? Could you not send the man within? Well, what says my lady? When do the men come?'

Eustace nudged the courier and glanced at the recent favourites among the vassals who had accompanied him. Now if Rannulf had not planned this, they would see some sport. The royal courier took a hesitant step. He had laughed when he recounted the tale to Eustace initially, but he did not laugh now. Rannulf's scowl was not inviting, and he had a reputation for acting first and questioning later. Moreover, the muscles hidden by that silly-looking shirt could strike through mail and bone to cleave a man in two. His voice trembled.

'I beg pardon, my lord. It is no fault of mine.'

'Why should you beg pardon for doing your duty?' Rannulf asked, but he deliberately broke the seal without looking for signs, which, indeed, he would have found, that someone had lifted it with a hot knife.

'Did not the lady send some verbal message to her lord?'

The messenger licked his lips; he was between the fire and the bottomless pit. 'She said – it is no fault of mine, indeed it is not – that she is not a servant and not to be ordered about like one.'

'What!'

Plainly, whatever Rannulf had expected, a message like that was not part of it. Eustace had certain satisfaction in the knowledge that Rannulf was not receiving unalloyed pleasure from his unmerited reward of the earldom of Soke. Meanwhile Rannulf had begun to read the parchment with staring eyes, and Eustace was further amused at the stunned, disbelieving incredulity in his face. Halfway through, Rannulf shook his head as if dazed and began again. Either Catherine had gone insane, or she had not written the letter.

He did not complete the second reading of the missive, either. It was unnecessary. 'The countess of Soke,' he muttered, 'denies her men.' He swallowed with an effort. 'What would you have me do? I can bring them if I go to summon them in person.'

'By that time they will be needed no longer. We have already delayed too long waiting for the levies of my father's ungrateful barons. Now he must march with what force he has at hand, and if his efforts are not attended with success, it is your fault and the fault of those like you.'

Rannulf did not reply; he had not even heard. His ears were filled with Catherine's voice in every tone he had ever heard her use to him, but whether he imagined the quivering fury of her brief tempers or the icy rejection of their long estrangement, he could recall no tone in which she would have spoken those words. There had always been the chance that she would refuse openly to summon the men because she and they leaned towards the rebels, but the way in which she refused was false. It came to him slowly, and then he did not know whether to shriek with laughter or roar with fury. So Catherine thought he needed to hide behind a woman's skirt! Well – perhaps she was right. Then both anger and mirth left him, and he was filled with a great desolation. The king, one of his frightened children, had rejected him, and Catherine, the other, had grown up and needed him no longer.

Geoffrey found him still standing where the others had left him, and his anxious inquiries aroused Rannulf sufficiently to permit him to dress and arm. Whether he truly absorbed the information that a large contingent of men had arrived, Geoffrey could not tell. Rannulf's eyes were dazed and withdrawn, his actions and orders the automatic result of long habit. For the next week more men drifted in, answering Rannulf's summons to his own vassals, but he did no more than receive them, waving them off into Geoffrey's care. He listened to what Geoffrey suggested about provisions and the order of the march, but to questions he replied only with vague grunts.

It did not matter that week, nor even while they were marching west, for Geoffrey and André had become an efficient team perfectly capable of handling routine military matters. When they arrived at Malmesbury at about midnight, however, and could see the campfires of another army on the far side of the Avon, the situation became acute.

'Where shall we make camp, my lord?' André asked in a solicitous voice for the second time in a few moments.

The face that turned to his showed nothing but blank incomprehension for the space of a short breath. Suddenly, terrifyingly, the expression altered to one of naked hate.

'How have I offended you, my lord?' André gasped

There was a tense, breath-held silence, and Rannulf let his eyes slide away from André, who cared for him as if he were a child. He began to laugh. 'You have offended me in nothing. Life has offended me. What did you say before?'

'Where shall we camp, my lord? Look.' André gestured to the fires of the army across the river.

Instead of answering the question or following André's outflung arm with his eyes, Rannulf lifted his head sharply and sniffed. Then, with a growing frown he watched the scudding clouds. 'Camp?' he asked, again vaguely, but now as if his mind was on a more immediate problem. 'Do not camp at all. Let the men eat and bait the horses. Do not move until I return.'

In the mass of milling footsoldiers and knights, it was almost impossible to find Northampton's camp. Most men were too tired, too busy seeking what comfort they could find, to wish to answer inquiries. Rannulf had his own methods of inducing co-operation, however, and after a few false casts which left certain individuals cursing him as they nursed bruised arms or shoulders, he found someone to lead him right. Simon of Northampton was huddled over a fire and raised a face twisted with misery to him.

'Go away!'

'Simon, there is going to be a storm – a bad storm.'

'You think that I do not know? Is not every bone in my body screaming? I am in agony, Rannulf. In Christ's name, have mercy. Go away.'

'We will never be able to ford the river in the storm, and it is my guess that Henry, knowing this, will either continue to ravage the town or form his men in battle array and challenge us.'

'Rannulf,' Northampton sighed, 'I do not care what he does. Go away and leave me in peace.'

'But Simon, this is a dangerous situation. If we withdraw, Henry will do nothing during the storm anyway, and we will be able to fall upon him as soon as it is over. On the other hand, if we seem to be powerless against him, those in the keep – if it still be ours – may lose heart and open to him. You must go and make this plain to Stephen. Indeed, I am sorry that you are not well, but—'

'Go away!' Northampton screamed. 'You are a little late with your news. The king has been told and will not withdraw.'

Rannulf shrugged his shoulders at this piece of information. He was a fool and should have realized that he would not be the only one to see which way the straws lay in the wind. Naturally, having been criticized for shifting his purpose at Wallingford, Stephen would now hold firm when he should shift. Rannulf shivered slightly in the damp blast of wind which caught and tore at his furred cloak. Shielding himself on the leeward side of his horse, he made his way back to where his men grumbled and crouched with their backs to the wind. When he tripped over Geoffrey's feet, he stopped and laughed harshly.

'Have you been to confession of late, my son?'

'Do we fight, papa?' Geoffrey came to his feet with lighting eyes. Then, answering the question, 'Yes, on Sunday as was meet. Nor do I have need to go again – I think.' The last was a slightly doubtful response to the expression which crossed his father's face.

'Face into the wind and see where it is coming from – and then use your wits and do not ask foolish questions. Nay, this is a time for miracles, and I have heard tell that those are brought about only by the pure in heart. Pray, Geoffrey – you are more like to be heard than an old sinner like myself – pray that the wind will shift.'

He turned from Geoffrey, leaving him to puzzle out the relationship between wind and battle for himself, to give instructions to André. Before they had a chance to do more than consider whether it would be worthwhile to try to set up shelters, a herald arrived to summon Rannulf to a king's council. His immediate reaction to the message was to refuse to go. Stephen certainly did not want him there and either he had been informed because the king had said generally to 'summon the barons' or because it was impossible to ignore so powerful a vassal.

More sober consideration drove him to follow the herald meekly. For safety's sake he had to be present to know what was going forward, even if he could exert no influence on the events which would transpire. His oath of homage to Stephen would end with his death, and Geoffrey would then be free to choose his own master. From the boy's reticence on political matters, Rannulf was certain that Geoffrey would swear to Henry – and that choice might well be the best way after all. A despot was better than a madman. Force or reason might control a despot. Nothing could control a lunatic.

In Stephen's tent the younger men drew aside a trifle, but Rannulf did not pass through their ranks to the front of the group. He had nothing to do or say, and listening might be accomplished as well from the background where he could lean against a tentpole and ease his still-aching leg. Stephen was glancing about now, checking the arrivals.

'Where is Northampton?'

'Sick, my lord,' one of the heralds replied. 'He will not come.'

Stephen grunted. Rannulf's lips twitched. He doubted that the king had seen him, but noted that he was not asked for.

'I have called this council,' Stephen began, 'to arrange the order of battle for the morrow.'

'My lord, the storm does not abate, nor does the wind shift. It may not be possible—'

'That, too, I have considered,' Stephen said sharply. 'Let us do one thing at a time and come to that anon. There are three fords. One below the town which enters directly into the Angevin's camp, one which leads directly to the gates of the keep, and one which comes up behind the keep at a bend a mile or two up-river. Now, has anyone a particular choice of passage and a reason for that choice?'

There was a babble of voices which soon sorted itself out into a general disposition of the troops. Rannulf's lips twitched again as he found himself relegated to following the king through the central ford. He felt a twinge of impatience, for he would have preferred to lead a group as his station and experience would normally entitle him to do. Nonetheless, he acknowledged silently that Stephen's force would be the most likely to see heavy fighting, and he had an urgent desire to fight. That part of the council was satisfactory enough and gave Rannulf no reason to regret his decision to hold his tongue. He was disquieted by the reserve of many of the older men. They did not hang back nor object; in fact they were far too indifferent and agreeable and, from his point of observation, Rannulf noted more than one exchanged glance.

'Now,' Stephen continued when everyone seemed sure of the part he had to play, 'Jordan has offered to cross the upper ford tonight. He has arranged a signal with his men who will permit him to enter through a small postern gate. If we are successful in crossing the river, the men of Malmesbury keep will issue out to help us.'

Rannulf closed his eyes wearily and thought he should have stayed in his own camp and gone to sleep. Nothing had happened here that was worth the hour he had spent on his feet.

'If we cannot cross the river, Jordan will destroy Malmesbury keep from within so that it cannot be taken and used against us and so that the Angevin's effort will be turned to naught.'

'No!' Rannulf shouted the word, surprised to hear his own voice but shocked past restraint. Jordan would never commit his keep to the flames – so much Rannulf could read in the indifference with which the man had attended to the entire proceedings. A good number of the barons also knew this, and Rannulf could read which from the expressions of resentment on their faces. They were not traitors in the absolute sense of desiring a victory for Henry of Anjou; they were merely men who did not wish to fight for Malmesbury, men from the north, from the southeast, and the far east who had little interest in what happened to the west and midlands. Rannulf looked for Warwick who would surely support him, but Warwick had gone with Eustace.

'So you are here, Soke,' Stephen remarked coldly. 'Why do you protest? Would you rather see another strong keep in rebel hands?'

A tide of colour surged up Rannulf's throat and stained his face. He, too, had little to gain from saving Malmesbury, but though he had been rejected he could not see Stephen destroy himself. The king believed in this plan and in the men who supported it. Rannulf feared that Stephen's spirit could not endure another breaking of faith.

'It is not meet nor fitting to ask a man to destroy his home and his livelihood,' Rannulf began reasonably. 'This storm cannot last above a day or two. The Angevin's men will suffer from it as much as we. Bid the men of Malmesbury to hold firm. If we cannot fight tomorrow or even the next day, it will be very soon.'

'My loyal friend Jordan has agreed willingly to this plan,' Stephen replied icily, 'and we will requite him in full measure and overflowing for his loss.'

How could a man be requited for the lands he had loved and the place in which he had spent his life? What would Stephen have to give after this disaster? This was the last chance the king would have to fight Henry with his full strength. Leicester had said, and Leicester was usually right, that a defeat would turn the tide in the Angevin's favour. To withdraw was to be defeated without even the chance of victory offered by battle.

'But wherefore this haste to destroy what was not lightly built? Perhaps if we had come here before the Angevin and our force was so feeble that we knew we could not withstand him, such desperate measures would be called for. Why should we act as if we are defeated before we even cross swords? Let us wait until the storm passes and then fight.'

The men whose lands were farthest west began to look questioningly at the king, and one said, 'It is true enough that a day or two cannot matter. A keep may be destroyed at any time.'

'Aye,' Rannulf continued stubbornly, 'and it must be considered that, while Jordan is loyal and willing, his men, who do not understand so well, may be loath to set flames to their home without apparent reason.'

'Why do you ever oppose my will?' Stephen shrieked. 'I have heard you say I am mad. Doubtless you have repeated that tale to all to break my men's faith in me. I am not mad! There is reason good and sufficient for what I do. Malmesbury is set too near the rebels' strongholds. Even if we were able to drive them off, they would return. I cannot be forever running to the west to support one keep.'

In the absolute silence which fell, Rannulf had more than enough time to wish his tongue had been cut out in his youth. He had exposed something far more dangerous than a little madness in the king. Stephen's courage had broken. He wanted Malmesbury destroyed because he was afraid to fight. Rannulf watched the faces of the men of the midlands turn to stone. They realized that Stephen was prepared to cede the west of the kingdom to Henry of Anjou and that their keeps would become the outer ring of defences. Some may have wondered why Stephen had marched west at all, but Rannulf knew. Eustace still desired to be king, and Stephen could deny his son nothing – in his presence. The trouble was that when Eustace was gone, the impetus was gone also.

By the next morning Rannulf had recovered from his misery of guilt. He had spent the past two weeks bringing himself to acknowledge that he was a useless and dangerous encumbrance to his family. Catherine was neither timid nor helpless; she could scheme better than he could and her connection with the rebel cause would stand her in good stead. Geoffrey knew nearly all there was to know of military science, and Leicester would stand behind him as a political bulwark. Rannulf became almost cheerful, driving his wretched men from the miserable shelter they had been able to find with the grim humour of impersonal despair. The wind was such that they could scarcely move against it at all, and sleet fell in silver sheets. Rannulf's fur cloak was glazed with it and pressed on his shoulders with five times its normal weight; water, melted from the ice by his body heat, trickled down his helm and face, making its way under his mail hood to send chill rivulets onto his back and chest. André's mount fell and could not rise on the sliding, ice-coated ground without help; Geoffrey's placed one foot awry and slid uncontrollably down a small embankment oversetting his rider into a little stream. Rannulf laughed heartily at both mishaps while he directed the small rescue operations, making both his son and his devoted retainer long to kick him.

They could see nothing funny in the situation at all, and it became less and less humorous as they struggled to advance towards the ford. The bank, which sloped gently into the water, was now a smoothly glazed slide, well coated with an even more treacherous layer of rolling hail. No horse or footman could prevent himself from careening down into the water once that surface was trodden on. The wind blew violently from the northwest, driving the sleet and hail so hard that it stung the eyes and lacerated the lips. To keep one's eyes open was torture; to close them was death. Both André and Geoffrey were willing to fight, but how they would be able to do so neither could imagine. Their sword hands were numb and they could not chance removing their cloaks. If the furred garments were laid aside, one invited death by freezing; to retain them, however, imprisoned one's arms and made fighting impossible.

The men grumbled and cursed, murmuring rebelliously that they would not fight. Even a madman like Stephen, they said, should see that God had set His face against this battle. Geoffrey and André rode up and down the ranks, speaking cheeringly, pointing out that it sleeted and hailed on the other side of the river as well as on theirs. True, the men snarled, but there the wind came from behind and, if it drove a man, drove him forward. It did not blind his eyes, nor numb his hands, nor freeze his heart. André made what replies he could, but he was chilled with a cold that had nothing to do with the weather. Never before had his confidence in his own skill and strength deserted him, not even on the bridge before Wallingford. When he met Geoffrey crossing through the ranks, he stopped and plucked at the huddled figure.

'Will you do me a favour?'

Geoffrey turned surprised blue eyes on him, tried to reply, and found that he could not speak because his teeth were chattering. Unwilling to display what might be taken as fear to his father's retainer, he simply nodded.

'If I come not alive from this meeting, will you greet your sister Mary from me and tell her – tell her—' Tell her what? He had no right to love, less right to confess that love to his lord's heir when he kept the secret from the earl – a remarkably foolish afterthought he realized, since to mention Mary's name was to confess. 'Tell her,' André said defiantly, 'that my last thought was of her.' If he died, it would not matter, and if he lived and Geoffrey carried the tale to Soke so much the better.

Again Geoffrey nodded, the surprise dying out of his eyes and a kind of romantic respect taking its place. As yet he, himself, had not been touched by the new-style passion called love, but the conventions of l'amour courtois, although new, were already familiar to him from the tales he had heard. No wonder André was so brave and devoted to his father. He was doing his *devoir* to his lady. Soon, the boy thought, I will find a lady of my own and I will be stronger and braver for her sake. No thought of marriage intruded into the romantic notion. Marriage was a thing apart from love, a thing to be arranged by one's father or one's overlord. Marriage was for the breeding of children, for the increase of lands, and for linking bloodlines. Love, Geoffrey glanced at André's face, love was something else.

Rannulf heard the men grumble also, but he made no

attempt to lift their spirits or stiffen their courage. He shivered impatiently in the saddle, wondering why the farce of forming the battle lines had been ordered. Surely it was impossible to attack. He wiped the sleet from his face again, and then cursed himself as the hail stung more bitterly while a new coating formed. What were they waiting for? To freeze solid where they stood? It took him two tries to kick his horse into movement, because his legs were so numb he could not direct them, nor really tell when they had connected. When he reined in again, it was directly to Stephen's left, and he no longer needed to ask for what they waited. The group around the king sat with their eyes anxiously fixed on Malmesbury keep.

'Perhaps the flames will not rise in this storm,' Stephen muttered.

'There should at least be some smoke,' an unknown voice replied.

A cackle of near-hysterical laughter rose in Rannulf's throat and was suppressed. The king had believed Jordan. He was waiting so that his army could see the keep of Malmesbury destroyed, see the discomfiture of Henry's troops, and take heart from the knowledge that what seemed like an Angevin victory could be turned into a defeat by strategy. As if any man could take heart from seeing a castle wantonly destroyed, a strong haven levelled into nothingness.

If only it were not so cold! Rannulf pinned his eyes on the opposite shore, on the ranks of men drawn up to resist them if they tried the crossing. Brief snatches of sound came across in the blasts of wind, rough but good-humoured curses and bursts of laughter. The force was smaller than theirs, but Henry's men were in good heart. There were sudden howls of cheerful greeting as a group of four men rode across the front of the line. One of them, Rannulf thought, must be the young Angevin. They stopped nearly opposite Stephen's group and looked across the river. Some discussion was taking place; the voices were too low to be carried even by the fierce wind, but the gestures were open and confident. Rannulf watched with a growing sense of envy, the longing to follow someone sure and bold struggling with his old affection.

Now a rider broke through the ranks of men and interrupted

the talk of the four leaders. From his excited gestures it could be guessed that he was a messenger with important news. Rannulf, for one, did not need, although he heard nothing, to guess what that news was. The last drop of warmth faded from his being, the little spot that had clung to the hope that men were not as weak and faithless as he expected them to be.

'There,' Stephen cried excitedly, 'the keep must be burning and we cannot see – Oh God, no!'

The drawbridge, plainly visible over the moat which was fed by a canal from the river, was being lowered. A hoarse, exultant cheer broke from the Angevin force, many of whom had turned their backs on Stephen's army to watch Malmesbury keep fall into their hands without a drop of blood being shed. Slowly a number of the men around Stephen drew back so that when the king turned his haggard face to his vassals, Rannulf was the closest man to him.

'He swore,' Stephen choked, 'on the Cross, on the Body and the Blood, on the relics of the martyrs. Traitor! All are traitors! He swore!'

There was a murmur of half-hearted consolation, an uneasy shifting of eyes and seats in the saddle. To some it did not matter at all; to some it mattered too much.

'Go and leave me alone,' Stephen screamed. 'That is what you wish to do. Go! Desert me! Traitors all!'

Now the murmurs and looks were angry on the faces of those in whom indifference did not rule. A number of men, some taking the words for a dismissal deliberately, some truly angered, lifted reins and set spurs to their mounts. Stephen's eyes, blazing, swept over the men who remained and fixed at last on the closest.

'What do you here, Soke? Do you remain to triumph over my discomfiture?'

'I remain to receive your further orders, my lord,' Rannulf replied woodenly. So much he still owed Stephen, for he had caused at least part of the trouble. 'Perhaps we can—'

'We can do nothing!' A sob broke the voice. 'You warned me – you alone.'

In a moment Stephen would begin to weep, and this was not the time or place for it. Rannulf spoke with deliberate stolidity.

'Well, Henry cannot remain forever in Malmesbury, and it is profitless for him to move west. He must cross the river and come to us. If we withdraw and wait for him, we may yet withstand him. Even the attempt to do so will put heart into the lords of the midlands, and—'

Stephen was shaking his head stubbornly. 'We have no food, no shelter, and it is so bitterly cold. I must have time, time to gather my strength and to think what to do. I will return to London.'

It was useless to argue, useless to say that he understood the difficulties concerning food and shelter, useless to explain that standing firm would bolster men's faith while the defeatist move Stephen planned would drive more men into Henry's arms.

'Very well, my lord,' he replied.

'Not you,' Stephen said softly, and when he looked at Rannulf his eyes were clear and sane and knowing. 'Can you not see that I am like a plague? Get you gone from me, lest the ill that I have become slay you. Go guard your own lands against Bigod, and release my son to come to me.'

Rannulf swallowed sickly. If Stephen had spoken one more harsh word, if his eyes and heart had remained shuttered, perhaps he could have freed himself. Now he was bound to the death or prison or exile which was Stephen's future. It did not matter. No one else needed him. 'I have taken the contagion already,' he muttered. 'Let me bide with you.'

'No, for I cannot withstand him.' Stephen did not name his son, but there was no one else of whom he could be speaking. 'And through him I might do you a hurt. Only Maud could have saved us – and Maud is dead.' Stephen's eyes held no tears, only such an emptiness of grief that Rannulf's throat closed and he could plead no more.

# Chapter 19

If the day and night spent at Malmesbury had been a cold purgatory, the trip from Malmesbury to Sleaford was a freezing hell. It did not seem to matter whether Rannulf's troop drove their horses to exhaustion, as they did in the first stretch between Malmesbury and Oxford, or whether they waited patiently in a friendly keep. The storm that had caught them, as if it were some malevolent, half-intelligent thing, seemed to lie in wait until they showed themselves and then attack with renewed fury.

Rannulf accompanied the king from Malmesbury to Oxford, hoping that Stephen would change his mind and order him to follow on to London. Not realizing he was sealing his vassal's fate, Stephen urged him passionately to care for himself. As the despair grew in Rannulf's eyes, Stephen changed his tune. He spoke cheerfully of new meetings when the turning of the tide should come, but he did not rescind his original order. Rannulf waited on the weather at Oxford, having no particular desire to be anywhere except at home. There Catherine would wake his desire to live, not for the things for which a man should live, not for duty and service, but for carnal pleasure. For the joy of seeing the sun rise and smelling the new-turned earth of spring, for kissing a woman and seeing grandchildren grow. Those things were well enough, but they should not draw a man from the path of duty.

Rannulf's long agony was over. He was not now torn in two, but he ached for those joys he had not even known were joys before Catherine awakened him to them. Catherine had given and Catherine had taken away. Rannulf was not aware of the blasphemy of his substitution. He knew only that her strength and courage had given him a glimpse of burdens shared so that they became pleasures and yet had removed his last excuse for clinging to the life he desired. He almost hated her for being what she was instead of the helpless, clinging thing that needed his protection.

Nature itself had seemed to set its face against Rannulf's desire to avoid his home. Northampton's troop arrived the day after Stephen left, and the sun came out the next morning. Perhaps the sun alone could not have forced Rannulf to move on, but he could not refuse to accompany his old friend, for Northampton was now nearly totally paralysed. It was under twenty miles to Towcester where Northampton's son met them, and it took three long days to cover the distance because Northampton had to be carried in a litter every step of the way. To make matters worse, no sooner were they too far from Oxford to make a return practical when it started to sleet and hail again. Rannulf would have been happy to go to Northampton's keep, but Simon's son was so plainly ill at ease in his presence that they rode forward the next day in spite of the inclement weather.

Warwick was their next haven. It was slightly out of the straight path home, but closer than any other place where they might rest. Here, too, they stayed only one night; here, too, Rannulf found that he was not welcome. Warwick was not at home, true, but it was not that which made the countess stiff and cold as the ice that bordered the river. Gundreda did not like him nor he her, yet it was Rannulf's habit to stop at Warwick keep in any journey he made, and Lady Warwick had often played hostess to him when she was alone. Ordinarily she was warmer than usual at such times, finding any masculine company that provided news and sensible conversation valuable when her husband was away. This desire to be rid of him in haste had nothing to do with their mutual dislike and was something new. Bitterly Rannulf thought how swiftly even those one had known for years changed with the breath of favour. Gundreda did not know that he and Stephen were reconciled, and Rannulf was too proud to tell her. He gathered his men and moved towards Leicester's keep. Rannulf was almost afraid to stop, but here at last he found someone who was glad to see him.

'I had begun to think that I was carrying the pox,' he said, sipping hot wine and standing well away from the fire.

'Why?' Robert laughed.

'Northampton's eldest boy could not sit nor stand quiet while I remained with him, and Warwick's lady all but told me to go.'

Leicester dropped his eyes. 'You had better let my daughter see to those hands of yours, Rannulf. They are so chilblained that they are bleeding. That is what comes of waging war in the winter. Are your feet as bad?'

'No,' Rannulf replied indifferently. 'Robert—'

'Then why are you limping so much?'

'I was hurt in the taking of Wallingford bridge, and the wound does not heal. Robert, there is no use dragging in side issues, particularly such bad fish as old wounds and chilblains. I must ask and you must answer. Is it the end?'

Leicester did not look up. 'For some it is the beginning.'

'For you, Robert?' The heavy, stolid man remained silent. 'Do you think I would ask such a question of you if my knowledge of the answer could hurt you?'

'No. I was wondering if I could find words with which to explain the unalterability of events and the uselessness of resistance. There is a pattern in things. Once a new pattern is formed, no amount of clinging to the old will save it. Those who will not change are only destroyed.'

'So much I know, but there are many ways of being destroyed, and all different for all men. For me to save life would destroy the soul. It is not so for others – I understand.'

'And Geoffrey and Richard?'

Rannulf smiled. 'Geoffrey's decision is different from mine, and he understands that my oath binds him only so long as I live. No one can blame a boy for loyalty to his father.' There was a hesitation, and then Rannulf continued steadily. 'I hope you will make so much clear where it will help my son in the new pattern of things.' Leicester's mouth thinned angrily, but he nodded. 'There is something more, Robert. Simon, I believe, is dying.'

'Northampton dying? Of what? Was he hurt?'

'No, he is only old. His body is – frozen. He may linger a while, but not in a state to steady a youngling in his path. Will

290

you guide Geoffrey and take Richard into your household?'

'I would do that without asking, but Rannulf, you talk as if you were already dead. You are not as old as Northampton.'

'No, but there will be more fighting. Eustace will not permit Stephen to make the truce he desires.'

'You have done your share and more, Rannulf. You cannot think you owe more to an overlord who—'

'Do not missay Stephen to me. He is torn in two – and that I understand too well. No, Robert, I have a lust to fight. I desire it. I need it. It will take no urging to thrust me into the thickest press.'

Leicester sighed. He would try once more. 'Rannulf, you see how the wind blows, but do you see how strongly? Do you know why Lady Warwick desired to be rid of you?'

'Of course. She thinks Stephen has thrown me aside and that Eustace waits only the merest chance to send home the death thrust. She did not wish to be tainted by me.'

'No. You must not speak of what I tell you now. You could not prevent it anyway. Do I have your word on it?'

Rannulf nodded. 'I will die for Stephen, but no man can save him. I will make trouble for no one.'

'I have already sent messages to Henry, and when the time is fitting for us both, I will do him homage.' Sure as he was that Rannulf had guessed so much, Leicester was relieved when his foster brother again nodded without emotion. 'If my vassals' keeps offer no resistance, Henry will most swiftly move eastward. To come back to Gundreda at Warwick – I know that she will yield all after a token siege or only a threat.'

'Warwick! But Warwick is with Stephen now.'

'Warwick knows nothing of this, and if he were told, he would not believe it.' Leicester shook his head. 'Even if he were there, he could not stop her. She does this for her children. You tell me Northampton is dying. His son waits only for that before he, too, gives Henry fealty. Who is left?'

His shock past, Rannulf shrugged. 'The quicker the better, really. There will be less blood shed, I suppose.'

'For God's sake, Rannulf, it will be such a little time. Could you not sit quietly at Sleaford?'

'No, I cannot. I told you that I lust after blood.' Probably

Catherine would follow Gundreda's path, give her promise of loyalty to Henry when he was away. Rannulf felt only relief. That would save Geoffrey and Richard and might well be what she had planned all along.

Leicester, unable to read Rannulf's thoughts and shocked by the viciousness of the tone, looked away. This was no normal desire for the thrills of battle. There was something desperately wrong with his foster brother. Leicester could do nothing. Rannulf never permitted any discussion of his inner emotional life, never admitted that he had one. Whether he endured joy or grief, he endured it alone, and that reserve showed no signs of breaking.

'Very well, if you must kill for reasons of your own, you must. But cannot you confine yourself to Bigod? Rannulf, listen to me,' Leicester said, grasping his foster brother's arm and shaking it. 'In a few weeks I will have Henry's ear. He likes Bigod as little as Stephen does. Confine yourself to fighting Norfolk and all will yet be well – I swear it.'

Rannulf's eyes were bleak and hard as the stones of the keep walls. 'Do not raise such hopes in me, Robert. It is not kind. If Stephen calls me, I will go to him. Would I not come to you, no matter what the cost, if you were in your death struggle?'

Then Leicester understood and reasoned no more. He urged Rannulf to stay with him, but Rannulf understood the turmoil that would be caused by Leicester's switch in loyalties. No matter what his personal reluctance his place was at home where he could quell rebellious ideas among his vassals and defend his borders against Norfolk.


Drenched and freezing foreriders brought the news of the earl's imminent arrival to Catherine. An hour later she was drenched herself as she embraced her sodden husband, held his face between her hands, kissed his eyes. In her joy at having him at home and safe, the night had come before she realized how cold and restrained his response was.

'Rannulf, are you still angry with me?' she asked out of an uneasy stillness which had fallen between them.

'Angry – for what? Oh, the refusal of the men of Soke and that message. No, I understood.'

'Then what is wrong? Where is Geoffrey?'

She worried about Geoffrey, Rannulf thought, even though she knew him so little. Doubtless she would fight for his children in ways he could not, fight as Gundreda of Warwick did.

'Geoffrey is with Northampton again,' Rannulf said civilly. 'Simon is dying, I believe. His older sons guard his land, and John is too sick still to nurse his father. If Bigod moves and I need Geoffrey, I will summon him to come to me.'

He had avoided her first question. 'What is wrong, then?' Catherine insisted.

'I am tired and I face ruin.' Now Rannulf spoke coldly. 'Is that not enough?'

'You run to seek ruin,' Catherine responded.

'Perhaps. It is my own affair. Let me be.'

'You are my husband. It is my affair also.'

'I bid you let me be,' he repeated sharply.

'I will not let you be. There comes a time when honour costs too high. Do you think I desire to be a penniless outcast? Do you think I am so silly a woman that I do not know what is happening? I have written to Leicester and received a reply, and I have letters from Gundreda of Warwick also.'

'Then do as she does,' Rannulf bellowed. 'Do more even! Here – here is a knife and my naked breast. Strike and save yourself the trouble I will cause you.'

Catherine snatched the knife and flung it across the solar, terror in her eyes. 'Rannulf, you would not – you would not!'

'Nay, I have sins enough without seeking everlasting damnation.'

'Rannulf,' she panted, 'we need you, all need you. I have no lust to be a widow again, to be put upon the block and sold to the highest bidder. Would you lay the burdens of these times on Geoffrey's shoulders? Would you see Richard's bright star dimmed?'

She clutched at him, but he pushed her away and began to laugh, the peals rising higher and higher until the solar rang with them. 'None needs me now – none of you,' he gasped when he had breath. 'You closed that passage to life upon me, Catherine – you!'

'I? I love you.'

The gasping laughter stopped. 'Aye, I believe it, but need me you do not. You taught me that when you kept your vassals from the war and yet set matters so that even Eustace could find no fault with me. Know that I call them *your* vassals. Widow you may be, but no man will have you without your will to it. Nor need I fear for my children. You will shield Richard against the devil himself, if need be. My death will free you and Geoffrey to flee to the Angevin, and Henry will receive you kindly for your father's sake and because of Leicester. None needs me but the dying king.'

He was near enough to catch her when she fell, ignorant enough to believe she had really fainted, not realizing that she only sought time to draw another arrow from her armoury with which to transfix him. The blue eyes fluttered open, tears trickling from their corners.

'You do not love me,' Catherine whispered. 'You cannot or you would not speak of your death to me. Naught will happen as you say, for if you die, I too will die of grief.'

'No one dies of grief,' Rannulf replied wearily, thinking that he and Stephen both would long since have been underground if anguish could kill.

'You are cruel and selfish. You think no worse can befall than your own death. What if you are taken prisoner or exiled? Then my estates as well as yours will be forfeit, and Geoffrey will not go to the Angevin but spend his life trying to free you or as a beggar in a foreign land.'

Rannulf laughed again, but more quietly. He did not wish Catherine to be torn apart between her love of him and her love of the children. A hurt now would save her much agony in the future.

'If I am imprisoned, you will do as Gundreda did for the sake of the children, and perhaps, save the gold to ransom me. If I go into exile, I will go willingly, and Geoffrey will keep the lands because I will order him to do so. You offer me love because you think with that you can bend me to your will and make me a traitor to the king. I have known it, but you are mistaken. Only one of us can rule in this household.'

His face was colder than on their unfortunate wedding day, and Catherine gasped with the pain of his rejection. He turned and left her before she could speak again, and later sent his servants to remove his clothing chests from her chamber. It was a public announcement of their estrangement which hurt Rannulf more even than it insulted Catherine, but it was the surest way to be certain that she would follow Gundreda's path.

No one was happy. Richard, overjoyed at first to have his father at home, could not understand why Rannulf was so moody and so bitter, why nothing he could do could please him or raise his spirits. Mary and André were no better off. Although Catherine had become little more than a pale shadow, she did manage to guard Mary so sedulously that she and André could not even exchange a glance. Fortunately the situation did not endure long. Scarcely was the first ploughing of February under way when an urgent message from Sir Giles reported suspicious activity on the Norfolk side of the border. The letter was directed to Catherine and was given unopened into her hands, Rannulf having summoned her to the hall for that purpose.

Happy or unhappy, Catherine did not permit herself to fail in her care for her appearance, but Rannulf felt she could have chosen colours that would have become her better. The dark blue gown over a pale grey tunic lent no colour to a face that had the blanched look of a long-time prisoner, and the silver embroidery of neck and sleeves had more lustre than her hair. He remained rigid with eyes fixed upon her while she broke the seal and read, but when she held out the parchment to him with a hand that trembled sufficiently to make the letter crackle and took a faltering half step in his direction, Rannulf could not resist moving closer.

'I know nothing of such matters,' Catherine whispered. 'Do you order all to your own liking. If you are content, I shall be also.'

'You know nothing, eh? But Sir Giles must think you know for he asks strange questions of an ignorant woman. Should he await attack or attack first himself?' Rannulf smiled coldly. 'Will you go to him?'

'It is the king's command that I guard the land against Bigod. I will go. Hugh Bigod may have thought that he could wrest keep and sheep, man and maid, horse and hamlet from a helpless woman. I am almost sorry I am here. I wonder what you would have done. Tell me, Catherine, would you have donned armour and led the men yourself?'

A faint colour rose in her cheeks at the gibe. 'Whatever I would have done, I would never have sought death as an escape from my troubles.'

'Nor do I,' Rannulf muttered. Even to quarrel with Catherine raised such a fire for living in him that he knew he could not yield life tamely.

Catherine saw her chance and leaped at it. 'Mayhap people do not die of grief, but there are worse things than death to a woman who loves. Do not condemn me to such pain. Swear that you will fight to live, Rannulf, not to die.'

'I swear,' he said hurriedly as he turned away, 'I swear. On this field I will fight to live.'


Four men at at ease at the high table of Warwick castle. Before them lay the remains of as excellent a dinner as late March could afford. The platters and trenchers were pushed back now to make room for pitchers and goblets filled with wine, and the flickering torches and steadier glow from wax candles lit the table, warming the yellow gold of the drinking vessels to a ruddy blaze. From the long tables in the hall rose the good-humoured noise of self-satisfied men who were not yet drunk enough to begin quarrelling. The wine in the goblets at the high table, however, sank only imperceptibly, and the voices of the men, although confident, owed nothing of that satisfactory emotion to the uplifting quality of the liquor.

'Well,' Henry of Anjou said gaily, 'I am becoming rusty for want of action. Since you have given us your countenance, Leicester, all we need do is knock on the gates and they are opened to us.'

'Are you complaining?' Robert of Leicester asked.

'Only that I will need to spend gold on a tourney, it seems, if I am to keep my skill with sword and lance. No, seriously, I have never been so glad, and it is not for the ease of achievement that I am glad but for the sparing of the country. It does my heart no good to see the land ravished. It is my land, and I do not have to destroy it.'

Leicester nodded his satisfaction. Here was one of the truly important differences between Stephen and Henry. Whether it was a basic love of the soil or only a long-range comprehension that a country burned and bloodied by war yielded little profit, Henry did have a true and deep consideration for the well-being of the land that Stephen never had.

William of Gloucester lifted his goblet and drank. He had taken no part in the foregoing discussion and could see no part for himself in the one which would follow. He had no interest in military objectives, since he had no intention of taking part in any military action. Altogether the presence and plans of his three companions were exceedingly dull, and he would not have come except that to stay away would have given too much food for thought to Henry's suspicious mind. He had lost interest even in baiting Hereford, for that gentleman merely gazed at him with lacklustre eyes. Leicester was no source of amusement, his monumental stolidity offering no weak spot to be pricked. Something would have to be done, and that right soon, to save him from extinction by boredom, Gloucester thought.

'We will have sufficient to do with sword and lance, my lord, if we go to relieve Wallingford. Stephen will not relinquish that readily because it is too close to his precious Oxford. He has even built a permanent camp decked out to look like a keep but almost defenceless at Crowmarsh. Still, it is a beginning. We should take that before he strengthens it and sends more men into it.'

Acutely, Henry said nothing, turning courteously to Leicester as if he wished to hear his approval of Hereford's suggestion. But Leicester did not approve – as Henry had known full well he would not.

'I am sorry, Roger, I cannot agree that Wallingford should be the next step. I hope I am no coward, but I agree with my lord that what can be gained without bloodshed, or with little bloodshed, should be taken first.' He held up a hand as Hereford appeared to be about to break into his rather ponderous speech. 'I have good reason for what I say. If we fight a well-entrenched and deeply hostile force, we are like to lose some of our strength. With each loss others will become bolder to resist.'

'Perhaps, but the men in Wallingford have resisted with great bloodshed and almost without hope for nigh on six months.'

'Nay, Hereford, you are letting your emotions rule your reason,' Henry said calmly. 'There has been much bloodshed at Wallingford, so much is true, and that has made both king's men and ours more stubborn. Neither will yield now unless they are literally destroyed. Besides, Wallingford has hope sufficient to its needs. They know I am here and that we have not forgotten them. We have shed a little blood also so that they have not starved.'

'Nor will we be able to free them if we are caught between two fires. Do not look so black, Hereford. I know that Wallingford is in good case. Waleran – and there is no use scowling at my brother's name for he has served your purpose well and did William Beauchamp little harm except in his dignity. Waleran, as I began to say, is looking about in that neighbourhood. Now and again he gives the men in Crowmarsh and the camp enough to think about so that supplies may be brought in. Wallingford is safe, and we must make sure our rear is safe.'

Henry frowned slightly. 'Safety is a good thing, but not if it is achieved at the cost of advances.'

'How will Earl Ferrars and the towns of Bedford and Stamford added to your victories stand in your opinion of advancement?'

'Most excellently, my dear Leicester,' Henry chuckled. 'If that is your opinion of seeking safety – to take Tutbury, Bedford, and Stamford – I shall hide under the bed when you begin to talk of war.'

Leicester smiled. 'My foster brother, Rannulf, earl of Soke, has roused Bigod. Once that monster is wakened, he strikes out in all directions. Stephen and Eustace are both safe as far east as Ipswich. I doubt much that they will return to help Ferrars or the others.' Hereford's head, which he had allowed to sink on his breast, came up at Rannulf's name, but Leicester again silenced him with a gesture. 'I did not say that Soke did this for our sake. In truth, I am sure as a man can be without proof or confession that it is his lady's doing.'

Interest gleamed in Henry's keen eyes. 'Her father was most sincerely our friend. Do you think she may lead him to us?'

Leicester shrugged, then shook his head negatively. 'I think not, although she has some power over him.'

'Can Soke be won by gold or soft words?'

Regretfully Leicester shook his head again. 'He can be won by nothing because he is bound by a lunatic's sense of duty and by a pitiful love which grows stronger as the king grows weaker. However, if Stephen yields or dies, Rannulf will not oppose you. Believe me, my lord, it would be most wise to let him go his own way. Moreover, he has not set his son against you, and Geoffrey will follow you willingly – if you do nothing to harm the father. They are blood and bone of each other, the children and the father.'

'He loves his children – good. When I am king, coddling the children will doubtless win the father. What else does he love? Every man rises to some lure.'

William of Gloucester yawned delicately and thought that one of the joys of his life had been removed when Soke's company was denied him. No one rose so easily to the lure; no one was so dangerous and therefore so satisfactory to torment. There would be no problem in catching Soke when Stephen was gone; he could put Henry in the way of doing so in five minutes. Henry need only set that dutiful idiot some difficult and dangerous task. Actually the sooner Stephen was gone and they could be united into one court the better. In the beginning when it was needful to play Maud and Stephen like fish, there had been some sport to this war, but the brainless bashing and slashing was a bore. And these idiots, taking one keep at a time, might be another ten years at it without accomplishing anything. William slid his lidded eyes over his companions and stifled another yawn; his decision hardened.

'When do you plan to move on Tutbury?' he asked.

'A day or two,' Henry replied cautiously. 'There is nothing to bide here for.'

'You will scarcely need me for that enterprise. Do I have

your leave, my lord, to follow some small plans of my own? Only for a short time.'

There was an immediate profit in the suspicion which leaped into Henry's eyes and was quickly masked. William's heavy lids drooped even more sleepily. Delightful. Henry would set spies on him whom he would need to avoid, for his plans involved what would certainly appear like trafficking with the enemy. And all for Henry's good too – how amusing.

'Do you wish to leave us, William? Perhaps we might be some aid to you in these plans.'

'Nay, my lord,' William replied. 'Of all things, your presence would be the last I desired.' He permitted an expression, frankly sensual, to appear on his face, adding, 'My plans concern a lady and a young, and rather handsome, man.'

The statement was literally true, for William's plans concerned Eustace and Constance. His expression was a blatant lie, assumed to deceive. Roger of Hereford stared fixedly at the wine in his goblet, trying to hide the revulsion he felt for William. It was bad enough to desert so serious a business in pursuit of pleasure, but somehow to do so for a pleasure composed of abnormal vice seemed to make matters worse. Henry did not know whether to believe William or not, but the colour of his complexion displayed the fact that the emotions he was concealing by a bland and unmoved expression were akin to Roger's. Leicester alone considered William without reaction other than a deep speculative interest, and William, enjoying himself for the first time in months, gave the stupid-looking earl full marks for an unusually keen intelligence.

# Chapter 20

Rannulf grunted with pain and tried not to wince away from the hands which were probing the angry-looking, suppurating wound on his thigh. The leech muttered angrily to himself about men who expected miracles of healing when they would not even offer the minor co-operation of permitting themselves to be bled. He had just offered that remedy to Rannulf and been refused curtly.

'I do not know, my lord,' Sir Giles said, 'that it is wise to refuse. It will abate your fever somewhat.'

'Aye, and lay me flat on my back for two days. Can we afford to give our enemies that much time?'

'Perhaps not, but you have so bedevilled them that I believe I can keep them from gathering their strength.'

Rannulf gestured impatiently. 'If I thought it would really help, I would do it, Giles. Four times these past months have I let them drain me white. So the fever abated – for two days or a week. Then the ague returns and I am no better.'

'Because you will not lie still and let the poultices and potions do their work, my lord.'

Rannulf cast André a glance full of mingled exasperation and affection. He wondered what he could have done to inspire such infuriating devotion. André was worse than Geoffrey, plaguing him constantly with appeals to rest, to attend to the leech's recommendations, to take this or that remedy suggested by this or that herb-wife or witch-wife. Rannulf had wondered, passingly, if André could be in Eustace's pay and desire to poison him, but as he was regularly worn down by the young man's nagging, regularly took the remedies, and certainly suffered no adverse effects except occasional nausea from the taste, it was obvious that the intentions were excellent if the result was not. Now he did not trouble to answer André, turning to Sir Giles again.

'Believe me, it is no lack of faith in your ability that makes me unwilling, but I am most anxious to drive them farther yet from our border. As long as the king continues to press from the south, our opportunity is great, for Bigod himself must remain there. If Stephen is called away, which I fear will befall any day now because of the ill news I hear, Norfolk's attention will turn to us. Then there will be a bitter battle, and I would as lief it took place on Norfolk's land than on ours.'

Sir Giles nodded reluctant agreement. The earl was perfectly right. The trouble was that he looked, and plainly felt, ill, and after more than three months of close contact as his battle companion, Sir Giles was deeply concerned for Soke's health. Nor was he concerned from the point of view of safety for the lands. His contact with Geoffrey had been reassuring in the extreme; the boy would be a worthy heir to his father. Geoffrey, however, was young and, more than that, Giles was growing very fond of Rannulf.

The earl bit his lip and stifled a groan as Geoffrey came in, pushing back his mail hood and wiping sweat from his face. 'How is it, papa?'

'How is it ever?' Rannulf snapped irritably, 'Well, what said the herald?'

'The castellan – if castellan he can be called who holds such a miserable daub of planks and mud – will be here anon to speak with you. I am sure they will yield on your terms.'

'Then why did you not wait to escort them in as I bade you?'

'I left Sir John and the men. A royal messenger hailed me in the road asking for you. I brought him hither and he is without.'

Rannulf and Sir Giles exchanged knowing glances. 'Make haste,' Rannulf said to the leech, bringing on another spate of grumbling and muttering.

When the leg was bandaged, Rannulf drew up his *chausses* and refastened his robe, signalling André to bring in the messenger. His face grew grimmer and grimmer as he perused the scroll, and, after a while, he handed it to Sir Giles as if he could not trust his voice to repeat its contents. There was an initial hesitation caused by Fortesque's unwillingness to display what might be an ignorance of higher strategy, and Rannulf, seeing his growing indignation, sent Geoffrey and André off with the messenger. They were to entertain him, the earl said significantly.

Sir Giles had come to the conclusion, after some thought, that no strategy could be deep or devious enough to account for the orders in the letter. 'My lord,' he said doubtfully, 'I am sorry if I am about to prove myself a dolt, but – but what is the sense to this?'

'You know as well as I,' Rannulf said furiously. He pulled himself to his feet, took a couple of steps, and returned to Sir Giles. 'There is no sense flying into a temper, as well I know,' he sighed then, 'no more sense than is in that command. What sense can there be in pulling me away from a successful campaign, dividing men who are fighting well together in a common cause all believe in, sending half those men to fight in a place they care nothing about and replacing them with men who care nothing for this land? What sense –' Rannulf stopped abruptly. There was no sense, but perhaps what Stephen wanted of him had nothing to do with the war.

'You should not go, sense or not. I do not mean for the danger to the lands either, but because, in truth, you are not well.'

'That does not matter. I will be as well or as ill with the king as elsewhere. I have given Stephen an oath of loyalty, and I must hold by that.' Rannulf had his private reasons for going to Stephen, but it was a good chance to impress the necessity for loyalty on a vassal's mind. 'But I will not permit the men to be broken up. Eustace may send part of his forces back to Stephen if he wishes. If not, so much the better for our purpose here.'

Rannulf took with him only his household guard, André and Geoffrey, whom he did not dare leave where Eustace could reach him. He was greeted by Stephen with a strict formality which puzzled him. If Stephen had not called him to have a friend to lean on, what was his purpose? It was not new suspicion. Stephen was pleasant, spoke standard words of welcome, proffered a civil invitation to dine, and dismissed him to rest. At dinner the king's behaviour was no clearer. He sat next to Rannulf, urged him tenderly to eat and even touched him caressingly from time to time, but he would not meet Rannulf's eyes. He spent the meal explaining his purpose. Rannulf was to go to Crowmarsh. That tiny keep, mud and sticks though it was, commanded the bridge at Wallingford, kept the men in Wallingford, and prevented them from going to Henry's aid. It was also a symbol of Stephen's power. As long as it stood, Henry could not turn his attention east. He spoke, indeed, so glibly and so much that Rannulf had no opportunity to open his mouth, and he went to bed with a dozen unanswered questions which had not been permitted to pass his lips.

'Rannulf.'

The whisper woke him, but he could see nothing for the tent flap was down and even the starlight was shut out. Rannulf's hand moved towards his sword and dropped away. A man who wishes you hurt does not wake you except with the blow he strikes.

'Who speaks?'

'I, Stephen. Nay, do not rise. I wished words with you that none would hear.'

The king dropped to the pallet beside him. Rannulf understood the formal greeting and talk. Eustace set spies upon his father, and Stephen still could not bear to cross his son.

'You called me mad, Rannulf, and perhaps for a time I was,' Stephen continued. 'But I am not mad now, and I would not have you think me so and therefore abandon my purpose.'

'Then why did you call me from a successful campaign?' Rannulf asked testily.

'I am old. I am tired. It is too late for me to drive Henry from this land at once. Nay, listen, I am not mad. Eustace and I plan to crush and drive out Bigod – to destroy him utterly. This land is fertile, easily defended, and the people are docile. Henry will not help Bigod, for he knows what he is and he is busy in the north and west. When we have a secure kingdom here, mayhap we can make truce or win back that part of the realm which we desire.'

Rannulf was silent; the plan was not mad.

'For this purpose,' Stephen continued, 'we need time. Henry

cannot come to fight me while Crowmarsh stands. In honour, he must relieve Wallingford and also he dare not leave an army faithful to me behind him.'

'Why me? Why should I be torn from the defence of my own lands and sent to Crowmarsh?'

'You are one of the few faithful left to me – faithful even when my eye is not upon you, I mean. Simon is dead. Warwick is dead of a broken heart. What Gundreda did killed him.'

Rannulf gasped with surprise. He had not heard that news, but Stephen laid his hand over his vassal's lips urging silence and Rannulf lay still, listening.

'I cannot permit what happened at Malmesbury to happen at Crowmarsh. If the keep cannot hold, I must at least have warning that it is attacked and about to fall. If it is yielded secretly and Henry comes upon me by surprise I will be undone.'

Rannulf was sick with disappointment. If Stephen's purpose succeeded, Eustace would rule Bigod's land, and that would be worse than having Bigod there. Yet to refuse Stephen or to go to Crowmarsh and yield it was outright treason, outright violation of his sword-oath. That was a different matter from a passive yielding to fate, and Rannulf knew he could not bring himself to it. He must go to Crowmarsh and hold it as long as it could be held.

'Never fear,' Rannulf said with grim hopelessness, 'I will hold it as long as any man can.'

To his surprise, Stephen was shaken with silent sobs. 'I will try to send you more men and supplies. Do not curse me, Rannulf, if I fail. This war with Bigod must come first.' He bent and kissed his vassal's lips. 'And do not hold the keep at the cost of your life. With aught else I will buy time, but not with that. Remember, not with that.' He rose as if to go, then bent close again. 'If you are taken prisoner, I will ransom you. Do not doubt my faith if it takes a little time. I will ransom you.'

Across the tiny moat, a thing to jest at and to fill with brush and mud in an hour, and across the silly palisade of sharpened logs, Rannulf gazed at the small hill where he had scolded

Geoffrey the day after the battle of Wallingford bridge. Now, again, he would have to impose his will upon his unwilling son. Geoffrey must leave him in Crowmarsh and go home. Rannulf cursed softly at himself for being so mazed between his illness and his distaste for his task that the true meaning of Stephen's last words had not come to him until after they were in Crowmarsh. The king wanted him to be taken prisoner. To Stephen's muddled mind, confinement would keep Rannulf safe and please Eustace. Perhaps Stephen did not understand that it would also give Eustace an opportunity to seize Rannulf's lands, or else Stephen knew but believed he could 'requite' Rannulf for the loss.

Rannulf laughed wryly. Eustace did not know Catherine. Still, Catherine could not don armour and lead the men in spite of his jest. Geoffrey must go home. For one thing, he must be free to serve as a focal point of loyalty to the men; for another he must not fight against Henry of Anjou in a desperate losing battle which might wake hatred in so young and so passionate a heart. Rannulf sighed, wishing that Geoffrey were a little older, wishing that he had not such a passionate nature, even wishing that the boy did not love him so much. Geoffrey counted as desertion what was only good sense.

He should have sent Geoffrey away before the boy had seen Crowmarsh and realized how indefensible it was. But then he had not known what Stephen's intentions were and later, when he had been training the raw ploughmen that Stephen had given him as levies, he had needed Geoffrey too much. Young as he was, the son of an earl had more authority than a bachelor knight like André, and Rannulf had been so often ill that authority other than his was a necessity. Now, although his eyes were glaring with fever and two bright spots of colour mantled cheekbones that protruded like a skull's in a pasty grey face, his illness did not matter; he had a disciplined fighting force that would follow orders. They were not many, but they were of very good heart, well trained and eager for the fray. And, as if God favoured his desire, a small Angevin force without either Hereford or Henry to lead it was approaching them.

The Angevin attack was truly a crowning mercy. Had

Geoffrey gone before the men had proved themselves in a fight, they might have lost heart with a leader who was much abed. But Rannulf knew he had strength enough in spurts to fight, and this first battle they would win. First, all but fifty of the men who were quartered at Crowmarsh would leave that pitiful defence to hide in the marsh and where else they could. Those who hid would include Geoffrey and the household guard. When Henry's men fell upon the little keep, the hidden troops would burst out and attack the attackers. According to the information Rannulf's scouts had brought in, the force sent to reduce Crowmarsh was small. It was a test of strength, perhaps, but is should be easy enough to drive them off in this first attempt. Geoffrey would aid in the fighting, but instead of returning to the keep as most of the others would when the attack was over, he would ride for Sleaford. From there he would send messengers to acquaint Stephen with the fact that Henry's men were finally attacking Crowmarsh and give particulars of the men and supplies necessary to repulse them.

Up to that point in the plan, Rannulf was sure of his son's obedience, for he had agreed readily to that much. Geoffrey's objection was to Rannulf's decision that his duty ended at that point and that he was to bide at Sleaford after the messengers were sent out. Unfortunately the boy's confidence had been badly shaken by the battle of Wallingford and Rannulf's inability to recover from his wound. He was certain Rannulf would die if he was left in Crowmarsh. What Geoffrey desired was to ride from Sleaford to where Eustace was besieging a keep of Norfolk's. There he would gather Rannulf's men, and those of Soke also if they would come, ride back to Crowmarsh and either drive off the Angevin troops or have a large enough force to escape from Crowmarsh when they pleased.

Rannulf bent to drop his head on his arms. He did not want Geoffrey to fight Henry, and, if Geoffrey went to Eustace, he might not return to Crowmarsh anyway. Eustace would never lose so excellent an opportunity. Like as not, Geoffrey would never see the vassals at all, would disappear, or die of some mysterious complaint. Thus far, Rannulf had tried no expedient beyond reasoning. He had asked for no promise, no swearing of oaths, hoping to bring Geoffrey around to his way of thinking without putting that additional pressure on him. Now the time for reasoning was over; Henry's men were on their way. A light step sounded on the planks behind him, and Rannulf lifted his head and turned.

'The men are ready. As soon as the light fails, we will go.'

Rannulf nodded and drew Geoffrey towards him. 'Look there,' he said, pointing to the hillock. 'Do you remember that place?'

A frown creased the fair brow. 'No, papa, I – oh, yes!'

The last words held a stricken note, and Rannulf seized the advantage. 'Do you remember what I said to you there?'

'I remember, but it had nothing to do with this case.'

'It is more true now than it was then, for now our enemies are closer upon us. Do not think I have lightly cast away the answers you gave me. I have thought of them much, but I know that for you to go to Eustace is but to invite the trap to spring shut, is but to give him our lands and murder your brother. Do you understand me, Geoffrey?'

'I understand that you have given me a sweet choice – that between murdering my father and murdering my brother!'

'I am not so easily killed. Besides, you have no choice at all. If matters do turn out ill, that must be your salvation. You must obey me. If I bid you sacrifice your life, would you say me nay? Of course not, your pride would uphold you. Then let it uphold you now. Down! Down on your knees!' Rannulf drew his sword and held the hilt out to his kneeling son, but Geoffrey turned his head obstinately and would not stretch his hand toward it or raise his eyes.

'Papa, for the rest of my life I will carry this. Do not make me do it!'

A spasm twisted Rannulf's face. He did not expect to die in spite of Geoffrey's fears, but he was ill and might not fight as well as in the past. If he should be killed, Geoffrey was too young a child to bear so heavy a burden of guilt.

'You must do it,' he said harshly, 'for if I should die, upon you rests the salvation of our family and the continuance of my line. If I am to die in battle, your presence could not save me. Such a death is no man's fault. Child, the pain of my loss

308

will fade. You will wed, and bed, and breed – and order your own sons to do things they will not like.'

Rannulf thrust the sword hilt towards Geoffrey so that it made a cross. 'Geoffrey, look up. Look at me. There is no cause yet to despair, but you are moved too much by love. I will take sword-oath of you that you will obey me. Lay your hand upon this cross – and swear.'

In the solar of Sleaford keep, Catherine waited for Geoffrey to come to her. Surely, even if Rannulf had sent no message, courtesy would compel his son to greet his stepmother. Surely he would not refuse to tell her of Rannulf's health and present situation. But he did not come in the morning. Boys are sometimes careless of courtesy, she thought; I will see him at dinner. But Geoffrey did not appear at the dinner table. He was out, the servants said, out hawking. He had not sat five minutes in the keep, only changed his clothes and his horse and ridden out. In a window seat which commanded the main entrance to the hall, Catherine waited for the eager huntsman's return. The afternoon passed, the long summer evening, and the night. When Geoffrey returned, Catherine did not know. She was up with the dawn to catch him when he broke his fast, but he was gone already. Another morning, another dinner hour, another night. Geoffrey had changed his hawk for hounds, but still he hunted. It is the cruelty of the very young, Catherine thought, the young whose hearts are so light, who think that none can suffer when they are happy or that none but they can suffer at all.

The third day it rained hard, and Catherine knew that Geoffrey must have stayed within the keep. When he still did not come, she thought for the first time that Rannulf might have bidden him avoid her. Did he think she would turn his son against him? The thought caused her such pain that she gasped for breath and shrank in upon herself. In a moment she had straightened her body and her chin lifted. If it were true that Rannulf had forbidden Geoffrey to speak to her, she had to know that. Calling her maids, Catherine assumed her own armour – a tunic of a deep rose to reflect colour into her face and a gown of greyish-blue silk so thin that the rose glinted through it. She decked her hair with threads of gold and scattered pearls and went to seek her answers from her stepson.

Geoffrey looked up at the fair vision before him with blank eyes. At first he did not recognize her, but suddenly he leaped to his feet. 'I beg your pardon for not coming to you. Indeed, I beg your pardon most humbly. I should have waited upon you at once, madam, but – but I have been so mazed. I do beg pardon, but I forgot – forgot that my father,' his voice choked on the word and he swallowed convulsively, 'my father had a new wife.'

Then he stared, amazed at seeing a fair woman blaze into glorious beauty before his eyes. Colour rose in her cheeks, her eyes sparkled, and her full lips lost their disconsolate droop and turned up mischievously at the corners. The silly boy had only forgotten so small a thing as a new wife – and not so new at that – in his lust for a holiday and his desire to chase the crane and the fallow deer.

'Nay, you are readily pardoned.' Catherine smiled and seated herself in a chair opposite the one Geoffrey had been using. Her lovely hand invited him to sit too. 'I should have sent a message to you. I should have remembered that you have been long at war and that pleasures are made more sweet by absence from them.'

Geoffrey merely looked utterly distracted at this civil speech and offered another slightly more coherent apology.

'I am not offended,' Catherine soothed. 'Nor do I mean to fret you with endless questions. Only tell me how my lord does and I will leave you to enjoy your pleasures in peace.'

'Peace and pleasure!' Geoffrey began to laugh. 'I think I shall never have peace or pleasure again.' He tried to check the near-hysterical laughter because he had been trained to shield women from trouble. They were powerless to make or mar, and therefore should be protected from worry over what they could not mend.

The colour receded from Catherine's cheeks, the animation from her eyes; a retransformation had taken place wiping out her sparkling beauty and leaving her only a fair woman with a nobly held head and frightened eyes.

'I – I did not wish to leave him,' Geoffrey sought for something to explain his distress. 'He is not well. A wound on his thigh festers and gives him much trouble.'

Men did not usually die from festering wounds, and Geoffrey knew it. Unless— Sometimes angry red lines grew out from a wound that had no apparent connection with the sore, or suddenly the neck would grow stiff and the jaws would lock. Then the men died, horribly, screaming through the locked jaw.

'He is not like to die?' she questioned sharply. Geoffrey winced away, as if she had touched him on the raw hurt. 'Where is he?' Catherine cried, getting to her feet. 'How can I come to him? Geoffrey, in mercy, tell me and let me go. If I can come to him, perhaps I can cure him. Oh, I am sure I can cure him.'

'There is no way for you to go where my father is, madam,' Geoffrey struggled with his exaggerated fear and then cried out despairingly, 'They are besieged, and he is sore sick. If he goes out to fight, his weakness will kill him; if he stays within, hunger and thirst will kill him.'

Geoffrey was nothing but a child, for all that he was considered a man in matters of war. Knowledge that a child was sick or afraid always brought Catherine a surface calm. Her face blanched parchment white, but she set herself to soothe her stepson and have the whole story from him. It did not take much effort; a few gentle questions, a few calming assurances, and it all tumbled out. Catherine patted the boy's heaving shoulders.

'Do not weep. You have done what is right, except in not coming to me at once with this tale. We will yet find a way.'

Geoffrey mastered his sobs, wiped his face, and looked into the quiet countenance of his stepmother. 'But I can do naught. He bound me with oaths not to go to Eustace or Stephen or return to him. He is right, but it is bitterly hard to sit here—'

'He bound you with oaths, but not me. Now tell me plainly, for I do not well understand matters of war, how many men and what weapons will be needed to free our lord or make the taking of Crowmarsh impossible.'

She was so sure. Geoffrey felt a flicker of hope. 'Not many men, unless Henry brings up the whole army – and then nothing could save the little hold. To make it safe now and en-sure my father's escape, our own vassals would be a force sufficient. What is mostly needed, more than men, is food and such things. The ground is such – nay, I cannot explain it to a woman, but any good knight experienced in battle would understand what was best to do an hour after coming there. Madam, you do not understand. There is no leader there ex-cept my father, and he is too weak to fight.'

'Do not trouble for that. I know such a man. Food and medicines for siege I also understand. Now, aside from the need to keep you out of Eustace's hands, is there any reason not to call the vassals from Norfolk's border? Will Norfolk overrun us?'

'Nay,' Geoffrey replied eagerly. 'Eustace would not dare permit that. He would sooner make truce or call up more men.' Catherine pursed her lips and sighed, and fear choked Geof-frey again. 'What good is all this talk?' he cried. 'How will you come by the vassals of Sleaford without me? Do you think they will come for a message not in my father's hand nor sealed by his seal? Even if there were such a message, do you think it would ever reach them?'

'I know nothing of the vassals of Sleaford. If they wish to come they may. The vassals of Soke will surely come, for I will fetch them myself.'

'You? You will go onto a battlefield? Into a camp of armed men?' Geoffrey was beginning to realize what Rannulf would think of this. 'It is too much for a woman to dare. Let us try—'

Catherine laughed. 'I have dared worse things than to out-face that fool of a prince. I have dared your father's wrath once or twice, and he has the right of life or death over me.'

'Madam, if you could bring them here, and I could speak with this man you say can lead them—'

'No, I must go myself, all the way to that place, Crow-marsh. An evil name for an evil place.' Catherine did not know what had happened, but from Geoffrey's fear something more than military problems beset Rannulf. Sickness of body and spirit was best nursed by a woman.

'Madam, madam, papa will not like it. Better perhaps for me to break my oath, lead them there, and return.' Geoffrey swallowed nervously. He could not decide which course of action would bring less of Rannulf's fury down on his head. 'He will slay us both,' he muttered.

'Nonetheless, I must go. You say that Eustace will not dare leave the lands of Soke and Sleaford exposed. Perhaps you are right, but from what else I have heard it is plain that he so hates our lord that no man can tell what he will do. What if, knowing Rannulf to be sure of freedom from Crowmarsh, he be taken with a madness of spite and think his loss small if Soke's lands are destroyed? Lord Geoffrey, I can gather supplies and lead my vassals to where my husband is, but I cannot gather together a force of untrained men and train them to protect the lands if Eustace should decide to depart. Also,' Catherine added as a clincher, 'I can cure your father's leg, which apparently no man can do.'

Geoffrey was glad to yield. He had no particular desire to have to confess that he had embroiled a woman in war. If he felt a twinge of conscience at letting Catherine walk alone into the lion's den, he was sure that his later punishment would be severe enough to ease that conscience. Moreover, what she said was true. He sprang to his feet and began to pace the hall, making plans. He would send the men-at-arms with her to Eustace's camp. She should try to come first to her own vassals, but if she could not find out in advance where they were camped, she should make a great noise upon entering the encampment. Thus, if she should be taken by Eustace, she would still need to fear nothing because it would be impossible to muzzle everyone who had seen her come. Her vassals would soon hear of her arrival and come to her rescue. When the men were ready to follow her, she could send the men-at-arms home. There was no need to come back to Sleaford for supplies. She should take what gold there was and buy along the way. She could also take a half-dozen of his father's famous horses. They could be bartered for great good.

The safest way was to skirt Norfolk's lands on the west and go due south, as near as might be by watching the sun, to Epping, or to Enfield if they missed Epping. There they were to turn sharp west and, going by Watford, would come to Crowmarsh near Wallingford. 'It is a little longer than the straight line that way, madam, but it will take you by two good markets and also avoid both the king's men and the Angevin's unless they have moved far and fast.'

Catherine listened attentively and nodded meekly. 'If you think it will be right to take your father's horses, I will, but he sets great store by them. Also, if you will be so good as to write down the way we must go, I will be glad. I might not remember, and my men have not travelled that way, my lord.'

Geoffrey was back beside her in two leaps. 'You must not call me "my lord" nor "Lord Geoffrey" neither. I would be Geoffrey alone to you, if you will favour me so far. So my mother would call me, and tender as a mother have you been to me this day – and as loyal to my father.'

Catherine put out her hand to stroke the golden curls. Geoffrey was almost as much hers as Richard was. 'Indeed, I will call you Geoffrey with a good will, and love you as I love Richard and Mary, if you will allow me.'

It was not until a day later, when her anxiety for Rannulf had sunk from a stabbing agony to a dull ache, that Catherine thought about the love she had promised Geoffrey. It was a strange way to love, to give him what he desired even though the desire was poison. To tear her men from Eustace was not such a great matter. Eustace hated Rannulf beyond all mending anyway, and probably that hatred would be carried over to Rannulf's heirs. Once her vassals had come to Crowmarsh and fought against Henry's men there, however, the gate to the other side might be closed. Catherine's eyes filled with tears. If she had to lose the struggle to save something for them, why could it not have happened before she had so enraged Rannulf? At least they could have comforted each other.

Had the future not been so dark, Catherine could have been amused at the way everything fell out to suit her. Within the hour in which she rode into camp, Eustace had called a war council, and to this council, uninvited, came Catherine, leaning gracefully upon Sir Giles' arm. The appearance of a woman at his council of war so surprised Eustace, for he had not heard of Catherine's coming, that he was struck mute.

314

'My lord,' Catherine said gently while Eustace's mouth still hung open, 'I have come for the vassals of Soke.'

'What!'

Eyes demurely on the ground, Catherine spoke louder, as if she believed the word gasped out in shock to mean literally that Eustace had not heard her. 'I have come for my vassals. I am the countess of Soke. My husband's son, the Lord Geoffrey, tells me that the earl, my husband, is pent in a place called Crowmarsh and besieged about by the Angevin's men. He has written to the king for succour – and to you – but no succour has he received. Therefore come I, as should a dutiful wife, to bring my men to my husband's aid.'

'What woman's folly is this?' Eustace asked. 'A breath of rumour is to a woman a high gale of truth. Where did you hear this nonsense? I have had no messenger. How do you know the king has sent no aid?'

'I have told you, my lord. My husband's son is in Sleaford. There is no rumour.'

Eustace turned pale but did not lose control of his voice. 'If this is not woman's nonsense, then it is a woman's lies and treachery. If Geoffrey of Sleaford is at home, why did he not come for the men?'

Sir Giles' mouth twitched, but it was still Catherine who answered with sweet calm. 'Perhaps you know that best. Also, they are my men, not his.'

It was incredible, the effrontery coupled with that modest demeanour. Eustace passed a hand across his face, dreadfully conscious of Sir Giles' hostile stare and the unwinking gaze of Rannulf's own vassals who trusted him not a whit. 'You lie,' he burst out, 'you have no letter from the earl of Soke. This is a scheme you have concocted for some womanish reason of your own – as a few months since you denied your husband your vassals for that he spoke to you not fair enough.'

'Alas, I greatly repent of that, my lord. Do not cast my foolishness in my teeth. I did not wish to deny my husband, only to keep my men from useless harm. In truth, I have no letter from Soke because he is so loyal a man that he had rather die succourless than draw his men from your purposes.'

That point took well, for Rannulf's vassals growled. Catherine lifted her head a little higher. 'I have, however, a letter to you from Lord Geoffrey reporting the sad condition of health and the great danger in which his father lies.' She pushed the scroll into Eustace's unwilling fingers and thought, from the brief glance she snatched at him, that she was near to her goal; the prince looked about ready to burst. 'Will you read it now, my lord, so you do not missay me more?' Catherine pleaded meekly – and all the men growled.

'I say this is a womanish folly. There is no need to read a letter which is a pack of lies because a serpent of a woman has worked on a child to do her will. Listen to her no more, I say. Take her out of here.'

Catherine shrank back against Sir Giles under the violence of Eustace's voice and gesture, but she did not drop her eyes from his face. 'If it be womanish folly to desire to have my husband out of a place – an indefensible place – to which he was sent so that he might be killed or taken prisoner – then womanish folly I gladly do.' Catherine released Sir Giles and sank to the ground tensing her muscles deliberately until her whole body trembled visibly. 'I am a woman and weak,' she cried. 'I cannot compel strong men to follow me, but upon my knees I cry out to my vassals and to Lord Soke's that they succour their lord who so well has cared for them—'

'Begone, you foul bitch!'

Eustace leaped to his feet, beside himself as he saw all his carefully laid plans being torn to tatters by the feeble hands of an idiot woman. Enraged beyond reason, he clapped a hand to his sword hilt. It was extremely unlikely that he realized what he was doing or even that in his blind rage he would have used the weapon, but the gesture was most ill-advised. All of Rannulf's vassals as well as Catherine's rose as one man, their hands also on their swords. Sir Giles, alone unmoved, bit the inside of his lip until the blood ran. She had done it again! Every man would follow her like a sheep to the slaughter, and he had not believed her when she planned it and told him how it would be.

316

# Chapter 21

'My lord!'

André's voice was shaking with excitement, and Rannulf looked up from the lists he was studying. He was annoyed at the interruption because he had been trying to calculate how long the supplies in the small hold would last. That was ordinarily woman's work, and Rannulf, unaccustomed to thinking about food portions, was encountering difficulties. He heaved himself to his feet, however, and began to draw on his mail hood.

'Where do they attack from this time? How many?'

'There is no attack, my lord. I would not break your rest for that! The king has sent us succour.'

'What!'

'Aye, come and see. There are some hundreds of knights fallen on our besiegers and driving them from their earthworks.'

'What do you mean, come and see, you idiot. We are not helpless. We must issue out to add our strength to theirs.'

'Yes, yes. I have so ordered, and the men will ride out as soon as the drawbridge can be got down in safety. You must not go, my lord, but if you—'

A blow sent André staggering halfway across the hall. 'I am not dead yet!' Rannulf roared. 'While I am alive, no men of mine shall ride to battle unless I lead them. Go bring my horse.'

It could not be the king, Rannulf thought, it must be Geoffrey. Bless him and blast him! Beyond that one swift passing idea, Rannulf wasted no time in trying to identify his supporters. It was sufficient that they were belabouring Henry's men with such ferocity as to draw all their attention. It was sufficient to ride out with couched lance and take revenge for insults flung up at men penned helplessly behind walls. It was sufficient when the lance was shattered to draw sword and see blood flow, to ease the pangs of body and heart in a furious expenditure of energy.

Above mere sufficiency, there was deep satisfaction in making a wall of men against which the Angevin troops beat fruitlessly and between which the heavy baggage wains moved safely into Crowmarsh. There would be no need now to count food portions – not for months. There were the last of the wains now. Rannulf shouted the commands that would make the men wheel in behind the carts, back up, and form a rearguard action. One more charge to drive the attackers well off and they could retreat into the hold. Even in that there was satisfaction, for with this augmentation in strength they could do more than defend themselves. If Henry sent no more men, they could attack and drive this small force away.

Rannulf's mood was as near mellow as it had ever been in the past year. He greeted his own vassals with hammerlike blows of affection and bear hugs, the men of Soke with a little more restraint but no less warmth. In a little while, however, he began to look around and frown.

'Very well,' he said loudly, 'come forth, oath-breaker. I will not eat you.'

The men nearest him looked very much surprised and glanced at each other, but no specific reply came to his remark. Rannulf's frown of puzzlement was quickly exchanged for an agonized anxiety.

'Where is my son Geoffrey?' he asked Sir Giles, who happened to be closest to him.

'In Sleaford keep, I suppose, unless he is out gathering troops. Did you desire him to come? Lady Catherine told me you had strictly forbade it.'

'How come you here then? Who summoned you from Eustace's camp? Where did you come by these supplies?'

Sir Giles uttered a half-laugh. 'By the Lady Catherine's doing is the answer to all questions, but if you wish to know whys and wherefores, ask her yourself. There she sits.'

Too stunned to utter a sound, Rannulf limped forward a few paces. There, indeed, she did sit, garbed in a travel-stained riding gown with a big smudge of dirt on her nose and her hair dark with dust. Rannulf opened his mouth, then closed it when he could get no sound out. Catherine raised her eyes to his, and there was trepidation in them, but there was also a – a twinkle.

'Woman,' Rannulf bellowed, 'are you mad?'

That was obviously a rhetorical question which required no answer, being only an opener for a tirade to follow, but Catherine did not wish to be scolded in public. 'No, my lord,' she replied in a low, respectful tone.

Thrown off his stride by her reply, Rannulf looked around. 'Why did you bring a woman to a besieged—' There was no sense in finishing that question because Sir Giles, to whom it was addressed, had retreated to the safety of the other end of the hall. Rannulf gaped at his wife again.

'If you will take a deep breath,' Catherine said gravely, 'you will be better able to speak.' She knew the further impudence was likely to make Rannulf completely speechless with rage. Catherine did not care if Rannulf bellowed until the roof rose. She could even love his roaring anger. Anything was better than the cold rejection she had suffered when he was last at Sleaford. She did, however, prefer to be bellowed at in private. Since he seemed to be safely paralysed, she rose and came to him. 'Do not blame Sir Giles. I forced him to take me. Moreover, there was no reason why I should not come. My lands, as you know, are settled on Geoffrey and Richard in the event that I die without an heir of my body. All that I love and desire is in this place. Wherefore should I not come?'

Rannulf's complexion could not change. The two fever spots burned in his cheeks above the all-pervading ugly grey, but his eyes went blank as if a shutter had closed in his soul. She had said she loved him, and he believed her, but he had not believed that love to be strong enough to make her ruin herself and the children for him.

'Come above to my chamber – such as it is,' he muttered. 'This is no place to speak of private matters.' When they had climbed the uneven stairs, he waved her to the one seat in the room. She was so calm, smiling at him, that Rannulf guessed she had not accepted defeat. Some new plan to recruit him into the rebel force was fermenting in that brain that should have belonged to a man. 'What do you think you can gain here? What do you want of me?'

Perhaps Rannulf was not as sick as Geoffrey thought, but he had much fever. It was no time to quarrel about loyalty and expediency. 'Lie down upon the bed,' she replied, frowning at the dirty pallet. It was a poor place for a sick man to lie, but she had brought no bed, grudging the baggage space. 'Let me see to your hurts. You have one wound that festers already, and all the others are like to do so.'

A wave of unutterable fatigue swept Rannulf. He watched as Catherine began to open a little casket. She had not denied that she wanted something. 'You came here for some purpose. I owe you a great debt. Ask, and let me make answer. If my answer does not please you, you can still go.'

It was well to humour a feverish man; to make him angrier could only hurt him. Catherine began to lay out her drugs and simples while she searched her mind for something to ask that would not be too obviously a sop. 'If you are so yielding,' she soothed, 'then give some dower to your daughter Mary. You are not well and this is a dangerous place. If aught befalls you here – or elsewhere – she will be penniless.'

Rannulf could have wept with pain and weakness and weariness, yet he had a greater impulse to laugh. She was offering him a comfit as if he were a sick child. Such a woman! She saw she could not accomplish her large purpose just now, so she would accomplish a smaller one while she bided her time.

'Let me sit to write,' he said thickly. 'I will give her the manor and farms of Donnington. Will that content you?'

'Most suitable, my lord. That will content me full well. While you write, I will go down to order hot water to wash you.'

The water was an excuse for Catherine to find Sir André. 'My lord has given Mary Donnington,' she said pointedly. 'I have spoken to your brother, and he will not approach Soke for you. There is no other way but that you screw up your courage and ask him yourself, and that in haste. Now that he has dowered her, others will ask for her, or he may begin to think on it himself. At least put it in his mind that you desire her.'

When Rannulf woke from the sleep of exhaustion which followed Catherine's careful treatment of his wounds, André was beside him. He looked around at the bare chamber, wondering whether his wife had really been there or whether he had been dreaming.

'Have I been out of my head?' he asked huskily.

'No, my lord.'

Rannulf turned his head sharply at the trembling voice. 'What ails you?'

'Do not slay me, my lord,' André whispered, going down on his knees by the pallet. Rannulf went rigid, wondering if Catherine could have opened the keep to their enemies while he slept.

'It is not because of the manor,' André hurried on, stumbling over the words, 'but because I was afraid someone else would offer first. Also, I spoke to my brother, and he says that I dishonour us all by my secrecy. He says that I must ask you or leave your service, and although I fear it will come to the same thing in that you doubtless have the right to drive me forth, yet I must ask. Do not cast me out, my lord. You may say me nay, but I love you also. I would never do your daughter a hurt, even though I desire her—'

'Mary!' Relief swept Rannulf, a relief so acute that it left his body bathed in sweat and his limbs trembling.

André swallowed convulsively. 'I have cast my eyes on your daughter,' he gasped, 'and my brother says I am damned. I know I had no right, but I meant no harm, and so good is she, so sweet, so—'

'Be quiet!' Rannulf ordered, afraid that he would burst into laughter and offend the poor trembling suitor. André dropped his forehead to the edge of the cot, his neck stretched as if he awaited a sword blow. So here was the secret behind André's devotion, and a simple secret at that. It was true that an earl could look higher for a husband even for a bastard daughter, but to Rannulf's mind it was a fitting reward to bestow on the young man for having saved Geoffrey's life.

'In part you are of better blood than she. You know that

her mother was a serving wench?' André nodded, his heart beating so hard with hope now that it nearly choked him. 'Go to,' Rannulf said after a rather long pause. 'Send your brother to me, and if he does not object to your throwing yourself away on a maidservant's daughter, we will see what can be done.' Rannulf had planned to offer André vassalage and a keep of his own anyway, so that he would lose nothing by this arrangement. To be tied in blood to Fortesque would be very useful also, in case Catherine was taken with any wild notions of which he did not approve.

He lay quietly waiting for Sir Giles, but it was Catherine who came in when the door opened. She smiled down at Rannulf and brushed the hair back from his face. 'You have agreed. I saw it in his face when he came down. How kind you are. I have been trying to tell you that those children desired each other for a year, but you snapped at me every time I mentioned Mary's name.'

Rannulf burst out laughing, and lifted himself so he could eat the soup she brought. 'You have won this battle, but you will have time for no others. When the men are rested, I will send you home and the vassals of Soke back to their own lands. They will obey me in this, Catherine, for you have no business here nor have they. I have supplies sufficient and, with my vassals here, men sufficient.'

Eustace was on the road himself only a day after Catherine. He could not stop her by force, he could not take the keep he had been besieging without the men she had spirited away, and he saw the failure of his entire plan to secure the east resulting from her action. Stephen's authority as king was his last hope to retrieve the situation. If he ordered her and the men back, perhaps they would obey. He found his father deep in the state of lethargy which had overcome him periodically since his mother's death. Stephen listened to him, but only shook his head.

'Oh, let them go. Take men from my forces. It is more necessary that Henry be detained than that we take this or that keep quickly.'

'But Henry will not be detained. Do you think Rannulf will

hold Crowmarsh now that his men are there? They will yield to the Angevin and turn upon us.'

Something flickered in Stephen's eyes. 'Nay, they will not. Besides, if Henry takes him prisoner, you need trouble about him no more.'

For one long moment Eustace stared at his father as if he had changed into a serpent before his eyes. Then he burst into roars of laughter. 'Wonderful,' he gasped, 'wonderful. I would never have thought of that way to be rid of him without a stain upon our honour.'

A quiver of shame passed through the weary king. Eustace thought that Henry must destroy so inveterate an enemy. That would have been his way because he would believe he could then win over the vassals. Rannulf's heir was only a boy. With his wife in the keep and available to be married to anyone the victor chose, Eustace would think he had all in his hands. Stephen did not believe that Henry would choose that path. He would rather try to cozen Rannulf into joining him or, if he could not make him yield so far, take ransom and an oath of neutrality from him. Stephen was not a murderer; to him it seemed that no one else could be.

Eustace, on the other hand, never doubted that Henry would murder a prisoner to achieve a purpose of his own. Nonetheless, he shook his head. 'It will not do,' he said. 'You must stop his vassals or Henry will have them and the east will never be secure.'

'I will recall them in time, some time. Let them at least bring Soke supplies. He will obey my orders. There is time.'

'But there is no time! I tell you Henry is on the move towards Wallingford. I wrote you that I had that news last week.'

Stephen rose and walked away from his son, his gait like that of a sleepwalker. 'For me there has been too much time. Oh, God,' he murmured, 'release me from this torment. Let me die.'

With those words repeating themselves like a litany in his brain, Eustace returned to his own quarters where he found a messenger from London awaiting him. The seal was his wife's and he had very nearly cast the scroll aside, but he had to do something or burst. He broke open the letter and began to read.

After five minutes of perusal, he threw the parchment to the floor with a muffled scream of rage. How could a man be so cursed? To have an idiot wife as well as an idiot father. Who could conceive of the stupidity of women? She had received Gloucester, had she, and Gloucester had spoken of how regrettable it was that Eustace alone did not have the management of the war. Gloucester, the foremost rebel spy.

Eustace kicked the scroll into the empty fireplace and tore his hair. His hand fell on an empty goblet and he hurled it across the room. A stool followed that, and he had just grabbed the edge of a table to overset it when he paused and put the end he had lifted gently on the ground. Ordinarily, whatever Constance was, Gloucester was not a fool. Ordinarily Gloucester did not make useless conversation. Therefore, if Gloucester had approached Constance, he must have had some reason. It was impossible that he should wish to seduce Constance; she was not sufficiently desirable. It was impossible that he should believe he could learn anything from her. Hurriedly, Eustace picked the letter out of the fireplace and began to read it again. Puzzling out what Gloucester had been hinting at through the fog of Constance's misinterpretation was not easy, but after a third reading he shuddered and sought for a safe place to hide the parchment. It could not happen, he thought, but he did not reply to the letter.

Instead he applied himself to a plan for meeting and defeating Henry. The Angevin's troops had been moving and fighting steadily for months; they must be weary. The area around Crowmarsh was more familiar to Eustace than to Henry. Rannulf's vassals had to be rescued from Crowmarsh. Rannulf himself would have to be dealt with in another way, but the idea of rescue was good for it would make the men grateful to him. Eustace rushed north again to fortify the land he had taken from Bigod, hurried back south to prod his father into taking similar precautions. He had news that confirmed his expectations. Henry's forces had arrived at Wallingford, but instead of assaulting and destroying Crowmarsh they had settled down to besiege it. Henry did not want to hurt these men; he wanted them to yield to him and join his forces. The siege might have another purpose. When there are sufficient supplies a siege is very restful to men weary of fighting. Eustace speeded his preparations, and soon all was ready. Men and arms were ready, the route was decided upon, the plan of attack perfected. Still Eustace did not communicate with Constance. If she went ahead with such a shameful plan, a plan to murder her father-in-law, on her own, it was no affair of Eustace's. The immunity and large favours she might promise Gloucester were not binding upon him. If they met Henry and defeated him, Eustace planned to string Gloucester from the ramparts of the White Tower by his thumbs or his heels.

'You should never have come here,' Rannulf sighed, twisting restlessly on the hard pallet. 'How many are there now encamped about us?'

'I do not know, my lord,' Catherine replied indifferently.

She had been in the hold five weeks, five weeks in daily and nightly attendance upon her husband, and they were further apart than ever. Rannulf had permitted the men and horses to rest for several days; he wished to try once more to drive off the small force that was besieging him. But the force did not stay to fight. When they were gone and Crowmarsh was free, Catherine had pleaded to stay one week – only one week to see if she could cure Rannulf's fever. Then she would go willingly. Otherwise, she said, her face burning and her eyes flashing, he would have to beat her unconscious or tie her screaming to her horse. Rannulf did not like the alternatives and he wished to be well. Her ministrations had already done him more good than any other treatment he had received. Before the week was out, however, Henry and his full army were upon them. Then they had really quarrelled bitterly.

'You cannot withstand a whole army,' Catherine had cried. 'Yield.'

'I have not been offered a chance to yield,' Rannulf replied. 'Can I yield if the terms are death? What terms will be offered, if I show myself ready to accept defeat without fighting?'

'You will never yield. You will see us all die to salve your pride.'

'So much will I humble my pride, that I will beg safe-conduct for you and for your men. When you are free, you can make what terms you like.'

'No, Rannulf, no. I had rather stay with you.'

But Rannulf quarrelled no more. He sent a herald with his petition. The herald returned with the reply that there was yet no one in the camp with sufficient authority to give or to deny safe-conduct. When Henry came, they would give him the message. Rannulf did not change his quarters as Catherine had feared, but he withdrew into some fastness within himself and thrust back every attempt of Catherine's to make amends. He resisted her with kindness, with more courtesy than he had ever shown her before, but with iron-hard determination. Five weeks had passed, but still there had been neither an attack nor an answer to Rannulf's request. He was certain that Henry was now in the besiegers' camp and that the refusal to communicate with him was deliberate, but there was nothing more he could do.

'I should go myself and see,' he said restlessly to Catherine.

'You have two able captains on the walls at this moment. Is no one but you able to count? With your ears you can hear that there is no fighting. The Angevin's men do nothing today that they did not do yesterday, and the day before, and the day before that. They build a dike and a palisade.'

'You should not have come here, Catherine.'

'Is that the sixteenth or seventeenth time you have said that this morning?'

Rannulf turned restlessly again. 'Are my arms and armour laid ready?' Catherine did not reply but shifted her body so that he could see the pile of accoutrements. 'I cannot understand why they do not attack. Now they have more than enough men, and defence here is laughable. Or why do they not ask us to yield? What nonsense is this earthwork with spikes above? We could not come out and do battle with a whole army, so why do they expend so much labour to keep us in? There must be some purpose in this. They can scarcely do it to give us the pleasure of picking off their men with our crossbows.'

'Oh, Rannulf, you have told me the purpose yourself. They hope that Stephen will come to save the keep.'

'He would be a fool to come. To keep Henry here while he swallows Bigod is his purpose.'

'Does not all the world know that Stephen is a fool?'

'Your life and liberty are as much at stake as mine, since the safe-conduct has not been granted. Catherine, you should not have come here.'

'Eighteen,' Catherine said, and could not help but laugh in spite of her weariness and depression. Rannulf cast a sharp glance at her, looked away, and laughed also.

A moment later, however, he had lifted himself upright and reached for a shirt. There were footsteps hurrying up the stairs. Catherine frowned angrily, but made no protest except to hold him back with one hand so she could tighten the bandage on his thigh.

'Do not rise, my lord.' André's voice came up the stairwell before his body appeared. 'Nothing is yet taking place, but a large army is coming from the east, and—'

'Do not rise!'

André stood well out of range because Rannulf's voice was that which usually preceded a well-placed clout. 'But there is nothing to disturb yourself for. They must have come to relieve us, not to attack. The men have all been called from the earthworks and are facing the river in arms.'

'If that is supposed to be a reason for me to continue to lie abed, I am sorry I agreed to give you my daughter. Little of value as she is, it seems a shame to cast her away on a fool.'

Since André was accustomed to such fond words from his prospective father-in-law, he did not blanch. Since it was also useless to argue with Rannulf, the young man sighed and began to help him dress and arm. Catherine remained seated quietly, her hands folded in her lap. Armed, Rannulf took a step towards the door but turned as André disappeared down the stairs.

'A paragon,' he murmured sarcastically.

She understood he referred to her hypocritical meekness in the presence of others, but she did not rise to the bait. When he passed down the stairs also, Catherine slipped to her knees and began to pray. Rannulf checked the defensive positions of the men who would remain in the hold, made sure that the drawbridge ropes and pulleys were well greased, that the horses were saddled, lances laid ready. It took time because he was meticulous in matters of fighting, but it soon became apparent that André had been perfectly right. There had been no need for him to rise so soon. He would have had time enough to accomplish all if he had lain abed some hours longer.

'André, your eyes are younger than mine,' he snarled impatiently. 'What are they doing now?'

'The same as before, my lord. From the gestures, arguing, and I should say many against one.'

That makes sense, Rannulf thought. Having gathered the men and come so far, Stephen has again stopped dead. Probably all are trying to bring him to order an attack and he, as usual, is full of doubts. The proof of Stephen's love for him was triply bitter. It merely showed the king again to be a fool, merely further demonstrated his instability of purpose, but it also shouted aloud that Rannulf's loyalty and devotion were inferior. He had been willing to yield to Henry; he knew he would have done it if he had had the chance, and his shame was a physical thing he could smell and taste. Her fault, with her beauty and her sweet voice and her tenderness – and her rebel sympathies. Rannulf hated Catherine, hated Stephen – and hated himself.

André looked at the sun. 'Well, it will soon be noon. They must – ah, that must be a herald.'

Rannulf sighed with relief. Let them fight or let them retreat. Let them do anything so long as it was done and ended. The herald forded the river, stopped, and then moved on with an escort. A short conversation ensued which seemed to find ready agreement from the leaders of the Angevin force. The herald turned away, but instead of riding back to the river he was led to the gates of the half-built wall and allowed to pass through, his escort remaining on the far side.

'I would have words with the earl of Soke,' the herald called.

'I am here,' Rannulf replied.

'The king desires you to come to him for the better judging of what is to be done in this case, and Henry, duke of Normandy, gives you safe-conduct to pass through his lines and to return if you so wish it.'

'I come,' Rannulf called. 'Lower the bridge,' he said quietly to the men-at-arms when he was mounted, 'but if you see the gate in the dike open, draw up again even if I be not over. Trust not overmuch to good faith.'

'I come also, my lord.'

Rannulf turned his head to see André also astride a horse. 'Pest! I thought you desired to wed my daughter, not me. Will I never be rid of you?' But if there was treachery in the air, it was better to have a friend, and he called out to the herald, 'Is there safe-conduct for my squire?'

'For your whole troop to the last man if you desire it, Lord Soke.'

Rannulf thought briefly of taking Catherine and her men with him, but he dismissed the idea. If there were to be a battle there was not enough time for them to be thoroughly clear of the area, and she would be safer within the keep.

'Come then,' he said to André.

A few minutes later he understood why the safe-conduct had been so broad. Robert of Leicester rode out and clasped his hand. 'I do not understand why Stephen wants you,' he said urgently to Rannulf, 'but Eustace is with him, so watch carefully where you walk and what you eat and drink.'

'Aye. Robert, why did you not gain safe-conduct for Catherine?'

'She did not need it. As Soke's daughter she would be safe whatever befell. Henry does not forget his friends.' It was not a lie, but Catherine had been left in the keep for just the purpose she had accomplished. If Stephen had not come and Henry had been forced to ask for Rannulf's submission, her presence would have been a large factor in Rannulf's agreement. 'If Stephen has shifted his purpose again,' Leicester continued, 'urge truce upon him.'

Rannulf bit his lip so suddenly and so sharply that blood beaded out on it. Leicester was offering him a last chance to secure a pardon from Henry. 'Robert—' He put out a hand helplessly, really agonized because he desired that pardon which would permit him to live in peace on his own land. 'I cannot. You know I cannot. Stephen has the advantage here. His army is as large as Henry's, and Henry's men are caught

329

between his and the hold of Crowmarsh. How can I urge truce on Stephen when he must know this is his last chance to hold his kingdom?'

'You pig-headed— Nay, if you were not you, I would not love you. Because it is to your honour and to the whole country's good that there be a truce. Stephen's case is hopeless in the long run. You must know that. Why then should one Englishman shed the blood of another? The wounds of this war are already bitter enough. Will you urge more fighting and make them harder to heal when all is over? Have you not sated your lust for blood?'

'Aye, I am sated. I am too weary to be angry at life.'

'Then for the good of us all, Rannulf, do as I ask you.'

'For the good of us all, perhaps Stephen should never have been king. It is too late now. I am sworn to him, I love him, and could he have shown his love for me in a plainer way? Nay, Robert, I will urge nothing. If it be possible, I will hold my tongue. So much I can do to content – to content you. I can promise no more.'

At first it seemed as if it would be possible for him to hold his tongue. He was shocked, when he was brought to Stephen, at the difference a few months had made in the king's appearance.

'Are you ill, my lord?'

'No more than usual,' Stephen replied significantly.

Rannulf felt a sickening twinge of anxiety and intermingled with it an even more sickening twinge of hope. If Stephen should die— Horrified at his selfishness, he stopped the thought, but as Stephen began to explain the general situation, Rannulf's sense of shame eased and he could not help but wonder if the thought had been selfish. The king was at the end of his physical and mental strength. Fond as he was of Rannulf, it was clear that he could not have mustered sufficient decisiveness to bring the army to Crowmarsh. He confessed as much, citing Eustace's change of heart towards Rannulf and his son's desire to keep Rannulf out of Henry's hands.

Rannulf was to escape no part of the knowledge of how right Robert of Leicester was. Stephen had sunk low, indeed, even in the opinions of the men faithful to him. During the council, the obvious disintegration in the spirit of men who had such a leader was apparent. All of them, knowing their force was superior and that they held the advantage, still did not wish to fight. All urged truce. All – except Eustace. Stubbornly, he urged battle, growing more and more excited as the barons, gaining confidence from their unanimity, grew bolder in opposing him. And Stephen was blown like a feather in a gale between the will of his son and the will of the barons.

'We need do neither – neither make truce nor fight,' he mumbled at last in despair. 'We can simply break camp and leave now without further parley with Henry.'

There was a perfect, stunned silence. Aside from the shame of such an action, it was about the only thing they could not do with safety. At the first move to break up, Henry's forces would certainly ford the river and attack them as they retreated. As soon as the barons gathered breath, a howl of protest went up.

'I do not care,' Stephen said, almost sobbing. 'I care little whether we make truce or fight. I am not afraid to fight.' That was true, Rannulf thought, watching the king. A man already in hell is not afraid to die. 'What do you think is best to do, Rannulf? You have not spoken, and I have fared ill since I turned away from your advice.'

Rannulf was so exasperated that he came within a hair of saying what was uppermost in his mind – that if Stephen wanted to do the best for everyone there, including himself, he should drop dead. Stephen was not fit to be king, nor, although his purpose was firmer, was Eustace. Robert had spoken the truth.

'I have too great an interest in the matter,' Rannulf said. 'I do not wish to rot in Crowmarsh, and if you mean to preserve that place, the Angevin must be driven away. My judgment, in this case, is of no value.'

'Your judgment is always of value, Soke,' Eustace snapped. 'You would vote for fighting. Are we not the stronger?'

'Yes, but—'

'Will not your men issue out from Crowmarsh and attack the Angevin's rear?'

'Yes.'

'You have forded the river. Is it now low? Can we not cross it easily?'

'Yes, but—'

'Are you willing to fight?'

'Yes.' Rannulf, eyes on the ground, muttered the affirmative reluctantly.

'You see, we cannot take out the men or the keep will fall into Henry's hands. We must fight,' Eustace urged.

'But who wishes to keep the mud hut!' a voice in the background exclaimed.

'The men must come out, it is true,' said another.

'So make truce and tear down the useless bauble. It has no power over Wallingford now that Henry is in the field, as we have seen. It is good for naught but to pen up good fighting men who could be used elsewhere. If it be destroyed no one will lose by that – and the Angevin will gain nothing.'

'Cowards all!' Eustace shouted, making the men hate him worse because of their fear that he had spoken the truth. 'We have the advantage here. We have them both before and behind. Father, you must give orders that we fight. When will we have a better chance?'

'I must consider,' Stephen replied, looking from Eustace to the scowling faces of his barons. If he ordered them to fight, they might all desert him.

As if the single additional evidence of Stephen's indecisiveness had catapulted him from his seat, Eustace leaped to his feet. 'Do not consider,' he screamed hysterically, 'decide! Cannot you see that your life hangs on this matter? Fight and you live. Yield and you die.'

'My son, you are distraught,' Stephen murmured dully.

'Father, I beg you. I will even beg you on my knees. We can win if you will only fight.'

Stephen touched his son's face, but he did not look at him. He gestured at the men of the council, and they made haste to leave. Sensing their departure, Eustace abandoned hope and dropped his head on to his father's knees.

'Why will you make me bear the burden of your death?' he sobbed.

# Chapter 22

William of Gloucester smiled vaguely at the pretty young man who was fanning him. The boy was the greatest find he had ever made, so pretty, so very quick to learn, so totally devoted – and mute. Blessing of all blessings, he was born mute and had been treated worse than an animal until William had rescued him, seeing and desiring the prettiness under the dirt and bruises. He was worth a great deal more than the mere satisfaction of a desire when he was cleaned and taught a form of sign language. He could not read nor write nor speak – except to William himself – which made him the perfect tool and confidant.

'It is as I thought,' William said to the receptive ears which could never find a way to relate what they had heard to a stranger. 'They would be twenty years more settling this war if I let them go their own way, and I am bored with it. It is time to make an end. See this paper here, my child? It tells me that Stephen and Henry have made truce. Thank God, Leicester thought with me in that matter – even if for different reasons. That hothead Hereford would have started the fighting again, Stephen would have retreated to another hold, and heaven knows how we would have tempted him out another time.'

A raised finger sent the boy running for cooled wine. William sipped, the pretty servant lifted his fan again, his eyes intent with interest.

'Aye,' William mused gently, 'I cannot think that aught more is needed. The truce is made, Crowmarsh destroyed, and both armies have turned their backs on each other. Dress yourself now in that garb of Eustace's livery which is laid ready and take this letter to the Lady Constance. It begs her to make ready for the king a favourite dish of his – smoked eels. Oh, yes, a great favourite.'

Eustace stared into the leaping flames at Bury St Edmunds. He could feel the sweat running down his face and back, his lips were cracked and painful with the heat, and he suspected that if anyone had laid a hand on his mail where it was nearest the fire the flesh would have been seared. Still he was not warm; still his teeth chattered with cold. This was hell. He need fear nothing, for he had tasted the worst that could be – burning flesh and freezing soul. I have not done it, nor have I condoned it, he thought. I have no part in the plan. I have not even sent word to London of how matters went at Crowmarsh. I will take vengeance; no paper of amnesty or pardon will hold me back.

There was no comfort in those thoughts; there was no comfort in anything. Eustace was all too conscious that he could not look into his father's face, and that his father seemed to know why. Eustace had fled from Crowmarsh, burning and pillaging on the way, but Stephen had followed him eastward and was again encamped before Ipswich. He was not encamped there for any reason, because he did not really prosecute the seige, but he might as well be there as elsewhere. He seemed to be waiting, not with patience and not with impatience, simply waiting, for the act that would release him from the pain of living.

'I will not go there,' Eustace said aloud. 'I will not go there.' But he knew that if it did not happen soon, he would go.

For a week his determination held, the ambition of a lifetime combating his knowledge of a lifetime of freely proffered love. On the morning of the 17th of August, a letter came to him from his father, an ordinary letter of business regarding a charter for Fountains Abbey. It would be well, Stephen wrote, if Eustace would take the trouble to ride the ten or fifteen miles that separated them so he could sign the charter also. He was growing old and very tired, Stephen continued, the monks had been kind to him, and he would like to be sure that they would have no trouble with the charter. When Eustace lifted his head from the parchment where he had laid it, the words were no longer legible, and the tears which had wiped them out had transferred the ink in comical smudges to his face. His struggle, however, was over. He would advise his father to abdicate the kingship and leave England to Henry. He would concur in the abdication, resigning his right to inheritance. They would retreat to the duchy of Blois and live out their lives in peace.

It would be impossible, of course, to explain in plain words what had brought about this change of feeling, Eustace decided, so he would not broach the matter to his father at once. He was able in his relief to greet Stephen with so light a countenance, with such clear peaceful eyes as he had not had since a child. Responding at once, warmth and life began to flow through Stephen. They made out the charter and talked generally, reliving happier days in the past. Eustace rode out for an hour to look with renewed interest at the progress the siege engines were making. It would be a proud thing to fling Norfolk into Henry's face, to say that they had accomplished more than Henry could but would not strive longer with him for a ravaged piece of earth worth nothing. He returned, still greatly uplifted, to find his father at table.

'Sit down,' Stephen said warmly, and thrust a dish across at Eustace. 'I know you do not like eels, but you must taste these. They have a most pleasant and unusual savour, and your lady wife had the kindness to send them all the way from London by your— What is wrong Eustace?'

Then everything happened at once. Stephen tried to snatch back the plate, his face white, his mouth distorted. Eustace, his eyes bulging with horror and remorse, managed to seize some three pieces of the eels and cram them into his own mouth. Stephen gave a choking cry and seemed to be trying to throttle his son. The servants pulled them apart, and one very handsome boy in Eustace's livery, seeing his master turn crimson and gag, silently pressed a goblet of wine into the prince's hands while the others continued to try to divert Stephen. In haste to get the eels down before his father could force him to disgorge or before his courage failed, Eustace drank and flung the goblet away. Stephen burst through the servants, and for a few moments more father and son struggled together. All

335

eyes were so intent upon this inexplicable conflict, that not a single person noticed how the handsome boy who had given Eustace the wine laughed perfectly silently and retreated gently towards the door until he had slipped away.

By the time the servants had the presence of mind to run and bring the vassals, Eustace was writhing in convulsions upon the floor. Some leaped to restrain him, some bellowed to the servants to summon the physicians. All knew any measure was too late, for the young man's face was blackening as his breathing failed. Rannulf first tried to urge Stephen away, and then, realizing that he would not leave his son to die alone even if the child knew him no longer, contented himself by removing all weapons from that place and watching the king to be sure he would do himself no hurt. It did not take Eustace long to die, but it took hours to convince Stephen that life was extinct and more hours to wrest the corpse from his arms. When the vassals had done so, however, Rannulf was alarmed by the king's quiescence. He ceased to weep and sat with staring eyes the rest of that day and that night. At first they thought he, too, would die, but as the days passed, he grew gentle and simple. If they bade him eat, he ate; if they bade him sleep, he slept.

The news did not take long to reach Henry's ears, but for once the young duke did not seem certain of what to do. He could have fallen upon the king's demoralized forces, squeezing them between Bigod and himself, beaten them and taken Stephen captive. Such action had many advantages, but it would violate the truce he had just signed and it would certainly bring inveterate hatred to him from any man still faithful to the king.

'Besides,' Henry said, looking into the faces of his councillors, 'he is my cousin, and once, when he could have had me prisoner, he sent me money and let me go.'

'We have broken so many bonds of faith already,' Hereford said miserably, 'what matter for one more? There is no need to treat Stephen harshly. He may be confined with all comfort and honour, or he may be sent back to Blois. We are all sick of this war, Harry. Make an end to it.'

'But will it make an end to it? What of men like your foster brother, Leicester? If we won this battle and took the king, would Rannulf of Soke take pardon of me and be my man?'

Leicester did not wish to reply because he wanted to protect Rannulf. While he sought for a way to temporize, Gloucester leaned forward.

'No, he would not, and neither would others. Nor should you be so sure you will win this battle. These men are desperate. If you offer them battle now, they will fight as they have never fought before, believing that to yield would only bring them death or exile anyway. Can you kill all, or take all prisoner? They will flee and hide themselves in their keeps, and you will have naught but war, rooting them out one by one. There is another, easier way. Stephen will be willing now to make peace, to name you his heir, and to bid his men do homage to you.'

'And how long will he keep those oaths? He will turn again and make trouble.'

Gloucester hoped so, because trouble was the spice of his life. 'Perhaps so, but not for some time. He is like a walking dead man. I think it will be long and long ere he recover what wits he ever had. Nor do I think he has long to live.'

Henry picked at his clothes and bit his lip. 'Aye, and that would give me time to gentle his vassals. You did not answer my first question, Leicester. Now answer this one. If I had oath of Soke, would he break that oath if Stephen called him to battle?'

'I think not,' Leicester replied slowly, then shook his head. 'If he were torn between two oaths, he would break his heart and die.'

Additional discussion could bring them no further, although the matter was argued out in council again and again in the weeks that followed. The news from London where Stephen's men had taken him was ever the same. The king walked and talked, ate and slept – but he did not live. An embassy was sent from Henry to discuss a final and lasting peace; they were well received and Stephen listened, but whether or not he heard, no man could say. The king's council also discussed the offer. Some found it suspicious; some found it good. To Rannulf, it was so desirable that it woke an agonized sense of guilt. He had wished for Eustace's death and even Stephen's to bring this about, and now he tormented himself by refusing to forward the proposal. At last he fled from his trouble and from the king who recognized him and smiled at him but did not need him because he was dead.

At first he could not even face Catherine whom he had not seen or written to since their parting at Crowmarsh. A few weeks of sober occupation on his outlying estates, however, brought back his sense of proportion. He was just about ready to take up his life again, to go back to Sleaford and make a blessed peace with Catherine, when news that Henry's offer had been accepted came from Leicester. The letter was strangely cold and formal. Rannulf realized he had made a dreadful mistake. His precipitate retreat to the most distant fastnesses of his property must have seemed like an act of defiance. He wrote to Leicester at once and explained as well as he could, but no reply came from his foster brother. Then, after another six weeks had passed, a summons arrived in Stephen's name to attend the formal acceptance of the treaty and acknowledgment of Henry as heir and co-ruler.

Soon upon that came a more serious blow, a curt order to submit his land charters and his patent of earldom to Henry for ratification. Ratification was the word used, but no promise was given that return of the charters with ratification would follow submission nor was there any indication that this was an empty formality. Rannulf considered refusal for two days, and then rode home to Sleaford to comply. He could not stand alone against all of England.

Rannulf did not at first explain to Catherine what had happened, and since he was a poor liar he avoided her company as much as possible. He thought more than once of asking her advice, but he could not imagine how she could help him and he could not bear to inflict more pain upon her than he already had. When at last it was time for him to leave for court, he told her only that. To his horror, Catherine said she wished to accompany him to see the new king. One lame excuse after another could not shake her determination and finally raised enough suspicion in her that Rannulf had no choice but to confess.

'I have marred all, as usual, with my haste,' he said bitterly.

'You would think I were a child, so ruled am I by my passions. I have made them all think I will not accept this final treaty which makes Henry co-ruler with Stephen.'

'Would you?'

Rannulf's face twisted. If Catherine was so doubtful of his intentions, how could he convince the others that it was not hate and spite which had sent him back to his lands? 'Aye, I would, and with a good grace. They say one cannot teach an old dog new tricks, but I would need to learn no new tricks. I am a faithful old dog, but my master is dead – his heart and head are dead even if his body will live a year or two longer – and I am ready to serve faithfully again. Besides, my heart and head are not dead. I am most curious to see what new tricks this new master will try to teach. How could I be so foolish? Oh, for God's sake, Catherine, do not weep! I have blundered and I must suffer for it.'

'Write to Robert. Explain to him. Will he allow this to happen to you? Will no man else speak a word in your defence?'

'I have written. I told you so. I am sure Robert has done and is doing all he can. Perhaps I am to be an example that it is not wise to stand against Henry's will and yield only when all hope is gone. Perhaps he thinks this too good an opportunity to seize some of my estates. I have heard that Henry is avaricious. Probably it has taken all of Robert's influence to save some of the lands for Geoffrey. Now do you bide here in quiet, and no harm will come to you. Geoffrey is safe in Leicester's keep and will remain there until Robert can wring a pardon for him from Henry. You need not fear Henry. He will love you for your father's sake, and Geoffrey will give you your own will in all things.'

'I will not bide. If you leave me, I will follow you.'

'Curse you for a stubborn bitch. You can do nothing for me. Whatever agreement Robert has made, I must abide by. If I protest, Henry may doubt that Leicester's word will bind me and may revoke all concessions.'

'Then I will speak for you. My father, as you fling in my face too often, was a good friend to Henry. He owes me my husband's life, lands, and honour. If that is not enough, well— They say that Henry is weak towards a beautiful woman. I am a beautiful woman. Perhaps I have what will buy your freedom. You do not want it anyway.'

'Catherine!' Rannulf roared, turning crimson.

'I will not yield without doing everything in my power.'

'You fool! I will tell you plain out what I had hoped you would not need to know. I have made a bargain through Leicester – at least I have offered a bargain – my life for my lands to go to Geoffrey. Will you have sense now and stay here?'

'No. I have made no bargain. I will fight as a woman fights while I can.'

'Go, then,' Rannulf snarled. 'I care not what you do, but if you go near that lecher – I will kill you.'

Mary was gone, a happy bride, to her own manor of Donnington so that Catherine had the order of their moving in her hands. It was as well that she had something to occupy her, and so did she apply herself to every petty detail that all went with oiled precision as far as their physical comfort was concerned. Well-trained servants travelled on before, so that when Rannulf and his wife arrived in London, their house was newly cleaned and furbished. The larder was full, dinner was waiting before the roaring fire in the hearth. Even the great curtained bed and Catherine's embroidery frame were set carefully in place.

Rannulf presented himself to Stephen soon after arrival, and he was kissed by a corpse's lips. There was nothing to hope for from Stephen. The king would sign what he was told to sign and probably would not even notice that Rannulf came to him no more. Stephen was no longer of this world. What was more significant was that Henry himself, although known to be in London, was not present. Neither was Hereford, nor Cornwall, nor Leicester, nor Gloucester. It might have been an accident, but on the following days they were absent also, and Rannulf felt they were avoiding him. He did not return to court again. There was no sense in embarrassing Leicester or some other men who owed him favours. He also felt a compulsion to watch Catherine whose meekness to him, since they had arrived in London, he did not trust. Rannulf found himself laughing wryly, recognizing that he was waiting with great eagerness for a denouement that most men would have fled to avoid.

Time passes, no matter how slow its crawling seems to some, at a regular rate; 13th January, 1154, finally arrived, but although Rannulf was glad the moment had come, the day dawned very ill for him with another bitter quarrel with Catherine. The cause was ridiculous. Catherine demanded that her husband be garbed as befitted one of the great nobles in the land. She had prepared the gown, laid out the jewels, and summoned the barber. Irritated by her tone, Rannulf said he would go as he was, becoming stubborner out of pure frustration as Catherine grew more insistent.

'Coward,' she screamed, beside herself with grief and fear for him, 'will you crawl like a singed cur, hoping to find pity? If we must go down in defeat, let us at least put on proud faces.'

For the first and only time in their marriage, Rannulf deliberately struck his wife. 'No living being has used that word to me and come scatheless away,' he bellowed back. 'I have lived in one pattern all my life, and fine clothes have been no part of that pattern. If any man cannot read my steadfastness in my face because my robe is plain, he is a fool.'

Then he was overcome with remorse, and would gladly have donned the robe to please her, but she threw it into the fire and retreated to the women's quarters. He would even have begged her pardon, though he knew he was right to have chastised her, but she would speak no word more to him until they came into the great hall of the White Tower. There she drew on the mask of the dutiful wife for all the courtiers to see, and no man or woman could outface her. We are a match in pride, Rannulf thought, just as the ceremony of homage was about to begin.

There were some dozen men who had the right of precedence over Rannulf, some who had been Henry's supporters from the beginning, but there was no difference in the manner in which Henry received homage of any of them. Nor, when he himself knelt to swear and receive the kiss of peace, could Rannulf detect any hesitation or reluctance in his new overlord's offer of hands and lips. Having done his *devoir*, Rannulf was ready to go. He was sure that nothing more would happen that day as far as he was concerned, for Henry could scarcely take homage of him one moment and accuse him of treason or some other crime in the next. He was bored by the endless procession of vassals swearing the same oath and hurt, although he saw the reasonableness of the behaviour, by the fact that Leicester had not come to greet him. Catherine, however, would not go willingly, and, although Rannulf could not see the point in staying to torment themselves, he did not wish to cross her again.

'Now are you sated?' he asked as Henry at last stepped down from the dais which had been raised in the hall for the swearing.

Catherine smiled sweetly for the edification of those around them, but her voice was thin with fury. 'It was for this moment that I waited. I do not yield all hope as readily as you do. I will fight with every weapon I have until my last breath, and I wish to speak with Henry.'

'I forbid it!'

'You are too late,' a cheerful, friendly voice interrupted. 'Madam, I am here, and you are too beautiful to be obedient, even if you are his wife. And, if you are not his wife – all the less should you obey him.'

Catherine sank to the ground with head bowed, but Henry lifted her to her feet immediately. 'No, no,' he laughed. 'You might ask for something in that position, and since I cannot resist a beautiful woman on her knees, I would say "yes" without thinking. A lady so lovely as you, madam, must stand upright before me. Ah, alack and alas, now I know you are Lady Soke. Look you at that black scowl your husband has for me.'

Rannulf tried to smooth away the expression knowing that this open, half-jesting flattery could mean nothing. He was successful, but only because he saw something that brought him even more disquiet than Catherine's behaviour. Geoffrey was smiling at him from behind Leicester's bulk. Robert's face was inscrutable, and for the first time in his life Rannulf doubted his foster brother's intentions to him. His world was shattering into ever smaller and more meaningless pieces, for his relationship with Robert had always been deeply satisfying.

342

It was a free love, freely given with no dependence, except for love, on either side. He did not need Robert, and Robert did not need him; they loved each other because they loved each other. If that was ended, there was nothing stable in the world.

'It is indeed my wife,' he said, and then spitefully, out of his bitterness, 'You might have saved your advice, my lord, for she is already as willful as she is beautiful.'

Henry chose to ignore the bitterness. 'All are alike,' he crowed while he thought that this was one lovely lady with whom he must not meddle. Henry was free with women, but not when they interfered with any more serious purpose, and Rannulf was not the kind to take that sort of affront to his pride meekly. He must be soothed. 'You are not alone, Lord Soke,' he said merrily. 'Look you how Hereford hangs his head like a whipped dog when his wife speaks, and I, alas, am no better. When my lady wife raises her sweet voice – I obey. A pox take all managing women, beautiful or not.' His eyes sought Geoffrey over Leicester's shoulder. 'You are Soke's son, are you not? Come, take your mother home. Nay, madam, we are all friends here. Do not look at me so, and do not fear. You, Soke, walk aside with me. I have something to say to you.'

A sidelong glance was cast at Rannulf from keen grey eyes. Henry had been delighted to see Catherine there for the fact that Soke had brought his wife indicated that Rannulf did not intend to run for his lands again and raise rebellion. He was equally delighted to see the iron control Rannulf had over his inner ferment. Henry had rejected Leicester's often-repeated plea that he be permitted to assure Rannulf of his safety. Henry wished to grant that favour himself and to test the strength of Rannulf's promise of submission. He was now sure of his prey, and began to exert the full strength of his charm to win Rannulf's heart as well as his homage.

He started off at a rapid pace down the hill, drawing Rannulf with him, by linking a hand in his vassal's arm. It seemed an odd habit, to converse while walking, but Rannulf soon realized that while they walked so quickly it was impossible for anyone to overhear more than one or two disconnected

343

words. Henry, apparently, had reasons for most of the odd things he seemed to do.

Rannulf had answered Henry's command with a formal, 'As you will, my lord,' grateful that Catherine and Geoffrey would be spared seeing his reaction to whatever blow Henry planned to deliver.

'Is that the truth?' Henry asked. 'Do you come willingly to this swearing?'

'Had I not come willingly,' Rannulf replied, 'I would not have come at all. I do not do things with half a heart. I wish to say only one thing for myself, and I will speak plain, for I know no other way. I once swore sword-oath to Stephen, and that oath I kept, letter and spirit. My overlord has renounced that oath and bade me swear instead to you. I have done so. This new oath also will I keep. I have obeyed Stephen; now, if I have life and leave to do so, I will obey you.'

'If you always use such plain words with me, I will have no complaint. Now, Soke, I am not a man of plain words. I love much speech and fair speech, but I will speak plainly to you. Some men are to be bound by love and duty, some by fear, some by lust, some by greed, and some by nothing at all. Of the last, we have too many in this land; of the first we have too few. On Leicester's word, and Hereford's also, you are of the first. Greatly would I cherish those few, had I the chance. I would like to know how to win your love.'

'I cannot tell you that,' Rannulf said, suspicious but truthful. If this was a game, it showed a cruelty of which he had never heard Henry accused. 'Love comes of itself, but I must have free pardon of you before I can even do my duty.'

'You had that when you did me homage.'

'I had?' Rannulf asked, a mingled hope and fear beginning to stir in him.

'Am I a monster? Shall I kiss a man's lips in peace one day and hang him for what is past the next?'

'Then why have I received no written pardon from you?'

Henry began to laugh. 'A pretty pardon that would have been. Perhaps you can tell me how I should have worded it, for I must have pardoned you for obeying the commands of the king of England. That would set me in a pretty case when

I gave you orders in the future. Stephen is still king of England and, though I rule with him and, no offence, he is not now fit to rule, I cannot pardon you for obeying him.'

It was no game. Rannulf's steps faltered in his relief, and Henry steadied him with a strong arm.

'Alas,' Henry said, 'I have trod amiss with you.' It was well with such a man to seem flexible and to acknowledge a fault now and again. Soke could be led easily, though it might be hard to drive him. 'Leicester said he should write and assure you of my friendship when you seemed to think I held your loyalty to Stephen a cheap and dangerous thing. I did refuse him, but only because I feared you might think me so weak that I plead for your support by proffering friendship before it was asked. I did not mean you to think I would withold my regard.'

Rannulf was mute, surprised, still a little suspicious. Henry read the emotions in his face. Now he had only to offer to Rannulf what was his own, and he would have gained a loyal and willing liege man, a workhorse of the finest breed, and all without cost to himself outside of a little conversation and a little wear and tear on Rannulf's nerves.

'I like to look forward,' Henry began again, 'and have all matters clearly settled. I do not wish, because of a word carelessly spoken or misunderstood, to fight my barons. It is bad for all to have a land torn apart by war. Peverel of Nottingham, Hugh Bigod, and the earl of Lincoln are the last sort of men of whom I spoke. They are to be bound by nothing at all. I will expect of you, that you keep them pent within their own lands where their borders touch yours. Keep them busy. I do not wish them to trouble me.'

This was the crux. Rannulf stopped and turned so that Henry faced him and they stood almost breast to breast. 'Are the lands still mine, then? I sent you the patent and the charters, and they have not been returned.'

'They have not?' Henry gasped in well-simulated surprise. 'But I gave orders that they be sent to your house in London after you came. I wished to try you, but not so high as that. Of course the lands are yours. What good to me is a penniless and landless vassal?'

'Catherine!' Rannulf said in a horrified voice, surprising Henry by the non sequitur. 'I have let her believe you wanted my head.'

Henry burst into laughter. 'Another slave to a lady's whim. You and Hereford should deal excellently together. Come and have a drink of wine with him, he is sadly oppressed these days. You can mend your wife's impressions later.'

'You do not know my Catherine,' Rannulf replied. 'If she thinks you mean harm to that which is hers, she is like to go summon her vassals and assault the White Tower. I must go to her.'

'Stay,' Henry laughed. 'At least let me find your charters that you may take them with you and not blame me if they be lost.'

Catherine, of course, had no such foolish notions. She knew what was and what was not within her power. She managed to conceal from Geoffrey, who bubbled with good spirits and sang the praises of the new king, how terrified she was, and she sent him back to court with a light heart. Then she sat with her hands folded in her lap, gathering her resources for a last battle. The scrape and slide of a horse pulled too suddenly to a halt in the courtyard made her bite her lips. Whatever the news, she must not give way to womanish weakness. She must husband her strength and plan what to do.

Her surprise was complete when Rannulf came bounding up the stairs with a step as light as Richard's. He burst into the room, his hands full of rolls of parchment from which the wax impressions of the Great Seal of England hung. So eager was he that he forgot his still-weakened leg, and he almost fell sprawling. Catherine leaped from her chair to steady him on his feet.

'Look, look,' Rannulf cried, not realizing that he had thrust here roughly away in his excitement. 'I have not read them through, but I do not think a word is changed in them. All is here, signed and sealed. And look here, Catherine, what I did not ask for, nor even think of desiring if the truth be told, a commission of warden of the northeastern parts.

'That is most excellent, my lord,' she said gladly, although she could not smile. That cold thrust of rejection meant that the passing of Rannulf's political trouble had not mended the rift between them.

Rannulf gave a shaken laugh and set the parchments down on the top of a high chest. 'He is a better man than I thought. He honours honour, and few do. I am sorry to have been so long in coming to you, but Leicester stopped me to ask my pardon for the part he played in this trial of spirit and to ask also that I release Geoffrey to be squire of the body to Henry. In a way it is bad, because I have need of him, but I suppose I can recall André to service, and there will be many who wish to give their sons to me for training now. Moreover, for Geoffrey, the training in the court—'

'Do I understand you aright, Rannulf?' Catherine interrupted, seeing that he would talk all night about things that meant nothing to her just now. 'Are we safe? Is our danger past?'

'As safe as a man may be in a mortal world full of erring beings, I believe we are,' he replied happily.

'And all things are exactly as you would have them?'

'Aye,' he said doubtfully, now conscious of her coldness and anger, 'everything is as I wish.'

Catherine stood in silence, wondering if it was worthwhile to abase her pride yet again and try once more to breach the wall between them. 'Not everything,' she said bitterly. 'You are still burdened with me. Give me leave then to go to Bourne, or to some other place pleasing to you, where I may live in peace.'

'Come, Catherine. Do not be so wroth for a tap. You missaid me, and I was so overburdened with fear that I could bear nothing with patience. I am sorry I struck you.'

'I do not care for that,' she cried. 'You want a helpless, mindless thing as wife, or no wife at all. If I could be that for you, I would, so much do I love you, but I cannot be other than I am. Will you love me, Rannulf, if I swear never to meddle again? Do you wish me to sign some charter or renounce my vassals' service in public? Bid me what to do, and I will do it. Tell me what will make me helpless enough to be again a woman in your eyes.'

'Catherine!' He took her in his arms, and she could feel his

347

hard body go soft, as if it would engulf her. 'I would not have you other than you are. Did you not know that for a word from you I would have cast all aside – life, name, honour – all. But then I would have hated myself and you also, and I knew I could not live and hate you. So I fled temptation. It was not too little love I felt, but too much.'

'Could you not have said that?'

'I wished to spare you pain. I did not wish you to be torn apart between conflicting loves as I was. I loved Stephen, too. I thought if I withdrew from you and angered you enough you would follow your father's faith and go to Henry. Then you and my sons would have been safe.'

'Did you never think of the pain you gave me?'

'I did not think at all. I could not bear to think.' He fell silent, backed away a little, and lifted one of her braids to trace the curving line with a forefinger. 'Look, Catherine, the realm has made peace and begun anew tonight. Let us also begin anew. If I have burdens, I will share them with you – I swear it.'

For a moment Catherine searched her husband's face seriously, then, helplessly, she began to laugh. 'Dreadful man,' she sputtered, 'you will not. As soon as a shadow falls, you will withdraw into yourself again and make me, incontinently and immodestly, run after you pleading to know what I have done amiss. You will not leave me a rag of pride, Rannulf.'

'Nay, for I need not fear that you will weaken me with your weakness. You are the only woman I have ever known whose heart, mind, and spirit I can admire. You are the only woman I have ever known that is deserving of the kind of love a man gives to a man.'

Laughing even harder, Catherine cast herself into her husband's arms again. What a compliment to give a wife! Doubtless, however, Rannulf believed he had given her the highest praise he had to bestow. Rannulf did not understand what was funny, but Catherine was warm and scented in his arms; she was happy, his world was whole and stable, he had bright new dreams of joy. He laughed with her.